CAKE

A LOVE STORY

J. BENGTSSON

To my parents, Les and Janet Wheeler, for giving me a sense of humor.
To my husband, Ben, for giving me a wonderful life.
To my children, Chris, Matt, and Lily, for giving me the greatest gift of all, being a mother.

HE THINKS HE'S PUT THE PAST
BEHIND HIM

1

CASEY: THE BEGINNING

On the morning of May 30th, I was just a twenty-three-year-old accounting student at Arizona State University enjoying the first weeks of summer break. On the side, I served up Bloomin' Onions as a waitress at Outback Steakhouse. I was a reasonably attractive twenty-something girl with a quick wit and easy smile. Really, there was nothing special about me... at least nothing special enough to predict that when I woke up that morning, life as I knew it would never be the same.

As the youngest of three rowdy kids in a loud, boisterous middle-class family, and the only girl, I had been a seriously rough-and-tumble tomboy. When I was young, my best friends were boys, and it wasn't unusual for me to spend hours outside riding bikes, bouncing a basketball, or climbing trees. But then, much to my dismay, puberty set in at the age of thirteen, and my scrawny little body started changing. I fought it for a while, not ready to give up my happy life as one of the boys. However, as my breasts formed and my legs lengthened and my hips shaped curves into my previously stick-thin frame, my friends started noticing.

Everything changed. The boys looked at me differently. They

whispered behind my back. They tried grabbing me in places I definitely did not want to be grabbed. Gradually, I stopped running around with the boys and found myself a group of nice, smart girls who were in my honors classes. No, they weren't as fun as the boys, but at least they weren't acting like horny little perverts.

Seeing as I was friendly with the smart kids, it goes without saying I was not among the popular crowd. Still, I had plenty of friends, and among the misfits I hung with, I was considered pretty hot stuff. I even sometimes caught the eye of boys from the in crowd. Some of the common 'compliments' I would receive from them were, "You're kind of pretty for a smart girl." Or, "You'd be hot if you didn't talk so much." Hey, in high school, you take what you can get.

It wasn't until midway through my junior year in high school that the hormones really kicked in, and all of the sudden, I was boy crazy. Once that happened, I started dressing nice, wearing makeup, and actually brushing my hair instead of just pulling it into a ponytail. I tried to play it cool when a boy took an interest in me, but all I knew about the opposite sex came from my two caveman brothers and the boys I'd played with for years. Potential suitors, I quickly discovered, did not particularly appreciate me making inappropriate jokes about their private parts.

Only one boy was brave enough to take me on: Tommy Schultz. We started dating midway through my senior year. Like me, he was one of the cooler smart kids. Tommy actually liked my sense of humor and thought I was fun. Together we experienced all the epic senior moments: senior picnic, senior trip, prom... and sex. He was my first, and I was in love. My immature brain really believed we'd be together forever. But the day after graduation he abruptly dumped me, explaining that he didn't want to be tied down his freshman year in college. I was heartbroken. He never looked back.

So off I went to college with a freshly broken heart. Even

though I'd grown up only a few miles from ASU, my parents wanted me to have the full college experience and allowed me to live in the dorms my freshman year. It turned out to be exactly what I needed to really grow and mature... and have a little fun in the process. In hindsight, I had to thank my former boyfriend. He'd been right. College was a hell of a lot more fun without him there too.

Luckily, the enormous student body afforded me the opportunity to start out with a completely clean slate. No one knew me as 'Tomboy Casey' or 'Talks too much Casey.' In college, I was just Casey, a girl with decent curves, cute dimples, a flowing mane of brunette hair, and what I had been told was an infectious personality. Yes, there were definitely times when I could turn off a guy's interest with a simple, ill-placed snort of laughter or a badly timed dick joke, but for the most part, I'd managed to reinvent myself into a somewhat polished young woman. Even if, at times, I had to rein in my raunchy sense of humor to appease the boys, the tradeoff was usually worth it.

Although I dated guys here and there, I didn't have another boyfriend until my sophomore year in college. Logan Adams was the son of a wealthy businessman and the 'backup' for the backup quarterback on the ASU football team. Logan was handsome, rich, and cocky as hell. Warning bells were going off in my head before he ever even opened his mouth. But, as many girls do, I overlooked his obvious flaws because he was so damn hot. And he did win me over with what I thought was his kind, sensitive side. Turned out there was nothing warm or fuzzy about him. It took me over a year to figure out that my boyfriend had a passion for sleeping with girls other than me.

After him, my love life was...well, non-existent. I was unattached and definitely not looking. There was a certain satisfaction in being single. I could do what I wanted, whenever I wanted. My main focus was not on finding a guy... it was to graduate on time the following spring. I was already on the five-year plan due to my work schedule and the difficulty in getting the classes I needed; no way was I going to make it six. And although I had a part-time job to help pay for my expensive tuition, my parents had sacrificed a lot to send me to college on their fixed income. I felt a strong sense of responsibility to really buckle down this year and get my degree completed.

Love would have to wait. And when it was time, I now knew the type of guy *not* to look for. Really, I wasn't that picky. Personality was way more important to me than looks... although if a guy were also hot, I'd consider that an added bonus. The older I got, the more I realized I shouldn't have to dumb it down or clean it up in order to impress a guy. Either I was good enough as I was or he wasn't worth my time. I knew my man was out there somewhere... I just never, in a million years, could have predicted who he would be.

Kate Mullin was a good friend of mine. We met as waitresses at Outback and stayed friends even after she left. We shared a quirky sense of humor and a love for reality TV. I'd known Kate for two years when she asked me to be a bridesmaid at her wedding. I was thrilled to be part of her special day. At lunch a couple of weeks before the ceremony, Kate dropped the bomb on me.

"Mitch thinks it would be best to pair you up with Jake."

Her words didn't immediately register with me, "Wait, what?" I asked.

"We're going to partner you and Jake up for the wedding," Kate repeated.

Then I understood, and my stomach dropped. Holy crap, she meant the rock star! I'd known Jake McKallister would be there – he was, after all, the groom's brother – but I'd just assumed I would be admiring him from afar.

"But…I thought Sarah was going to be his partner," I sputtered. "That's all she's talked about for the past four months."

"I know. I love Sarah, but sometimes she comes on too strong."

"Sometimes?" I joked. "Remember Aaron?"

"Oh, god." Kate rolled her eyes and laughed. "Yeah. That was bad."

"I was going to tell her he was gay, but it was just so much fun to watch."

"You're awful," Kate proclaimed, shaking her head. "Anyway, Mitch is worried that Sarah will be all over Jake and that she might make him feel uncomfortable. Jake doesn't like fawning."

"And you think I won't fawn all over him?" I replied in a raised voice.

"It's not your style, Casey."

"Have you *seen* the boy?"

"Yes," Kate affirmed. "I have seen him."

"Then you understand that you're giving me way too much credit, right?"

Kate nodded her head, laughing.

"I mean, I've never met anyone famous before… not to mention gorgeous-famous. There's no telling what I might do to that poor boy," I claimed, only half-joking.

"And if you do, I'm sure he'd be happy about it."

I gasped like I was offended…which I wasn't. The reality was I'd never be bold enough to hit on a guy like Jake, so such a scenario was absurd.

"Mitch just wants him to feel comfortable at the wedding. If Jake wants to get laid, that's his business…we just aren't going to facilitate it."

"Right, because the last thing you want is all eyes on the hot singer and his busty blonde."

"Yeah, for sure," Kate agreed. "Look, Casey, if you really don't want to partner with him, I'll talk to Mitch and we'll find someone…uh…someone more deserving of spending the evening with a famous, smokin' hot rock star, okay?"

"Well, now, hold on there, missy. Let's not be hasty," I replied, a sly smile spreading across my face. "I didn't say I wasn't interested. I'm just conveying to you that the idea of it scares the crap out of me. But, yeah, I can suck it up for one night…take one for the team. I mean, it's *your* wedding, and that's the type of person I am: selfless."

"Ahhh…yes, Casey, you are an amazing human being. Thank you for your sacrifice."

I nodded stoically as if I were doing Kate a huge favor, and then gasped after realizing the implications of pairing with Jake. "Oh, god, Sarah is going to be so mad."

Kate cringed. "I haven't figured out how I'm going to tell her yet."

"She'll never forgive you. It's like she called dibs on Jake the moment you announced your wedding."

"I know."

"Sarah is still going to go after him… I hope Mitch realizes that."

"Yeah, he does, but at least Jake won't feel obligated to hang out with her the entire time."

"That's true. Does Sarah even know if Jake is single? Isn't he dating that pop star?"

"That was a while ago. I don't think they're still together," Kate said.

"That doesn't mean he doesn't have a new girl. I mean, all this effort Sarah is putting into nailing a rock star, and it could all be for naught. It just seems such a shame."

"You be nice, Casey. Sarah will be mad enough as it is. And I don't think Jake has a girlfriend. He didn't ask for a plus one for the wedding, so I'm just assuming he's single."

"Single, but banging the groupies," I sang out.

"Casey! God, you can be so crude sometimes." Kate grimaced as she tried to suppress a smile.

"That's why you love me," I declared.

"Yeah. You're right."

"I guess I should tone it down for Jake. He probably won't appreciate my raunchy personality as much as you do."

"I don't know about that. He does have four brothers."

"True. But I've heard he isn't...uh... how do I put this nicely... the most interactive guy."

"Where did you hear that?"

"Like...everywhere? Duh!"

"Well, don't believe everything you hear or read about him in the media. Mitch says Jake gets a bad rap, and that he's actually a pretty well-adjusted guy."

"Seriously?"

"That's what I'm told," Kate affirmed, putting her hands up. "But then, what do I know? The first time I'll meet the other half of Mitch's family will be on our wedding day."

I could hear the annoyance in her voice and knew this was an issue for her. In the two years they'd been dating, Mitch had yet to take Kate to California to introduce her to his father, stepmother, and half-siblings. Mitch's mom and dad had never married, and split while he was still a baby. Growing up, Mitch had lived primarily with his mother in Arizona and only visited his dad and half-siblings in California on assorted holidays and during the summer months.

When Kate first told me she was dating Jake McKallister's half-brother, I assumed she'd already met Jake. But the reality was, Jake and Mitch weren't close. They shared a father, but not much else. Their relationship was more like that of distant cousins: they didn't dislike each other, they just lived their own lives and knew very little about one another. Kate had told me that Mitch was surprised Jake was even coming at all.

"Don't you worry," I replied to my obviously distressed friend.

"I'll take care of our handsome musician. If there's any fun in that gorgeous body of his, I'll do my best to bring it out of him."

"There's the Casey I know and love."

After the initial shock wore off, nervous excitement set in. All week before the wedding, I worried that Jake and I would have absolutely nothing in common... nothing to talk about. I had zero experience with guys like him. I'd never been the type of girl who went for the bad boy, tattooed rocker types. Although I had to admit, my current dating pool – the clean-cut jock or the self-important intellectual – had not yielded the best results either.

Regardless, what was I going to say to a guy like him? Jake McKallister might have been a rock star, but he was no ordinary one. His road to the top had been brutal. Jake became famous as a child...but not for his musical aptitude. In fact, he became famous for something entirely not of his doing. At thirteen years of age, Jake McKallister had been the victim of a stranger abduction. The violent kidnapping, which was witnessed by his traumatized younger brother, struck a nerve with the American public. His disappearance and the subsequent search efforts played out over television sets across the nation. Incredibly, Jake had managed to survive over a month in captivity before making a shocking escape, which ended with the stabbing death of the very man who had kidnapped him.

Police immediately declared the killing self-defense and refused to provide any further comment. Then, presumably in an effort to protect the privacy of a minor, the court system sealed all documents relating to Jake McKallister's kidnapping. Although no specifics had ever been released to the public, that didn't stop the media from speculating on every tiny detail. The general consensus about the kidnapping was that Jake had been horribly abused during his time in captivity, and that had he not killed his abductor, he would not be alive today. That became especially telling when the kidnapper's DNA linked him to several other missing and murdered boys. Jake had not survived just a stranger abduction but a serial killer.

The sensational story lit up the news channels and printing presses for months. The media hounded Jake. He couldn't step foot outside his door without cameras in his face. I couldn't imagine what it must have been like for him to survive what he had, and then to be treated so harshly by the media.

As with all big news stories, Jake's eventually faded from the headlines; and he, presumably, went on to lead a private life. But as it turned out, that was not the end of his story. Jake resurfaced a few years later as a solo rock musician, and was almost immediately catapulted into superstardom. He was hailed as a musical prodigy, and truly, his talents were undeniable. With his soaring rock anthems and haunting ballads, and his knack for writing one mega hit song after another, Jake was arguably the world's most famous rock star.

Yet, despite all his success, Jake was a bit of an enigma. He lived a giant life, but little was known about him privately. Aside from work-related appearances, Jake was rarely spotted out in public. He didn't frequent typical celebrity establishments, seldom appeared on television, and steadfastly refused all interviews... much to the dismay of the collective media worldwide. Really, though, who could blame him for snubbing the media after how they'd treated him as a child?

Jake's silence only seemed to fuel the fire of mystery surrounding him. Rumors swirled. Reports of him being homicidal, antisocial, suicidal, or a drug addict were front-page fodder for the trash magazines. And without Jake telling his side of the story, that was the version most people believed.

To be fair, the handful of times I'd seen Jake on TV, he'd seemed like a fairly personable guy. He smiled and interacted like any other person would. And when he performed, Jake was really engaging and energetic. I'd always wondered if maybe Jake wasn't the recluse he was portrayed to be. Maybe he just liked his privacy. Plenty of people had survived traumatic childhoods and had turned out to be perfectly normal adults. I mean, talent and looks alone couldn't have gotten Jake to where he was today, not without at least some social skills. Besides, getting up on stage in front of thousands of people... that took tenacity and resolve, certainly not common traits found among deranged, homicidal loners.

No, it wasn't so much Jake I was worried about, but myself. I always turned into a blabbering idiot when I was around reserved people. There was always that need to fill in the blanks. I could almost picture the look on the poor guy's face when I started jabbering on endlessly about trivial stuff. He was going to think I was such a weirdo.

2

CASEY: THE INTRODUCTION

The day of the wedding rehearsal, I was a nervous wreck. It had started out bad after having to clean my roommate's puke off the bathroom floor – don't ask – and things just continued downhill. Well, okay, there really wasn't much worse than cleaning up puke; but still, every little thing that could go wrong did. So it wasn't so farfetched for me to believe that my first meeting with Jake was going to be a disastrous affair. And the closer it got to the rehearsal, the worse the uneasy feeling in the pit of my stomach became. As I drove to the hotel, I reviewed the little list in my head of topics that I could talk about with Jake if conversation lulled. Usually, I didn't have a problem chatting with men, but then Jake McKallister was no ordinary man. I'd never been so anxious in all my life.

After I checked into the hotel, I began the arduous task of picking what to wear to the rehearsal and then later at dinner. I tried to predict what Jake would like: sophisticated? Cute and flirty? Sexy? In the end, I decided to dress in what I would feel most comfortable in, since – let's be honest – he probably wasn't even going to talk to me beyond the required niceties, so there would be no reason to try and impress him. I chose casual chic, or at least as chic as my limited income could afford: tan slacks that accentuated my butt, and a white peasant top. After the outfit was picked, I smoothed my dark hair with a flat iron and applied limited makeup... just enough, really, to give my skin a natural glow and to accentuate my big, brown eyes – which, I felt, aside from my dimpled smile, were my best feature.

I arrived at the rehearsal a few minutes late and anxiously scanned the room for the groomsman I was paired with. Jake was nowhere in sight. I sighed with relief; and, if I were being completely honest, just the slightest bit of disappointment. The rehearsal started without him, so everyone was paired with someone except for me. I consoled myself by observing Jake's family instead. And there were plenty of them to observe. The whole McKallister clan, minus Jake, had come from California the night before. Brothers and sisters, ranging in age from teens to the mid-twenties, parents, and a set of paternal grandparents named Jim and Sue. The only reason I knew that was because their grandchildren called them JimSuey, which I thought was pretty inventive.

Both of Jake's parents, Scott and Michelle, looked to be in their early fifties. Scott was tall and handsome... for an older guy. You could tell in his earlier years he'd probably been quite the stud muffin. The way he was dressed, as well as the way he carried himself, told me a lot about him. This was a blue-collar man who worked hard for his money. He had an easy rapport with his kids, and it was clear to me they adored him.

One thing I found surprisingly similar to my own family was the way the McKallisters all teased each other. Just in the short time I was observing them, I heard Scott razzed by his sons for the shirt he was wearing, a patch of thinning hair on his head, and his incorrect use of the phrase 'on fleek.' Obviously, Scott was used to this type of treatment, because he had plenty of insults of his own to sling back at his boys. Just by his interaction with his kids, I could tell Scott was the fun parent, not the disciplinarian. That job, I was certain, went to Jake's mom, Michelle. She seemed more serious than her husband and kept reprimanding her kids when they teased Scott or got rowdy. But she also found her brood humorous, as evidenced by the smile she was always attempting to suppress. Michelle's navy blue top set off her gorgeous light blue eyes, and her auburn hair shone below her shoulders. She dressed nicely and was well kept, but she wasn't dripping wealth. She just seemed like a normal, middle-class mom.

I couldn't catch the names of all Jake's siblings. There were just too many of them. I did figure out that Jake had two sisters and four brothers, including Mitch. I wasn't sure who was older or younger except for the two teenagers. Looks-wise, they were all good-looking people. I could see a slight similarity between them and their famous brother, but it wasn't obvious. They all had their own look, except for the youngest boy, who was clearly trying to channel his big brother in both appearance and mannerisms.

The rehearsal lasted about an hour, and after it was over, I walked up to Kate.

"Sorry, Casey."

"Is Jake not coming?"

"I'm not sure. He was supposed to be here. No one seems to be able to get in touch with him."

"Geez, I hope everything is okay."

"Yeah, hopefully he just missed a flight or something."

"He'll be here, don't worry, and if not, I'll be a vision of loveliness walking down the aisle by myself."

"That you'll be, Case."

～

That evening at the rehearsal dinner, Jake was still a no-show. But word had arrived that his flight had been delayed by three hours leaving Frankfurt, causing him to miss his connecting flight to Phoenix. Mitch and Kate's wedding actually fell right in the middle of his eight-month world tour. Jake had just taken the weekend off to attend the nuptials and would be on a plane back to Europe Sunday night. Although he was not expected to make it in time for the rehearsal dinner, he would definitely be at the wedding the next day. My nervousness dissipated knowing I would not have to talk to him that night.

About halfway through the dinner, a commotion arose outside the banquet room. A shrill scream could be heard coming from the main dining area. I whipped my head in that direction, startled, and instantly worried that perhaps there was an active shooter in the restaurant. I was seconds away from diving under the table for protection when the door to our private room swung open, and Jake McKallister coolly walked in.

He was clutching a duffle bag in one hand and a backpack in the other. Slung casually over his back was a guitar case... the only indication that he was, in fact, a universally renowned rock star; because, certainly his attire did not scream it. He was simply dressed in a light gray, body-hugging, button-up shirt, severely scuffed up leather boots, and faded black denim jeans molded effortlessly onto his noteworthy ass like a glove. This clearly was not the universally accepted rock star uniform of black leather, chains, body piercings, and guy-liner. No, the way he was dressed almost seemed to confirm that Jake McKallister was the real deal, a talent far beyond his years. He didn't need any trickery or costumes to prove he was someone special.

Judging by looks alone, Jake was indeed something special. Hypnotizing was more like it. The minute he walked in the room, it was as if he drained all the oxygen from it. Everyone seemed to be holding their breath in admiration of the young man who had sauntered in so nonchalantly. Wow, slow clap for the smoking hot rock star!

Not known for my subtlety, my mouth dropped open just at

the sight of him. I'd seen him plenty of times in magazines and on television but, in person, Jake McKallister was truly striking. I scanned his famous face as if it were the first time I'd ever seen him... his beautifully rugged bone structure; his tanned, unblemished skin; his full, delectable lips; and those show-stopping eyes... lord. I couldn't even really tell what color they were – like an extremely light, translucent, greenish-gray shade. And as if that wasn't impressive enough, those babies were framed in long, dark lashes. I gulped. I couldn't remember ever seeing eyes as pretty as his. But maybe it was more about the history behind them that made them so striking. There was something so hauntingly expressive about them – as if the story of his life, no doubt an excruciating one, was hiding just behind the surface.

Jake's brown hair was shoulder length and fell in careless waves over his handsome, clean-shaven face. Some strands hung over his eyes. He didn't make much of an effort to remove them. As opposed to some of those vain men who incessantly flipped and ran their hands through their long locks, something told me Jake's hair was not so much a fashion accessory as it was a protective shield. It gave him a dangerous 'leave-me-alone' type vibe.

As handsome and talented as he was, even at first glance, it was easy to see why the media would describe him as reserved. There was an unapproachable quality to him, almost like he was daring people to bother him. Jake made me nervous just looking at him. If I weren't already paired with him, I wouldn't dare go up and talk to him. In fact, I was actively regretting my decision to be his partner for the wedding. He was so far out of my comfort zone.

Still, I couldn't help but admire his physical attributes. My eyes traveled the length of his body. He was an impressive guy. He had to be around six feet tall, with long legs and a long, lean, muscled torso. He took care of himself and was strong and powerful, that much was obvious. A few buttons of his shirt were open, exposing a strapping chest as the fabric clung to his sculpted muscles. My body tingled in response. *Keep on dreamin', girl! You're not even in the same league as this guy.*

Jake's brother, whom I'd seen at the rehearsal, went over to greet him as he propped his guitar against the wall and then dropped his bags. After a quick exchange, Jake turned toward all of us in the rehearsal party just as a commotion from the entrance caught his attention. A girl from the restaurant burst through the door and lunged for him. Jake didn't even flinch, not even when she was inches from grabbing onto his arm. His brother and the restaurant manager simultaneously pulled her back, pushing her from the room. The manager then shut the door on a gaggle of teenagers ready to take the girl's place.

I saw a flash of annoyance cross Jake's face, but he immediately masked it. He replaced that second of irritation with a strained smile like he knew he was being watched and had to put on a show for us. As Jake moved across the room, he radiated strength and prominence. He was an imposing figure. I wondered how old he was. From what I remembered about him, we were close in age, but the way he carried himself made him seem so much older. There was a maturity to him that went far beyond his years... one which could only be acquired through living and learning. And there was no doubt in my mind Jake had lived through more than his fair share. By all accounts, he'd grown up quickly and had learned some pretty tough life lessons at a very young age.

Jake walked directly over to Mitch and Kate. He hugged his brother and apologized for being late. He then took a step back and shook Kate's hand, introducing himself. Jake was neutral in his expression, but he seemed genuine upon meeting his future sister-in-law. As for poor Kate... well, I had to smile. She was blushing and smiling like a fangirl meeting her idol for the first time. Even though Jake was about to become her brother-in-law, she was still hopelessly star-struck.

We all were. Jake exuded a dynamic presence. It wasn't just the fact that he was a beautiful specimen of a man or that he was universally famous; there was something else about him – something that made you feel that you were in the company of someone special. My attraction to him was instantaneous. Of course, a quick glance around the room at all the swooning women told me I wasn't the only one having that reaction.

And something also told me Jake was well aware of the response he was eliciting from his female admirers. Really, he was a bit of a walking contradiction. He might have been a reserved person, but he was no shrinking violet. He had the commanding, quiet confidence of a person who knew exactly who he was. All that worrying I'd done about him being introverted or broken was for naught. If anything, Jake McKallister appeared to be the complete opposite of what I'd imagined. This was a guy who could get any girl in the room, and he knew it.

As Jake turned toward the crowd, he scanned the wedding party. I felt my heart race as his pretty eyes rolled over me. He didn't linger. In fact, I doubt he saw me at all. He was clearly seeking out his family, and when he found them, he cut across the room. Hushed whispering filled the air. Jake paid no attention to it, although there was no way he couldn't have heard it. As he passed, every head turned. Jake didn't reciprocate. There was no need. He was the star, and as such, was used to displays of adoration. I wondered what it must feel like to command that kind of attention everywhere you went. Surprisingly, it didn't seem to bother Jake. In fact, he appeared to be totally unaffected by the way he was affecting everyone else. I wasn't sure if he was an expert at guarding his emotions or if he really was that indifferent to others' opinions. Strangely enough, his apathetic attitude didn't come across as cocky. Maybe it was just the knowledge of who he was and what he had survived that made him somewhat immune to the typical stereotypes. I'd always been attracted to smiley, outgoing types, but even I had to admit,

I found everything about Jake McKallister to be incredibly appealing. Suddenly I wanted to know more... much more... about him.

With all eyes on him, Jake greeted JimSuey and then his mother, father, and two sisters before settling down between his three brothers. Then, as if someone flipped a switch, Jake's demeanor changed completely. It was like the wall came down around him. Here, amongst his family, he was entirely comfortable, and it showed. I watched him interact with his siblings in an easy, relaxed way. The strained smile from earlier was replaced with a genuinely charming lopsided grin. I was surprised to see him throw his head back when he laughed. To me, that had always been a sign of a person with a good sense of humor. The wariness in his eyes also vanished. This Jake did not even remotely resemble the same guarded guy who'd walked in five minutes earlier. Was this the Jake McKallister that was shielded from public view? Was this the real man behind the mask? I found myself becoming more stalkerish as the minutes passed. I had to will myself to stop staring.

When the waitress came around, Jake ordered chicken tacos and water – not that I was spying on him or anything. The waitress stumbled on her words a bit and seemed flustered. Being a server myself, I probably wouldn't have been able to keep my cool around Jake either. It seemed all eyes, including mine, were still trained on him. A few times he looked up from his conversation to scan the room. People would quickly look away, pretending like they hadn't been staring at him the entire time. But he knew. He had to know. None of us were being real subtle with our gawking. He was like some exotic zoo animal that we were all peering at through the cage, trying to get a better look at.

Toward the end of dinner, Jake's father, Scott, slightly drunk and boisterously entertaining, told a colorful rendition of his path to fatherhood, much to the embarrassment of his wife and kids. The story went something like this: after becoming a father to Mitch at twenty-three years old, Scott met Michelle and they had their first son, Keith. Then, two years later, they had a daughter, Emma. They decided that was enough kids for them. But then three years later, they had an "oops" – Jake. And just eleven months after Jake, they had a "make an appointment now" – Kyle. A vasectomy followed. And as Scott told it, it was the best decision he ever 'didn't make' because, after having to live through the "the twin toddler terrors," as he called Jake and Kyle, more kids was the last thing he wanted. But then, as Scott remembers it, five years later his wife was begging him to have just one more baby after the boys started school. So "poor, suffering" Scott went and had the vasectomy reversed, and a year later, their youngest son, Quinn, was born. But Michelle was unhappy again because she worried that Quinn would be lonely without a sibling close in age, so sixteen months later came their youngest child, daughter Grace. During the entire story, the McKallister kids were covering their faces in mock humiliation, and Michelle was shaking her head and rolling her eyes.

When Scott was done embarrassing his family, Jake's older brother Keith grinned and said, "Geez, Dad, seriously? Was that really necessary?"

Scott raised his glass and jokingly nodded his head, as if he'd just done a valuable public service for the community.

"Well, all I can say after that story is… Jake, I bet you've never been so happy to be an 'oops.'" Everyone burst out laughing as Keith patted his brother Kyle on the shoulder sympathetically. Kyle raised his hands in defeat, then pretended to cry. Jake slapped Kyle on the back supportively. It was such a cute, light-hearted moment for a family who had undoubtedly lived through some very dark times.

After dinner was finished, Sarah, who had been trying to get Jake's attention all evening, made a beeline for him. During the rehearsal, she'd been flirting with Kyle, whom she was partnered with for the wedding. But now that his brother was in the picture, Kyle didn't stand a chance. I watched him saunter off with an annoyed look on his face as Sarah introduced herself to his brother. Jake scanned her appreciatively with his eyes. With her shiny blonde hair, high cheekbones, and tall, model-worthy body, Sarah was stunning. Every guy thought so.

Girls, on the other hand, weren't as impressed. Sarah might have been beautiful on the outside, but her insides needed a little work. The first time we met, I, at least, tried to give her the benefit of the doubt; but damn, Sarah was a difficult one to like. Just after being introduced, and getting an unimpressed once-over from her, I attempted to break the ice with a joke. Instead of laughing, Sarah just stared at me like I was some annoying little gnat, then turned her attention to someone else. She made me feel like a total idiot, and from that point on, I didn't like her. But sadly, our paths still crossed occasionally because Kate and Sarah had been friends since birth, and their families had lived next door to each other growing up. So occasionally when I went out with Kate, Sarah was there, too. And when she was with us, the guys fought over her. It was as if Kate and I didn't even exist. Occasionally one of Sarah's rejects would head in my direction, but any guy who was interested in Sarah was not a guy I wanted to get to know. That's why I hated the idea of her hitting on Jake. Once she had her claws in him, the rest of us were toast. *As if, Casey.*

Of course, I guess I couldn't blame him for looking. She was practically thrusting her cleavage in his face. What straight man wouldn't react to that? Hell, even I was impressed. I noticed Jake's eyes lingering a second too long on those impressive orbs. Sarah saw it too and took it as a sign to up her flirting. After all, she'd been waiting for this day to come for a long time now. So I watched as she boldly asserted her intentions, giggling and jiggling. If Jake wanted to, he could be having sex with her in a matter of minutes. However, the jury was still out on how he felt about her overly assertive behavior. I saw him look past her a few times. Was he planning an escape, or was that just wishful thinking on my part?

Then Sarah made a big mistake. She placed her hand on his chest. As if someone flipped the switch again, Jake's walls went back up. His relaxed smile from earlier instantly faded and the strained one was back. His body seemed more rigid, and his face took on that same unapproachable quality.

Sarah saw it too. But instead of conceding defeat, she changed her tactics. The horny sexpot wasn't working. She became instantly more mature, her face taking on a serious tone. I imagined her telling him some heartbreaking tale of the trials and tribulations she faced on a day-to-day basis in the cutthroat world of high-end modeling. That was sure to win his sympathies. I wanted to laugh. Sarah was pulling out all the punches. But why wouldn't she? In her eyes, Jake was the ultimate prize: a sexual encounter she could brag about for years to come. But just as Mitch had predicted, Sarah's fawning didn't go over well with Jake. He looked incredibly uncomfortable and didn't seem the least bit interested in Sarah. Huh... maybe her charms were not foolproof after all.

Just then, Kate's mom, Angie, came up to me.

"Quite a looker, that one," she remarked, glancing toward Jake.

I blushed. Had I been so obvious in my stalking? Angie must have taken my silence as surprise.

"Hey, I may be old and married, but I'm not dead."

I laughed. "Don't explain yourself to me. I agree with you. He's smoldering eye candy."

"Poor boy doesn't know what hit him. Sarah is a force to be reckoned with."

"I'm sure he meets Sarahs every day. Somehow I think he can handle himself just fine," I replied.

"Oh, I'm sure you're right. Hell, if I was thirty years younger,

I'd be giving it a shot, too... oh, crap, who am I kidding, I would never have had a chance at a guy like him."

"You and me both," I laughed.

"Hey, don't sell yourself short. You're every bit as gorgeous as Sarah, you're just more subtle in your beauty."

"Yeah, well a flat chest will do that to a person," I deadpanned.

"Big boobs or not," Angie grinned, "I think you're adorable."

"That's the nicest thing anyone has ever said to me," I joked.

Angie laughed, giving me a quick side hug. "Okay, girl, I'll see you tomorrow for the big day," she said with genuine warmth and enthusiasm. "I'm so excited."

As soon as she left, I turned back to the 'Jake and Sarah show'. Thank god, I hadn't missed much. Sarah was still working her charms on what now appeared to be a completely uninterested Jake. Then, all of the sudden, his oldest brother Keith swooped in, made some excuse, and pulled him away. Jake's brothers were his escape route, and I was certain they had 'saved' him many times before.

I smiled, impressed. Jake had just gone up a whole bunch of notches in my book. As he went back to his family, I walked to my chair to gather my things. I knew I should probably go over and introduce myself, since we were paired together for the wedding, but he kind of terrified me for reasons I could not explain. So I took the coward's way out and made the decision to wait until tomorrow, just before the ceremony; then I would say hi.

As I was preparing to leave, I heard Kate call my name. I turned around and, to my horror, saw her walking up... with Jake. *No... oh, god... no.* Instantly, I felt weak in the knees.

Jake stared at me impassively with that face... with those eyes... wary of another Sarah episode, no doubt. Swooning girls must surround the guy all the time, and I got the impression he did not entirely appreciate the adoration. I was determined not to be that girl.

"I just wanted to introduce you guys. Jake, this is my very good friend, Casey Caldwell. She'll be your partner for the ceremony tomorrow. She can fill you in on anything you missed at the rehearsal."

Jake politely reached out his hand. I put mine in his. "Nice to meet you," he said.

"You too," I managed to say before I gazed up at his gorgeous, famous face and, for some reason, all rational thought left my brain. For probably the first time in my life, I became hopelessly and completely tongue-tied. I could not come up with even one tiny thing to say to Jake. Not only was I not *that* girl, I wasn't even a girl who could carry on a normal conversation with the guy.

Jake let go of my hand and looked away, no doubt sensing the awkwardness too. An uncomfortable silence followed. Panic took over. My list, my list… what the hell was on my list? The three of us stood there uneasily for a few seconds before Kate prodded, "Casey, maybe you can tell Jake what he missed."

"Yeah, sure," I mumbled. Then I had to think. What had we even done in the rehearsal? My mind was a giant blank. More silence.

"Okay, so I'll leave you guys to it. I have to talk to my mom about the wedding before she leaves," Kate claimed, before scurrying away like a coward.

Kate just left me dangling off the ledge. What a traitor! Jake and I watched her walk away. I had the impression he felt as betrayed by her as I did. Reluctantly, he turned back to me.

Jake cleared his throat. "So…uh… is there anything out of the ordinary I need to know, or is the wedding pretty standard fare?"

And then he did it. He scanned the crowd looking for his brother to come and save him… from me. *Oh, no you don't, asshole! You will not reduce me to a 'Sarah.'* My voice miraculously returned. Jake McKallister was about to meet the real Casey Caldwell.

"Yes...pretty standard wedding fare... except, you know, for the dance moves at the end."

This got Jake's attention immediately. Where he might not have really noticed me before, Jake gaped at me now, his eyes opened wide with surprise and confusion. "What do you mean, the dance moves?"

"You know, at the end, the whole wedding party... we're all doing that dance."

The color nearly drained from Jake's face. He looked truly shocked. He was shaking his head. "No. Nobody told me."

Now, any normal person would have shut it down there. I mean, this was Jake McKallister, a goddamn worldwide celebrity, who was certainly not known for having a sunny personality. But oh no, not me. I had the unfortunate disease others had referred to as verbal diarrhea. Once I got started, the words just poured out of me.

"Yeah, they surprised us with it at the rehearsal this afternoon. Have you ever seen on the Internet where the whole wedding party dances down the aisle in celebration?" I asked.

"I...maybe...I don't know." Jake stumbled over his words.

"Well, that's basically what we'll be doing," I continued in a pleasant, conversational tone of voice.

Jake just stared at me in consternation before saying, "I just can't believe no one said anything to me."

"Well, I think it was a last minute thing, you know?"

"Still, I mean, you'd think that's something they'd mention," he replied, shaking his head. His eyebrows were furrowed in frustration. The initial shock was wearing off and now Jake just looked pissed. It was definitely time to stop. He was getting agitated. It was entirely possible he wouldn't find my little prank humorous. Best-case scenario: he laughed. Worst-case scenario: he would seek a restraining order against me. That should have been enough for me to shut the hell up, but... nope. Instead, I just upped the ante.

"Yeah, that is weird, huh? Anyway, no worries. The dance is really easy. I'll teach you… it goes like this, one-two-three hop then skip then back two-three-four hop then skip. See, it's pretty easy."

To illustrate my terribly choreographed fake dance, I did a ridiculous 'stand in place' version. My arms were flailing all over the place and my feet were doing something close to Irish dancing. Jake's mouth dropped open in horrified incredulity as he watched me.

"You want to practice?"

My rock star partner stared at me like I had two rotating heads before regaining his composure and shaking his own head in annoyance. "No, not really."

"Okay, suit yourself. Oh, shoot…I almost forgot… at the end, just as we leave the church, we all have to jump in the air and click our heels together."

"What?" Jake blurted out with a seriously irritated look on his face. I'd crossed the line of his tolerance. "Are you serious?" he asked me, not so much as a question but as a complaint.

He'd just given me the cue I needed to end my little ruse. I smiled, shook my head and answered, "No."

It took a few seconds for my response to register with Jake.

"Wait…*are* you kidding?" he asked in disbelief.

"Yeah, I'm just kidding," I grinned. "No dancing… just your standard wedding fare."

Jake stared at me in surprise – no, total shock – and for a second, I worried that the worst case scenario was about to become reality. But then a smile, so dazzling and so sincere, spread across his handsome face and he said, "Seriously? You were just messing with me?"

"We were having an awkward moment." I grinned, shrugging. "I thought it might lighten the mood." No way was I going to tell him my true motivation behind the prank.

Jake stared at me a second before he started laughing. Oh,

minimize our accomplishments... whatever," I said in mock annoyance.

"Oh, god, I'm so sorry. I didn't mean to sell your school short."

"It's okay. It's a common error."

Jake grinned, and his eyes gleamed with mischief. "So?"

"So, what?" I demanded, with just the right amount of flirt back.

"Are you a party girl?"

I laughed out loud. "Seriously? Way to stereotype, rock star."

Then it was Jake's turn to express his amusement. By the look of respect on his face, my retort had made an impression on him. "Yeah, who am I to talk, right?"

I nodded, feeling happier than I had in a long time. "And to answer your question... I know I seem super cool and everything, but I'm actually kind of a nerd."

Jake looked me up and down appreciatively and said, "You don't look like any nerd I've ever seen."

Ahh...swoon!

"Well, this might sway you...I'm an accounting major."

"Shut up!" he exclaimed in surprise. "Accounting?"

I nodded proudly.

"Damn, you *are* a nerd."

"I told you," I said, touching his arm spontaneously. The conversation was so effortless that I wasn't thinking. Recalling his reaction to Sarah's touch, I immediately removed my hand and tried to play it off like it was no big deal. "Oh, sorry, I got overly excited... like a puppy." *Please don't be mad.*

Jake grinned. "It's okay. My arm didn't mind."

And truly, he seemed fine with it... totally unaffected. *Huh. Okay.*

"So how did you end up at ASU, the world's biggest party school?" Jake teased while emphasizing 'world.'

"My family lives six blocks from the school. It was the cheapest alternative."

"Ah…okay."

"And before you assume I'm totally boring, I'll say that I may have dabbled a bit in the party scene from time to time."

"You being boring was the furthest thing from my mind," Jake answered, with just the right touch of sincerity.

Another compliment? He seemed to be enjoying my company. What were the chances? Jake was staring down at me with gleaming eyes and the most charming expression on his face. Damn… he was so beautiful to look at I almost felt like apologizing for gazing upon him.

"Did you ever watch the movie *Ted 2?*" He asked.

I knew exactly where he was going with his question. *Ted 2* had bashed ASU for its party reputation and for its students being dumb. Jake was teasing me. I loved it. I smiled coyly and said, "I did."

Jake grinned, his eyebrows raised.

"What?" I demanded, dramatically slapping a hand on my hip.

"Nothing."

"Go ahead, Jake. I've heard every joke there is about ASU."

"I didn't say anything."

"How many ASU freshmen does it take to change a lightbulb?"

"I don't know."

"None, it's a sophomore course."

He laughed out loud.

"Why are rectal thermometers banned at ASU?"

He shrugged.

"They cause brain damage."

Jake laughed again.

"And finally…why aren't ASU cheerleaders allowed to do the splits?"

"I have no idea," he replied, throwing his hands up in defeat.

"Because they stick to the ground."

"Oh, god." Jake shook his head and winced. "Never mind about *Ted 2*."

Damn, this guy was actually super cool. My breath caught in my chest. I was so excited to be talking to him that I felt the need to inhale deeply a few times and regroup.

"So I have to ask, Casey, do you actually want to be an accountant?"

"Yes, actually I do," I acknowledged, nodding. "That's how college works, Jake. You study the thing that you want to be."

"Yeah, no, I get that…it's just… I can't think of anything more boring to do in life," he said, smiling, and then added, "No offense."

"None taken…and it is boring, but I love numbers."

"You must be good at math, then."

"Yeah, I'm good at math."

"Like how good?"

"Decently good."

"Decently good? What does that mean?" he asked.

"I don't know. I don't want to be one of those cocky nerds," I said.

Jake considered the issue for a moment. "Can one really be academically cocky?"

"You have no idea how cocky nerds are nowadays. It really has become an epidemic," I related with a seriously concerned face.

Jake shook his head in amusement. "Wow, where have I been?"

"I doubt you run into too many of them in your line of work, but trust me, they exist."

"I believe you," Jake said, his eyes twinkling with enjoyment. He took my breath away. He then asked, "What year are you in?"

"Wow you have a lot of questions, don't you?"

"I know," Jake agreed. "I'm usually not this talkative."

"Really? Huh? 'Cause right now, you're just a regular chatty pants."

Jake stared at me in surprise. "Did you just call me chatty pants?"

"I did."

Jake shook his head, laughing, "My god, Casey, people have called me a lot of things in my lifetime, but I've never *ever* heard that one. That's impressive."

"Well, thank you," I nodded. "And to answer your question, I'll be a senior this year."

"To tell you the truth, I forgot what question I asked you."

"That's okay...we can't all be as smart as me."

"Uh-huh, says the ASU student."

"Oooh... that was a low blow." I said, hunching over like I'd actually been hit. Hot, talented, nice... *and* a sense of humor? *Be still, my wildly beating heart.*

"I know. Sorry."

"Hey, never apologize for a well-placed comeback."

He looked down at me with a sexy tilt of the head, and I could feel a tingling of excitement race through me. Wow. I was really crushing on this guy. We stared at each other for a moment, not speaking, then Jake flashed me the cutest smile and I returned the favor.

"So, uh, how do you know Kate?" he asked, breaking the silence.

"We were waitresses together at Outback Steakhouse until she moved in with Mitch and quit. I'm still there serving up Bloomin' Onions five days a week."

Jake nodded. "Actually, I'm more of an Aussie Cheese Fries kind of guy."

"No way...so am I!" I exclaimed, probably more excited than I should have been, but Jake didn't seem to mind my enthusiasm. "... only in the girl version, of course."

I nodded in concession. Nice. I liked his confidence. He seemed so sure of himself.

"And besides, I have a good excuse."

"Yeah, yeah, I know – concerts, groupies, Europe, those pesky first class flights not leaving on time. Excuses, excuses. Wah, wah," I teased.

"Geez, tough crowd."

"Excuse me if I don't cry you a river, but I had problems of my own – real life problems – trying to get here on time today."

"Oh, really?" Jake replied, looking genuinely curious. "Real life problems, huh?"

"Yep."

"Am I going to get to hear your little sob story?"

I sized him up with my eyes and considered. "I'm not sure if you can handle it."

"Oh, trust me – I can handle it."

"Okay, but I'm warning you now that my story involves bodily excretions."

Jake reacted with surprise. "Wow…you really know how to build excitement."

"Do you want to hear my story or not?" I asked in a demanding tone, all the while flashing him a devious smile.

"Yes. I'll be quiet."

"Thank you," I sassed. Unlike his conversation with Sarah, Jake seemed completely engaged in ours. "So last night my room-mate hooked up with some random guy at a bar. The two of them got pretty drunk. Anyway, I guess he got up early to try and sneak away before she woke up, as these winners often do, but decided to use the bathroom first. I woke up to my roommate screaming. Apparently, this idiot had clogged our toilet before slipping out the front door, and now it was overflowing all over the floor and there was literally crap floating across the linoleum."

"God, no," Jake winced, shaking his head.

"Oh, yes. And it gets worse. I ran in and my roommate was as white as a ghost. She was looking at me with that face."

"What face?" he asked, completely mesmerized by my tale of woe.

"The barf face," I revealed dramatically.

"No?"

"Yes," I confirmed.

Jake laughed.

"So I'm like, 'Oh, no... no no no'... and as soon as I say that, she pukes... and it's like projectile vomiting. I only narrowly escaped a direct hit. My roommate starts bawling and says she can't deal with it and runs out of the bathroom. Now normally, I too would be running for the hills, but with the wedding rehearsal at four o'clock, that was not an option. I still had to shower and pack and run errands. So, while you were all cozily nestled up in your first class fantasy seat, I was living the life of a real live Cinderella, scooping up poop, mopping up puke, and plunging the murky depths of a toilet."

Jake just stared at me with a combination of disgust and awe. *Crap.* I'd gone too far. Why did I always have to push the limits of social acceptability?

He shook his head and said, "Wow."

"See? I told you, you couldn't handle it." Nervous dread crept into my voice.

"No. It's not that," Jake refuted with a serious look on his famous face. "I just didn't realize how bad the real world had become since I started living it up in first class."

I burst out laughing, and after a moment, Jake joined in. So loud was my amusement that people around us turned to stare. Sarah gave me a malicious once-over.

"I think you're the funny one, Jake McKallister," I claimed, after catching my breath.

Jake looked pleased by my assessment. "Are you going to call me by my full name all the time, Casey Caldwell?"

"Possibly. I haven't decided yet."

Jake ran his fingers through his hair. There was something so sexy about the way he did it. I gulped. "You know, this might come as a surprise to you, but most people I meet for the first time don't entertain me with stories of vomit and crap."

"Seriously?" I questioned, pretending to be surprised.

"Yeah, most people just ask for an autograph or a picture," he affirmed.

"So then, this must have been quite a treat for you?" I replied with an innocent look on my face.

Jake laughed. "You have no idea."

Just then his mom called and told him it was time to go.

"Okay," he replied, then turned back to me. "That was not a setup. She actually really wants me to go."

"I know…I got that. ASU student, remember?"

"Oh, yeah…I forgot," Jake nodded. "Well, I guess I have to go make her happy."

"Ah…you're a good son."

"That's up for debate."

"I don't want to keep you. It was really fun talking to you, Jake McKallister."

"You too, Casey Caldwell," he replied, and then rewarded me with a cute, almost shy, little smile. He cocked his head just a smidge and hair fell over his eyes. I swallowed hard. I'd never seen any man as sexy as him in all my life. Everything about him made me quiver. He lingered there a second, staring at me with that look on his face, almost like he didn't want to leave. "Okay, well, I'll see you tomorrow, then."

"Yep…I'll have my dancing shoes on."

"Yeah, you do that," he said, as he walked away laughing. Jake stopped by the door to gather his belongings and just before exiting, turned around and smiled at me. It was a sweet, friendly smile, and it was meant just for me.

After Jake left, I just stood there, possibly in a state of shock. A shiver ran through my body. I couldn't believe I'd just had that conversation... with Jake McKallister, of all people. I felt the butterflies in my stomach. I could not remember a time when I'd felt that comfortable around a guy I was attracted to. The conversation just flowed so naturally. He might have been famous, but he acted like a normal guy, albeit the hottest normal guy I'd ever met. I went over every little part of our conversation again in my head, committing it to memory. Damn, Jake McKallister had been flirting with me! That was so totally unexpected.

"CASEY," squealed Kelsey, one of the bridesmaids. "I can't believe you talked to him for so long. Weren't you nervous?"

"At first, yeah, but he's actually super cool," I replied in a daze. "And funny."

"Seriously? I thought he was supposed to be mute or something," Savannah said.

My eyebrows rose unintentionally. "That's totally rude."

"I was kidding. Geez, don't be so sensitive."

I was sensitive. Weird. I had only just met Jake, but already I felt the need to defend him. He was so much more than what people imagined him to be. If that was the 'real' Jake I had just been talking to, it made me wonder why he didn't let the world see him for the amazing guy he really was.

Sarah was standing nearby and had obviously overheard our conversation. She walked over, looking beautiful but annoyed. "I'm still pissed they gave Jake to you. I should have been the one talking to him."

I was instantly annoyed with her. *Gave* him to me? Did she think the only reason he was talking to me was because he'd been 'assigned' to me? Bitch. Although I wanted to punch her in her smug little face, I took the high road instead, for Kate's sake. "I had nothing to do with it. I was as surprised as you were."

"Yeah, well, just so you know, being paired with him doesn't mean he's yours, Casey. I'm still going to hang out with him tomorrow."

"I never said you couldn't."

"I wasn't asking for your permission. I was just making sure you understood that," Sarah stated, and then walked away.

I wanted to scream at her, but I kept my cool. I knew what she didn't: Jake wasn't interested in her. Was she so oblivious that she hadn't picked up on the whole brother running interference thing? Still, it made me nervous. When Sarah wanted someone, there was usually no denying her.

"I saw you two laughing," Molly recounted, interrupting my thoughts. "What did he say that was so funny?"

"I don't know," I said. For some reason, I didn't want to share with others the conversation I'd had with Jake. "We were just chatting."

"About what, though?" Molly pressed.

"My school, where I worked, stuff like that."

"But what did he say about himself?"

"Nothing really. He was more asking me questions."

I then realized we hadn't actually talked about him at all. Oh, crap. Was I being too pushy? Did I come across as one of those annoying girls who talks too much? Actually, I *was* one of those girls, but that was beside the point. I thought back to our conversation. Jake had been the one asking the questions. And if he'd thought I was too chatty, he could have left with his brother when he'd had the chance. No, clearly Jake had enjoyed our conversation. At least I hoped he had.

"Why would he ask you questions?" Molly asked, looking perplexed.

"I don't know." I grinned at the off-handed insult. "He must have found me unbelievably interesting."

"That came out wrong. I didn't mean it in a bad way," Molly

laughed. "I just meant, he's a freaking celebrity. Why weren't *you* asking *him* questions?"

I threw my hands up in the air for effect. "It was a natural, free-flowing conversation. I guess I didn't think to ask him about his life in the limelight. Sorry."

It took a few more minutes of stupid questions before the others finally stopped badgering me about Jake. Excusing myself, I slipped away from the girls and drove back to the hotel. Once back in my room, I changed into a pair of gray ASU sweats and a pink tank top, and then brushed my hair into a high ponytail. I had numerous missed calls from my mother. I smiled. I knew she was dying to know how the day had gone. My mom was into celebrities and read *People* magazine faithfully. All week leading up to the wedding, she'd been giddy with the excitement of knowing that I was going to have the unique opportunity to meet, and maybe even hang out with, one of the world's most elusive stars.

Because I only had one bar in my room, I took the elevator down and went outside by the pool to make my phone call.

"Did you meet him?" My excited mom answered my call with a question.

"Oh yeah, I met him."

"And?"

"And I'm in love," I sighed dramatically. "I'm already planning our wedding."

"Wow, that was fast. Does Jake know?"

"No. I'll just invite him and hope he shows up."

"Yeah, that sounds like a smart plan. Did he seem to like you, though?"

"Yeah. I mean, he was super nice to me. We actually talked for a while."

"Really? I wouldn't have thought he was a talker."

I thought back to when I'd called Jake 'chatty pants' and his shocked reaction.

"Well, I don't think he normally is, but he was talkative with me."

"Really?" Mom seemed genuinely surprised.

"Yeah. I mean, he comes across kind of distant, but once you get to know him, he's actually a really personable guy."

"And you got to know him?"

"Well, not really. I mean, he was asking all the questions, but we had a really fun conversation. We were kidding around. I'm telling you, Mom... we had a little spark going on and, maybe it was just my imagination, but I think he might be in love with me, too," I said as I lazily twirled my hair.

"Huh. How much time did you say you spent with him?"

"Like fifteen minutes."

"Boy, you move fast."

"Gotta be quick when you're dealing with rock stars. They're flighty creatures."

She laughed.

"Seriously, though... Jake really impressed me. He has a great sense of humor and is so genuine and self-assured – but not in that cocky 'I'm better than you because I'm famous' kind of way. His is more like a quiet confidence. And his eyes... oh, god... did I tell you about his eyes?"

"No."

"They were so pretty I wanted to lick them."

"Oh, no, Casey, please tell me you didn't?" Mom gulped, actually sounding seriously concerned – as if I, of all people, would be that inappropriate with a freakin' celebrity. I couldn't help but laugh at her lack of faith in me.

"No, mom, geez. Obviously, I managed to control myself," I huffed before adding, "but just barely."

"Well, thank goodness. I don't know about you sometimes."

"Anyway, back to my new favorite subject. Jake is my total dream man. Good job, nice guy, laughs at my jokes, and he's easy on the eyes. What more could a girl want?"

"Oh, you were actually serious about being in love?"

"Yep," I giggled.

"Oh, boy. That's what I was afraid of… just don't come home pregnant with a rock star's baby."

"Wow… what a cliché," I said, rolling my eyes.

Mom laughed.

"Although it's not a bad idea. I think we would make a pretty cute baby."

"Casey! Don't even think it!"

"I'm just saying."

"And *I'm* just saying… condoms are your best friends."

"Yeah, yeah. God, you're so old-fashioned."

"If I were old-fashioned, we wouldn't be talking about condoms and you getting pregnant with a rock star's baby."

"True," I conceded. "You're the best mom in the world."

"That's more like it. Now, I want to hear every detail of your conversation."

So I recounted every moment of it for my mom. She was horrified that I'd pulled a prank on Jake and even more appalled that I'd told him my poop-puke story. But she loved that he seemed to think it was funny. She was also pleased when I told her what a nice, normal guy he seemed to be. We both agreed it was surprising that Jake had opened up to me so easily. For a guy who was supposed to be so damaged, Jake McKallister sure did seem to have it all together.

3

JAKE: A NEW BEGINNING

I t had already been a long twenty-four hours when I walked through the festively decorated double doors of the Mexican restaurant. I was frustrated and on edge. Everything had worked against me today. And it wasn't for lack of effort. It was just one of those days where you took one step forward, then two steps back. It was like the universe didn't want me in Arizona. I wished I could have had a buffer and left a day earlier, but due to a tight touring schedule, that just wasn't possible. So instead I flew for twenty-one fucking hours before landing in Arizona. I started my day in Austria. Then spent a three-hour delay in Frankfurt due to a threatened airline strike. That caused me to arrive in Los Angeles too late to catch my connecting flight to Arizona. So I was booked on another flight that made an inconvenient stop in Las Vegas first. Just thinking about it pissed me off.

As a general rule, I didn't like being late. I especially didn't like being late to my brother's wedding rehearsal. It made me look like I didn't care. Which I did, or I wouldn't have made that shitty trip to begin with.

I stifled a yawn. Even though I'd slept most of the Atlantic crossing, I was still tired. Four months of non-stop touring was taking a toll on my body, especially my weak knee. I realized that I wouldn't be able to mask the symptoms for much longer; it was getting worse for every day. Tour after tour, always the same damn thing. The swelling and pain... there was no way I was going to be able to delay surgery this time around. I'd already put it off for too long, choosing to go back out on tour instead of getting it taken care of. But now I resigned myself to the fact that I'd be going under the knife after this tour for sure. Thinking about my knee made me think about how I got the injury; and that, in turn, made me think about him. I hated thinking about him. It put me in a bad fucking mood. I took a deep breath and tried to redirect my focus elsewhere.

I yawned again. Damn, why was I so tired all the time? Of course, I knew the answer – I'd spent the better part of the last seven years on the road. I sometimes felt like I was getting too old for the gypsy lifestyle. I needed time away from the grind and the constant schedules. Every year I promised myself that I would take a much-needed break, and every year I broke that lofty promise.

The restaurant had a festive party atmosphere, but I was anything but cheerful. Of course, I had no plans to let my sour mood ruin the party. I was a pro at concealing my true feelings. I'd had years of training and had learned to work a crowd with the best of them. No one liked a miserable asshole. If I'd learned anything in my twenty-three years, it was how to pretend to be someone I wasn't. With that in mind, I put my game face on and approached the hostess. Her bored expression instantly transformed. Doubling in size, her eyes bugged out and her mouth dropped open. If I wasn't so tired and frustrated I might have considered her cartoonish reaction amusing. Now I just found it annoying.

"Hi. I'm here for the rehearsal dinner," I explained. "Can you point me in the right direction?"

The hostess continued to gape at me, apparently unable to process what I was saying. She blinked several times, as if trying to convince herself that she was seeing what she thought she was seeing. I waited patiently. I was used to this reaction... very used to it. I'd tried many approaches in the past but had come to the conclusion that it was best to just wait it out.

"You... you're Jake McKallister." She ignored my question in order to state the obvious. Her eyes danced with excitement.

I wanted to tell her not to waste her energy because, really, I wasn't worth her enthusiasm, but instead I nodded and gave her a quick smile. Over the years I'd perfected responses to the most common questions I got from people. I didn't want to appear ungrateful or cocky or uninterested, but I also didn't want to encourage a conversation.

"The rehearsal dinner, for McKallister? Do you know where I go?" I repeated.

"Oh... yeah, I'm sorry... um... I just... you... um... it's in the back. See the green wall? Just there," the hostess replied, slightly out of breath.

I smiled and said, "Thanks." As I walked passed her I heard her whisper, "Oh, my god." I focused on the green wall as I made my way through the restaurant. I purposefully avoided looking into the shocked faces of the diners. Making eye contact only encouraged interaction. Damn. When had I become so jaded?

A sweaty, overweight man wearing a tan suit and about three pounds of jewelry rushed up to me. "Jake, so nice to have you here at El Rancherito," he announced, then reached out to take my hand.

He gave me a creepy smile and looked me up and down. I had an instant feeling of unease. If there was one thing my unfortunate childhood had afforded me, it was the ability to pick the creeps out of a crowd. Against my better judgment, but not wanting to cause a scene, I reluctantly shook his big meaty paw.

"My name is Leo," he revealed. "And I'm the manager here.

Anything you want... anything at all... just ask." Leo said this
with such smarmy eagerness that I really did believe he would do
anything I asked, legal or not. I nodded, pulling my hand away.

"What a surprise to see you here. This wedding, is it for a
family member?"

"Yes. My brother," I responded.

"Oh, wow... I didn't make the connection. But of course –
McKallister," Leo said, giving me another full body once over.
What the fuck? I wanted to nail him in the nuts. It's not that I was
homophobic – I got hit on by gay guys from time to time, and
usually, it didn't bother me. But this douche... he was sizing me up
like some pedophile getting off on the idea of what had happened
to me as a kid. I ran into guys like him occasionally. It was just a
vibe they gave off, and Leo definitely had it going on. "If I'd
known, I would have prepared better for your arrival. Forgive me."

Yeah, like preparing some basement dungeon, you fucking
perv. Holding my tongue, I simply nodded and asked, "Is this the
room that the rehearsal dinner is in?"

"Yes... yes it is," Leo affirmed. He was abruptly silenced by a
shrill scream. I turned to see a teenage girl rushing toward me.

"This way," Leo instructed, pointing toward a decorated door.
I opened it and slipped through just as pervy Leo caught the
screeching girl. I shut the door behind me, thankfully trapping
both of them on the other side. The commotion caused every
member of the wedding party to glance my way as I came in the
room. I always seemed to make an entrance, whether I liked it or
not. I dropped my bag and set my guitar against the wall just as
the door swung back open and the girl from the restaurant burst
in. Kyle, who had already been on his way over, rushed toward
her. Leo came up from behind in hot pursuit. Both grabbed her a
split second before she latched onto me. Leo slipped his arms
around her waist and carried the kicking and screaming girl out
of the room, shutting the door behind him.

Trying hard not to let my annoyance play out over my face, I forced a smile and turned toward the startled faces of the wedding party. So much for my plan to slip in quietly and keep a low profile. But then, who was I kidding? Even though I wanted the focus to be on my brother and his bride-to-be, it was unrealistic to think the wedding guests would feel the same way. Ignoring their stares, I walked over and greeted Mitch and met my future sister-in-law before retreating to the relative safety of my family. I hadn't seen most of them since I started my current tour four months ago. It was great to just relax and laugh with my brothers.

After dinner, a woman strolled up to me. She was the picture of cool confidence as she flashed me a perfect smile. Her blue eyes sparkled under a thick layering of mascara. Her blonde hair was long and straight, her nails perfectly manicured. She was wearing skin-tight jeans and a cleavage-baring top... to a wedding rehearsal dinner, no less. It told me everything I needed to know about her. She was an easy mark, and she wanted me to know it. My eyes diverted directly to her impressive rack. She smiled as I looked up.

"Hi, I'm Sarah," she said, batting her eyes. "I'm a huge fan."

"Oh, thanks," I replied. She proceeded to tell me about the numerous concerts of mine she'd been to. I nodded, and we chatted about a couple of them. I pretended to know what she was talking about, but in reality, I'd done hundreds of concerts in my years as a professional musician. There was no way for me to remember specific dates. The entire time Sarah talked, she shook her breasts at me. To say it was a distraction was an understatement. Sarah was hot, and I wasn't immune to her obvious charms, but I met women like her everywhere I went. They were a dime a dozen in my line of work, and although this one was clearly attractive, I hadn't come all the way to Mitch's wedding to nail some random chick and then try to avoid her the rest of the weekend. No, this was a family weekend, and I didn't want any distractions.

Once she started getting all touchy-feely with me, I signaled discreetly to Keith, and he immediately came over and pulled me away from Sarah. I went back to my family and spent the next five minutes being grilled by my mom about what I was eating, how much sleep I was getting, and if I was being sexually responsible by wearing a condom. When my mom started inquiring about my sex life, that was when I decided to seek out new company. I headed over to talk to Mitch, who was standing with his mother.

"Jake," she said with a smile on her face. "I don't know if you remember me... "

"Of course. April, Mitch's mom."

"Wow, I can't believe you remember... what has it been, thirteen years? I think you were maybe nine or ten when I last saw you."

"At the water park, right?"

"Oh, my gosh, you do have a good memory."

"He wasn't a baby, mom," Mitch laughed.

"This is my daughter, Melanie," she said, as a teenage girl joined our conversation.

"Oh yeah, damn. You were like two years old the last time I saw you. You're Grace's age, right?" I asked the teenage girl.

She looked at me, all excited and flushed. She just nodded.

April grinned at her daughter's reaction. "She's a huge fan."

"Sweet. You like rock music, huh? Most girls your age are more into pop."

"No, not me," Melanie said. "I love your music. My mom took me to one of your Arizona concerts last year. It was the bomb."

"Why didn't you tell Mitch? I would have gotten you backstage passes."

Melanie glared at her mom accusingly. "I told her to but she refused."

"In my defense, we hadn't seen you for years. We didn't even know if you remembered us. It seemed rude to ask."

"And then I called Mitch to ask, but he refused, too," Melanie continued, not letting it go. Clearly, this was a sore spot with her.

I glanced at my brother, confused. He looked uncomfortable. Why the hell would he refuse to ask me for tickets? Did he think I would deny him? Fuck, what kind of person did he think I was?

Not wanting to get into it with him on the day before his wedding, I just said, "I get a certain number of tickets per show to give to friends and family, and if no one asks for them, they just go unused. It's kind of a bummer. Next time I'm in town, I expect you guys to call me for tickets, okay?"

"Well... if you insist," April said, smiling. "And next time you're in town, I would love to make you a home-cooked meal. I'm sure you get tired of takeout on the road."

"Oh, yeah... definitely."

"And I'll invite Mitch and Kate, and we'll make a party out of it."

"Okay, that sounds good."

Kate walked up to our little group. She put her arms around my brother and kissed him. The look on their faces and the obvious love they had for each other gave me pause. It was an emotion I'd never known and probably never would.

"Sorry to disturb you all," Kate said. "But can I steal Jake away for a minute? I want to introduce him to the bridesmaid he's paired up with for the wedding."

"Oh, okay, sure," I responded politely as I allowed her to lead me away.

"You know, Jake, I wanted to thank you for flying all the way here for our wedding. I know it wasn't easy for you, and you had to rearrange tour dates and everything."

"No, it was fine. I wanted to come."

"Well, I'm just really happy to finally meet you... and the rest of your family, too."

"You hadn't met my family?" I asked in surprise.

"Nope... not until today."

"Not even my dad?"

Kate shook her head. "I've wanted to, but Mitch is... you know..."

No. I didn't know. I guess I'd been on the road so much that I hadn't really paid much attention to family dynamics. Had there been a rift between Mitch and our family?

"Huh," I replied.

"Anyway, I'm just happy everyone is here," she said, then pointed to a young woman with brown hair who stood with her back to us. "That's my friend."

Kate called to her and she turned around. To be honest, when I first laid eyes on Casey Caldwell, I looked right through her. Nothing about her stood out to me; not because she wasn't attractive, but because I couldn't be bothered to invest myself in another stranger. I was just going through the motions, distracted. The required pleasantries were as much as I was willing to give. Lately, that had really just been my life.

The introduction led to an unbearably awkward silence. Great. *Get me the hell out of here.* Trying to come up with something to say to my wedding partner, I asked her some lame question about the ceremony while I searched for my brothers in the crowd, hoping they would come and rescue me sooner rather than later. I wasn't even listening to her answer... until she did something so unusual, so out of the blue, that I was forced to pay attention. Casey Caldwell played a joke on me.

It might not seem like a big deal to most, but to me, it was a downright shocking thing to do. People who met me for the first time just assumed, because of my dark past, that I couldn't take a joke. It was a reaction that I'd grown accustomed to and one I'd come to expect. Only those closest to me knew I had a good sense of humor.

But here was some random girl playing a joke on me. I was more than a little intrigued. All of the sudden this indistinguishable stranger blossomed before my very eyes. My fatigue vanished, and for the first time in a long time, I was wide awake. And I was shocked to discover just how beautiful this girl standing before me was. How had I not seen her before? God, those shiny brown eyes, that smoking hot body, and those dimples! I was mesmerized.

As if making up for lost time, I hung on her every word with unmasked enthusiasm. Casey probably thought I was some inexperienced little boy the way I was smiling and flirting. But I couldn't help myself. The way she called me out... her witty comebacks... her boldness... I was awestruck. She was unlike any girl I'd ever met, and I felt an immediate and intense attraction to her. She had it all: funny, smart, confident, interesting, and sexy. And the way she interacted with me... there was no fussing, no excited babbling, no declarations of undying devotion. Casey just talked to me like I was any other person, completely unaffected by my stardom. It was clear she wasn't a groupie. In fact, I wasn't even sure if Casey was a fan, and the idea of meeting a girl with a totally clean slate appealed to me more than I could ever say.

When my mom called me away, I didn't want to leave. It was such an odd reaction for me. Usually, I couldn't wait to get away from conversations with strangers, but after ten minutes of talking to Casey, somehow she was no longer in that category.

Leaving the restaurant I was distracted, anxious... giddy.

"What?" Kyle questioned, eyeing me suspiciously.

"What do you mean, *what?*" I asked.

"You're acting weird."

"How am I acting weird?"

"I don't know... you're like all cheerful and shit."

"So you think it's weird when I'm happy?" I asked.

"Sort of, yeah."

"Thanks," I mumbled. His assessment annoyed me.

"So?"

"So, what?"

"Jesus Christ, Jake! What's going on?"

"Nothing. I just met that girl," I mumbled. "Damn, she's a smoke show."

Kyle eyed me skeptically. "Yeah, well, I hate to burst your bubble, J, but she was hitting on me earlier."

"Seriously?" I asked, my stomach dropping. I was way more disappointed than I should have been after just meeting the girl.

"Yeah, during the rehearsal."

"Casey was hitting on you?" I questioned, trying to clarify Kyle's claim. It just didn't seem like her, but... God, how would I know? Maybe she was just putting on a show for my benefit.

"I don't know what her name was, dude, but her tits... damn."

"Wait. Are you talking about the brunette or the blonde?"

"The blonde with the enormous..." Kyle finished the sentence by holding his hands out like he was juggling melons.

I felt instant relief. "I was talking about the brunette, Casey."

"The last girl you were talking to?"

"Yeah."

"Did she have big tits, too?"

"What's it with you and big tits today, Kyle?"

"So that would be a no." Kyle grinned, ignoring my question.

"Shut up. I don't care about big tits. You know I'm more of an ass man. And before you ask – yeah, she had a nice ass."

"Well, to each his own. I prefer the busty blonde, myself."

I made a face. "You can have her."

"Oh, wow, thanks, bro. It's so nice of you to give me your leftovers," Kyle replied sarcastically.

I ignored his comment.

"So, this Casey girl must be pretty hot to get you all worked up."

"Yeah, she's hot, but it's not even that. I actually had fun talking to her."

"Holy shit! No fucking way!" Kyle teased. "Talking, huh?"

"Shut up. I'm not kidding. She's the first girl I've met who just talks to me like I'm a normal human being."

"Jesus, what's wrong with her?" Kyle asked gravely. "Clearly, you aren't normal."

"God, I almost forgot how annoying you are," I said, shaking my head in irritation.

"Well, hell. I've only been off the tour for two weeks, and you're already starting to forget my character flaws. That's just unacceptable!"

"And I have two more full months to enjoy a Kyle-free tour. How lucky am I?"

"Keep that shit up and I won't come back." Kyle grinned.

"Promise?"

"Shut up. You know you miss me."

"No. Actually, I don't miss you at all," I lied.

"Yeah, you do. You're bored without me. Admit it."

I didn't respond.

"Admit it!" Kyle pressed again.

"No. You realize I could fire you at any time, right?"

"Yeah, but you won't. Face it, Jake, you can't live without me," Kyle said dismissively.

He was right. I would never fire Kyle. As annoying as he was, Kyle was more than just my little brother... and I needed him by my side. Over the years, there would sometimes be grumbling amongst the crew that Kyle was a freeloader getting a paycheck simply for being my brother, but I didn't see it that way. Kyle's job title had always been somewhat murky, but officially he was on security detail. He liked to tell people he was my personal bodyguard, but really, he just hung out with me and kept me sane. My world was filled with 'yes men,' and Kyle was there to say 'no.' He never let me take myself too seriously. If I was feeling full of myself, Kyle was there to knock me down a few pegs with a well-placed insult. He reminded me of who I was and where I came from. I shuddered to think who I would be without him. There were only a few people I trusted in this world, and Kyle was at the top of that list. So yeah, maybe I did pay him to be my brother and to kick my ass when necessary. Who cared? It was my money. And truthfully, I did miss him. I couldn't wait for him to get back to the tour in August, after he finished his stint on a reality show that was about to start filming.

"Whatever. I don't even know what we're talking about anymore." I shrugged.

"Me neither," Kyle laughed. "Oh, wait… it had something to do with you being normal."

"Not being normal… just being treated normal."

Kyle smiled mischievously at me.

"What?"

"It doesn't take much to win you over, does it?" Kyle shook his head. "Seriously, if the groupies only knew."

I shrugged. "Well, I thought it was cool. Plus, Casey is really fucking hysterical. You would not believe the shit that comes out of her mouth," I swore, shaking my head in amusement.

"I heard you laughing."

"Yeah, she cracks me up. The first thing she did was punk me."

"What do you mean?"

"When I asked her if there was anything important I needed to know from the rehearsal, she told me all I missed was learning the dance routine."

"What? There's a dance routine?" Kyle asked, confused.

"No, dumbshit, that was the punk."

"Oh. Wait, what?"

"Jesus Christ, Kyle, try to follow along." I shook my head impatiently. Sometimes he was so damn stupid.

"I'm trying. You're confusing me."

I sighed and proceeded to recount, in detail, the entire story for Kyle, taking care not to leave out the part where I almost pissed my pants from the horror of it all.

Once I'd completed my tale of woe, Kyle nodded his approval. "That's pretty funny, actually."

"Yeah. Casey was so chill. I can't remember a time I was that interested in something a girl had to say."

"Wow, that's deep." Kyle rolled his eyes. "You should put that on a bumper sticker."

I laughed.

"So are you going to hit that?"

I shook my head. "Something tells me she's not that type of girl."

Kyle scoffed. "You're a fucking rock star, Jake. With you, every girl is that type of girl."

"Trust me, not her. Casey doesn't seem impressed with all that."

"Or so she says."

"What's that supposed to mean?"

"Maybe it's all an act to get you interested."

I gave Kyle a dirty look. "Not everyone I meet has an agenda, asshole."

"I'm just saying… you never know."

"So you want me to live my life never trusting anyone's motives?"

"Don't you already do that?"

"No." *Yes.*

Kyle shrugged. "Better safe than sorry, right?"

"Jesus, K, that's fucked up. With that thinking, I might as well get used to being alone with just my hand for company."

"Isn't that the way it is already?"

"Shut up!" I shook my head. "Anyway, Casey isn't like that."

"And you know this because you talked to her for what? Fifteen minutes?"

"No, I know this because I consider myself to be a pretty good judge of character. For example, I know you're a piece of shit," I said pointedly.

Kyle laughed out loud. "This is true. So... did you get her number?"

"No."

"Why not?" Kyle shook his head like I was an idiot.

"I'm going to see her tomorrow. Why would I need her number?"

"For emergencies."

"Like what? If I fall and can't get up?"

"No, if you fall and can't get up and need a quick blow job." Kyle smirked.

I shook my head. "I think I'll be okay. Besides, Casey would require a lot more effort than I'm willing to put forth tonight."

"Damn, Jake, you're so romantic," Kyle mocked.

"Yeah, whatever. Anyway, she probably already has a boyfriend."

"Why do you think that?"

"I don't know. She just has a very relaxed vibe to her. Like a girl who isn't looking for a guy, so she can act herself around them."

"So why isn't he here, then? This is a wedding for one of her best friends. Why wouldn't he be here, too?"

"I don't know, Kyle, maybe he is here."

"Very doubtful."

"Why?"

"Because if I were some girl's boyfriend and I saw her talking to you, I would be at her side in a frickin' second," Kyle admitted.

"I don't know, Kyle," I said, feeling myself getting frustrated. "And I don't care. I just think she's hot. That's all."

I headed back over to the hotel with my family in the giant SUV my parents had rented. My brothers and I were getting pretty rowdy, verbally assaulting one another like only brothers can. My older sister Emma yelled at us to shut up. My mom yelled at her to stop yelling. My dad laughed.

God, how I'd missed my dysfunctional family. I left home at sixteen, and often felt like I missed out on so much growing up. But my life was different back then. This closeness I share with my family now, it didn't exist when I was a teenager. During that time in my life, I actively tried to push them away. Going out on the road on my own had been the perfect way to distance myself. But the longer I was away, the more I missed my family, and the more I appreciated what I'd left behind. I spent the short stretches of time at home between tours trying to reestablish the bonds. I was lucky; my family never blamed me for the way I acted. In fact, they'd welcomed me back with open arms. After that, I never took them for granted again.

Kyle slammed into my side after a violent push from my incredibly irritated sister. I had been deep in thought and hadn't seen what he'd done to piss her off. Emma was more of an introverted person, preferring peace and quiet to the chaos that a rowdy family of eight always seemed to provide. When we were kids, Emma loved getting Kyle and me in trouble. We couldn't do anything without her telling Mom on us. I'd always viewed her as the enemy. But after the kidnapping, when I was so scarred and afraid, it was Emma who would sit silently for hours in whatever room I was in, just reading a book. We never spoke, but it was what she didn't say that stuck with me all these years. She was there for me unconditionally when my life was at its worst. I'd never forgotten her loyalty.

"Stop it, Kyle!" she screamed.

Kyle raised his eyebrows in amusement. I could tell from the look in his eyes that he was not even close to stopping whatever he was doing to irritate her.

I pulled him back. "Relax, idiot."

"Fuck off," he whispered in my ear so Mom wouldn't hear.

"Stop now, or I'll tell mom what you did in Greece," I whispered back.

He scowled at me. "You wouldn't dare."

"Try me," I replied.

"Then I'll tell her what you did in Japan."

"Go ahead. Because by the time I'm finished telling her what you did in Russia, she won't even care."

Kyle glared at me. I glared back. Finally, he sat back up, ignoring our sister.

Emma glanced over at me, then looked away. I saw the slightest smile on her face. That was Emma... always subtle.

I smiled as I breathed in, feeling relaxed despite the turmoil in the car. My life on the road was filled up with constant schedules and lots of pressure. I rarely, if ever, took the time to relax and goof off like other guys my age. Sometimes, on the road, I felt so old and isolated, especially now that Kyle was gone. Really, I shouldn't have felt that way because I traveled with a sixty-plus crew. We spent a lot of time together... too much time. Every day was a new city or new country or new audience. I mean, we all worked great as a team, and we were friendly with each other but, on a personal level, I held them at arm's length, never letting them get too close. When they had parking lot parties at the venues after shows, they invited me, but I rarely went. And if I did go, Kyle was always with me. It just felt weird hanging out with them during off hours. They always seemed a little nervous when I came around, like they had to be on good behavior. It was clear they viewed me more as their boss than their friend, and I was okay with that.

It wasn't that I was trying to be a guarded asshole, but I was not good at opening up to people. Only those I genuinely loved and trusted ever really got to know me. Everyone else in my world was approached with caution. Just like Kyle said: a lot of people had ulterior motives when it came to me. There was a big payday to be had for information about my life, especially if that information included something about the kidnapping.

Crewmembers, a manager, even random hookups had sold me out in the past, even though they had nothing but lies to sell. It's not like I would have trusted those people with my deepest, darkest secrets. Hell, not even those closest to me were privy to that information. Because of those betrayals, I found it incredibly difficult to know whom to trust – so as a general rule, I trusted no one, especially not the damn media. When I was a kid, those assholes had made my life a living hell. Now that I was an adult and could speak for myself, I decided I didn't owe them a fucking thing. I refused all interviews. The media didn't take kindly to my insolence, so as punishment, they destroyed my character on a daily basis.

It was no wonder that, outside of my family, I only considered one person to be an actual friend... and he was a fifty-something-year-old man. All my childhood buddies had disappeared after the kidnapping, although I had to take the blame for that. I couldn't stand the way they stared at me, with a weird combination of both pity and embarrassment. And I hated the way they tried to pretend nothing had changed, even though my whole world had been turned upside down and then crushed. Being around them reminded me of who I once was and who I would never be again, and so I shut them out of my life completely and never looked back.

Several lonely years followed. Really, I only had my miserable self to keep me company, as I'd pushed my family away as well. Back then I saw no future for myself. Living seemed pointless. It was rare for me to go more than a month or two without attempting suicide. After one such attempt, my frustrated mother steered me into the living room, where we kept all our musical instruments, and forced me to sit at the piano. I hadn't touched it since the kidnapping. Music was just another reminder of all I'd lost. Before the kidnapping, music had been my life. I could play just about any instrument I touched. I started writing songs when I was eight or nine, and I joined a band at eleven. I loved being on stage performing, and I truly believed that one day I would be a famous musician. But that was when I was still young and carefree... and still brave and fun and adventurous. That was when I still had tons of friends and went through life with a perpetual smile on my face. That was before Ray... before I lost my faith in humanity... before I lost my innocence.

In the blink of an eye, it was all gone – my whole life – just completely destroyed. My childhood hopes and dreams seemed so foolish and far away. Life had stopped being worth living. But there was one person who refused to allow me to give up, and refused to give up on me. And that day when she sat me down at the piano, placing her fingers over mine and pressing down on the keys for the both of us because I didn't have the strength or desire to do it on my own, she brought me back into the land of the living. I played the piano for hours that day, letting the music flow through me and lift up my tattered soul. I could almost feel the open wounds start sealing themselves shut. Music became my savior; my only friend. I poured all my sadness and fear and anger into it. Hours upon hours upon hours. It was all I did all day, every day. All the terrible thoughts in my head eventually made their way out onto paper and then into songs. My voice returned. Somehow singing the words that had been trapped inside my head for so long gave me hope for my future. Maybe I would be all right. Maybe living wouldn't be so pointless.

And then, unexpectedly, everything I'd ever wanted as a young, innocent kid dreaming of rock stardom came true. In the beginning, stepping out onto the stage was a terrifying experience. After hiding myself away for so long, just the thought of opening myself back up to a cruel, unforgiving world was incredibly daunting. But if I wanted to be a musician, I knew I needed to get comfortable on stage... and fast. Touring cured me of those fears. I spent so much time on stage that it became like second nature for me. Soon there were no more jitters, and I found performing to be uplifting. There was something truly amazing about connecting with an audience who hadn't come to my concert to gawk or pity me. They had come for the music, because a song I created made them feel something. It was a powerful connection. Standing up on the stage in front of thousands of strangers and feeling the roar of the crowd beneath my feet made me feel alive again. I became stronger and more confident. The unwavering support of my fans gave my self-esteem the boost it so desperately needed. Without their support, I would still be a scared, lost kid making music inside my head for my own sanity.

And really, my fans were the perfect, superficial friends. They were always there if I needed a quick pick-me-up, and always there to make me feel like I was a pretty damn cool guy. And for the most part, they weren't invasive. Mostly they just wanted a small piece of me, like a picture or an autograph. The interactions were always surface level – a smile, a few pleasantries – and then we went our separate ways. I was never expected to dig deeper, like I would have to do if I had real friends.

I approached women with the same wary caution that I approached everyone else who tried to get close to me. I liked women. I liked flirting. I liked sex. I didn't like talking. I didn't like commitment. I didn't like messy emotions. For that reason, casual, one-night stands worked best for me. In and out, so to speak. And before you feel sorry for the duped women... don't. Their interest in me was just as superficial as my interest in them. Maybe I only wanted sex, but they only wanted the bragging rights of bagging a rock star.

Getting women into bed wasn't hard. Usually it was just a matter of picking the one that looked like she'd be the least amount of work. For example, women who wanted to get to know me – out! Women who wanted a second 'date' – out! Women who wanted to heal me – oh, god, get in line. For some reason, the fact that I was viewed as damaged goods was a huge selling point for women. The need to fix me was strong. I imagine it was the same irrational need that pushed some women into marrying death-row inmates. Not that I considered myself on the same level as a cold-blooded killer, but still, I was sufficiently fucked up... so all the more reason to stay the hell away from me.

Then I met Casey, and all my flawed reasoning about women went out the door. For the life of me, I couldn't get a read on her. She didn't fit into any of the little stereotypical boxes I'd created. She wasn't a friend or a foe or a fan. She wasn't trying to fix me or fuck me or bask in my fame. From what I could tell, Casey seemed totally genuine. She really did appear to be just a cool girl, with no ulterior motives, having a friendly conversation with a guy. Why was that weird to me? Was I that screwed up that normal in everyone else's world was not normal in mine?

Later that night, my brothers and I found a little table tucked out of the way in the interior atrium area of the hotel. It was a chill little spot with a fishpond, waterfalls, and trees. All the rooms of the hotel opened up into a view of the inside tropical paradise. Keith smuggled a bottle of Jack Daniels in his backpack and we took turns taking swigs. We allowed Quinn, who was only sixteen, one pull, but only after threatening him with death if he told our parents. Mitch had two mouthfuls and quit. He alluded to the fact that Kate would kill him if he were hung over for the wedding, then went on to tell us we shouldn't be hung over in the morning either.

The bottle kept going around, and after four passes, I started feeling the effects. I was a bit of a lightweight with alcohol. I didn't like the feeling of being out of control, so getting drunk was way too stressful for me. I didn't even know why I was drinking the whiskey in the first place; probably peer pressure from my idiot brothers. The next time the bottle went around, I abstained.

Since the mood was light and fun, I decided to ruin it. "So, what was that all about earlier, Mitch? Why wouldn't you ask me for concert tickets for your little sister?"

"What do you mean?" he asked, but it was obvious from the look on his face he knew exactly what I meant.

I stared at him until he was forced to elaborate.

"I don't want to get into it with you... not today."

"What do you mean, get into it with me? I'm just asking a question."

"Jake, drop it," Keith tried.

"No. Obviously, he has a problem with me. I just want to know what it is," I pressed.

Mitch sighed. "It goes both ways, Jake."

"What's that supposed to mean?"

"You really want to know?" Mitch challenged.

"I wouldn't have asked if I didn't," I responded, defiantly.

"Okay. You know I live in Phoenix, right?"

I nodded.

"A few months ago, your tour rolled through Phoenix... where I live. You'd had the tour stop on your calendar since... well, since the tour was announced. Did you ever call or text? No."

"Did you ever call or text me? I don't think so."

"You never contacted me once, Jake. You knew I lived there, and you didn't even bother."

"Sorry if I'm a little fucking busy when I'm on tour."

"Yeah, 'cause a text takes so much time," Mitch shot back. "Anyway, I just assumed you didn't want my company or that of my mom and sister."

"Jesus Christ. Your feelings were hurt?" I replied, antagonistically. Another reason why I shouldn't drink.

Mitch laughed, but it was a bitter sound. "You've made it pretty clear that I don't factor in your life, Jake. I'm not going to beg for your friendship."

"What the hell?" I protested. "What did I ever do to you?"

"Jake, stop," Kyle gave me a warning glare.

"I just flew for twenty-two fucking hours! Don't tell me to stop!" I raised my voice at Kyle, then turned my attention back on Mitch. "Why'd you invite me, then? So I could bring the wow factor to your wedding or so I could sing at it?"

"Don't accuse me of trying to use you or your fame, Jake. That's the furthest thing from the truth... and insulting, too. And you were the one who offered to sing at the wedding, so don't dump that on me now."

Mitch glared at me. I slunk back in my chair. He was right. I had offered. If I was going to be a belligerent asshole, I needed to get my facts straight.

Mitch's shoulders drooped, and he said, "I don't want to fight with you. I invited you because you're my brother and I love you and I want you to be here."

His admission stopped me in my tracks. Okay, now I felt like a fucking dick.

"I'm sorry, Jake. I shouldn't have said that about not factoring in your life." Mitch ran a hand through his hair nervously. "Look, it's no secret – you and I have never been close. I wanted nothing to do with you when I was a teenager. You wanted nothing to do with me when you were a teenager. But now that we're both adults, I want to change all that – but I don't want you to think that I want to change all that because you're famous. It's like... if we haven't talked in two years, and then I call you for concert tickets, I'm just using you – and that's not the relationship I want to have with you. Do you understand what I'm saying?"

I didn't say anything for a second, then nodded.

"It's just... God, you're so intimidating sometimes," Mitch said, shaking his head. "You have this huge life. I don't have a whole hell of a lot to offer. I guess I've always felt like you were the one in control of our relationship, and I kept waiting for you to reach out to me. I was putting it all on you, and that was unfair. I just... can we... is there a way for us to just start over?"

Kyle kicked me under the table, flashing me a serious *Stop this shit now* look.

I hadn't needed his kick in the shin. I already realized I was in the wrong and that I was being a jerk on the eve of Mitch's wedding. I blamed Jack Daniels.

I sighed, gave Mitch a serious look, and then said, "I'll start over with you on one condition."

"Okay?" Mitch hesitated. "What?"

"You stop talking like such a fucking woman."

Mitch looked surprised by my comment, then burst out laughing. The tension in the air dissipated.

"I've never heard so much talk about feelings come out of one guy's mouth in all my life. Damn Mitch, grow a pair."

Mitch laughed. "Give me a frickin' break! I'm getting married tomorrow. I'm emotional."

The light mood came back to the conversation. Mitch and I had cleared the air, but I definitely needed to make more of an effort with him. Maybe I would just make a trip to Arizona after the end of my tour so we could hang out or something. I didn't have a ton of people in my life. I couldn't afford to lose any.

About an hour later, Mitch excused himself. Apparently, he needed his beauty sleep, or at least that's what we all razzed him about. A few minutes after he left, I saw Casey walk by, and I felt a flutter of excitement.

"That's her," I whispered, pointing in her direction. "That's Casey." Earlier in our conversation, I'd filled my brothers in on the joke she'd played on me.

They all looked over.

Then suddenly, and without warning, Kyle called out, "CASEY!"

Instinctively I ducked.

From my crouched position, I declared angrily, "What the fuck did you do that for?"

"Get up. She's looking this way." Kyle smirked, leaving me no choice but to sit back up in my chair. Casey was looking up from her phone and scanning the area.

Kyle nudged me. "You're up, Romeo."

"I told you I wasn't… " I started berating Kyle until Casey saw me. An adorable smile spread across her face, and she waved. A weird feeling washed over me, and I set aside my trepidation as I waved back earnestly, motioning for her to come over.

4

CASEY: THE ENTOURAGE

I felt a tingle run up my spine as I walked anxiously toward him. My heart immediately raced as Jake's handsome face got closer. He was sitting with his three brothers, one of whom was shoving a bottle of whiskey in his backpack.

"You look lost," Jake remarked.

"No, I'm just one of those people who likes wandering around hotels late at night in my pajamas," I replied, as I attempted to casually walk toward them.

"I didn't know there were people like that," Jake said.

"Homeless people," his brother chimed in.

I laughed, then raised my phone and said, "No bars in my room. So... what are you guys up to?"

"Just a little male bonding," one of the brothers answered. "I'm Keith, by the way. Jake's big brother. And the guy with all the tats, that's Kyle; and this is baby Quinn and that ugly dude – oh yeah, you met him already – that's Jake."

"Keith, Tats, Baby, and Ugly Dude... got it," I repeated, then turned to Jake and said, "See, I pay attention."

He laughed at our inside joke.

"So Jake was just telling us about the prank you pulled on him earlier. That was pretty funny," Kyle stated.

"Oh, well, thank you. To be honest, I hadn't meant to punk him, but we were just standing there awkwardly and I was nervous and when I'm nervous, word vomit just spills out of my mouth."

Although I was careful not to show it, I was pleased that Jake had been talking about me to his brothers. "But I have to say, Jake really was just too easy."

"That's what they all say," Keith deadpanned.

"Hey!" Jake exclaimed, acting offended.

I laughed. These were some fun guys.

Then Jake turned to me in surprise. "Wait, hold on a second. You were nervous?"

"What part of that uncomfortable, cringe-worthy introduction do you not remember?"

"I remember wanting to get the hell away from you as fast as possible, but then you went all rogue on me and I'm like, *what the fuck?*"

I laughed. "Yeah, well, just so you know, I was plotting my escape, too."

"I don't doubt it." Jake nodded. "So why would you prank me then?"

"I don't know. You asked me some bullshit question and the expression on your face... you looked miserable," I razzed him. "Like you were just trying to come up with something to fill the awkwardness."

"I was," Jake confessed.

"It just struck me as funny. I couldn't help myself. You were a good sport, though."

Jake's eyes shone brightly.

"So what do you do, Casey?" Keith asked.

"You won't believe this. She's an accountant," Jake said, almost proudly.

"Seriously?" Kyle asked.

"Well, an accountant in training. I'm a senior at ASU," I corrected.

"No shit? I thought accountants were all nerdy, math types," Kyle said.

"I scored a perfect 800 on the math portion of the SATs, and I was a member of the math team and the debate team in high school."

"Shut up," Kyle replied with mock horror. "Did you have any friends at all?"

Amusement danced across my face. "I had a few, but they weren't the cool kids, like I'm sure you and your brothers were."

Kyle was still shaking his head like he couldn't wrap his mind around such an oddity. "So were you like one of those girls who blossomed late or something?"

"Kyle!" Jake admonished his brother.

"What? Too personal?"

"Way too personal," Jake replied.

"I'm just saying... she's a hot nerd. Who knew they existed?"

I burst out laughing and everyone else joined in. I couldn't help but be flattered by his flawed assessment.

"According to Casey, nerds have become cocky creatures," Jake said, referring to our earlier conversation.

"No shit?" Kyle replied. "I don't know any nerds, so I can't speak to that."

"I do," Quinn jumped in, "And she's right. They're like the new bullies in school, always putting people down for not being as smart as them."

"Thank you!" I exclaimed, redeemed, and gave Quinn a high five.

"Damn, I wish we'd had those kinds of bullies when I went to school," Jake said. "Somehow I can't see getting too worked up about a bully with glasses and a pocket protector."

"So, do you have a boyfriend, Casey?" Kyle asked, abruptly changing the subject.

"Kyle!" Jake forcefully scolded. I saw them exchange a look.

"What? It's just a question."

"Sorry, my brother doesn't have any manners," Jake announced, looking kind of embarrassed. I wasn't sure what was happening, but I was pretty sure they'd had a conversation about whether I was single or not. *Ooh... interesting.*

"No boyfriend," I replied with a sly smile on my face. "And thanks for pointing it out, Kyle. I'm also not a lesbian, in case you were wondering."

All four brothers dissolved into a fit of laughter. I smiled proudly as I waited for them to stop. I could tell they were impressed with my response.

"Actually, that *was* going to be my next question," Kyle shot back, playfully.

"Well, then, I'm glad I cleared it all up for you."

"You want to sit down?" Jake asked unexpectedly.

YES. YES. YES. I desperately wanted to join them, but playing it cool seemed the best strategy with this particular group of hot guys. "Oh, well, I don't want to disturb your brotherly male bonding, or... uh... whatever this thing is that you got going on here."

"Please... hot, single, non-lesbian nerds are always allowed in male-bonding sessions. It's an unwritten rule, right, guys?" Kyle said.

All the brothers nodded their heads, even the teenage one.

"Oh, yeah... 'cause this whole thing I got going on here" – I motioned to my face and body in an overly dramatic fashion – "Very hot."

The guys laughed, and then Jake pulled out a chair for me. I stared at him for a second. His eyes were sparkling and he seemed eager for me to stay, so I sat down. It's not every day you get an invitation like that. And to think I'd been feeling pretty damn lucky earlier in the evening just to have met and chatted with him. But this... this exceeded all expectation. Just wait until my mom heard about this!

5

JAKE: A WEIGHT IS LIFTED

*R*eally? *Wipe the goofy smile off your face, idiot. What are you doing? Could you be any more obvious? You're practically drooling.* What was it about her that got me worked up like this? My heart was beating faster; my palms were sweaty. I'd never had this kind of a reaction to anyone before. I hated losing control like this, but it felt weirdly exciting too. Casey was so fun, and so random. I loved the way her mind worked. She was smart and interesting and hot all in one stunning package. It was obvious my brothers loved her too. Even Kyle seemed to be fascinated with her, and he was notoriously hard to please when it came to women.

I, for one, couldn't take my eyes off her. Casey looked so hot in her simple tank top and sweats. It accentuated her tight body and rounded butt. Her hair was swept back into a high ponytail, and she was wearing minimal makeup. A natural beauty... that's what Casey was. God, it was so attractive. I was used to heavily made-up girls hitting on me, so Casey's wholesome look was a welcome change of pace.

And her fun-loving, sunny personality was like a magnet, drawing me in. Enthralled, I hung on Casey's every word, experiencing a sense of pride every time she said something that made my brothers laugh. She had a zest for life that I found incredibly attractive. There had been a time, long ago, when I was like her. I had nearly forgotten that feeling until her joy swallowed me up. It was as if her light was beckoning my darkness, daring it to crawl out of the shadows.

Her laugh jolted me from my self-absorption. I felt that weight lift off me again. How was she doing it? Why was I reacting to her like this? Could it be as simple as Casey just made me happy? As much as I hated to admit it, Kyle was right. It was weird for me to feel true, unfiltered happiness. Yet all it took for Casey to make me happy was a laugh or a smile.

And when she laughed, she did this cute little flip of her head, and her ponytail would whip around and nearly hit me in the face. When I mentioned that her hair was like a deadly weapon, she made a point to smack me in the face with her ponytail every time she turned her head. Was she for real? No girls ever joked with me like that. *Ever!* I loved it.

The round table we were all sitting at was really only meant for three people, so adding the fifth person meant that Casey had to sit close enough to me that our legs touched. I was treated to her incredible scent. It was a clean, fresh fruity fragrance; probably just her shampoo, but it was so enticing that I fought the urge to bury my nose in her hair like a goddamn stalker. It was like she wasn't trying to impress, and that impressed me even more. I was so used to women throwing themselves at my feet that I'd never experienced the rush of actually pursuing someone. And judging by the reaction in my body when she was near, Casey was definitely the type of girl I would want to pursue. I shook my head. I was getting all caught up in thoughts of her. I needed to keep it together. I needed to back off and try to retain some level of cool. Then it occurred to me – I was acting like the fangirls who were always fawning over me.

6

CASEY: CAKE

A nd there we stayed for well over an hour, talking and laughing. The McKallister boys were endearing, all sporting a similar goofy sense of humor. Keith, the oldest, was the most talkative and obviously the leader of the bunch. He had an easy smile and a light, friendly personality. His eyes danced with excitement as he spoke. I liked him instantly. Keith was a catch. Not only was he a good-looking guy with short dark hair and a trimmed beard, but he owned his own skate shop business and had been in a committed relationship with a woman named Samantha (Sam) for the past three years. Keith talked about her in a loving way, saying she and I had similar personalities and that he would have to introduce me to her the following day when she arrived for the wedding. Nothing was more attractive than a guy who was dedicated to his woman.

Kyle was a year younger than Jake. He was tall and thin with shaggy brown hair and a careless, hippie look. His body was littered with tattoos. Really, by looks alone, he should have been the famous singer. He had a rougher exterior and temperament, and could be a bit harsh and crude – definitely the troublemaker – but he was funny as hell and had a charm to him that was

undeniable. I had no doubt Kyle got his fair share of female attention. In fact, his brothers had basically confirmed that for me
when they mentioned his string of past hookups. Even though it
was Jake who had invited me to join them, Kyle was the one who
was dishing out the pickup lines, good-naturedly hitting on me
all while keeping one eye squarely on his brother to gauge his
reaction. Obviously Kyle thrilled in getting a rise out of his
famous brother.

With his shoulder length hair, liquid eyes, and chiseled
features, Quinn, the youngest, looked the most like Jake. Just
sixteen, he carried himself with the awkwardness of youth, but I
had a feeling it wouldn't be long before Quinn came into his own
– that is, if his brothers didn't break him first. He was teased
relentlessly, yet to his credit, the kid took everything they dished
out with a smile on his face. It was clear that he desperately
sought his older brothers' approval. Any attention they lavished
on him, negative or otherwise, seemed to thrill him.

Of course, the brother who surprised and charmed me most
was Jake. I saw no signs of the insecure, despondent, and broken
young man that he was made out to be in the press. Instead, he
had a relaxed smile, a quick wit, and an easy-going personality. If
Jake had emotional issues related to the kidnapping, he sure
didn't show it. He was the epitome of a cool, confident, and
charming guy. At some point during the conversation, I
completely forgot who Jake was. It didn't feel like I was chatting
up a famous celebrity. He was just a normal guy, one I really
enjoyed talking to.

It was after one in the morning when we made the collective
decision that it was time for bed, and we all walked to the elevator. As we were waiting for it to arrive, I turned to the
McKallister boys and said, "Well, guys, thanks for letting me
crash your party. That was really fun."

All the guys agreed with me.

The doors opened, and just as I was about to step in, Jake

grabbed my arm gently and said, "Let's take the next one. I'll walk you back to your room."

I was floored by his offer but tried to play it off like I got invitations like that all the time from gorgeous, famous musicians.

"Yeah, sure. That would be nice," I replied casually. Inside, I was dying of happiness. I could not have been more flattered. Jake seemed to like being around me. Why? I had no idea... but I wasn't complaining.

The brothers said goodbye as the elevator door shut, and then Jake and I were standing there alone.

"Well, that was fun. Thanks for inviting me, Jake McKallister."

"You know, my middle name is Ryan if you want to throw that in, too," Jake offered.

"Nope, I'm good," I announced, smiling up at him.

Jake leaned in and focused on my eyes, "You're a cool girl, Casey Caldwell."

"Me?"

"Yes, you."

"I think you have me confused with someone else."

"Nope... pretty sure I don't."

I stared up at Jake skeptically. "You don't meet a lot of normal girls, do you, Jake?"

"No. Not really," he admitted, flashing me a sheepish grin.

"That's what I figured. Most of the normal girls you meet are probably screaming in your face or having to be physically extracted from you."

"Pretty much, yeah."

"Speaking of being physically extracted, did you know you were originally paired up with Sarah for the wedding?"

"Really?" Intrigued, Jake stood a little straighter. "I didn't know that."

"Yeah, I think Mitch was worried that the two of you would be banging each other through the wedding ceremony, so they decided to pair us together instead."

Jake's eyes grew wide with surprise.

"Apparently, they consider me to be rather harmless. I'm not sure if I should be offended. I mean, I know I'm no Sarah, but I don't consider myself to be toe fungus either," I argued.

Jake scoffed.

"What?" I asked, slightly offended that he didn't correct my musings.

"Mitch got it all wrong."

"What? The banging part, or the fungus part?"

"The part about you being harmless," Jake said matter of factly.

I could not have been more shocked by his statement. What did that mean? Did he think we would be a better match than he and Sarah? What was going on in that famous head of his?

"You think I'm dangerous?" I questioned with surprise in my voice.

Jake smiled. I stared at him for a few seconds before smiling back. What the hell was going on here? *And stop staring at me with those amazing eyes.*

Without even thinking, I said exactly what was on my flustered mind. "Damn, I can't get over your eyes, Jake. Such a light greenish-gray color, but the iris is, like, outlined or something, making them pop. Whoa, hold up," I said dramatically as I examined them closer. "And then they have these very subtle flecks of amber, yellow, and blue around the pupils, like peacock eyes. So pretty."

Jake gazed at me a second before looking away, and I swore he might actually have blushed a little bit.

"I guess you hear that a lot, don't you?"

"That I have peacock eyes?" Jake laughed. "No. That is a first."

"No, I meant, you must hear that you have pretty eyes all the time," I corrected.

"Um... not as often as I hear they're a weird color."

"Not weird... unique." I smiled in admiration.

Jake shrugged. "If you say so."

"I do."

"I never really liked my eyes," Jake admitted.

"Seriously? I would kill for that color."

Jake shook his head. "They draw too much attention."

"That's the point."

"Not when it's negative attention." Jake shrugged.

"How can having awesome eyes give you negative attention?" I asked, not buying his argument.

Jake didn't respond immediately, almost like he was deciding what to tell me. "One time, when I was a kid, this woman, who I'd never met before, came up to me at the mall and told me I had evil eyes."

"Really?" I asked, surprised.

Jake nodded.

"Oh, my god, what a bitch."

Jake laughed. "I know. Who says that to a kid, right?"

"How old were you?"

"Probably ten or eleven."

"Please tell me you punched her in the vagina," I blurted out, rather crudely.

Jake's eyes widened in surprise at my vulgar comment, and I immediately regretted my choice of words. But Jake just shook his head in amusement as he choked out a laugh. "No, I didn't punch her in the vagina. I don't hit girls. Geez, Casey."

"What did you do, then?"

"Then? As if there could not possibly be another viable option to vagina punching," Jake laughed. "Anyway... I gave her my best crazy look and responded in an eerie voice, *and now I've cursed you.* You should have seen the look on her face. She was praying as she ran away."

"No way! That's genius."

"I was a little shit back then."

"Maybe a little." I grinned. "But she deserved it."

"Damn right she did," Jake said, as his expression turned mischievous. "Oh, and remind me not to mess with you. You went straight for vagina punching. I didn't even know that was a thing."

"Oh, yeah...it's a thing," I giggled.

"And how many have you punched in your lifetime?"

I started calculating in my head.

"Seriously? You have to count?" Jake's voice rose in mock surprise.

"I'm just playing with you. I've never punched anyone in the vagina, but if some bitch says that to you again, I will protect your honor."

"Wow, I feel so special."

I looked up at him in all his glory. He was irresistibly attractive. At that moment, I could not imagine ever meeting anyone as good-looking or as intriguing as Jake McKallister.

"You're easy to talk to," I stated. "I wasn't expecting that."

"Yeah, I'm sure," Jake replied, his expression changing.

"I didn't mean that disrespectfully," I backtracked.

"I didn't take it that way."

I searched his face for any hint of offense. That had definitely not been my intention. Jake seemed to sense my trepidation, though, and smiled warmly in response. My insecurities melted away, along with my dignity. I was seriously swooning. How could I not when he stared at me all adorable like that? I was only human.

Hushed whispering caught our attention. A couple of women giggled as they pointed excitedly in our direction.

"Oh, shit... let's go," Jake whispered. He pushed the elevator button multiple times as if he were willing it to come quickly. As luck would have it, the door miraculously opened. We stepped in, and Jake hastily pushed the close door button.

"What floor?"

"Four." The doors closed just as the women came into view. Jake looked immensely relieved as the elevator started moving.

"We just dodged a bullet there," he stated.

"Yeah, they looked pretty needy," I replied.

"Needy doesn't even begin to describe it."

"So you have some pretty freakin' awesome brothers. And your dad is a riot. It must be interesting at your family dinners."

"You have no idea," Jake agreed.

"Your dad's story was... " I started to say, but was interrupted.

"Embarrassing. I know."

"No. I was going to say cute."

"He had a little too much to drink I think," Jake said, attempting to explain away his father's casual betrayal of the entire McKallister clan.

"I don't know... I thought it was pretty funny. In fact, I was thinking I might just call you 'Oops' from now on."

Jake balked. "You better not."

"Oh, you don't like that, huh? Then I'm definitely going to call you that. Oops McKallister... it kind of has a ring to it, don't you think?"

"Okay, I see where this is going. Two can play this game. From now on I'll call you 'Poops' Caldwell."

"Poops?" I nodded as if I was seriously considering the validity of the unflattering nickname he'd created for me. "That's pretty funny, actually. Okay, yeah, that's good. That will be our Hollywood couple name... OopsPoops."

"Or Poops... Oooops?"

We laughed easily together. Every light moment we shared drew me in deeper. This was definitely the type of guy I could fall head over heals for. In fact, I suspected I was only one mortifying stumble away from complete humiliation.

The elevator door opened on four, and we got out.

"You know," I said, catching his eye. "I think we should just stick with Jacey."

"Wait a minute!" Jake erupted in mock indignation. "Since when did we get a Hollywood couple name? I've known you for about six hours."

"Oh, um… oh, geez… this is awkward… I just thought… uh…" I stammered. "Is it too early? Oh, man, that's just embarrassing."

I searched Jake's face for a reaction. It lit up. His eyes danced with amusement. Whew. That could have gone south quickly. Thank goodness this guy understood sarcasm. With hot guys, a good sense of humor was never a given.

As I took in his handsome features, I noticed for the first time a faded inch-long, raised scar on his jawline and then another faded one on his cheek. I wondered how those imperfections came to be, but I would never dare ask him. I had a feeling Jake's good nature extended only so far.

We started walking again. I hadn't realized we'd stopped. Somehow, we had made it down the hall on my floor and paused in front of my door. It felt as though I was floating – like an out of body experience.

"This is my room," I said with clear disappointment in my voice. God, how I wanted to take another lap around. We stood there for a couple seconds, and then Jake nudged me good-naturedly. I nudged him back. We both smiled. I wondered what Jake was thinking. Had he walked me to my room in hopes of getting something? I realized that I would be pretty powerless under his charms if it came to that.

"Well, it's been fun, Casey."

He gave me a quick hug. I could feel his muscles under the fabric of his shirt, and it made me tingle in all the right places. I wanted to hold onto him and not let him go. How big of a slut would that make me if I invited him in?

Instead of acting on instinct, I used my brain. "It has. Thanks for walking me to my room."

"Yeah, no problem," Jake replied, then hesitated like he wanted to say something else but thought against it. "Well... I guess I'll see you tomorrow."

"Yes, tomorrow," I agreed.

Jake started walking away, then turned and said, "Oh, and by the way, I think our Hollywood couple name should be Cake."

I laughed out loud. "Cake? Oh, my god, Jake... I *love* it! Short and sweet."

"Yep, short and sweet," Jake agreed. He continued on his way. "See you, Casey."

"See you, Jake McKallister," I called after him. Jake turned back toward me, rolled his eyes, and smiled. I watched his really extraordinarily nice butt walk away before going into my room and shutting the door. I flung myself onto the bed and mouthed *Oh, my god* over and over again as I pounded my fists into the mattress. I silently cheered my good fortune. Jake was a perfect gentleman, which made me like him even more.

7

JAKE: CONFLICTED

W hat the hell was happening? The last thing I needed in the middle of a tour was a girl, even one as amazing as Casey. I had to stop acting like some horny middle-schooler. I wasn't myself with Casey. She brought someone out in me that I didn't recognize. Chatty, flirty... shit, I'd been this close to inviting myself into her room. Not to have sex, but to keep on talking to her. Me? Talking? It certainly wasn't what I was known for. Usually the less I knew about a girl, the better. Made it easier to get her out of my bed afterward. Yeah, it was a douchebag way of thinking, but what could I say? I'd had a fucked-up life; emotional attachments had never been my strong suit. But damn, this girl was different from anyone I'd ever met before. I had to get it under control before I did something stupid and crazy... like fall for her.

I maneuvered my way back to my room, avoiding the women who were riding the elevator looking for me. What made it more difficult was that the elevators were fashioned from see-through glass, so I was actually having to duck and hide. I took the stairs and waited until the coast was clear before darting down the hallway to the room I was sharing with Kyle.

As I burst through the door, Kyle looked up at me in surprise. "That was quick. She's probably not real impressed with your stamina."

"Shut up," I shot back, breathing heavily as I sank down on the sofa next to Keith. "I'm not interested in your annoying commentary right now."

"Geez... testy."

"Leave him alone, Kyle," Keith said, and then turned to me. "Why are you panting?"

"Why are you here?" I countered. Keith had his own room that he was sharing with his girlfriend.

"I wasn't tired. And I wanted a drink. Why are you panting?"

"Dodging fans," I replied.

"Oh, great," Kyle huffed, rolling his eyes. "Did they follow you here?"

"I don't know. Probably."

"They better not start knocking."

"I hope they keep you up all night, asshole," I spat.

I was in a foul mood. The whole thing with Casey had me questioning myself, and I didn't like it one bit.

"Fuck you!" Kyle exclaimed.

"No, fuck you! I can't believe you did that to me."

"What? Call over a girl you're clearly crushing on? So sorry. Shoot me."

"I'm not crushing on her. I met her six hours ago. And asking her if she has a boyfriend? Dammit, Kyle. Obviously, she knew we'd been talking about her."

"So? Now she knows you're interested."

"I'm not interested," I protested loudly.

"Uh-huh," Kyle said knowingly. He knew me better than any other human on the planet, and sometimes I hated the power he had over me.

"Fuck you! I don't need you playing matchmaker. I can get a girl all on my own."

"Not with that attitude, you can't," Kyle joked under his breath.

I glared at him. "I swear to God, Kyle. I'm about to punch you."

"Okay, okay," Keith intervened. "Will the two of you shut up for like two seconds? Jesus Christ. You're giving me a headache."

Keith took a swig from his beer.

"Where did you get that?" I asked, momentarily forgetting my hate for Kyle.

"In the cooler. Help yourself."

I got up and grabbed a beer. Leave it to Keith to bring a cooler full of beer to a wedding. First the Jack Daniels and now this? It was the most I'd had to drink in a long time, but tonight I really felt like I needed something to take the edge off.

I'd nearly finished off my first beer when Keith stated, "It's too bad you aren't interested. I liked her."

I didn't respond.

"I was surprised that you even invited her to sit with us," Keith pressed.

"It wasn't like I had much choice after Kyle's little stunt," I said through gritted teeth, glaring at my younger brother.

"Hey, I just called her over. You're the one who extended the invite." Kyle grinned smugly.

That pissed me off. "Well, if you hadn't called her over, then I would never have invited her to sit down."

"Tomaytoes... tomahtoes," he replied in an accent.

"Shut the hell up, Kyle!"

"What are you so defensive for? Sounds to me like you're trying to convince yourself you don't like her, when by inviting her to sit with us, you clearly do."

"Was that such a problem for you guys? Jesus!"

"No. It wasn't a problem at all, Jake. Casey is really fun to hang out with," Keith said, trying to defuse the argument between Kyle and me. "I didn't mean it like that. I just meant you don't usually bring girls home to meet the fam. I mean, how long did you date Krista? Three, four months? I met her once backstage at a concert, and you didn't even introduce us."

I frowned but didn't refute his claim. He was right. I'd never been captivated by any girl I'd dated or slept with. Introducing her to my family seemed a moot point since I knew she wouldn't be around long enough for it to matter.

Keith shrugged. "Yeah, well, anyway, I think you should try dating a nice, normal girl like her some time."

"As opposed to what?" I asked.

"Your groupie sluts."

I got up and grabbed another beer. I popped the cap, took a swig, and sat back down before responding. "I like my groupie sluts."

"Yeah, well, I hate to break this to you, but those limber ladies aren't marriage material, my man," Keith laughed.

"Who says I want to get married?"

"I'm not saying now... I'm saying someday you'll want to grow up and have a big boy relationship. And all I'm saying is that it should be with a girl like Casey."

"If you like her so much, why don't you date her?"

"Can't."

"Why?"

"Because she likes you, dummy." Keith rolled his eyes.

"No, she doesn't," I argued.

Keith gaped at me like I was a crazy person, then shook his head in disappointment. "You're an idiot."

I gave him a dirty look.

"Seriously?" he said.

"What?" I asked, feeling annoyed.

"Oh, come on, Jake. You guys have chemistry. You know it. She knows it. The fucking goldfish in the lobby pond know it."

I couldn't help but laugh at that. "I just... I don't want to give her the wrong impression."

"What impression is that?"

"That I'm interested."

"You're not?"

"I mean, she's cool and all but..." I hesitated. "It's just not a good time to get involved with someone, you know."

"Who says?"

"I say." I sneered at Keith. "I'm insanely busy, Keith. I just don't have time for a relationship right now."

"So, tell me exactly when will be a good time, Jake, because for the past seven years you've been perpetually busy. If that is going to be the deciding factor, then you might as well prepare now to be alone forever."

I stared at Keith. I wanted to argue with him, but we both knew he was right. I was always making excuses, using my schedule as a reason for not wanting to get close to a girl, but the truth was... God, the truth was so much more depressing. We sat in silence, drinking our beer.

"So if you aren't interested," Kyle broke the quiet moment, "Can I have a go at her?"

I gave Kyle a death stare. He loved pushing my buttons.

"I'll take that as a no."

8

CASEY: SMITTEN

I had trouble sleeping that night. All I could see when I closed my eyes was Jake's face, Jake's smile, Jake's hair. I liked everything about him, including his awesome family. I was hopelessly smitten with a guy I would probably never see again after tomorrow.

When I woke up in the morning, the only thing on my mind was Jake McKallister... and I couldn't stop smiling. I ran our conversations over and over in my mind, laughing to no one. God, I had it bad. I was seriously crushing on Jake. How had this happened? How had I become one of those horrible clichés – the love-struck groupie who fell for the rock star? Stupid. This guy was gorgeous, talented, rich, and famous. The girls in his world were models and singers, not waitresses. Yet Jake gave off all the signs of being interested. Of course, maybe he was only interested in a booty call, but if that were the case, then why didn't he push for it? Obviously, he had to know I was into him. It wouldn't have taken much to sway me. No. I'd convinced myself that Jake was into me, and no amount of self-doubt could shake me of that belief.

9

JAKE: UNDENIABLE ATTRACTION

"Wake up, dipshit!" Kyle's voice broke into my dreams. I bolted upright, unsure of where I was or what was happening. Kyle was standing in the doorway, grinning.

"Your alarm is going off."

"Oh, god. What the...?" I reached over and turned it off. "I'm so out of it. Fucking jetlag! What time is it?"

"Eight. You're fine."

I'd been having quite the dream when I was so rudely interrupted. I turned so Kyle wouldn't catch sight of my morning wood. Kyle remained in the doorway.

"What?"

"Nothing."

"Are you waiting for a tip?" I asked grumpily.

"I wasn't, but I wouldn't turn one down if you offered."

"Well, then, here's my tip... if you don't leave now, you'll see dick."

Kyle made a gagging sound and walked out of the room.

I rubbed my tired eyes and thought about the dream I'd just been having. She was even invading them. A smile spread across my face as I thought about all the funny things Casey had said yesterday. Damn, she was smart and feisty and fun. Keith was right. I liked her. There was no denying it.

I yanked off the sheets and walked to the bathroom. I turned on the shower and took a piss while the water warmed up. Stepping into the steaming flow, I let it roll over my tired body before dunking my head under the steady stream. Water saturated my hair and ran down my sides. As I soaped up, my hands slid over the rough, raised skin that crisscrossed my body, a reminder of the childhood horrors I'd survived. I had long ago come to terms with how those scars came to be, but that didn't mean I openly discussed my past. It was one of the main reasons I pushed women away. I hated revealing my scars because that meant having to explain them. This was why my 'groupie-sluts,' as Keith so eloquently put it, were so perfect. The encounters were quick and impersonal. No girl was ever around long enough for me to have the conversation. Hell, most of the time, they weren't around long enough to even see me without a shirt on.

My thoughts turned back to Casey, and I wondered what she would think of my scars. She was different from the others, but that didn't mean she would be any less curious. At some point, she would want details, and I knew I couldn't give that to her. What had happened to me was something I would never share with anyone. It was just the way I dealt with the trauma. But unfortunately, people always wanted more from me. My pleas for privacy were never accepted. This had always been the major deal breaker when it came to women. One or two trysts in bed and they were, all of the sudden, my personal therapists, prodding me to open up and share my feelings. Fuck that! That part of my life was off-limits to everyone... including any woman who tried to get close to me.

But then, I'd never really been too invested in those relationships to begin with. There was no real trust. The few "girlfriends" I'd had were really just about sex for me. There was no emotional connection. We didn't have light, fun conversations. We didn't laugh together. We just got together often for sex, and then, by default, we hung out in public occasionally. I guess I could see why the girl might consider us 'together,' but I never did. My relationships never went deeper for me emotionally. In fact, I spent most of my last relationship just trying to get out of it. But Casey excited me in ways that went beyond just sex. She made me feel, I don't know, normal, and my attraction to her was undeniable. So then why did I feel so conflicted? Why couldn't I just let go? Why couldn't I just allow myself to be happy... just this once?

Later that day, after arriving at the church with my family, Mitch walked up to me in the groom's room looking worried. *Uh-oh. What now?* I thought we'd cleared things up last night.

"What's up?" I asked, with apprehension in my voice.

"I was just... um... what do you think about just hanging back here until the ceremony starts?"

"You don't want me to usher?"

Mitch's face was twisted in distress. Obviously, he was sufficiently concerned about offending me. "It's not that I don't want you to. It's just... I think having you as an usher might be counterproductive to getting people to take their seats."

"Oh. Yeah. Probably," I said, feeling a little bummed. Any chance I got to hang with my brothers I took. But I understood what he was saying.

Mitch then started backtracking. "I mean if you want to, then that's cool too. Whatever you want."

"I'll wait back here, Mitch. No big deal."

"Are you sure?" He seemed uncertain.

"Yeah, I'm sure."

∽

The ushers left for their escorting duties soon after. As Mitch got ready with our Dad and his best man, I waited on the sofa by myself playing on my phone until I got bored and started thinking about Casey. Once I did, I couldn't get her out of my mind. I still had forty-five minutes to kill, so I decided to go looking for her. I walked out of the church and was heading over to the rooms in the other building where I knew the bridal party was getting ready when I saw a group of teenage girls lingering. They weren't dressed for a wedding, and they had cameras and cell phones at the ready. Crap. I froze in place and contemplated going back inside the church, but by now I was already halfway there. I had not yet been spotted, so I made the split-second decision to keep walking. I'd only covered half the remaining distance before a girl screamed my name. I looked up, smiled, waved, and then like a coward, ran the rest of the distance. I quickly ducked inside the building, feeling instant relief but also worrying that the entire hoard of excited teens would follow me inside. I turned around and locked the door. If anyone was coming behind me, they were screwed, but I figured that was preferable to an invasion of enthusiastic teenage girls.

I wandered from room to room looking inside for Casey. I passed an older woman, and I asked if she knew Casey. She didn't. Finally, I rounded a corner and there she was. I stopped dead in my tracks and gazed at her in awe. Casey was wearing a shimmery, flowing bridesmaid dress. The color was so unusual, a greenish-yellow mix, but it was perfect with her tanned skin and shiny brown hair. The dress fell just above her knees and I was treated to a view of her perfectly toned legs. Holy shit. I gulped. I was awestruck by her beauty. My eyes scanned upwards. Casey's hair was again pulled back into a ponytail, but now it looked glamorous, slicked back tightly, with curls cascading down her back. A couple of small flowers were pinned into her hair. Even the makeup she was wearing, more than last night, was still subtle and radiant. The sunlight from the window illuminated her, and she reminded me of a meadow full of wildflowers. I just stood there and stared at her, mesmerized. Casey was smiling as she chatted easily with a young girl. She was arranging flowers in the child's hair. She must have sensed my presence and looked up. When she saw me, a bright smile crossed her face. I wasn't sure if I'd ever seen anyone as beautiful in all my life.

10

CASEY: SPY GAMES

I tried to keep my mind off Jake by throwing myself into the wedding preparations. It wasn't until I was at the church that I actually saw him again. I was helping one of the junior bridesmaids put a flower crown in her hair when I looked up and there he was, staring right at me.

"Oh, hey," Jake said. "I was looking for you."

You were looking for me? I wanted to blurt out, but instead I just smiled widely and gazed up at him in all his gorgeous glory. Jake was dressed in a black tailored tux that fit him to perfection. Good Lord, was he fine. "Wow."

Jake smiled.

"Oh, no. Did I say that out loud?"

"You did."

"Well, crap. How awkward," I joked. "Still, I stand by my observation. You definitely clean up nicely."

"I'm not really sure how to take that." Jake grinned.

I smiled coyly and shrugged my shoulders.

"Well... puke green is a good color on you."

I laughed out loud, but it came out more like a snort. I

covered my mouth quickly, and both Jake and I laughed. The preteen flower girl looked up at me in horror, like I'd committed a mortal sin by snorting in front of a hot guy.

"You like this, huh?" I said, as I stood up and twirled in my dress. Jake nodded.

I turned to the girl, who was staring in awe at Jake. "You're all set, Kayla."

"Oh... okay, uh... thanks," Kayla replied, without even looking at me. Still staring at Jake, Kayla started to walk out of the room. Then she stopped, gathered her courage, and asked Jake, "Can I get your autograph?"

"Sure." Jake replied agreeably. "What do you want me to sign?"

"Oh, um... let me... " Kayla started looking around the room for a pen and some paper. While we were waiting, Jake glanced at me. I smiled, and he gave me one back. A tingle shot through my body. I could not have been more attracted to him if I tried. Kayla eventually found something for Jake to sign, and he wrote her a little note and handed it back to her.

"Thank you so much," Kayla said. "You're so nice. I wish I had my phone so I could take a picture, but my mom made me give it to her for the wedding. My friends would be so jealous."

"Find me at the reception tonight and we can take a picture then, okay?"

"Really? That would be so sick. Okay... thanks," Kayla rambled as she skipped out of the room. Then from down the hall, we could hear her squeal, "You're hot!"

Both Jake and I looked at each other and laughed. He shrugged like he was saying, *What do you want me to do about it?*

"Oh, my god, Jake, you're so hot!" I exclaimed in my best preteen voice. "Can I get your autograph?"

"I can do better than that," Jake stated, and then bent down and kissed my cheek.

I gasped in mock adoration. "I'll never wash this cheek again."

Jake wrinkled up his nose. "Gross."

I smiled at him. He was just so cute staring down at me with that twinkle in his eye and the adorable lopsided grin on his face. He was clearly flirting with me, and it was making me weak in the knees. I wanted to jump him and give him a proper kiss, but I wasn't nearly bold enough.

"Aren't you supposed to be somewhere? Like ushering?"

"I was told my help was not required."

"Really?"

"Yeah… apparently they felt I couldn't handle the inherent pressures of being a wedding usher." Jake shrugged.

"Well, it's a tough job… walking people to their seats and all," I acknowledged.

"Right, because ushering is so much more demanding than performing in front of thousands of people every night."

"Exactly," I agreed. "You know, Jake, have you considered that maybe Mitch and Kate don't want you distracting their guests."

"I wasn't planning on breaking out in song," he remarked, sounding a bit miffed.

"You don't need to sing. You're just a walking distraction."

"Oh really? Are you distracted by me?" Jake asked and took a step closer to me. There was obvious suggestion in his voice. Damn, he was hot!

"I meant, you're a distraction to other people. You have absolutely no affect on me at all." I grinned.

"No?" Jake said as he stepped right up to me. "Are you sure?"

"Yep. Totally sure," I lied.

"What about now?" he asked, as he put his hand on my hip. He was so close to me now that I could feel the heat of his presence creeping through my body. I actually trembled. Jake didn't seem to notice, thankfully.

I fanned myself. "Nope, nothing." I grinned as I placed my hand on his beautifully dressed chest. He was staring down at me; our eyes locked.

"Hey, guys. What's up?"

Jake and I jumped. So focused were we on our little flirt-fest that neither one of us knew that we had company. We each took a step back, and I looked over to see Sarah standing in the doorway. She was trying to act casual in the face of what she'd just witnessed, but I could tell she was pissed. Sarah had staked her claim on this guy months ago, and I'd basically pulled up at the last minute and started building a house on her land.

Sarah strolled in. Each of us bridesmaids was wearing a different color, and she looked beautiful and confident in her light blue dress. Although the color I'd chosen complimented my skin tone, I suddenly felt frumpy and very green. Sarah smiled radiantly at Jake as she stepped between us. She turned to me, out of Jake's line of vision, and flicked me the meanest *get lost* look imaginable. "Um, Casey? Kate's looking for you. She needs your help with the veil."

I knew this was a lie to make me disappear. With me at a safe distance, Sarah would be free to work her charms on Jake. And if that happened, our burgeoning flirt fest would be over. I agreed with Sarah on one point: Jake was something special. And I was not going down without a fight.

I said in my sweetest voice, "Actually, Sarah, would you mind helping Kate with the veil? I was just about to take Jake to the church and coach him on what he needs to do for the wedding. Kate actually asked me to do that, but I haven't had a chance yet because I've been helping the flower girls."

"Kate asked specifically for you, though," Sarah said, not giving up easily.

"I'm sure she'll understand. She has her mom and her sister to help. I know Kate would want Jake up to par with all the wedding plans," I countered. Sarah flashed me the look of death. She knew what I was doing, but it would make her look like a bitch if she denied me. Then I turned to Jake, who seemed mesmerized by our conversation. "Are you ready?" I asked. Jake jerked his head up and nodded.

"See you later," Jake said politely to Sarah. She smiled sweetly at him, but inside, I knew she was fuming. Jake and I walked out of the room. Neither of us said a word until we were far out of hearing range.

"How close did we just come to a girl fight?" Jake whispered. "I'm not gonna lie, that would have been hot."

I looked up to see that he was smiling.

"Oh, you'd like that, would you?" I replied. "Girls fighting over you?"

"Let's just say I wouldn't be opposed to it."

I rolled my eyes like I was annoyed with him, but in reality, I loved his flirty little banter. It was so incredibly charming. I walked with him to the exit.

Jake stopped suddenly. "Not that way."

"What?"

"We can't go that way."

"Why not?"

"Fans."

"What?"

"There are teenage girls out there. I promise you – you don't want to go that way."

"Seriously?"

"Yes, seriously, Casey," Jake said, looking exasperated.

I laughed.

"What's so funny?" he asked, frowning.

"I don't know. It's just funny to me," I replied.

"I'm glad I could amuse you."

"Oh, don't be so dramatic. I'll save you," I said, as I grabbed his hand and led him in another direction.

"Where are we going?"

"I know another way out."

We came to a door that I'd used yesterday to bring in the dresses. I opened it slowly and peeked out. Jake was right. There was a group of girls, not from our wedding party, who were

milling around. These were probably youths from the church
that had gotten wind of Jake's presence and were waiting by the
back exit where the bridal party would walk out under the
covered awning into the church.

"Okay, on my count," I whispered, like I was a spy on some
mission.

"What?" Jake asked in confusion.

"I don't know, I just always wanted to say that. One, two...
three!" I grabbed his hand, yanked him out of the building, and
pulled him behind some bushes.

"You didn't even tell me what the count was," Jake
complained.

"Oh, sorry... it was three," I whispered.

Jake laughed. "Yeah, I get that now."

"Shhh!" I inclined my head towards the fans.

"What exactly are we doing?" Jake whispered.

"Getting you to the church without you getting mobbed," I
explained. "It's okay, I've done this before."

"You've done this before?" Jake asked in amazement. He was
enjoying the silliness of the situation.

I put my finger to my lips, and we tiptoed and ducked at the
appropriate moments. I made all these ridiculous gestures with
my hands as if I were on some covert mission. Jake just looked at
me with amusement in his eyes. At one point, he narrowly
missed stepping in a pile of cat poop, which most definitely,
would have taken the fun out of our little game. We were both
whisper-laughing. It was fun... like playing spy.

It took us about two minutes to get to the front of the church.
I raised my arms in victory and whispered, "Ta dah!"

"Congratulations, you got me across a parking lot" – Jake
smiled, and then pointed toward a group of people filing into the
church – "into an even bigger group of people. What now,
Bond?"

"Now we blend," I instructed, and started walking nonchalantly toward the entrance. I looked at Jake, who was studying me with interest. "Try to look uglier if you can," I whispered. Jake suppressed a snort. We casually merged with the people filing into the church. Once in the building, guests started noticing Jake, so I grabbed his hand and walked him around a corner. When we were out of sight, I squealed and started running with him down a hallway, giggling like a little girl. Jake gamely followed me. I led him to the back room where the bridal party was supposed to gather in exactly six minutes. I pushed him in and shut the door behind me. There was no one there yet.

I put a hand on Jake's shoulder, panting. "Whew, that was close."

Jake shook his head in amusement. "You're crazy fun, Casey."

At that moment, I was insanely happy. Jake just seemed to get me and my quirky humor. I felt like I could be myself with him, snorts and all. I stood on my tippy-toes and gave him a quick peck on the cheek.

Jake looked surprised. "What was that for?" he asked.

"For being a good sport," I replied.

A wide smile spread across his face. He stared down at me for the longest time, breathing heavily from our little excursion. Finally, he said, "So where were we when Sarah so rudely interrupted?"

I took a step forward until we were nearly touching. "I think we had gotten to about this point," I recalled, placing my hand on his chest.

"Oh, yeah, I remember now," he said, and then leaned down like he was going to kiss me. At that very moment, footsteps could be heard coming from the outside corridor. Kate and the others were coming. We looked at each other.

I sighed and rolled my eyes. "Oh, good lord... this way." I grabbed his hand again and led him to the back door. I opened it and instructed, "Follow the corridor to the end. You'll come to the groom's room."

"Okay." Jake brushed past me and started walking away. "Maybe we can finish this later," he said over his shoulder.

"I'm counting on it."

11

JAKE: STOLEN FUTURE

E very time I was with her I felt like I was on top of the world. She was just so much fun... and sexy... and beautiful. I could feel myself falling under her spell, and in the moment, I could imagine all the possibilities. I felt like I was in control, and I knew exactly what I wanted. But then I would walk away from her and be plagued with self-doubt. This girl had easily broken through the barriers it had taken me so long to erect. It happened so fast and without warning. Casey was the first girl I'd ever been attracted to, who made me feel something. My pounding heart was proof of that. Honestly, I hadn't thought it was possible. I'd always viewed myself as a lost cause when it came to love and affection, but with Casey, the promise of living the normal, simple life that I'd always craved actually seemed possible.

But then reality would set in. I knew myself, and I knew my limitations. It wasn't just the scars that held me back; there were demons that lived inside me, ones that rarely surfaced in my everyday life, but they were still there, lying dormant and waiting for the right trigger. And usually, that trigger was sexual intimacy. A certain touch, a simple phrase, a breathy whisper – any of those things had the potential to elicit flashbacks so realistic that I would be transported back into the nightmare of my youth. It had happened before, and I never wanted it to happen again. The only surefire way I knew of preventing a flashback was to not get too emotionally close to women, to not let my guard down around them, and to never trust anyone on an intimate level. I would rather die alone and lonely than have to relive the horrors.

But I was young and still had needs. I liked women, and I liked sex. So over the years, I'd figured a way around the problem: if I was horny enough and kept my sexual encounters to quick, impersonal romps, I could outrun the flashbacks, so to speak. But Casey was already affecting me on an emotional level that went so much deeper than anything I'd ever experienced. I didn't know if it would be possible to just have a casual encounter with her. And, honestly, I didn't want that anyway. I'd already had my fill of casual. I wanted more. I needed more. Yet I couldn't have more. No matter how perfect Casey was for me, there was never going to be a white picket fence and a beautiful wife and a team of kids running around. Not for me. There could never be a future with anyone because the minute Raymond Davis put that gun to my head he stole any chance of me ever living a normal life.

So I knew I had to cut her loose before things got too complicated. It wasn't just for my sake but hers as well. It was unfair to pull her into my life when I knew full well that I couldn't give her what she deserved. The longer I pretended that I was someone else, someone whole, the more attached we would become and the higher the chance of my destroying her life once the flashbacks destroyed mine. I had to stop being stupid and selfish. I had to stop leading her on. How could I break this off before it ever really started? What would I even say to her? Clearly, she knew I liked her; so really, anything I said would be confusing. Should I make excuses? Should I lie? Should I tell her it was for her own good? In the end, I chose the path of least resistance... I would just ignore her. She would think I was a total jerk, but it was better that way. It was only one day. I could ignore her for one goddamn day, and then I would be back in Europe, and I would never think of her again.

12

CASEY: THE BRUSH OFF

As I walked down the aisle holding my flowers, my eyes
focused on Jake. My stomach did a little flip. He was so
gorgeous. There was this strange, raw chemistry... a powerful
connection that I couldn't explain. I'd liked plenty of guys before
him but had never experienced anything close to this. It was
almost like a magnetic force field attracting me to him. I couldn't
see anything or anyone else in the church. Just him. He stared
straight ahead with that same detached look on his face that he'd
had when I first saw him. Was it because he was in front of a
bunch of strangers? This definitely wasn't the guy I knew. I tried
to catch his eye, but he was all business. So distracted was I with
Jake that I tripped on the first step, falling to the side. I caught
myself with one hand and managed to push myself upright in one
quick motion. I attempted to suppress a giggle but it was too
funny to hold in. Jake caught my eye, and his facial expression
softened. A slight smile crossed his face, but then he looked away
again and the mask went back up. I got an instant feeling of
unease. What was going on?

The ceremony was followed by almost an hour of pictures.
Jake stayed close to his family the entire time. I tried to get his

attention once or twice, but he refused to engage me. Even when I was standing next to him for a picture, he still didn't talk to me. It wasn't like I was expecting him to flirt with me in front of his family, but he could at least look at me and acknowledge my existence.

After pictures, we moved into the reception hall. Dinner was not starting for an hour, so the guests were all wandering around and chatting. Jake stayed next to his parents. I wondered if they had asked him to hang out with them for the wedding. I thought it was a little odd that a twenty-three-year-old man would stick next to his parents as they mingled with other people, but what did I know about their relationship? Still, why didn't he even look in my direction? I had an uncomfortable feeling that Jake was actively trying to ignore me. I just couldn't understand why. He'd been so flirty with me and had even said that we would continue our conversation later; but then nothing. Weird.

Dinner began. Jake was assigned to sit with his family, and I was with the bridal party. I glanced at him several times – okay, every minute or two – throughout the evening, but he never once reciprocated. The longer this went on, the more I realized that I needed to accept the truth: Jake McKallister was definitely not into me. I felt crushed. I didn't know why. I had just met him, so why would it hurt this much?

After dinner and during the speeches, my friend, and co-worker JD came over and sat next to me, thankfully taking my mind off Jake. Of course, JD started up with his incessant flirting. He always felt a need to sweet-talk me, even though he and I both knew it was never going to happen. JD, with his black wavy hair and chiseled good looks, was the biggest player I'd ever met. His booty count was in the fifties, and he loved bragging about it. I had no interest in being another notch on his belt. Still, I found his efforts entertaining. We talked and laughed for a while. At one point I looked up to check on Jake for the thousandth time and was shocked to find him staring right at me for the first time all evening... and he actually looked annoyed. It took me a second to realize why. JD. Was he... could it really be? Was Jake McKallister seriously jealous of JD Owens?

I wanted to laugh out loud at the preposterous assumption that Jake had made about JD. Did he really think that any guy, much less JD Owens, was on a level playing field with him? Did he not realize he was in a league all his own? But the look on his face was clear: Jake McKallister was jealous. I smiled and waved at him as if nothing at all was amiss. His frown turned upside down, and he tentatively waved back. He then turned back to his sister, ignoring me once again.

"Whoa... you know him?"

"Sort of. We were paired for the wedding, remember?"

"I know, but you guys weren't interacting or anything. I just assumed he was keeping to himself."

"No. We actually met yesterday at dinner. I hung out with him and his brothers later at the hotel, too."

"Oh, you hung out at the hotel." JD nodded.

"Yeah, wipe that smirk off your face. Nothing happened," I said.

"Uh-huh," JD said knowingly.

I laughed and wagged my finger at him.

"So what's he like? He seems stand-offish."

"Yeah, he seems that way, but when you get to know him, he's actually really nice." I must have voiced it with googly eyes because JD picked up on it right away.

"So wait... hold up here... Do you, or do you not, have something going with Jake McKallister?" JD asked in surprise.

"No... I mean... I don't know. We kind of hit it off last night, but... yeah. I have no idea what's going on. He's pretty much ignored me since the wedding started."

"Well, he's not ignoring you now," JD said. I glanced back, and Jake quickly turned away like he didn't want me to know he'd been staring. Something told me I now had Jake's full and undivided attention.

"What the hell?" I mumbled. "He made it pretty clear he wasn't interested, so then why would he even care if I'm talking to you?"

"Probably because I'm devastatingly handsome."

"Oh, yeah, right. That must be it." I shook my head.

"Seriously, though, Case... he seems legit pissed that I'm talking to you."

"Well, too bad," I responded, feeling a little pissed myself. Jake had spent the better part of the day ignoring me. He didn't have the right to be jealous.

"Shall I continue to irritate him?" JD asked.

If Jake wanted to play games, then so would I.

"Please."

JD put his arms around me, and I laughed loudly enough for Jake to hear. He turned around again upon hearing me enjoying myself and saw me in JD's embrace. His eyes instantly met mine, and I swear he looked hurt. I quickly pulled out of the hug, feeling strangely guilty.

Then suddenly, the sound of tapping on the microphone broke the moment. Mitch said, "I just want to thank everyone for being here tonight. You've all given Kate and me a day to always remember. We are so grateful for our amazing friends and family. Here's to all of you!"

Glasses were raised in celebration.

"And to my beautiful wife... I feel so lucky. You made my heart beat faster from the moment we met. Now I know why... .you were the one, Kate. You've always been the one. I'm so excited to spend the rest of my life with you."

More glasses were raised.

"So I'm not sure if any of you are aware of this, but my younger brother Jake is a minimally successful professional musician," Mitch went on. "And, you know, he's still working on trying to build a fan base, so he begged me to let him sing tonight." The crowd laughed. "Okay, okay, relax – I was just kidding. In reality, I begged Jake to sing Kate's favorite song, a little tune called "Pride," and he graciously agreed. So, Jake?" Mitch motioned to Jake, who immediately stood up and walked over to the stage. Kate clapped happily. Quinn followed his brother onto the stage. "Jake will be accompanied on guitar by our youngest brother, Quinn."

The McKallister boys slung the guitars over their shoulders and strummed the strings a few times as they waited to perform.

"You know, when people find out that Jake is my brother the first question I'm always asked is... can you sing? And I'm like... noooo... and people always seem so disappointed... like why?" Mitch expressed in a whine. Everyone laughed, including Jake. Mitch turned to him and said, "Anyway, I think we can both agree that you inherited your musical talents from your mother's side of the family because our dad... ." Mitch shook his head sadly.

Jake nodded and laughed.

"At least you all inherited your good looks from me," Scott called out.

"Yeah, right, Dad," Mitch said. "Anyway, lucky for us that Jake's mom gave him a voice, because we all get to enjoy it tonight. Thank you for playing for us," Mitch said, nodding toward Jake before replacing the microphone. He exchanged a few words with Jake and then walked back to Kate. He kissed her before sitting down. She looked giddy with excitement.

Jake adjusted the guitar, stepped up to the microphone, and to my surprise, glanced over at me before he started playing. His was the only instrument, and the sound was sweet and gentle. Then he began singing. Jake's voice was warm and rich and wonderful. He'd created this song out of nothing, and it was simply beautiful. Quinn then joined in on guitar and sang backup vocals. People around me listened and sang and swayed to the music. I looked on in amazement at how he was affecting every-one. To be able to touch so many people with such a simple, heartfelt song was really inspiring. Jake's talent was undeniable. An overwhelming sense of pride filled my chest. I couldn't take my eyes off him. His voice mesmerized me. His words seemed to fill the air around me. Just as he sang the last words, his eyes locked with mine. I felt powerful electricity pass between us. It was a brief moment, but it happened. Jake looked away as the song ended, and the audience erupted in applause.

13

JAKE: THE GREEN-EYED MONSTER

After the song, the dinner wrapped up with the maid of honor's and the best man's speeches. Then the bride and groom had their first dance. I glanced over at Casey. She was still sitting with that guy. I shook my head. I was pissed. It sure hadn't taken her long to replace me. My stomach was tied up in knots, I was so frickin' jealous. I hadn't even known I had that trait in me until tonight. I guess I'd never actually liked any girl enough to get jealous over her actions. I hated the idea of another guy getting Casey's attention. She liked me; I knew she did. And I liked her. So what the fuck was I doing over here while that asshole was sitting with her, making his play? God, I was such an idiot. I'd led him right to her.

I mean, really, what did I expect? Casey was a beautiful woman with an amazing personality. She wasn't going to be single for long. And judging by the guy hanging all over her, she might even be off the market by the end of the night. Just the idea of her being with another guy, and having the life with him that I wanted, filled me with anger. It was just a cruel twist of fate that had put me here, watching from a distance, and him there, sitting beside her. If I hadn't been in the wrong place at the wrong time all those years ago, my life would have been so different. A fucking twist of fate! That's all that separated me from the guys who had what I didn't.

Yeah, yeah. Stop with your pity party. I'd done this to myself. It had been my decision to walk away. Casey had every right to hang out with whomever she wanted, especially after I'd been such a giant douchebag to her. I'd seen her staring at me. I could feel her confusion. I could taste her disappointment. What was I doing? How could I really predict how Casey would react to me and how my body would react to her? And really, why was I so worried about screwing things up? Any woman who dated me obviously knew about my past. It wasn't like Casey would be going in blind. I mean, wasn't the common assumption that I was irreversibly damaged? So it should come as no surprise to her when I fucked everything up.

I watched Casey laugh at something the douche said, and anger rose up through me again. *No. Sorry.* I couldn't stand another second of this shit. I might not be able to have her, but I sure as hell wasn't going to let him have her either. It was at that moment I realized it was impossible to ignore Casey Caldwell. I couldn't when she went all James Bond on me and saved me from the fans; I couldn't in the church when she adorably tripped on the step and instead of being mortified, started giggling good-naturedly. And I definitely couldn't when she was chatting up some asshole guy who just wanted to get her into bed.

14

CASEY: CONFESSIONS

"Don't look now, but lover boy is on his way over," JD reported. "Damn, he sure knows how to command a room. No wonder it's so difficult to score at this wedding."

I grinned, keeping focused on JD so Jake wouldn't get spooked and head in another direction. A few moments later, I felt a nudge, and when I looked up, Jake was standing next to me. He'd taken off his coat and bowtie when he performed and now was wearing a white collared shirt unbuttoned a few notches.

"Hey!" I exclaimed, a little too loudly.

"Hey yourself," he answered back, smiling warmly. The Jake I knew from earlier was back, in all his sizzling sexiness. My whole body tingled with anticipation. I wanted him, and I wanted him to know.

I touched his arm and let my hand linger there on his warm skin. His eyes met mine, and we smiled at each other.

JD loudly cleared his throat to let us know he was still there. In fact, I'd completely forgotten about him. We both looked over.

"Hi, I'm JD," he said, as he stood to shake Jake's hand.

"Hey, nice to meet you."

"Great song, by the way," JD complimented. "I'm a big fan of your music."

Jake focused his full attention on JD. "Oh, yeah? Thanks, man."

The three of us stood there for a couple of seconds before Jake asked, "So, how do you know Casey?"

"JD's a friend of mine. We work together," I answered, before he had a chance to.

JD smirked, then nodded. "Yeah, what she said."

"How long have you worked together?" Jake asked. I sensed some strain in his voice.

JD looked at me. "What, like three years? Has it been that long?"

"Yeah, I think so," I replied, distracted. What was Jake doing? Why all the questions? Was he trying to assess our relationship or something?

"We haven't dated or anything like that," I blurted out, then instantly regretted it when I caught sight of JD's arched eyebrows and amused grin.

Heat burned my cheeks. I was so embarrassed. Jake hadn't asked if we had dated. Now he was going to think I was assuming he was jealous. *Oh, god. Shut up, Casey!*

Jake nodded but didn't respond. His expression was neutral. Had he seen the little non-verbal action playing out in front of him? What was he thinking? Was my second chance with him slipping away?

"Well, then, you won't mind if I steal my bridesmaid?" Jake wasn't really giving JD a choice in the matter as he grabbed my hand, pulled me out of my chair, and led me away.

"Oh, no... that's fine," JD called to our backs.

"See ya later," I threw over my shoulder.

"Not if I can help it," Jake whispered in my ear.

I didn't respond until we were on the other side of the room.

"That's big talk for a guy who's been ignoring me all evening," I stated, calling him out on his behavior.

Jake hesitated a second. The serious look on his face wiped the smile right off mine.

"Oh," I whispered, as my cheeks reddened. A knot instantly formed in the pit of my stomach. He really *had* been ignoring me... and on purpose, apparently. I felt like an idiot for thinking there was anything between us. "I'm embarrassed."

"Don't be, Casey. Let me explain," he started.

"No," I interrupted, putting my hand up and backing away from him a step. "You don't have to explain yourself, Jake. We just met. I mean, you're not into me, and that's okay. I just... I totally read things all wrong."

"No, you didn't. You read them right."

I looked at Jake in surprise. *WTF?* "Okay, now I'm really confused."

"I know. I'm sorry. I'm a fucking idiot."

"Yeah, you are, and you're starting to piss me off, too," I admitted.

"Sorry. Casey, please, just give me a minute to explain, okay?"

I looked at my wrist like there was a watch on it and replied, "Your minute starts now."

Jake seemed surprised that I was playing hardball with him.

"Tick tock, Jake."

"It's true, I've been avoiding you," Jake rushed out his words. "But it isn't because I don't like you. Obviously, I do. It's just... I'm in the middle of a world tour. I've been on the road for four months. This weekend was just supposed to be a quick detour and then it was back to Europe. I have up to five shows a week. I have a bunch of band and crew members that rely on me to keep things going. I'm just not in a place where I can really develop a new relationship."

"Okay. Why didn't you just say that? You didn't have to ignore me all day."

"I know, but every time I'm with you I get all giddy and weird and shit... and I can't think straight... so instead of trying to explain all that to you, I decided to take the immature, idiot approach and just ignore you."

I thought about what he said for a second before grinning and saying, "Well, I guess nothing says affection like ignoring the person completely. In a screwed up way, it's kind of a compliment."

"You're not mad?" Jake asked, looking immensely relieved.

"No... guys' brains just aren't as evolved as girls'."

Jake smiled and shook his head in amusement.

"I do have to ask, though. Your dastardly plan was working perfectly. Why did you ruin it all and come over to me just now?"

"I... " Jake looked embarrassed. "I saw you with JD, and I got jealous."

"Huh... interesting." I nodded, thoughtfully. "So now what? Are you going to go back to ignoring me?"

"I want to hang out with you, but... "

"But you don't want to lead me on? I get it. Who says I want a relationship with you anyway? Maybe I have some big summer plans that I don't want you to ruin either."

"I didn't... I... " Jake stumbled over his words. "You wouldn't be ruining my plans."

I shook my head. "I'm just kidding. Seriously, though, why does it have to be so complicated? I wasn't asking you to get down on one knee, Jake. You're a fun guy. I like hanging out with you. I just wanted to do more of that tonight... that's all. And I'm still up for it, if you are. It doesn't have to be anything more than that. I mean, it's either that or you continue to ignore me and I continue to talk to JD to make you jealous."

"You were trying to make me jealous on purpose?" Jake asked, in surprise.

"Only when I figured out that it bothered you."

"That's whacked." He grinned.

"Well, it got you over here, so… " I smiled up at him.

He shook his head like he found me amusing.

"So what do you say? One evening of fun… no strings attached," I said, maybe a little too eagerly. "Do we have a deal?"

Jake nodded. "I'm down if you are."

Of course, I realized that the deal I was offering was for Jake's benefit only. But I'd already decided that I would take what I could get from him. At least he'd been honest with me and hadn't tried to sweet talk me into sleeping with him, all the while knowing he was going to dump my ass the minute he stepped foot on the plane. I understood that Jake was a complex guy with a demanding life. That he was even willing to take the time to get to know me made me feel special. And he'd admitted that he liked me. Maybe after his tour ended he would look me up. But if I never saw him again, then I would just have to deal with it. Spending time with Jake was worth the risk, in my opinion. I mean, really, what girl wouldn't jump at the chance to spend an evening of fun with the hottest, most charming musician on the planet?

One of my favorite songs came on. "I love this song. Do you want to dance?" I asked.

Jake's lips tightened into a frown. "I don't dance."

"Oh, that's right. I almost forgot about your allergic reaction to yesterday's fictional wedding dance."

Jake nodded.

"Wait, though. You're a rock star. Don't you have to dance on stage?"

Jake laughed out loud. "Obviously, you've never been to a rock concert before."

"No, actually, I haven't."

"Let me guess – you're more of a pop music kind of girl?"

"I listen to whatever's on the radio."

"Who is your favorite musician?"

"Well, you, of course."

"Oh, uh huh, right. Name one song of mine," Jake challenged.

"Pride."

"Too easy. Name one I haven't sung in the last thirty minutes."

I stood there a moment thinking, then a smile broke out across my face.

"I knew it," Jake laughed. "Who is it? Beyoncé, Bieber, or Spears?"

"All the above," I laughed. "But, like I said, I just listen to what's on the radio. I don't really pay attention to the artist. I'm sure I've heard a lot of your songs, but just didn't know it was you who sang them."

"You know there's an app for that?" Jake grinned.

"I know, I know. It doesn't bother you?"

"What? That you're not a Stan?"

"A what?"

"A superfan."

My eyes narrowed in bemusement. "I've never heard that term."

"It's from an Eminem song, but you probably aren't familiar with him either."

"I know who he is, Jake, but I'm definitely not a Stan."

"Well, I'm not vain enough to think everyone is a card-carrying member of my fan club."

"Wait a minute. Are you telling me they still have fan clubs?" I asked.

"Uh… yeah. They've moved online, but they still exist."

"Wow, who would have guessed?"

"Anyone who knows anything about music, for starters."

"Yeah, yeah." I waved him off. "Anyway, I'm going to make up for lost time. I'm now officially your number one fan, Jake McKallister."

"No, Lexi in Ohio is my number one fan."

"Oh, so sorry. I stand corrected," I laughed. "Okay, here's

another confession... I've never been to a concert before, of any kind."

"Ever?" Jake asked in surprise.

"Nope. It's not that I didn't want to, it's just I never really had the means. When I was younger, I would beg my parents to let me go to a concert or to buy albums, but we always lived on a fixed income and just didn't have excess money. Then when I got older and started making my own money, I still never went because I needed that money for trivial little things like food."

"Yeah, that seems way more important. I actually haven't been to that many concerts either... only like maybe 700 or so," Jake teased.

"So, yeah... we're sort of on the same page on that then," I said, quirking an eyebrow.

Jake nodded in agreement.

"Hey, I have an idea," I said brightly, realizing I could barely contain my excitement when I was with him.

"What?"

"Maybe you could be my first," I teased, pausing before adding: "Concert, that is."

"Yeah, I would love to pop your concert cherry." Jake smirked.

I bust out laughing. Just then a slow song came on.

"You want to dance?" Jake asked.

My mouth dropped open. "I thought you didn't dance."

Jake cocked his head and said in his sexy way, "I slow dance."

"Oh, do you, now?" I squared my shoulders and let him lead me out onto the dance floor. Once we stopped, he reached his arm around me and pulled me close. I wrapped my arms around his neck, and he moved his hands to my hips. I leaned into him. We stared at each other. I felt that familiar chemistry between us again. We swayed gently to the music, not speaking for a long time, just enjoying the feel of our bodies pressed against each other while moving in rhythm to the music. I was lost in his embrace. He kept dipping his head into my shoulder. His hair tickled my bare skin, sending shock waves radiating through me. He held me close. Absently, I stroked the long strands of his hair. It was a bold move, but it just seemed so natural at the time and Jake clearly didn't mind. The song ended and was replaced with a dance tune. We reluctantly broke apart and walked back over to where we had been standing.

Jake's mom came over to us, introduced herself to me, and then turned to Jake and said, "You might want to tone it down a bit... you wouldn't want to draw attention away from the bride and groom."

He looked surprised, but he nodded anyway. Once his mom left, Jake leaned down and, with his hot breath tickling my neck, said, "I'm really hot. You want to get some air?"

"Yeah, good idea," I echoed, fanning myself as I followed him out of the reception hall. We walked down a long hallway, then turned right, and came to a stairwell.

"Where are we going?"

"A place I found last night when I was dodging those women."

"They followed you?" I asked in surprise.

"Yep," he said like it was an everyday thing. And, yeah, it probably was.

Jake pushed open a door. "This way. Every floor has one of these."

I followed Jake through the passage that led outside. He put his hand on the small of my back to guide me out to the little balcony, and the simple, polite gesture sent shivers down my spine.

"Sorry about that back there with my mom. I hate when she does that."

"Does what?"

"Reprimands me like I'm five."

"That's what moms do," I replied.

"Yeah, well, my mom does it a lot. I think she thinks I'm an idiot."

"She might be on to something," I smirked.

Jake cocked his head and lifted an eyebrow.

I grabbed his arm and shook it. "I'm just kidding. I can tell you're a smart guy."

"Oh, yeah? And how can you tell that?"

"Just by the way you carry yourself. You seem intelligent."

"I seem intelligent?" Jake asked in amusement.

I nodded.

"I dropped out of school at thirteen."

"Oh, damn… never mind."

Jake dropped his shoulders in playful defeat.

"Like totally out of school, or were you one of those weird homeschoolers?"

Jake laughed. "I was a weird homeschooler."

"Was it your choice to leave school?"

Jake didn't answer right away. *Oh, god, was that too personal? Should I avoid asking him questions about himself?*

"I was suspended for fighting and then refused to go back after that. But, you know, for obvious reasons, it was easier for me to be at home," he finally said. "Plus, I had a lot more time to work on my music. If I hadn't been a weird homeschooler, I don't think I ever would have gotten good enough to do it professionally."

I nodded, then decided I should probably clarify my joke. "You know I was only kidding about the homeschooler stuff, right?"

Jake shook his head, his eyes shining bright. "No, you weren't."

"Yes, I was." I demanded, and smiled up at him. "I'm sure there are plenty of perfectly normal homeschoolers."

Jake laughed out loud. "See? Another off-handed insult."

"Sorry," I apologized. "I have a problem. I'll try to control myself."

"No, please don't," Jake replied. "Everyone is so careful around me all the time. It's nice to hang out with someone who isn't worried about offending me. I mean, like, you've pretty much insulted me in every conversation we've had. Well done, Casey."

"Well, thank you. I really do try."

"I can tell and I appreciate it." Jake grinned.

I laughed. It made me feel so much more relaxed knowing Jake wasn't easily offended. I stopped worrying about being careful around him. He was like anyone else – only way more talented, and much hotter.

"Wait, though, you didn't just pick up music once you dropped out of school, did you?"

"No. I've been playing the piano since I was three."

"Geez, you overachiever."

Jake laughed. "Hey, that wasn't my fault. I would much rather have been outside playing."

"And you play the guitar, too. Any other instruments?"

"Um… " Jake had the grace to look embarrassed.

"What?"

"Nothing."

"Oh, no, now you gotta tell me."

"I play a few others."

"Like how many others?"

"Maybe like thirty or so."

"Thirty?!"

"Or so," he clarified.

"Good Lord. What are you, like, a musical genius?" I squealed.

"No. It just comes easily to me. And I like to know how things are played," Jake said, as if it were no big deal.

I stared at him in shocked surprise. "Well, damn. I'm impressed. I had no idea there were even thirty instruments to play."

"Seriously? Casey, there are thousands."

"Really? Wow, you must think I'm totally ignorant," I sighed. "In my defense, I don't come from a musical family."

"You're more book smart. Nothing wrong with that."

I melted a little inside. Jake was a sweet guy. I liked the way he made me feel special.

"So how old were you when you first started touring?" I asked.

"Sixteen."

"Of course," I rolled my eyes.

Jake shrugged his shoulders.

"I knew you started out young, but I didn't realize you were that young. Damn, at sixteen I still had braces and slept with stuffed animals. And here you were playing in front of thousands of people."

"Hardly. If a thousand people came to see me play, that was a big crowd. It's not like I started out in super stadiums. You need to think on a lot smaller scale, Casey."

"Proms?"

"Well, not that small," Jake ran a hand through his hair. "More like fairs and colleges and rec centers."

"But now you play in front of thousands of people, right?"

"Yes."

"Do you ever get scared before you go out on stage?"

"No."

"Never?"

"Um... maybe sometimes, I guess, when I'm going to be on TV or something. But once I start performing, I'm fine."

"It doesn't freak you out having all those people screaming for you?"

"No. It's an awesome feeling, being up on that stage with the music and lights and the roar of the crowd."

"Ew... that sounds horrible to me," I said, making a face. "You're brave. I'm more of a cerebral person myself. About as daring as I get is reading the last page of a book before starting it."

"Oh, god. I hate reading. One of the worst pastimes I could think of."

"Do we not have anything in common at all?"

Jake shrugged. "Maybe you should take some risks, Casey."

"Maybe you should read a book, Jake."

We both stared at each other for a second before bursting out in laughter.

"So, did you go on tour by yourself when you were sixteen?" I asked.

"Yeah. I mean, the label sent a guardian with me, but he was pretty useless."

"Why didn't your parents go?"

"Because of my younger siblings. They couldn't just leave, and my dad had to work. I think that's why my mom is so over protective now. She had to stop mothering me before she was ready."

"There probably is some Freudian message in all that," I said, giving him a side glance.

"Don't even go there," Jake gagged.

I laughed, then looked out over the railing.

"Wow, that's a long way down."

"Are you afraid of heights?" he asked.

"No, not really. Just afraid of falling to my death."

"Trust me, Casey, there are a lot worse ways to die."

Seeing that those words were coming from a person who had first-hand knowledge of such things, I was a bit jarred. I looked at Jake, but he didn't seem to be affected by what he said. It was more like he'd been stating the obvious.

"You know, I read that if you were to dropped a penny from the Empire State Building and it hit someone in the head, it would crack their skull," Jake said, still looking over the edge.

"No way is that true," I replied.

"I read it on the Internet, Casey, so of course, it's true," Jake proclaimed. "Shall we try it?" he said, as he pretended to drop a penny.

"First of all, we aren't on the Empire State Building." I grabbed his hand and laughed. "And secondly... you aren't taking into consideration terminal velocity and air resistance."

"Huh?"

"The penny is too light. The wind will kick it around."

"Huh?" he repeated.

"For your theory to work, your penny would have to be coming down like a rocket. There are too many factors that will stop that from happening – mainly air."

"Wow, Casey... way to take the fun out of that theory," Jake huffed, pretending to be pissed. "I forgot I was dealing with a college student."

"Oh, I'm sorry, Jake. Would you rather I dumb it down for you?"

"God, no," he laughed. "I'm just learning so much from you."

"Oh yeah, I'm sure. Everyone loves a smart girl."

"I don't know about everyone else but I like that you're confident in your smartness. And before you tell me smartness isn't a word, I already know that."

"I wouldn't dream of it," I said, although I had been seconds away from correcting him.

Jake's hands gripped the railing as he leaned further over the balcony. "Man, I gotta say, this wedding is way more fun than I thought it would be."

"I know. I'm having the best time," I replied.

"I've been so busy with the tour that I haven't really taken any time for fun."

"Really? That's surprising."

"It is?"

"Yeah, I mean... aren't you people supposed to be wild and crazy?"

"And by 'you people'?" Jake asked, in amusement. "You're referring to rock stars in general?"

"Yep."

"Well... if you must know, I'm kind of a disgrace to 'my people.'"

"Oh, really? And why is that?"

"I'm not a drug addict."

"Oh." I caught his eye, surprised by his answer. "Are you saying most rock stars are drug addicts?"

"I'm saying the vast majority of us are, yes." Jake nodded.

"Why?"

"Easy access to anything you could ever dream of and the money to make it happen."

"And you've never done drugs?"

"Well, I wouldn't say never," Jake responded honestly. "When I was younger, I smoked weed on occasion but never did anything harder than that. I'm not a big fan of being out of control, so I just stopped."

"It wasn't hard to quit?"

"No, because I wasn't addicted in the first place. I only did it a handful of times. What about you?"

"I'm a good girl. I've never touched drugs."

"That's good."

"I mean... my friends were nerds. The only peer pressure we put on each other was to get the highest test grades."

Jake shook his head. "A whole other world."

"Definitely. It's a lot easier when no one you hang out with is cool."

"Yeah. I can imagine it would be. So when did you transform into bad-ass Casey?"

"Well, you know, I think she was in me the whole time," I said, trying to sound as awesome as possible. "But my first year in college is probably where I blossomed."

"Did you party a lot?"

"Kind of. I mean, I went to a lot of parties, but I've never been much of a drinker. I don't really like the taste of alcohol. If I drink, it has to be one of those frou-frou sugary drinks, like a daiquiri or a margarita."

"I hate sugary drinks. I'm not a fan of sugar in general."

"No way! I *love* sugar. That's my downfall. I could eat Mitch and Kate's whole damn wedding cake if you let me at it," I bragged.

"Jesus. How do you stay so thin?"

"Two words: spin class."

Jake ran his eyes over my body and nodded, looking impressed.

"Do you drink?" I asked him.

"Yeah, but not a lot. I like beer."

"Yuck. It tastes like urine."

Jake raised his eyebrows. "When have you ever tasted urine?"

"I haven't, but I assume that's what urine would taste like."

Jake winced, then shook his head. "It doesn't."

"Ew... there is only one way you'd know that." I wrinkled my nose in disgust.

Jake nodded.

"Oh, my god! That's disgusting... you drank urine?"

"Once."

"Well, I should hope it was only once! Jesus," I said, shaking my head.

Jake laughed. "And it wasn't on purpose."

"And again, I should hope it wasn't on purpose," I said, still shaking my head in disbelief. "So tell me, Jake, how does one accidentally drink urine?"

"It was while I was on tour a few years ago, and we were hanging out after a concert. Anyway, I got a call and left, and some other guy took my seat. Well, one of his friends decided to play a trick on him when he left for the bathroom, and replaced his beer bottle with one from the fridge, which the friend had conveniently peed in earlier. Anyway, I came back in, took my seat, and picked up the beer thinking it was mine. Some of the guys started screaming for me to stop, but it was already too late."

"Oh, no... oh please, no," I squealed, covering my ears. "Don't even tell me!"

"Oh, yes. And I took a giant frickin' swig, too. The minute it hit my palate... oh my god, I just knew. And by that point, it was already going down my throat."

"No, you didn't?!" I cried. "You *swallowed* it?"

Jake looked at me with a sheepish grin. "I heaved for hours."

"So gross... so, so gross. What did you do to that guy?"

"I gave him a beat down and fired him," Jake admitted. "Then I hired him back once I got the taste of urine out of my system."

I shook my head in wonder. "Guys are so different than girls. If a girl had done that – which she never would have – but if she had, god forbid, that would have been the end of the friendship for sure. And guys, they just pat each other on the backs and go, *Great idea, man.*"

Jake nodded, smiling.

"Whew, I think I could have gone without hearing that little story," I said, fanning my flushed face.

"Yeah, well you told me your poop and puke story yesterday, so now we're even."

"True, true. So tell me something – less gross – that I don't know about you, Jake McKallister."

Jake thought about it for a few seconds, and then his face turned serious. "Okay, I can tell you one secret, but you have to swear you'll never repeat it."

Instantly, I was extremely interested. Any secret of Jake McKallister's had to be noteworthy. "I swear."

"Because if you told anyone, I would be so pissed."

"Your secret is safe with me," I promised.

"Okay... oh, god... this is so embarrassing... I'm just going to blurt it out... I watch *The Bachelor.*"

I gasped in mock horror. *"The Bachelor...* oh, Jake, no."

"Shhh... someone will hear you," he whispered, and put his finger to my lips. "I have all the seasons... including *The Bachelorette."*

Damn, he was just so cute. Trying to keep the smile off my face, I proclaimed, "I'm sorry, Jake. This is just too much for me to comprehend. I think I need to leave now."

Jake pulled me into his arms unexpectedly. "Don't go." He stared down at me with such heat I thought I might melt in his arms.

"I'm not going anywhere... trust me," I whispered.

Jake smiled at this. "Good," he whispered back.

"And, you know, it's not like you're the only one with a shocking secret. I have one of my own, actually."

"Oh, really?" Jake replied, as he pulled out of the hug and looked down at me with interest.

"Well, it's not as scandalous as your *Bachelor* admission, but I feel like I need to be honest with you," I said, with an earnest tone to my voice.

"Okay," Jake responded, sounding a bit worried.

"Do you want to know what my secret is?" I asked him.

"I'm not sure," Jake replied. "You don't have a penis or anything, do you?"

"What?" I gaped, before bursting into laughter. "No... not that big of a secret," I exclaimed, smacking him in the arm as I continued. "How would me having a penis be less shocking than you watching *The Bachelor?"*

"I don't know," Jake said. "You got all serious, and I got worried."

"So naturally your first thought was that I'm transsexual?" I shot back.

Jake shrugged, as if it were a natural assumption.

"You're funny, Jake McKallister."

"Okay, so the suspense is killing me... what's this big secret?"

"Well, now I don't even want to tell you, because you were expecting something grand."

"Come on, please," Jake begged.

"Okay," I said, eyeing him skeptically. "But you can't make fun of me, okay?"

"No promises," Jake announced. "Just spit it out."

"I collect banana labels."

"You collect what?"

"Banana labels."

"Banana labels?" Jake repeated like he hadn't understood correctly.

"Yes."

"Okay, hold on. Let me just make sure I'm hearing you right. You collect the little labels that you peel off bananas?" Jake asked incredulously.

"Yes."

Jake looked at me like I was crazy, then burst out laughing.

"You said you wouldn't laugh at me."

"No, I didn't. And that... oh, my god, Casey... that is hysterical. I mean, that beats my secret hands down," he claimed.

"Shut up," I replied, but I was enjoying his amusement on my behalf.

"And you collect these labels *why?*" Jake asked.

"When I was a kid, my mom was looking at a banana and said that it was from Ecuador. I'd never even heard of that country, so I researched it. I thought it was the coolest thing that I was eating fruit that came from another country. After that, I always checked where a banana was from. If it was a new place, I'd learn as much as I could about the country, and then I would peel off the label and paste it on a piece of paper with a whole written overview of the country. Pretty soon I had so many, I had to put the labels in a binder."

"You have a *binder* even?" His voice rose to almost a squeak.

I nodded.

Jake burst out laughing again. "Oh, god... Holy crap. That is hilarious. I love it," he said, shaking his head. "You're seriously one of the most interesting people I've ever met in my life. I'll never be able to look at a banana sticker again without thinking of you."

I laughed with him, enjoying the moment. "Well, we can't all be as interesting and talented as you. The majority of us were only gifted with mediocre skills."

"Says the girl who knows the square root of every number," Jake replied.

"Right, because *that* is a noteworthy talent. You, with your beautiful voice and creative mind, moving a room full of strangers to tears; and mine, cold and calculating, eliciting a room full of yawns from uninterested onlookers. You're probably an artist, too, aren't you?"

Jake smiled coyly.

"I knew it!" I exclaimed. "Do you paint or draw?"

"Both."

"Of course you do. I'm a terrible artist. Even my stick figures end up with extra appendages."

"That's okay. You're good at other things."

"Oh, really?" I challenged. "Like what? I'm very interested."

"You're good at making me laugh."

"That's not difficult," I said, rolling my eyes. "You laugh all the time."

"With people I know, yeah, but not with people I've just met."

"Seriously?"

Jake looked at me in surprise. "You know who I am, right?"

"Yes."

"Then you know I'm not exactly known for my sense of humor."

Stunned that Jake would be so blunt, I struggled to find the right words. This guy was so misunderstood. I'd only known him for 24 hours, yet I knew enough to know that he was so much more than what was reported in the media.

"You want to know the first thing that I noticed about you at the restaurant last night?" I asked.

"Okay," Jake replied, looking interested.

"You throw your head back when you laugh."

"So?"

"So, that's how I can tell if a person has a good sense of humor or not. And you, my friend, have one."

Jake stared at me.

"What?" I asked.

"What else have you figured out about me, Casey Caldwell?"

"Honestly? Not much. You're not the easiest person to read."

Jake nodded.

"Is that intentional?"

He gave a cryptic look.

"See, that's what I'm talking about," I said. "Are you trying to be ambiguous?"

Jake didn't answer immediately, as if he were considering whether or not he should answer my question, and then his shoulders drooped a bit and he said, "It's a defense mechanism. Sorry."

I stared at Jake. His honesty floored me. This guy continually surprised me. "Don't apologize," I answered. "I find your mysterious ways intriguing. Figuring you out is like a puzzle."

Jake grinned his sexy little smile, and then bent down and whispered in my ear, "You want to put a few pieces together?"

His hot breath on my neck sent shivers down my spine. Excitement coursed through me. Was this really happening? Was Jake actually inviting me into his life – the real one, not the life that people had imagined for him?

"Yes, please," I replied, breathlessly.

Then, all of the sudden, Jake's expression changed completely. He fixed me with a fiery look, then leaned in close just inches from my face, leaving no doubt what he wanted. The heat between us was smoldering. I eagerly awaited the kiss I was being promised. Jake's lips lingered just above mine, making me want it even more. But as with everything else about this guy, I never knew exactly what to expect. Jake always seemed to keep me guessing. And this was no different. Most guys would have been halfway down my throat by now, but Jake was in no hurry. Instead, he teased me with the promise of something more. The wait was agonizing and thrilling all at once. This boy knew how to seduce a girl. When his lips finally touched mine, a bolt of electricity surged through me, traveling straight to my pleasure spot. I actually groaned. No guy had ever elicited that strong a response in me with just a single kiss. Of course, this was no ordinary kiss... and no ordinary guy.

Jake's lips lingered on the same spot, drawing out that first contact. I felt weak in the knees. Then he started kissing my upper lip in a slow, leisurely fashion before moving on to both. His style was unhurried and seductive, and it was making me crazy. I wanted to devour him, but he controlled the kiss. I was trembling. Our bodies were pressed into each other. I was lost in him. And then he went in for the kill. Our lips were locked in a steamy kiss, and I was taking him in greedily. His hands were on my face; mine were in his hair. I was tingling all over. It was an incredible kiss, like nothing I'd ever experienced before. When he finally pulled away, my head was spinning and I actually felt a bit faint. We both kind of stood there, stunned by the raw and powerful chemistry between us. I leaned into him for support.

Jake's gorgeous eyes were all I could see. I stared at him in awe for a minute before throwing myself at him, kissing him fervidly. This time, I was in control – which meant, of course, that the kiss was totally out of control. I was animalistic in my approach, although Jake didn't seem the least bit turned off by my intensity. He matched me action for action. I thought I knew what passion and lust were until I met Jake McKallister. This guy took me to new levels.

Jake left my lips and kissed behind my ear and down my neck. My body was shaking. "Oh, god," I whispered, breathlessly.

He worked his way around until he was back at my lips. Then his tongue got in on the action. But he was in no hurry. Jake's tongue lazily wandered around the entrance, making me want to beg him for more. In fact, I wanted him to devour me. This kiss was rocking my world. My legs wobbled. Every nerve in my body tingled as I pushed against him. I felt like I could do him right there, without caring who saw. I had never been so careless with my virtue but Jake did something for me that no guy had ever done... he made me weak with lust.

Suddenly Jake's phone buzzed, startling us both. He ignored it until it stopped. We kissed through the intrusion. A minute later the phone started buzzing again. Jake and I separated slightly, and he pulled out his phone to check who was calling, then returned the phone to his pocket and jumped right back into our kiss. I pressed up against him. Just as we started getting hot and heavy again, Jake's phone buzzed for the third time.

"Fuck," he groaned, as he pulled his phone out of his pocket. This time Jake answered it.

"Hey, what's up?" he said, slightly out of breath. There was silence before Jake said, "Okay, I'm on my way. Thanks." He ended the call and turned to me. "They're going to have some games and cut the cake. We have to get back."

15

JAKE: FIRST REAL KISS

I held Casey's hand while we walked back. I don't know why. I just did. It felt comfortable. It felt right. She smiled up at me with such a happy, trusting look. I wanted to wrap her in a hug. She made me feel so... I don't even know how she made me feel. All I knew was that I liked it. A lot. Things were getting more complicated by the second. My emotions were all over the place. How was I supposed to just walk away from her after that kiss? It rocked my world.

Up until tonight, I'd never really found kissing to be very enjoyable. For some reason, to me, kissing seemed more intimate than sex. But I did it anyway because it was a means to an end. Girls wanted at least some foreplay, a little reassurance that they weren't totally being used. So I did what I thought was necessary to get them into bed. Usually, it didn't take much before they had their legs wrapped around me and we were going at it. Of course, I wasn't totally selfish. I made it worth their while; if for no other reason than I had a reputation to uphold. Over the years I'd learned what satiated a woman, and I did my best to ensure she would walk away feeling compensated.

Yeah, I was using them; but hell, they were using me too.

Women didn't go after me because of my winning personality – they went after me because I was a rock star. For whatever reason, nothing turned women on more than a bunch of sweaty guys up on stage belting out song after song. Hey, I didn't make the rules. I just took advantage of what I'd been given. And as brief as the encounters were, they were mutually beneficial. I got my rocks off, and they got bragging rights with their girlfriends. Win-win.

But that kiss had nothing to do with the rock star. That was all me... and all her. It wasn't a trade off or a means to an end; it was genuine emotion. The first real kiss I'd ever had in my life. Was it really possible to meet someone and just know they were the one for you? I'd always thought that was crap, but now I wasn't so sure. What I did know was this was not the last time I was going to kiss Casey Caldwell.

CASEY: THE RULEBOOK

As we walked back to the reception, Jake took my hand. No words – he just reached down and grabbed it. And instead of being awkward, it was like our hands molded into one. The connection I felt to him at that moment was electrifying.

Just before walking back into the reception hall, Jake dropped my hand. "I have to go back to my family for a bit. Can I find you later?"

"I'd like that."

"Okay. See you soon." He smiled and then walked back into the hall and headed straight over to his family. Before reentering, I tried to smooth down my hair and my dress. I was in a serious state of disarray. It looked – and felt – like I'd had sex. I was slick between the legs and wanted nothing more than to lock myself away with this sexy man I'd just met. So much for playing hard to get. How had Jake been able to reduce me to a quivering fangirl so easily?

The wedding party separated by gender for the garter and bouquet toss. I went through the motions, but I wasn't really connected to what was happening. In fact, I almost got hit in the head by the bouquet and watched, impassively, as women went after it like their lives depended on it. I, for one, didn't feel like I needed the bouquet. I'd already won the biggest prize at the wedding – the affections of an amazing guy who kissed me like he meant it.

I watched Jake with his brothers. They were having so much fun. For his part, Jake seemed to have completely disengaged from our balcony kiss. I wasn't so lucky. The memory of it clouded my mind. I wanted more. I felt desperate to get back to him. I hated being that girl. I'd always prided myself on being independent and level-headed when it came to guys, but Jake – damn, he was like a drug. This must be what it felt like to be addicted. I was still a bit disoriented when Sarah and two other bridesmaids cornered me.

"What the hell, Casey? You know I like Jake. Why are you doing this?"

"Yeah, totally uncool, Casey," Julia piped in.

"Wait, what am I doing?" I replied.

"Oh, please. You know damn well what I'm talking about. You've been throwing yourself on him since the second you met him. It's actually pretty pathetic."

"No more pathetic than your half-assed attempt to lure him in yesterday."

"What's that supposed to mean?" Sarah questioned with venom in her eyes.

"It means… you don't have dibs on him, Sarah. Jake's a big boy. He makes his own decisions and can choose who he wants to hang around with."

"How can he choose when you're monopolizing all his time?"

"Do you see him with me now?" I said dramatically. "No, because I don't have a leash on him, Sarah. Jake is free to hang out with whoever he wants."

"And that's you? Is that what you're saying, Casey?"

I threw my hands up in the air and sighed. "I don't know what to tell you. Jake isn't here now, so be my guest," I huffed, motioning in his direction.

"Right... I'll be rude and interrupt him when he's with his family."

"What do you want me to do, Sarah?"

"Back off!" she demanded in all her mean girl glory.

"No," I replied defiantly.

"No?" she answered in disbelief.

"No. I like him, and I'm not backing off."

"You act all high and mighty, Casey, but you're nothing special."

"Thanks," I replied sarcastically. "I appreciate that."

"You know what kills me? You were the one acting all unimpressed by Jake at the bridal shower. *Long hair guys aren't my type,*" Sarah mimicked me. "Now suddenly you're hot for him? How does that happen?"

"There's no sinister plot going on here, Sarah. Once I met him, I discovered that he's a great guy and I enjoy hanging out with him. That's it."

"Well, we would all like a chance to hang out with him, but we can't because you're draped all over him and not giving anyone else a shot."

"You had a chance. He wasn't interested. Let it go."

Sarah glared at me. "You're such a conniving slut, Casey."

"Jake doesn't think so."

Sarah stared at me a second before her eyes went big and she mocked, "Oh, wow... you actually think he's into you, don't you? That's hilarious. What do you think is going to happen here? You think Jake is going to whisk you away on some magic fairy ride? You think you're going to be his girlfriend and marry him someday?"

Yes. "No. Of course not. I didn't say that."

Sarah had me completely flustered.

"You didn't have to. I can see it in your eyes. Please tell me, Casey, you don't actually think he likes you, do you?"

When I didn't immediately respond, Sarah laughed out loud, but she didn't sound happy in the least.

"Oh, my god, you're delusional. I actually kind of feel sorry for you. You understand that he's a rock star, right?" Sarah was talking down to me like I was some stupid little girl. I'd never been good at defending myself against girls like her. Boys I could handle, but mean girls... they intimidated the hell out of me. So instead of engaging her any further, I turned to walk away.

But Sarah grabbed my arm. "I hope you know... he only wants one thing from you," she said through gritted teeth.

I yanked my arm from her grip and stormed off. The encounter left me feeling shaken. I started questioning the moments I'd shared with Jake. Was that really all he wanted from me? To get me in bed? Because if that was what he wanted, it wouldn't take even the slightest bit of effort on his part. And really, what was I expecting? It wasn't like we were going to start dating. Jake had been perfectly clear about that.

I found an empty table toward the back of the reception hall and sat down. My feet were aching in the heels, so I took my shoes off. I closed my eyes and tried to calm down. Suddenly I felt like crying. What was I doing? I was seriously falling for a guy who had candidly admitted to me just an hour before that he wasn't interested in a relationship. By making my 'no strings attached' deal with him, I'd basically tricked him into hanging out with me by dangling the possibility of sex in front of him... knowing I had no intention of honoring the tease. I tried to pretend we could just be friends, but the attraction I felt toward him was off the charts. And either Jake felt the same way about me, or he was just a master at seducing women – which, given his profession, probably wasn't too far-fetched. Could he just be that skilled at playing women that he was able to bring me to my knees so effortlessly? Maybe Sarah was right. Maybe I was just another notch in his belt.

"Damn, you're hard to find sometimes, Casey Caldwell." I opened my eyes, and upon seeing Jake's adorable smile, all my self-pity disappeared. I smiled back up at him. "What are you doing over here all by yourself? Are you hiding from me?"

"Actually, yes."

Jake's face changed. He looked confused, like he was trying to figure out what he'd done wrong.

"It's not you," I sighed. "I just got bitched out for hogging all your time. Apparently, there are other girls here who would like the chance to have sex with you tonight."

Jake didn't seem all that shocked by my words, which made me feel even more insecure.

"And, despite what happened on the balcony, I don't sleep with guys on a first date – not that this is even a date, but you know what I mean. So if that's what you're expecting, maybe you should just go and explore your options... hit up Sarah. She's a sure thing," I revealed, finally breathing after my speech. "Plus my feet hurt," I whined.

Jake stood there silently. I couldn't read his face. He appeared to be thinking. Was he really contemplating his choices?

"Well, it was really nice meeting you, Casey. Maybe I'll see you around sometime," Jake said, then turned and walked away. My mouth dropped open. It felt like I'd been punched in the stomach. I didn't know what I'd been expecting, but it definitely wasn't that. I thought we had more of a connection than for him to just dump me on the spot so he could find a more willing hookup. Such a jerk!

I was so upset that I didn't comprehend when Jake stopped a few feet away, swiped a white rose out of a vase, and grabbed a couple of napkins off the table next to him. He then turned around and came sauntering back over to me with a mischievous smile on his face. It took me a second to understand what was happening.

"Oh, my god, that was... oh, my god... that was just mean!" I exclaimed. "I really hate you." I shot my leg out to playfully kick him, but he dodged me easily. What I really wanted to do was grab him and kiss him.

"You were just too easy," he said, stealing my line from last night's prank.

"You got me good," I acknowledged, laughing from both relief and happiness. "For a second there I seriously thought you were the biggest jerk *ever!*"

"I know. I could see the venom in your eyes. But, really, Casey, you had it coming," Jake defended, shaking his head and smiling. He pulled a chair up close to me, sat down, and then handed me the rose. "For you."

"Ahh... so sweet. Thank you," I replied, as I inhaled its scent.

"You're welcome." He sighed, then added, "I guess the only thing left to do is take care of your other problem."

I stared at him, confused.

"Give me your damn feet."

My mouth dropped open in surprise.

"What? I'll give you a foot massage."

"You're seriously going to rub my dirty, stinky feet?" I asked incredulously.

"I brought protection," he revealed, proudly holding up two white napkins.

"Wow, you're just full of surprises."

Not about to turn the guy down, I swung my legs up and deposited them onto his lap.

Jake wrapped my feet in the napkins and dug into my tender arches. "And just so you know, I don't have a foot fetish or anything, so this sort of grosses me out. I'm only doing this to impress you."

"Well, then you've accomplished your goal."

His capable hands massaged so thoroughly that I lost the ability to speak intelligible words. Instead, I just moaned and groaned. That was until he hit a particularly sore spot on my heel and I actually began whimpering with pleasure.

"Holy shit, Casey. You sound like you're having little foot-gasms."

I laughed loudly at this. "You have no idea how good that feels."

"I'm getting a pretty good idea."

"So speaking of foot-gasms, Jake, why would you stay? I mean, I took sex off the table."

Jake's eyes fixed on mine. "I'm not a Neanderthal, Casey. I don't need to have sex to have a good time."

"And are you?"

"Am I what?"

"Having a good time?"

"I wouldn't be here with your stinky feet in my lap if I weren't."

"Yeah, you'd be in a broom closet with Sarah." I was kidding – mostly.

Jake shook his head, but he was grinning. "God, it's all about sex with you, Casey."

I gave an apologetic look. "I know. Sorry. You intimidate me. I mean, it would take no effort on your part to get with pretty much any girl at this wedding."

Jake didn't refute my claim – probably because he knew it was true. In fact, he was actually giving what I said quite a bit of thought. What was I getting myself into?

Finally, he sighed, and said, "Sometimes having sex just isn't worth the consequences."

"What does that mean?"

"It means that with sex comes expectations."

I waited for him to explain his comment, and when he didn't I said, "And?"

Jake exhaled dramatically, as if he were expected to explain himself to a child. "If I'm going to have meaningless sex with someone, I need a quick exit strategy; otherwise she's going to want to follow me around – or worse, talk. In a setting like this, there's no way to disappear after getting it on, so sex wouldn't be worth the consequences... get it?"

"Wow, you've really given this a lot of thought."

He nodded in agreement. "I've learned from experience."

"I'm sure you have. So, then, I guess it's a good thing we aren't going to have meaningless sex tonight." I laughed. "Because I would definitely be following you around trying to talk to you."

"I know." Jake grinned. "You'd be the worst."

I gasped in mock anger and then reached out and smacked him.

"I'm just kidding. With you, it wouldn't be meaningless sex," Jake retorted, laying on the charm.

"Well, you won't have a chance to find out, now, will you, BFF?"

"Oh, I didn't realize that's what we were."

"Your rules, not mine."

"My rules?" Jake questioned.

"Well, isn't it you that has some fancy-schmancy world tour that you don't want to disturb with a needy ho?"

"Oh right, you're the needy ho. I forgot."

"Uh-huh."

Jake smiled his sexy smile and continued rubbing my feet in silence for a minute before saying, "What if I want to revise my rules?"

"I'm listening."

"Friends with benefits, maybe?"

"Yes, but you forget my number one rule: no sex on the first date."

"What about the second date?"

"I have no steadfast rules about that. But we would have to

have a second date to find out, and that seems unlikely since you're leaving tomorrow for Europe."

"I'm leaving for Europe, not another planet. It doesn't seem all that far-fetched that we might see each other again, Casey."

My heart leapt inside my chest. Did he want to see me again? Refusing to allow him to see my excitement, I shrugged, then replied simply, "Yeah, I guess... if I'm not dating someone else by the time you get back."

Jake grinned at me. "How likely is that?"

"You don't think I can get me a guy in three months time? I go to ASU, Jake... it's not that hard!" I exclaimed with indignation.

He held up his hands in surrender. "I have no doubt you could find a guy in an instant. I just meant, how likely are you to find a guy who rubs your feet when they're sore, or who finds your first date rule charming?"

"Honestly?" My shoulders drooped. "Not very likely." Seriously? Was Jake McKallister really trying to sell himself to me? There was absolutely no need. I already found him irresistibly adorable. "But then how likely are you to find a girl who makes you laugh, and who also has a binder full of banana labels?"

His expression turned serious. "Honestly? I don't think another girl like you exists in the world."

Ahhh... damn you, Jake.

"Still, that doesn't solve our current problem. What about tonight?" I asked.

Jake thought for a minute. "Is making out considered sex in your little rule book?"

"Well, now that you mention it... No, making out falls within the realms of acceptable 'no sex' behavior."

Jake looked at me blankly. "I have no idea what you just said."

"Yes, Jake. We can make out. God, do you need me to show you the rule book?" I said, rolling my eyes dramatically.

"That might help," he said, smiling that adorable smile of his. "Because, honestly, you're confusing the fuck out of me."

I laughed. "You have a bit of a potty mouth, don't you, Mr. McKallister?"

"I travel with like sixty dudes year round. There's no swear jar."

"I'm going to start fining you, but instead of putting money in a swear jar for every f-bomb, you'll owe me a foot rub."

"The punishment needs to fit the crime, Casey."

I nodded. How could I argue with that? Jake dropped his eyes to my legs then boldly placed his hand on my knee. His fingers lazily traced my skin. I shuddered. He grinned, looking up at me from behind his hair. He knew exactly what he was doing to me.

"You have nice legs," he commented absently.

"Thank you. Too bad for you they're attached to my stinky feet."

"I know. That part of it sucks."

Jake's hands continued to roam. I looked up to make sure we were not giving the room a show and found one set of angry eyes fixed on me.

I grabbed Jake's hand and moved it down a few inches. "Probably not the best place for this."

"Probably not," he said, but that didn't stop him. I pulled my dress down to hide his hands.

"God, she's glaring at me."

He swung his head in that direction.

"Don't look! Geez, Jake," I squealed, as I palmed his face and turned it back to me.

"Who? Sarah?"

"Yes. She really hates me now."

"So what?" Jake replied matter of factly. "You weren't friends to begin with, were you?"

"No. I've only met her a few times. She's Kate's friend, not mine."

"Then don't worry what she thinks."

"I already know what she thinks. According to Sarah, I'm a conniving slut."

"Ouch... she seriously said that to you?"

"Yep."

"Bitch. You want me to go rough her up for you?"

"Hmm... that is such a sweet offer," I joked. "But she'd probably just like it."

Jake grinned then scanned the reception with his eyes. Upon seeing so many party-goers watching him, Jake swiftly removed his hand from up my dress.

"Does it bother you when people stare at you?"

"Someone's staring at me?" He joked.

I playfully pushed him. "Seriously, do you not even notice it?"

Jake's smile faded a bit. "No. I notice it. I just choose to ignore it."

"You choose to ignore it?" I asked in surprise. "That's an interesting strategy."

"There's not a lot I can do about it. If I stare them down or ask them to stop then I look like a douche."

"True. You'd look like a whiny, ungrateful celebrity."

"Exactly. Nothing worse than those sniveling assholes." Jake grinned.

"No doubt," I rolled my eyes.

"I don't think most gawkers are trying to be rude, though. People are just mesmerized by fame. They lose their common sense and forget their manners. It's a strange phenomenon. I mean, I'm just a normal guy, but people don't want to see me that way. It doesn't really sell records, you know?"

I nodded.

"So you have to give the public what they want." Jake shrugged.

"And what do they want from you?"

"Well, see, with me, it gets a little complicated because I've got two personas going on. The wild, brooding, sex-crazed rock star

– that's standard protocol. But then I've got the whole deranged, doomed victim thing going on, too."

I shook my head. "Again, overachiever."

Jake nodded, amused.

"So, how do you decide which persona to be?"

"I don't. They do."

"And how do they decide?"

"Usually by whether they're fans or not. My fans, who buy my records and go to my concerts, they perceive me to be the hip musician. And then there are those who aren't fans, but who think they know who I am because of media reports. Those are the ones who consider me to be a victim."

"Huh. Wow." I exhaled. "Being you is so complicated."

"You have no idea," Jake smiled, but there some melancholy attached to it.

"And you're okay with people thinking you're someone that you're not?"

"Yep," Jake replied, dismissively.

"I would hate that."

Jake shrugged. "Because you care what people think of you."

"And you don't?"

"Nope."

"Really? Not at all?" I asked skeptically. I didn't believe him for a second.

Jake sighed. "I used to when I was younger but then I grew a very tough, impenetrable skin. Now I don't give a shit what people say about me."

I looked at him in surprise. "Wow. I want one of those skins."

Jake shook his head. "No, you don't."

We sat there quietly for a minute before I whispered, "Do you care what I think?"

Jake seemed surprised by my question. After a few seconds, he replied, "Yeah."

I smiled. "So then you aren't as bulletproof as you think you are."

Jake smiled back but didn't answer.

God, he was incredible. I found him so intriguing... a play in contrasts. There were so many layers to him, so many things I wanted to know about him; but instinctively I knew Jake was the type of person that needed his layers peeled back slowly and with the utmost care. He seemed so strong and in control, but there was a vulnerability to him that took my breath away. What surprised me most about Jake was his willingness to allow me tiny little glimpses into his innermost thoughts. I hadn't expected those small morsels of honesty from him, certainly not after knowing him for such a short time. He trusted me. Why, I had no idea; but he did. And I intended to live up to that trust.

I ran my finger down his arm. Now it was his turn to shudder. He looked me in the eyes with a smoldering expression, and then trailed a finger up my leg. I shivered as wetness formed between my legs. It didn't take much with this guy. We sat there gently caressing each other's skin, not talking for several minutes, until Keith came bounding up to us. We quickly removed our hands.

"Hey, sorry to disturb you two," he said with a smirk, as he looked between us. "But JimSuey are leaving, and they wanted to say good-bye to you."

"Oh, okay. Where are they?"

"Over at the table."

"Sorry, but the foot rub is now over." Jake lifted my feet with a slight bow.

"Damn," I sighed as I swung my legs back down and set him free.

Jake stood up and said, "I'll be back soon."

Keith watched him walk away and then turned back to me with a shit-eating grin on his face. "Sooo, how is everything?"

"Good. And you?"

"Great." Keith smiled knowingly at me. "Are you enjoying my little brother?"

"I am," I said. "Very much so. Thanks for asking."

"He's dreamy, isn't he?" Keith rolled his eyes and had a dopey look on his face.

"That he is," I agreed.

"You two... " Keith paused. "I'm liking it."

"Yeah?"

Keith nodded, looking impressed. "I'm kind of surprised, actually."

"Wow, thanks."

"I'm not surprised by you," Keith explained. "I'm surprised by my brother. Jake's not usually so, uh, engaging."

"Really? Huh. Well I find him quite engaging."

"It must be the company," he said, assessing me with a mixture of wonder and curiosity. "Nice job, Casey."

"Well, thank you, Keith."

We smiled at each other in amusement.

"I gotta go, but I still want to introduce you to Sam. I'll find you later."

I nodded as he walked away. Dang! I was really digging these McKallister brothers. I glanced over to see Jake with his grandparents. He'd asked me to wait there, so that was what I intended to do. I'd wait there all night if I had to.

17

JAKE: GUILT TRIP

All I wanted was to get back to Casey. After saying goodbye to my grandparents, I had every intention to hurry back over to her. But my mom was by my side before I could make my escape.

"Are you having fun?" she asked.

I could hear the edge in her voice.

"Yeah," I said, then looked in Casey's direction, distracted.

"Jake?"

"What?" I said, turning my full attention on her.

"How long has it been since we've seen you?"

"I don't know. Since the start of the tour?"

"That's right. It's been more than four months."

"I guess. Why?" I asked, but I already knew where she was going with this. Cue the guilt trip.

"Jake, you know this is our only chance to spend time together as a family, but I feel like you've been preoccupied with other things," Mom said with a sour look on her face. "You do your own thing all year round, but right now is family time, and I'm asking you to honor that."

"I have been spending time with family... What are you talking about?"

"I'm talking about that girl hanging all over you. Every time I turn around, you've gone off with her somewhere. Does she not even care that this is your brother's wedding?"

"She's not doing anything, Mom," I said, shaking my head, annoyed. "You always do that."

"Do what?"

"You always have that accusatory tone."

"I don't have a tone, Jake."

"Yeah, you do, Mom, and the underlying message is that any girl who hangs out with me is a gold digger."

Mom shook her head. "That's not what I meant."

"Yeah, I'm pretty sure it was. But it doesn't matter because I don't need you to tell me who I can and can't hang out with."

Mom sighed. "Look, Jake. I've seen how you operate. This girl, she'll be here today, gone tomorrow. This is Mitch's wedding day: it only happens once. All I'm asking is that you prioritize your family and not some girl you're never going to see again."

Of course, that was how my mom would view this. Admittedly, that really was how I normally operated. Casey wasn't just my average hook up, but there was no way in hell I was going to admit that to my mom. I looked over at Casey sitting there alone waiting for me. Then I turned back to my mom. Dammit. She was making me choose. I didn't want to choose. I wanted time with both.

"Please, Jake," Mom begged.

I hesitated a second before reluctantly replying, "Okay."

And so I stayed put with my family. Every once in a while, I would glance over to see Casey still sitting there, expecting me to return. Shit. I had to let her know what was going on before she thought I was ignoring her again. So the next time she looked my way I pointed toward the bathrooms and held three fingers up.

She didn't understand my reference at first but, after I repeated it again, Casey looked toward the bathrooms and nodded, raising her own three fingers.

I excused myself to use the bathroom a couple minutes later. Casey was no longer at the table. I turned the corner, and there she was, smiling at me. I felt my heart start racing. She was so frickin' hot.

"Hey." I grinned.

"Hey, you." She smiled back. "Why the secret rendezvous?"

"Because my mom is pissed that I'm not spending enough time with the family. She basically gave me a guilt trip. I just didn't want you to think I ditched you."

"I didn't think that," Casey said with scrunched eyebrows. "But, Jake, I don't want to keep you from your family."

"You're not. Look, I'm going to try to sneak away once things start wrapping up. I'll tell them I have jetlag or something like that. I was thinking we could hang out a little later... that is, if our deal is still on?"

"Of course."

"Can I get your number? I'll text you once I slip away."

Casey gave me her number. And for some reason, I texted her back so she would have my contact information. I never did that with women. If they asked for my number, I'd just tell them to give me theirs and I would text them. Which I never did. With Casey, I was worried that if I didn't get the right number, I might not see her again. Jesus. I was so fucked.

She texted me back. "Room 442."

"I would invite you to my room, but I'm sharing with Kyle."

"You couldn't afford your own room?"

"I didn't think I was going to need my own room. I wasn't planning on meeting Casey Caldwell."

She smiled up at me like she was happy with my response, and then said, "Text me when you can break away."

"I will. How late is too late?"

"For you, no time is too late," she replied. "Now get back to your family."

18

CASEY: OVERSHARE

We parted ways. I actually slipped into the bathroom, since I was already there, and when I rejoined the party, I saw Jake surrounded by at least ten women. He must have been cornered on his way back from our secret meeting. I shook my head. Damn, he had his hands full. He couldn't go anywhere without women throwing themselves at his feet, present company included. Jake looked up as if he sensed me staring, and upon seeing my amused reaction, he grinned. My heart fluttered. Now that I'd gotten to know him as a person, I found him even more attractive than when I'd first laid eyes on him – if that was even possible.

He focused his attention back on the adoring crowd. I noticed his relaxed posture. Jake didn't seem tense and reserved like he'd been yesterday at dinner. That he could turn it on and off so completely intrigued me. I marveled as Jake played the part of the hot, lady-killing rock star. He knew exactly how to conduct himself in a way that would make them swoon. Jake was affable, but not overly so. Confident, but not cocky. Sexy without being off-putting. He was the epitome of the enigmatic, unattainable guy that girls could only dream of getting.

Unfortunately, Sarah and a few other bridesmaids had noticed Jake free from my evil clutches and joined the group of women. She inched her way closer and closer until her breasts were in his line of vision. I watched her give it the old college try one more time. Jake shut her down immediately, though, and she backed off. I knew it was petty, but I couldn't help but smile. Jake glanced at me again, gave me the quickest little knowing glance, like he wanted me to recognize he'd done that for me, and then turned his attention back to the women. Oh, god, he was so flippin' awesome. I wanted to throw my arms around him and hug him. Who would have thought that only a day after meeting him, Jake McKallister and I would have our own nonverbal communication going on? I felt like the luckiest girl in the world.

The little flower girl who was promised a picture earlier in the day tentatively broke through the circle of women to ask Jake about the photo. Jake rewarded her with his undivided attention and a photographic memory to last a lifetime. She seemed even more smitten after her brief encounter with him. In fact, everyone was smitten with him. He really did appear to be the genuine guy that he'd presented to me. After a while, Jake's family pulled him away from the crowds and took him over to their table.

I was standing there by myself for a minute or two before Kate came up to me. We hugged. "It was an amazing wedding, Kate, and you're the most beautiful bride."

"Yeah, yeah, enough about me," she joked, then took my arm and led me away from everyone. She whispered, "What the hell is going on between you and Jake?"

"Is it that obvious?"

"Casey, the entire wedding party is following Jake's every move, and you seem to have his undivided attention."

I looked at my friend for any sign of accusation. Suddenly, I felt terrible that I had been part of diverting focus away from her and Mitch on their big day. I should have toned it down with

Jake. "Oh, no, Kate, I'm so sorry. I didn't mean to take away from your wedding... I swear."

"Relax, Casey. No one was looking at you anyway," Kate laughed.

"You got that right."

"We knew Jake would draw a lot of attention no matter what he did at the wedding. But we don't mind. Mitch and I are just glad he came," Kate said.

"And you aren't mad at me?" I asked.

"No. I mean, who could blame you? Jake's gorgeous. Anyone in here would trade places with you in an instant."

"Except you, of course." I smiled mischievously at her.

"Oh yeah, right, except me." She winked and held up her finger. "Because I'm married."

"To his brother," I added.

"Right, to his brother," she repeated, then whispered, "He is hot, though."

"Mitch or Jake?"

"Shut up!" Kate hissed. "I'm a little tipsy right now so you better not say anything."

"I won't," I promised. "And I know Jake's not trying to be disruptive on purpose."

"I don't think he's being disruptive at all. I love having him here. I mean, how many brides can say that Jake McKallister sang to them at their wedding?"

"Only you."

"Damn right. Okay, no more avoiding my question. What's going on? Spill!"

I sighed. "Honestly, Kate, I have no idea what's happening. Jake's a complicated guy."

"Duh," Kate replied eloquently. "What were you expecting?"

"That's the thing – I wasn't expecting anything. He's totally out of my league. I mean, he seems more the type to go after the Sarahs of the world, not the Caseys, right?"

Kate shrugged and then nodded, like she begrudgingly agreed with my assessment.

"I figured we might exchange a few words here or there, but I truly didn't expect him to have a conversation with me... or to be this incredible guy who is so friggin' charming and sweet and funny."

Kate was staring at me in awe before shaking her head. "Damn, girl."

I looked around and whispered, "And I definitely didn't expect him to kiss me."

"He kissed you!?" Kate squealed in a low voice.

"Shhh! Yes. And I mean, like, holy crap, Kate, Jake is smoldering. He's like sex on a stick."

Kate burst out laughing. She fanned herself. "The imagery... good god, Casey, I'm not going to be able to look at him now without thinking that."

"Sorry."

"So what do you think? Is he just trying to get in your pants, or do you think he actually likes you?"

"Well," I smoothed down my dress. "He's not getting in my pants, and he knows it."

"What do you mean, he knows it?"

"I told him I don't sleep with guys I just meet, and he didn't run in the other direction. So either he's incredibly overconfident in his wooing skills, or he doesn't mind just enjoying my company without the promise of anything more."

"How did *that* conversation come up?" Kate marveled.

"You know me... I tend to overshare."

"Geez, Casey." She shook her head in amusement. "I'm still trying to wrap my brain around how the two of you went from that awkward moment last night to him shoving his tongue down your throat."

"Well, it didn't stay that awkward for long. After you left, we totally hit it off. Then, later, I was walking through the lobby of the hotel and I hear my name and there's Jake with his brothers and he's calling me over."

"Wait, the brothers got together? They didn't invite Mitch?"

"No, I think he was there. They said something about Mitch leaving just before I got there."

"Oh, huh. I didn't see him last night. I'll have to ask him. Sorry, go on."

"So Jake invited me to sit down with him and his brothers, and then later he offered to walk me to my room."

"And?" she asked suggestively.

"And... nothing. He was a perfect gentleman."

"Bummer."

"I know, right? But I was also impressed. If he'd pushed, I probably would have slept with him... I mean, who wouldn't, right?"

"Not me... I'm married," Kate said, but she was nodding her head anyway.

"To his brother," I added, continuing our little game.

"Yep." Kate nodded and then gave a little burp. "And I looove Mitch."

"Yes, you do." I patted her shoulder. "Anyway, we've just kind of been hanging out today. He's an intriguing guy, that's for sure."

"Wow. I'm just... shocked. I never thought the two of you would hit it off like that. I'm really happy for you."

"You act like we're dating," I protested. "One step at a time, sister."

"I know. I'm just excited for you. Would you ever have thought this possible yesterday... you kissing Jake?"

"Ha, no way. Things like this just don't happen to me," I acknowledged.

"Things like this don't happen to anyone, Casey."

Mitch walked up and took Kate's hand, kissing her cheek. "What are you two talking about?"

"I'll give you one guess," Kate teased.

"Um, let's see... you wouldn't by chance be talking about my brother, would you?"

"Uh-huh... but more importantly, we're talking about your brother's interest in my girl Casey here." Kate gestured toward me with her hands.

"Yeah, what's up with that? You guys seem to have really hit it off."

"We did. He's a great guy."

"Yeah, he is... and tough to compete with," Mitch admitted. "Not that I'm complaining."

"Yeah, he can definitely draw a crowd."

"Where is he now?" Mitch asked, looking around. "He's not usually hard to find. I only have to look for a crowd of people or look toward where that crowd of people is staring."

Mitch was right. We found Jake right away, using Mitch's Jake-finding technique.

"Well, we better go off and mingle." Kate hugged me. "Have fun."

"Okay, you too," I answered.

Kate was walking away when she turned and winked at me.

I stood there by myself after they left, trying to figure out what to do. Jake was still busy with his family. Aside from JD and the bridesmaids, I really didn't know many people at the wedding – and since the other bridesmaids had all joined Team Sarah, and I didn't dare go chat with JD after Jake admitted he was jealous, I just kind of wandered around aimlessly.

Thankfully, Keith walked up with his girlfriend, Sam. He introduced us and we instantly hit it off. She was very easy-going and friendly. We chatted for so long that Keith got bored and excused himself.

"I thought he would never leave," Sam complained. "I mean, how much girl talk could he stand, right? I was seconds away from talking about tampons to make him go away."

"I know, geez. He's fun though. I met all the brothers last night. They're a sick bunch of boys."

Sam nodded.

"And they all seem to love you. They were raving about you last night."

"Oh, were they now," Sam's eyes lit up. "Those McKalli boys. God, I love them. They are so fun to be around. Just like their dad."

"Not like their mom?"

Sam slapped her hands over her mouth, looking horrified. "That didn't sound right, did it?"

I laughed. "I'm just kidding."

"Michelle and the girls just aren't as outgoing as the boys," Sam attempted to explain herself. "When I first met Michelle, she terrified me."

"Really? Why?"

"She can come across as a little stand-offish and overprotective," Sam confessed. "But once you get to know her, she's actually a really nice person." She paused. "So anyway, enough about that. Keith said that you and Jake hit it off last night. He said you guys had mad chemistry."

"Keith said that?" I asked, feeling a flutter of excitement pass through me.

Sam nodded.

"I felt it for sure, and it was totally unexpected. Jake's just… wow."

"He is wow." Sam smiled warmly. "I love Jake. I've known him for three years. He takes such a beating in the media, and it's so not deserved."

I shook my head. "No, it isn't."

Sam's eyes sparkled. "You're totally crushing on him, aren't you?"

I nodded, flashing her my best puppy dog eyes.

"Ahh." She gave me a quick side hug. "I approve."

"Oh, good. Maybe you can let him know."

Keith came back then and told Sam he wanted to introduce her to someone. They said goodbye to me and left. I wandered around for another forty minutes or so until I got a text. I'd been holding my phone in my hand just in case.

"Your place in thirty minutes?"

"I'll be there." I followed the words with a variety of different emojis.

19

CASEY: ADVENT CALENDAR

I hurried back to my room, which was a few floors down from where the reception was held. I jumped in the shower to rinse off, then quickly got dressed in some yoga pants, a tank top, and a thin zip-up sweatshirt. I was going for comfort, not sexpot. Plus, I didn't want Jake to think I was trying too hard to impress him. I checked my hair. Aside from taking out the flowers, I kept it as it was because it still looked cute. By the time all that was done, I only had time to brush my teeth before the knock came at the door, exactly thirty minutes later.

I opened it to find Jake standing in front of me, his hair wet, wearing ripped up jeans and a cutoff muscle tee that hung down past his nipples. He obviously had gone the comfort route as well. In fact, it looked like he threw on whatever he had lying around, and that seemed somehow so endearing. Plus, what he was wearing couldn't have looked hotter. The shirt showed off his cut muscles, and for the first time, I noticed that he had tattoos: one coming halfway down his right arm and another wrapping around the left side of his torso. I wondered how many others were hidden under his clothing. I'd never desired to date a guy with tattoos; but then, I'd never met Jake McKallister. Everything about him was incredibly sexy, including his ink. I had to force myself not to drool at the man standing before me. He grinned. I smiled back. Oh, lord, I was in so much trouble.

"For you," he said, as he handed me a bouquet of flowers. It took me a second to realize they were actually just a collection of plant stems. No flowers. Some still had dirt attached to the end. I burst out laughing. It was probably the most charming thing a guy had ever done for me.

"My goodness. These are gorgeous. It's almost like you put this arrangement together on your way over here," I remarked.

Jake smiled and shrugged.

"You better get in here before someone spots you."

"Too late," Jake said, motioning over his shoulder. I saw some women staring in our direction from the other side of the indoor courtyard.

"They didn't see you rip the plant out of the pot, did they?"

"I'm thinking they probably did."

I laughed and shook my head, "Get in here."

Grabbing his shirt, I pulled him in and promptly shut the door on the stalking women. Concerned about having unwelcome spectators peeking through the interior window, I went to work sealing off any open areas with the curtains. But no matter how I tried, there were still wide-open gaps. Jake watched me in amusement.

"Are you just going to stand there?" I asked, exasperated.

"I'm not really sure what you're doing. Every time you close this side, the other side opens up."

"Duh…a little help would be appreciated here. Unless, of course, you don't mind having an audience."

"It depends on what we'll be doing," Jake said mischievously.

"Does it matter? We're still going to have strangers peeking through the window." As if on cue, a woman's face appeared in an opening in the curtain. We both jumped in surprise.

"Oh, shit! What the hell?" Jake exclaimed, no longer finding it amusing. He came over to help me seal the curtain shut, and he pushed a chair and an ottoman up against the curtain to keep it in place.

"How rude," I whispered.

"Sorry. I should have been more careful coming over here," Jake apologized.

"It's not your fault," I said, looking back at the window. How was I going to relax now, knowing there were women standing right on the other side, probably with their ears up against the glass? There was only one option now: the bedroom. The hotel suite had a sitting room and then another room with a bed. I'd intended to stay in the sitting room with Jake, hanging out on the couch, but that was not going to be feasible, now that I had the creepy image of that woman's face peering through my window.

"Let's go in the other room, okay?"

"Good idea," Jake said, seemingly relieved to be leaving the fishbowl. But first, he walked over to the door and deadbolted it. I grabbed his hand and led him into the room with the bed and shut the door. Even though we had just met, I felt safe with him. I trusted that he was the man he'd presented to me. There was no uneasiness, just excitement.

As soon as we were away from prying eyes, I boldly stepped up against his body and started kissing him. I'd been waiting to get my hands on him again since the balcony. Jake seemed surprised by my forwardness, but he met my bravado with his own intensity. It immediately became heated. Jake actually ran his hands partway up the back of my shirt. My hands grabbed his scrumptious ass. We ground into each other as our lips and tongues labored. We kissed for several minutes, the force of it making me weak in the knees. Finally, when I felt I couldn't take any more without other things happening, I ended the kiss.

"Okay, yeah...wow...you're a decent kisser."

"Decent?" Jake smiled. "Stop, you flatter me."

I took a step back and stared up at the man who made my

insides turn to lustful mush. He just looked so damn hot with his wet hair hanging in those transparent green eyes. Did he look in the mirror every day and smile at what stared back at him? I reached up and moved a couple strands of hair gently away. Jake instinctively ran his hand through it.

"Sorry, is it a mess?" Jake asked.

"No, I like it." Feeling overwhelmed with affection for him, I wrapped my arms around his waist and hugged him. It just felt so natural. I could feel Jake's body relax as he responded by hugging me back. "You're a pretty awesome guy, you know that, Jake McKallister?"

"I don't know about that." He shrugged.

"Well, you're awesome to me."

"Then I guess that's all that counts, right?"

I snuggled up closer. "Damn, you smell good. What's that cologne?"

"I'm not wearing cologne. It's probably just my deodorant, Eau de Right Guard," Jake responded with a laugh.

"Oh…oops…well, it smells great on you. Manly."

"Thank you. You're just all full of compliments, aren't you?"

"I know I am. I'm just happy. I haven't met a cool guy in so long."

"Probably because you go to ASU."

"Probably," I conceded. "So how did you slip away from your mom?"

"I told her I had jetlag."

"And she bought that?"

"I'm not sure. She didn't look happy, so she probably knew I was lying."

"I don't want you to get in trouble."

"Casey, I'm twenty-three years old. What's she going to do, ground me?"

He had a point. Jake was an adult. He made his own choices. I had to stop worrying about it. "So, what do you want to do?"

Jake raised his eyebrows at me like I was crazy. We both laughed.

"Well, I know something that I definitely don't want to do. Absolutely no sex! I'm not that kind of guy," Jake said, mimicking me. "If that's what you want, I'm sure there's a sweaty guy with a comb-over in the bar right now who's a sure thing."

I threw my head back and laughed. "Okay... I deserved that. I'll try to keep my hands off you."

"You do that." Jake nodded.

"You're not really my type anyway," I teased.

"I'm not?"

"Don't sound so surprised. Do you think every girl just falls for you the instant she sees you?"

"No, but... " Jake stopped himself.

"But what?"

"I don't know...you just seem... "

"I seem what?"

Jake looked serious. "Into me."

"I'm totally into you... but that doesn't mean you're my type. I've never gone for the bad boy, long hair rocker guys."

"Huh?" Jake smiled. "So then, what's your type? And please don't say the douchey frat boy."

I looked up at him with guilt strewn across my face.

"Noooo, " Jake scoffed. "Yuck, Casey... come on!"

"What? You should talk. What's your type? The anorexic model?"

"Hardly," Jake replied, and then added, "I like a little meat on the bones." He ran his hands over my curves.

"Well, then, lucky for you that I eat."

"Yeah, that is lucky." Jake agreed, his eyes still roaming my body. "I actually think your type is the long-haired rocker... you just don't know it yet."

"Oh really? What makes you so sure?"

"Just a hunch," he said, smiling his most charming smile.

"Well, I have to hand it to you, Jake – you make a good case for your kind, that's for sure."

"My kind?" he repeated. "The things you say are so random."

I perked up and said, "Let's play a game."

"Uh oh," Jake groaned. "No more spy games."

I shook my head, then spoke like I was addressing a child. "No, silly, not the spy game. Let's play slaps."

"Oh, in that case, you're on!" We both jumped on the bed and sat Indian style.

"Ladies first," I proclaimed and held my hands upright. Jake slid his long fingers over mine, palms down. I turned quickly before he was ready and slapped, but Jake snapped his hands back so fast that I barely saw them move. He smiled in victory. Over and over I tried to slap him, but he was just too quick for me. We laughed uproariously. Jake was just fun like that. We traded positions and he slapped numerous times until the backs of my hands were red. I finally admitted defeat.

"Damn, I thought I was good at this game, but you're expert level."

"I'm a guitarist. You had no chance."

"What does being a guitarist have to do with anything?" I asked.

"I'm quick with my hands," he replied, then proceeded to demonstrate on his air guitar. He was, indeed, quick with his hands and fingers. I nodded my approval.

Jake taught me how to play my very own air guitar. After putting on a little concert, we started playing rock, paper, scissors, and then made up our own handshake.

Later, while we were still sitting on the bed, crisscross-applesauce, I asked, "Have you always had long hair?"

"Yeah, pretty much."

"Is it to give you rocker cred, or do you just like to hide behind it?"

Jake tilted his head as he considered my question. Hair fell into his eyes. "Maybe a little of both."

"Do you ever wear it up in a man bun?"

"Only when I'm trying to look sexy," Jake said, emphasizing the word *sexy*.

I moved the hair out of his eyes with my finger. "I don't really get the whole man bun craze. Only a select few guys look manly with that hairstyle. The rest just look like girls."

"Gee, thanks." He grinned.

"Easy there, stud. I never said you were one of the rest. In fact, let's test my theory."

I jumped up off the bed and walked over to my toiletries bag. I found what I was looking for – a black hair tie – then flung myself back onto the bed playfully. I crawled until I was sitting up on my knees behind him.

"Seriously?"

"Yes."

"Then I can do it myself."

"No. What's the fun in that?" I said, slapping his hand away. "I'll make you look pretty."

"I can't wait," he replied sarcastically.

"Now be quiet," I sassed, and turned his head around so he was no longer staring at me.

"You're bossy."

I nodded in agreement as I started pulling his hair back. It was still damp and hung just above his shoulders. I ran my fingers along his strong neckline as I smoothed the strands back. He shivered. Over and over I ran my fingers through his hair until I'd gathered it into a ponytail. Jake barely had enough hair left over for the bun, but I managed. I turned his head to look at the results. Good god.

"What category do I fall into?" he asked. "And you better not say *little girl*."

"Neither."

"Neither? I thought you said there were only two categories?"

"That was before I saw you in a man bun. Now I realize there's a third category," I explained.

"Yeah? What's that?" Jake asked, genuinely curious.

"Hot as hell," I expressed confidently.

"Well, that's better than being in the girl category." Jake smiled.

"Uh-huh, now turn back around. I'm not done." He turned his head away again and I ran my fingers up and down his neck. Jake shuddered. I spotted yet another tattoo, this one on his back, just below the neckline of his shirt. Damn, he was like an advent calendar. Every time I opened a flap, a new prize inside was revealed. I was so turned on by him. I swooped down and kissed his neck. I think I might have audibly groaned as I ran my tongue in swirly motions over his naked skin. I could hear Jake gasp.

"I changed my mind. I like the way you do my hair," he whispered, breathing heavily.

As I kissed his neck, I wrapped one arm around his stomach and the other hand slithered up his shirt. Jake tensed as my hand passed over raised skin. Holy shit, were those scars? I'd almost forgotten about his horrible past. Instinctively, I knew better than to react. I just ignored it and continued to swirl my tongue over his skin and to explore with my hand. Jake's body gradually relaxed under my touch, almost like he was giving me his trust. Then he turned around and pushed me on the bed and climbed on top of me. We started kissing. It got hot and heavy fast. Our hands were everywhere. I was groping him through his jeans and his hand was between my legs. I was losing it. I didn't care about the rules anymore. I just desperately wanted him.

Jake let out a groan, then rolled off me. He sat up, looking totally flushed.

"Sorry," he panted, giving me an apologetic look. "Probably shouldn't have done that."

I grabbed for him, wanting to pull him back down on top of me. "It's okay."

"No. That was not part of your damn rule book."

"Fuck the rule book."

"Who has a potty mouth now?"

"Oh, god, this is a bad time for you to be a Boy Scout, Jake." I frowned and sat up in frustration.

Jake smiled, then leaned over and grabbed the remote. He turned on the TV.

"Seriously?" I asked, folding my arms in front of me.

"Yep," he said, nonchalantly.

I sighed loudly, then climbed over next to him, and we sat shoulder to shoulder propped up against the backboard.

Jake flipped stations until he found *Family Guy*. We watched the entire episode, laughing hysterically at every little thing. When it was over, Jake turned the TV back off and we just talked. It was such a natural, free-flowing conversation.

My phone rang at about 2:00 am. I picked it up to see that it was my mom and ignored it.

"Who's that?" Jake asked.

"My mom."

"Your mom?" Jake raised his eyebrows.

"Yeah, why?"

"It's 2:00 am," he declared. "Does she always call you so late?"

"No. She's calling to find out how the day went."

"She can't wait until the morning?" Jake still seemed amazed.

"No, because she wants to know about you."

"About me?" Jake asked in surprise, a smile slowly spreading across his face. "Why? What did you tell her about me?"

"Yesterday after the rehearsal dinner, I called her and told her I met you."

"Uh-huh. What else?"

"I told her you were really hot and that you were a super cool guy and that you laughed at my jokes."

"Uh-huh, and?"

"Well." I smiled sheepishly, "I also might have accidentally, um... mentioned that I was, you know, possibly going to marry you someday."

Jake's eyes got big with surprise. He had definitely not been expecting that. But luckily, he got the joke and laughed. "Oh, really?"

"Yeah."

"You accidentally mentioned that?"

"Yep. It was weird. It just kind of popped out. You know how that sort of thing goes," I said casually.

"Yeah, totally. Just the other day I accidentally proposed marriage to someone."

"Right? So you know it's a pretty common error."

Jake shook his head, amused. "So, what did your mom have to say about that?"

"Um...oh, yeah, she was happy. She asked if *you* were aware of the fact that we were getting married, and I told her that I was just going to invite you and hope you showed up."

Jake grinned.

I reached up and pulled my hair tie out of Jake's man bun. I folded the hair tie a couple of times until it was ring size.

"So anyway, whew –here it goes," I exhaled noisily. "Jake, will you... "

He slapped his hand over my mouth playfully before I could finish my fake proposal and tried to unravel the hair tie ring with his other. We were both struggling for the fake ring. Finally, I pulled away far enough to unfold the hair tie and shoot it into his face. But the band had no elasticity to it and just kind of plopped onto the bed between us. We stared at each other in surprise then burst out laughing.

"Phew, that was close," Jake said, wiping his forehead with the back of his hand.

"Damn, I almost had you," I replied in a crazy voice.

He rolled away from me, his hands out to keep me at a distance. "Do you seriously joke with your mom about that kind of stuff?"

"All the time. She even told me to have fun tonight but to not get pregnant."

Jake's mouth dropped open. "She did not?"

"She did," I nodded proudly. "Where do you think I get my sense of humor?"

"So you're saying that all I have to do to win over your mom is to not knock you up tonight?"

"Yep. Pretty much."

"Wow, that's good to know." Jake shook his head, still seeming surprised.

"You have a wide berth." I grinned, grabbing his hand and leaning in for a kiss. I loved that he didn't take things too seriously and that he understood immediately that I was only kidding. Most guys probably would have been running for the door.

"So I gotta ask...what's a guy like you single for?"

Jake looked at me for a second before countering, "What's a girl like you single for?"

"Oh, that's easy, guys are assholes," I blurted out. "No offense."

"No worries," Jake replied. "My kind isn't easily offended."

"Ha! Funny. And you...why are you single?"

"I'm twenty-three."

"That's your answer?" I laughed.

"What? Would you prefer that I had a girlfriend?"

"No, I'm just curious why you don't."

"I don't know. I haven't been looking."

"No?" I said, tracing his fingers. They were so long and masculine.

"No," he replied.

"Why aren't you looking?"

"'Cause I have been insanely busy. My days aren't all spent like this, Casey."

"All work and no play?"

"Something like that."

"Do you ever sleep with fans?" I asked, as I turned his hand over to reveal heavy calluses.

Jake grinned, looking away sheepishly.

"What?" I asked innocently and then tickled his hand.

"This feels like a trap," he replied, pulling his hand away from me.

I laughed. "So, do you?"

"I'm going to take the fifth on that."

I turned over and propped myself up on my elbows. "Sir... just answer the question," I replied, like a cop interrogating a witness.

Jake huffed and changed his own position on the bed. His body was touching mine now, and I was acutely aware of his manliness. He gave me a seductive glance, and I felt my heart beat faster.

"You're trying to distract me from my line of questioning," I complained.

"Yes, I am, actually. Is it working?"

"With you...it's always working," I admitted

"Yeah?"

"Like you don't know," I scoffed.

Jake reached over and ran his finger along my forearm, sending shivers through my skin. "You think I'm some man whore, don't you?"

"Pretty much, yeah. I mean, can you blame me? You have a very detailed exit strategy when it comes to women."

Jake grinned but didn't respond.

"I think it's funny."

"What's funny?"

"You...juggling a continent worth of horny women. It must be exhausting."

"You have no idea," he joked.

"When was your last one night stand?"

"Why do you care?"

"I'm just trying to get to know you better," I said innocently.

"By asking me who I've slept with?" Jake questioned, his voice high-pitched. "That's a terrible way to get to know someone."

"I'm not a jealous person. I'm just curious, is all."

"You're curious?" Jake laughed. "Oh, well, in that case, my last one night stand was in Australia."

"Australia?" I asked. "Am I supposed to know when you were in Australia, Jake?"

"You would if you were a stalker, Casey."

"Well, then, lucky for both of us that I'm not. Now, back to Australia."

"Oh god," he moaned.

"Jake, you can make this easy or you can make this difficult," I said, with as much authority as my voice could muster.

"It was three weeks ago. There, are you happy now?"

"Three weeks?" I blurted out. "You poor thing. How have you managed to survive?"

Jake shrugged, then held up his right hand. I bust up laughing and pushed him away from me. Jake looked insanely pleased with himself.

"I'll have you know that I haven't had sex in seven months."

"Seven months?"

"Yeah, since my last boyfriend."

"He was that bad, huh?" Jake responded, shaking his head in disappointment.

"Yep. That bad."

"So does that mean you haven't had a second date in the last seven months, or that you haven't found a guy interesting enough to jump in bed with?"

"Honestly? Both," I sighed.

"Well, if you want, I can end that dry spell for you," Jake offered. "Strictly for health purposes, of course."

"Oooh...so smooth, Jake."

"You like that?" He replied. "I've got more where that came from."

"No. I get the idea. It really is shocking that you don't have a girlfriend."

"I know, right?"

"You dated Krista Allen for a while, didn't you?" I asked. Krista was a pop star with a wild reputation. During their time together, she was often photographed partying without him, sparking endless breakup rumors on social media.

Jake rolled onto his back and rubbed his eyes with his hands. "Um... I guess... yeah."

"You guess?" I laughed. "Either you did or you didn't."

"Okay, then, we did."

I stared at him incredulously. "Wow, so sentimental."

Jake rolled his eyes.

"So I take it the relationship didn't end well?"

"Do relationships ever end well?"

"True. Are you still friends?"

"Um." He shrugged, frowning. "I'm thinking not."

"Uh, oh, what happened?" I asked, leaning in so as not to miss anything.

"I don't think she likes me very much."

"Why?"

"I broke up with her over text."

I gasped. "No, you didn't!"

Jake grimaced as he nodded. "I broke up with her, then turned my phone off."

"That's terrible!" I burst out laughing. "Way to man up."

"I know. Not one of my finest moments. But in my defense, I tried to break up with her in person, but she shut me down both times."

"What do you mean, she shut you down?"

"She wouldn't let me break up with her."

"Seriously?"

"Yeah. The first time she was like, 'Wait a second are you trying to break up with me?' and I nodded, and she put her hand up and said, 'Oh, no, you don't,' and she stormed out. That night she was back acting like nothing happened."

I couldn't help but be impressed. That chick had balls. If that had been me, I would've crawled out of there with my tail firmly tucked between my legs. "What did you do?"

"So, like, a couple days later I tried again, and she said that I couldn't just make that decision by myself and that there were two of us in the relationship, and I was being selfish, and she just kept talking and talking... "

"And we know how you feel about talking," I added.

"Exactly! So I finally just gave up."

"You gave up on breaking up with her?"

Jake nodded.

I laughed.

"I stayed with her another month and then broke up with her the day after she left on tour."

"I guess I can see why you broke up with her over text," I said, then added, "Why'd you want to break up with her in the first place?"

"Why? I don't know...I guess because we didn't really have anything in common."

"You're both famous singers. How much more in common can you get?"

"Okay, well, that part, maybe, but Krista likes to party and I don't. She likes being the center of attention and I don't. We really had no business being together."

"Then how did you end up as a couple?"

"You know – the same old boy meets girl story. We met, had

sex, and then she wouldn't leave," Jake replied with a smirk on his face.

"Shut up!" I laughed.

"The sad thing is… I'm not kidding," Jake confessed.

"How long were you together?"

"Like five months."

"Were you in love with her?"

"God, you ask a lot of personal questions."

"I know, right?" I replied, realizing how personal I was being.

"You're worse than my mother." Jake teased. "And that's saying something."

"Oh, geez…sorry. I don't know why I'm interrogating you. You can tell me to shut up if you want."

"Wait a minute. Why didn't you tell me that hours ago?"

"What? I thought you liked hearing me jabber on and on."

"I do, actually. And to answer your question, no, I didn't love her. I mean, I've felt affection for people, but I don't think I've ever really been in love."

"Really?" I asked. I was stunned he would open up to me like that.

"I feel like real love would smack me in the face… You know what I mean?"

"Yeah, I know what you mean," I replied, tracing his fingers with mine. Jake raised his beautiful eyes to meet mine. He stared at me for longer than usual.

I broke the moment by bringing my hand up and lightly slapping his face. Jake looked surprised. I smiled coyly. Then he understood.

"Hey, it was worth a shot," I said, shrugging.

A wide grin broke out across his face. He leaned over like he was going to kiss me, but instead he playfully slapped me in the face. I slapped back and we started rolling around trying to slap each other. I got up and straddled him as he tried to protect his face. We were both breathless from laughing. I bent down and kissed him. It was just a quick peck, but Jake drew me in, and before long we were making out.

After a couple of hot and heavy minutes, Jake rolled out from under me. He turned to his side and swore, "Okay. Shit. Stop already."

"It's okay," I puffed. "I want to."

"Do I need to remind you that you don't sleep with guys on a first date? Your words... not mine."

"Well, technically, this isn't even a date, so the rules don't really apply."

"Oh, *now* you tell me." Jake exaggerated his words.

"Sorry. I don't mean to be leading you on. I just wish we weren't so rushed. I want more time with you, but that isn't going to happen."

"I want more time with you, too."

"You do?"

"What part of tonight makes you doubt that?"

Come to think of it, Jake was definitely acting like a man who was enjoying every minute of our time together.

"Um, let me see... probably the part where you were ignoring me."

"Oh, that." Jake shrugged. "I already explained that I was an idiot. What more do you want?"

I leaned in and kissed him. "Nothing, actually. I really like you, Jake."

"I really like you too, Casey."

We lay on the bed for a while, not really talking, just enjoying each other's company.

I broke our quiet reflection. "What do you look for in a girl?"

"I don't know."

"I mean, women are throwing themselves at you. They go to your concerts. You're their fantasy. All you have to do is show interest, and they're basically yours. I have to assume there are a lot of hot girls throwing themselves at your feet all the time. So how do you choose?"

"Whoever is the hottest."

Jake's eyes gleamed with mischief.

"So what do you find hot? Do you like big butts?"

"I like a shapely ass," he replied as he slapped mine. "But not so big that you can set a soda can on it."

"Boobs?"

"Yeah… she has to have them."

I laughed. "Obviously. I meant, real or fake?"

"Real, of course."

"Even if they're small?" I asked.

"Even if they're small," Jake replied. "They have to move."

"Good call. Hair: long or short?"

"Long. I like pony tails."

I flipped mine in his face.

"Oh, and most importantly, I like a girl who has a little crinkle on her nose when she smiles." Jake flipped to his side and traced the crinkle on my nose.

"Wait a minute… are you describing me, Jake McKallister?"

"Maybe," he flirted.

"God, you're cute…and you know it."

Jake shrugged, flashing me the most adorable lopsided grin.

"Don't look at me like that!"

"Like this?" he replied, as he repeated his smile.

"Yeah, like that."

"Oh, sorry. Being delightful just comes so naturally for me."

He was so flippin' awesome. I leaned over and kissed him. Jake pulled me down on top of him. I dug my fingers into his side, tickling him. Jake grabbed at my hands as I tore into his side with my fingers. He twisted away as best he could before flipping me over on my back and getting on top of me in one swift move. He started tickling me.

Then it became all out war. We were rolling around on the

bed, laughing and wrestling. Soon, the tickling stopped and the mashing started. He was licking my neck with his tongue. I felt wildly out of control. My hand snaked its way down his stomach and found his erection straining through his jeans. Jake groaned. I stroked him for a moment before he pulled back panting. He put his hands up as if to stop me. "Okay...okay, you... that's... "

20

JAKE: THE GOOD PILLOW

I pulled myself out from under her and sat up, panting. I groaned in frustration. "I'm really trying to respect your wishes, but you aren't making it easy."

"I know, I know... sorry," she apologized.

I was trying to calm my body down. A few more seconds and I would have been beyond control. This girl did things to me that I never could have imagined. Spending this time with her had been beyond all expectation. It was hands down the most fun and most connected I'd ever felt with a girl in my entire life.

"You make me all hot and bothered. I'm having trouble controlling myself. I'm sorry," she kept apologizing.

Heat rose through my body and I felt flushed.

"This is only going in one direction. Maybe I should go."

"No. Don't. I like the direction we're going," she pleaded, looking all disheveled and vulnerable.

"I don't want you to regret this in the morning."

"I won't, I promise."

"It's really late, Casey. I won't be able to function tomorrow if I don't get a couple of hours of sleep."

"You can sleep here. I just... I just don't want this to end."

God, she was the cutest, sexiest girl ever. "I don't either," I admitted.

"Please stay," she begged.

I hesitated. I wanted to stay, I really did, but my brain was telling me to go.

"Pretty please with sugar on top. I'll give you the good pillow."

I loved when she said stuff like that. "Oh, well, why didn't you say that in the first place? The good pillow makes all the difference."

"Yah!" she squealed then hugged me. "I'll be good. I promise."

I grinned. I liked this girl so much.

We both got off the bed and pulled down the sheets.

"So, where is my good pillow?" I asked.

Casey picked up all the pillows and stacked them on my side of the bed.

"I don't need *that* many."

"I know, but you can have first pick."

"Christ, how many pillows does one bed need?"

Casey crawled onto the bed, making a point to show her ass to me. She looked over her shoulder to make sure I was watching. She needn't have worried; Casey had my undivided attention.

"Are you okay if I take my jeans off?"

"I'm okay if you get butt-ass naked."

I raised one eyebrow at her and she started backtracking.

"But that's probably not a good idea, is it?"

"No, probably not," I agreed, trying to keep the smile off my face.

I pulled off my jeans and could feel Casey's eyes on me as I climbed into bed.

"Yep. I pegged you for a boxer kind of guy the minute I saw you."

"Uh huh. And what are you? A thong girl?"

"No... I'm more a granny panty kind of girl myself."

I choked on my laugh. "Let me see!" I demanded, grabbing for her.

"Oh, no, you don't," she wiggled away. "If you want to see what I'm wearing under these Lulus, then you have to come back and find me after your tour ends."

"Fine," I said, pulling the sheets up. "But I know you're wearing a thong because I've been checking out your ass all night, and there have been no granny panty lines whatsoever."

Casey laughed out loud. "Oh, you're an observant guy. I like that."

"Only observant when it comes to your ass," I countered.

I found a couple of pillows and piled the other four on top of her head. She squealed and threw all four onto the ground before turning to me and nestling into my body, her head resting on my arm and chest. Normally I hated this. I was definitely not the cuddling type. It usually made me feel claustrophobic and intensely uncomfortable, but with Casey, it felt amazing. It was like she fit right into the nook of my body.

We lay there a few minutes before she said, "Can I ask you something?"

I tensed immediately. Suddenly, I wanted to jump up and bolt out of the room. I knew what she was going to ask. That was how people always started the conversation when they wanted to ask something about the kidnapping or about my scars.

"What?" I responded solemnly. Why had I thought Casey would be any different? Anger and indifference spread through my body like fire.

"You could have anyone. What... what do you see in me?" Casey asked, her voice heartbreakingly sweet and vulnerable.

I was shocked. It was not the question I'd been expecting at all. Suddenly I felt bad for the way I'd assumed the worst of her. My heart softened, and my body relaxed once more. I didn't respond right away. I wasn't sure exactly how to answer her question. A pang of guilt gripped me. She thought I was some great prize. God, if she only knew. Was it fair to drag her down with me? Or maybe Casey could lift me up. Maybe this girl was brave enough to save me from myself.

Finally, I spoke the only word that came to mind: "Everything."

I could feel her smile on my chest. We didn't speak after that, but about a minute after she asked the question, she raised her head and gave me a simple kiss on the cheek before settling back into the crook of my arm. After that, we both fell fast asleep.

21

CASEY: HE PROMISED

The next morning, we overslept.

The first word I heard in my sleepy haze was Jake swearing. "Shit!" He jumped out of bed and grabbed his phone. "Shit, shit, shit," he swore again. "I'm in trouble. I have like fifty missed calls."

"What time is it?"

"10:38."

"Shit," I agreed. Jake was expected at a family barbecue in less than an hour, and I was working at 2:00. I watched him read some texts and swiftly answer back. In between texts, he was pulling on his jeans.

"I'm so sorry," I apologized, feeling awful. It was my fault he was late. "I shouldn't have begged you to stay."

Jake stopped rushing and looked at me. All of a sudden he seemed to relax. He pulled me up to my feet and wrapped me in a warm hug. Then he bent down and kissed me on my lips.

"I wouldn't change a thing about last night."

Relief spread through my body, and I smiled. "Me neither."

Jake slipped into the bathroom while I waited on the bed for him. Just as he came out, there was a knock on the door.

"Who would be knocking on my door?" I asked, confused.

"My brother."

"Your brother?" I questioned. "What's he doing here?"

"Apparently, we have a bit of a crowd outside."

"Are you serious?" I hastily slipped my sweatshirt on and followed him into the sitting room. "How would they even know you're here?"

"Probably the women from last night. Maybe they called their friends, I don't know."

"Do you think they've been outside the room all night?" I whispered.

"Probably," Jake said, shrugging nonchalantly.

I stared at him a second in disbelief. He acted like it was no big deal. I laughed. "Okay, then."

Jake turned to me with a serious look on his face. "Casey?" he said, hesitating. I knew what he was going to say. Some half-assed apology for why I was never going to see him again. I felt a lump form in my throat.

"It's okay, Jake. We had a deal. You don't need to say anything at all."

He stood there looking at me. There was another knock on the door.

"Hold on a second, Kyle," Jake called out then turned to me and gave me a hug. "I'll call you."

"Okay." I nodded, assuming his words were a brush off.

He lifted my chin with his fingers. I looked into his gorgeous eyes and, at that moment, anything seemed possible. Jake said with sincerity, "I promise, Casey."

I smiled at him now. He leaned down and kissed me. Then just as suddenly, he pulled away and answered the door. Kyle slipped in.

"How many?" Jake asked.

"Maybe like ten."

"Any cameras?"

"No paparazzi that I could see, but that doesn't mean they aren't hiding in the planters. Here." Kyle handed Jake a hooded sweatshirt. "I have two security guards out front."

"Okay, thanks. How mad is Mom?"

"She's mad."

"Great. I might need to bring the security guards in with me," Jake only half-joked.

"Well, hey there, Casey," Kyle said to me, grinning.

"Well, hello to you, Kyle," I replied, sticking my tongue out at him. He laughed.

"What?" Jake asked, entirely missing our little exchange because he'd been pulling his sweatshirt over his head.

"Nothing," Kyle replied.

"Is he giving you a hard time?" Jake asked me.

"Nothing I can't handle."

Jake looked between the two of us, then shrugged and put the hood over his head. "When I leave, lock the door behind me. Don't answer if anyone knocks unless you know for sure who it is. They should follow me, but you never know."

I studied him like he was speaking a foreign language. Was this seriously his life? "Why would they knock on my door?"

"To ask questions about me. But it sounds like it's just fans, not reporters. You should be fine. Text me if you need me to send security before you leave."

I was determined to show him I wasn't fazed. "I'm a big girl."

Jake shook his head. There was a look of concern on his face. "You aren't used to dealing with people like this. If someone's out there waiting for you, go back inside and text me. I'll send the guards. Promise me you'll do that."

Hating to see the worry in his eyes, I conceded. "Okay, I promise."

"Good. Okay. I'll call you."

I nodded. Kyle opened the door, and Jake ducked out. I heard girls screaming his name. I shut and locked the door like Jake had told me to do, and then looked through the peephole. I could see some movement as the women followed Jake. What the hell was that? Did he deal with this on a daily basis? How could he seem so grounded and normal under such circumstances?

I quickly packed my bags and peeked out the window. I took one last look around the room before leaving. No one was outside the door anymore. Jake was right; they'd followed him. Poor guy.

I drove home in a daze. All I could think about was Jake. I replayed every moment with him. I must have looked like an idiot in my car because I had a gigantic smile on my face the entire way. When I arrived back at my apartment, I was feeling tired but giddy. I'd spent the night with the hottest and sweetest guy I'd ever met in my life, and I just had this strange feeling that however unlikely it was, Jake and I would be together again. I could feel the connection. It was raw and powerful. And I knew he could feel it, too. Yeah, he was a rock star, and yeah, he was rich and famous, but people like him were still human beings. Was it so crazy for me to think Jake could be falling for me?

As soon as I walked in the apartment my roommate, Taylor, called out, "Casey? Is that you?"

"Yeah, it's me. But I'm still not talking to you," I answered. Her poop and puke debacle was still fresh in my mind.

I heard a squeal, and then my roommate came around the corner. She wrapped me in a hug and kissed my ear until I squirmed away laughing. "I'm so sorry. I love you, Casey. Please forgive me," Taylor begged endearingly. It was always impossible to stay mad at her.

"I hate you, you know that?" I said, smiling.

"I know, but I LOOOOVE you," she replied and hugged me again.

"You only love me because you want to know about Jake."

"Uh, yeah. I called you over and over. I texted you hundreds of times, literally... look at your phone. Would it have killed you to respond to me?"

"I was occupied the entire time."

Taylor looked at me with excitement. "Please tell me you were occupied with a certain hot musician that shall not be named?"

"Maybe... " I replied coyly.

"What? No... NOOO! Seriously? Did you sleep with him?"

"That is none of your business," I replied.

"Casey, honestly... don't mess with me like this," Taylor demanded. "Just tell me."

I couldn't stop the smile that formed on my face.

"NO YOU DIDN'T!" she screamed. "YOU SLEPT WITH HIM, DIDN'T YOU?"

"Shhh," I shushed her. "The neighbors are going to hear you."

"YOU SLEPT WITH HIM?" Taylor repeated, making no effort to quiet down.

"No," I refuted, making hand gestures for her to stop yelling. "I didn't sleep with him, all right?"

"So were you just kidding, then?" Taylor asked, looking flushed and confused.

"I didn't sleep with him, Taylor," I conceded. "But we might have made out a little bit."

Taylor squealed again in excitement. "OH MY GOD! Casey, you better spill it. And don't leave out anything. I want to hear every single juicy detail about our hunky rock star."

"Me too," our mutual friend Anna announced from the doorway. Until then I'd had no idea she was there.

"Well, first of all, there is no *our* in this story. I have dibs," I proclaimed. "And second, I have to be at work in a little over an hour. I don't have time."

"Five minutes," Taylor begged. "Come on, you've got to give us something."

I sighed. "Okay, five minutes, but then I have to get in the shower."

"Deal," Taylor said, looking like an excited child. "So? Spill it."

"We met at the rehearsal dinner. I was terrified to talk to him, but once I did, we just kind of hit it off. We hung out at the wedding. Then we hung out after the wedding."

"No way is that detailed enough," Taylor complained. "How did you hit it off?"

"I don't know. We just did. He's a cutie, and we laughed so much. Jake's actually a really funny guy."

"Seriously?" Anna asked. "Isn't he, like, introverted?"

"No. I mean, I can see why people might think he's reserved when they first meet him, but he's really personable, actually."

"Really? Huh. That's surprising considering...you know... everything."

I looked at Anna with disdain. I knew what she was implying, and I didn't like it.

"Just because you read something about him in the media doesn't make it true," I replied, a bit too brashly.

"To be fair, Casey," Taylor explained. "It's not just Anna who thinks that... everyone does."

"Well, I don't. And neither does he," I replied, defiantly.

"Wow," Taylor said.

"Wow, what?" I asked.

"You're, like, defending him and everything."

I dropped my shoulders and sighed. "I know. I already feel protective of him. I hate that people think he's something that he's not."

"I'm sorry, Casey. That was a stupid thing for me to say."

"It's okay. I thought the same thing before meeting him, too. It's weird. Jake knows how he's viewed, and it doesn't seem to bother him at all. He makes jokes about it."

"Well, he sounds awesome," Anna said, obviously trying to make up for her earlier blunder.

"I don't care about his personality. I just want to know how hot he is," Taylor declared.

"Pretty damn hot. He's totally your type, Tay. Tall, lean, muscled, long hair, tattoos."

"Are you frickin' serious?" she whined.

"Oh, yeah," I said, fanning myself.

"I hate you," Taylor said, grimacing. "I mean I really, really hate you!"

"Hey, you're the one who asked."

"Is he a total fuckboy?"

"I don't know. He seemed genuine, but I'm sure he's had his fair share of fangirl booty. I mean, at the wedding, women were practically throwing themselves at his feet. He could have had his pick of the place."

"And he picked you," Anna replied.

"Well, he didn't really pick me. We were paired together. But he did spend way more time with me than I was expecting, that's for sure."

"Yeah, and you guys did more than just spend time together," Taylor pointed out. "Obviously, he was way into you if you guys made out."

"I mean he acted like he was."

"So tell me again why you didn't sleep with him?"

"You know I don't sleep with guys on a first date."

"Well, I know, but I would have thought you might relax those lofty standards for a guy like him," Taylor said. "I mean he's Jake freakin' McKallister."

"What can I say? I like getting to know a guy before spreading my legs for him."

"I'm just saying, Case, rock stars are usually a one-shot deal."

My shoulders drooped. "God, I hope not."

"I mean, you said it yourself – women were throwing themselves at his feet."

I shrugged.

"It might've been your only chance."

"He promised to call me," I replied in a meek voice.

Taylor raised her eyebrows. "I'm sure he did."

Blinding insecurity smacked me in the face. What Taylor was saying made sense, but it didn't mesh with the scenes in my head. We'd had a connection. Or at least, I thought we had. Was I being naïve? Was Jake gone forever?

"I'm never going to see him again, am I?" I whined, as I sank lower into the sofa.

"Don't listen to her, Casey. It sounds like Jake was really into you," Anna said. And just like that, she was my new best friend.

"Or... he was into you because he was trying to... get into you," Taylor lamented.

I left then to take a shower, a sinking feeling spread through me. I knew what we'd experienced last night was real – but was it anything more than just a good time for him? What did I have that was different from any other girl he met? Nothing. So then why had he stayed? I'd laid it out for Jake in the beginning. He could have left at any time, but he didn't. He spent the whole night with me and respected my decision not to have sex... even talked me out of it when I started pushing too hard. Taylor was wrong. Jake wasn't the guy she was making him out to be. He liked me. I hadn't just imagined his interest; it was real.

I picked up my phone and looked at his number, memorizing it. Maybe I should text him. No. I couldn't appear like a needy one-night stand. The decision over whether we continued whatever it was we had going on would have to be left up to him. Then it hit me: that's what made me different than the other girls. I had Jake McKallister's phone number. I had his frickin' number!

22

JAKE: THE CRUSH

I t had been a great night… probably the best of my life. When Casey and I finally fell asleep entangled in each other's arms, it was as if lying together was the most natural thing in the world to do. By the look of contentment on Casey's face when she was asleep, I could tell it was normal for her to feel safe and protected. I was the complete opposite. Nothing about my past had provided me with safety and security, so it came as quite a shock to me when I woke up in the morning rested and relaxed. I hadn't stressed at all with Casey. I was like a goddamn normal human being for a change, and the thought made me so happy. Maybe I *could* have a normal life with a nice girl. Why not? Crazier things had happened.

I'd totally overslept, though, and from the pissed off texts I'd received, I knew I was going to pay for it. After a rather uneventful return to my room, winding through a few eager fans, I opened the door to find my mom sitting on the couch. *Shit!*

"Nice of you to finally join us, Jake," she said through pursed lips. She definitely didn't seem like she thought it was nice.

"Sorry. I overslept. My phone was off for the wedding, and I totally forgot to turn it back on last night."

My mom just stared at me with a pissed look on her face. There was a tray of food from the breakfast I'd obviously missed. I glanced over at Keith, who was packing my duffle bag and trying to disappear from the conversation.

"That wouldn't have been a problem if you'd stayed in your own bed last night," she spat out.

Of course, I had no retort. What could I say?

"I thought we talked about this last night. You promised you were going to prioritize the family over just another female admirer."

I saw Keith glance over at me, then back to Mom. Obviously, my brother wanted me to tell her that Casey was more than that, but I had no intention of admitting to something that I really didn't understand myself. I scowled at Keith, non-verbally warning him that this was none of his business. He shook his head and looked away.

"Sorry," I apologized, knowing that nothing I could say would appease my mom.

And, as predicted, she wasn't ready to accept my rather insincere remorse. "We had plans this morning, remember? Plans we had to change because you weren't here."

"I'm sorry, Mom. I messed up," I acknowledged. If I'd learned one thing about women in my few short years, it was to recognize their superiority and just apologize for my very existence.

Mom shook her head, looking immensely disappointed in me. "Would just one night without sex have killed you, Jake?"

Kyle coughed out a laugh, and Keith started choking from the force it took to hold one back. I was close to losing it myself, but I knew this was not the moment to laugh in my mom's face. It was no secret she was not a fan of the one-night-stand lifestyle I typically favored, but usually, she just kept her opinions to herself.

"Well, actually, if you must know... I didn't have sex; and, surprisingly, no, it didn't kill me." I smirked. Keith and Kyle lost it. I started laughing, too. Mom stood up, not finding it nearly as funny as my brothers and me.

"Pack your stuff. We're leaving for the barbecue in thirty minutes," she said, then stalked out of the room. But I swear I saw the tiniest of smiles on her face.

The barbecue was at the home of Kate's parents. It was a get-together only for the families of the bride and groom. Still, what with my family and Mitch's mom's side of the family and Kate's relatives, there were around twenty-five people. I really was not looking forward to spending my last day stateside making conversation with a bunch of people I didn't know when there was a girl who made my blood boil only thirty minutes away. I couldn't get her out of my head. I could still feel her fingers trailing up my body, her lips on mine. I'd already decided that, if time allowed, I was going to stop by Casey's work... surprise her. I just wanted a few more minutes with her before flying back to Germany.

I played the part of an interested partygoer, enduring the enthusiastic admiration of a bunch of strangers with a smile and polite thanks. I ate – no, I savored – the barbecue chicken and steak that I'd been deprived of in Asia and Europe, and most importantly, I spent the required amount of time pretending to be a good son to my irritated parents. But I was restless. I kept checking the outside clock on the wall of their house. 1:00. 2:00. 3:00. *Oh, god, shoot me now!* My flight was scheduled to depart at 6:45pm. With each tick of the clock, I was losing time with her. Finally at 3:45, I couldn't take anymore.

"Kyle, I need to leave by 4:00," I said. We had already decided he would drive me to the airport since my parents weren't sure how long the BBQ would be going on.

"Why so early? The airport's only like twenty-five minutes from here, and it's a Sunday."

"I just… I need to get there. I have some business I need to take care of, and I can't do it here. I'm just going to say my good-byes, and then can you drive me?"

"Yeah, sure."

So I went around and apologized and thanked the hosts for having me. I said my goodbyes to Mitch and Kate and then my parents and siblings. By the time I was sitting in the car it was already 4:05. My leg was fidgeting and I was wringing my hands together.

"Let's go," I demanded, rather abruptly.

"What the fuck is wrong with you?" Kyle asked.

"Change of plans. First I need you to drive me to Outback Steakhouse. It's just off the 17."

Kyle turned and looked at me in shock. "Dude, seriously?"

"Yeah, seriously."

Kyle stared at me for a second, then shook his head and laughed. "Way to play hard to get," he commented, as he put the car in gear and started driving.

"There's no point. She already knows I like her."

Kyle shook his head like he was disappointed in me, but there was a smile on his face when he said, "Amateur."

We sat in silence for a while before Kyle asked, "So, just exactly how much do you like this girl?"

"Enough to risk missing my flight just to see her again."

Kyle laughed. "Well, damn… Jakey-boy has got himself a crush. I never thought I would see the day."

"Just shut up and drive," I said, trying to keep the stupid smile off my face that always seemed to come when I was thinking about her.

"I'm driving, dumbass. And just so you know, if you're late, it's on you."

23

CASEY: NO BABY TALK

I was about three hours into my shift when one of the other waitresses grabbed my arm. Her face was flush with excitement.

"What's going on?" I asked in surprise.

Kaitlin stared at me, a weird look on her face.

"Are you okay?"

"Tony needs you up front," Kaitlin replied breathlessly, and let out an inexplicable little squeal.

"Okay," I said, looking at the strange expression on my co-worker's face. "What? Am I missing something here? What's going on?"

"That's what I want to know," Kaitlin replied, grabbing my arm and steering me toward the entrance of the restaurant. "You've been holding out on me, girl."

"Kaitlin, geez... what is... " As I turned the corner, there he was, standing in the waiting area. I could not believe my eyes.

"Jake?" I asked in total shock.

He smiled.

"What are you doing here?"

"Thought I would stop by before catching my flight."

I stared at his handsome face for a second before walking over to him in disbelief and hugging him. "I can't believe you're here. This is such an amazing surprise. Thank you," I said, and without thinking, kissed him on the lips. There was a collective gasp from my co-workers and a few customers as well. Not caring about our audience, I lingered there a second, feeling the familiar heat between us. It wasn't until I pulled back that I noticed Kyle.

"Oh, Kyle, sorry. I didn't see you there," I said as I went over to hug him.

"Story of my life," Kyle smirked.

I laughed, then turned to Jake and asked, "How much time do you have?"

"About enough time for some Aussie cheese fries," Jake replied, then turned to Tony, my manager, and asked, "Can I get a table in Casey's section?"

"Of course," Tony replied, and turned to another server named Sami and said, "An order of cheese fries – make it a double." Sami ran off to the kitchen. Tony then guided Jake and Kyle through the restaurant and sat them in a booth. The entire dining room was whispering and staring. The other servers had stopped working and just stood there looking dumbfounded. As usual, Jake ignored the hoopla surrounding him. His eyes were on me. I couldn't believe he'd come to my work. It spoke volumes about his interest in me. How could this possibly be happening? I smiled at him and our eyes met. Just a simple look from Jake made me tingle from head to toe. Good god. For a moment, I forgot where I was and what I was doing. I couldn't concentrate on anything but Jake. I wanted nothing more than to slide into the booth next to him, but I had four active tables. I shook my head, extracting myself from my trance, and excused myself in order to take care of my customers. As I walked away, I turned my head to find Jake still staring at me in that smoldering way.

I smiled and mouthed to him, "Stop."

Jake shrugged like he didn't know what I was talking about, but the smug look on his face told me he did.

I got back to my tables, and after several minutes of serving the needs of my customers, brought two glasses of water to the only people in the restaurant that mattered to me. As always, Jake and I chatted effortlessly. Kyle had fun acting like the put-upon third wheel. I saw Tony heading my way and quickly retreated back toward my other tables.

"Casey?" Tony called to me. I stopped and turned back.

"I know. I'm sorry," I said, not even trying to defend myself.

"Why don't you take your break now?"

"I have four tables."

"I'll cover them."

"Really?" I asked.

Tony nodded.

"Thanks." I was shocked. It was totally unlike Tony to ever give us a personal break if we had friends or family visiting the restaurant, but Jake obviously was different. He was famous, and Tony wanted to make him happy.

"Thanks a lot." Jake smiled at Tony. "I really appreciate that."

"Yeah. Yeah. No problem." Tony beamed.

I sat down and scooted into the booth. Jake wrapped his arms around me, and I stared up at him all googly-eyed.

"Okay, if this is going to work, we're going to need some ground rules," Kyle said. "Keep it above the waist. No tongue action and absolutely no baby talk."

Both Jake and I bust up laughing. We chatted for about five minutes until two orders of cheese fries arrived. We wolfed them down. Cameras flashed around us as people snuck pictures of Jake. Several teenage girls were bold enough to walk up to our table and ask for his autograph, which Jake promised to sign on his way out. When one of my co-workers asked for an autograph, Tony stepped in and reprimanded him.

The co-worker slunk off with his tail between his legs.

Jake looked at me in surprise and then whispered, "Geez, now I feel bad. Your boss is kind of scary."

"You know what's even scarier?" I replied. "He's on his best behavior because you're here."

Jake cringed. "It's kind of like a Cinderella story here, Casey. The damsel in distress in need of saving."

"Oh, and in this little fantasy world of yours, are you the knight in shining armor?"

"I believe it's Prince Charming, but yeah."

Kyle rolled his eyes. "Oh, god, please. I can't take any more of this witty banter. Shoot me now."

"No one's forcing you to stay," Jake shot back.

"Yeah, yeah, who's the one watching the clock? I hate to break up this little love fest, but we've got to get you to the airport."

"Yeah, I know," Jake replied, then turned to me. "Can you walk me to the car?"

"Yes," I said, gazing up at him. *I'd follow you anywhere.*

Jake scooted out of the booth and was instantly surrounded by those he'd deflected earlier. He signed autographs and took pictures for about five minutes before he announced to the crowd that he had a plane to catch. He posed for a picture with Tony and then with the wait staff before he took my hand and led me out the front door. I could only imagine the conversations going on in the restaurant about Jake and me.

We walked up to the car and Kyle said, "Okay, well, it was good seeing you again, Casey."

"You too," I replied, and gave him a hug. Kyle was an interesting guy. It was obvious he and Jake were close. I couldn't help but wonder what conversations they'd had about me. Kyle got into the driver's seat to give us some privacy.

And then it was just Jake and me... and the people from the restaurant who had spilled out to gawk. Jake leaned against the car like he didn't notice the audience, and I forgot about them too as I folded myself up into his arms. Nothing felt so warm and wonderful.

"My roommate told me that I should have slept with you last night," I admitted.

"Your roommate is very wise," Jake said in an accent.

"And she said that because I didn't have sex with you, I would never see you again."

"Your roommate a bitch," Jake continued in his little accent.

I grabbed his shirt and laughed. "I really like you, Jake... and it's not because you're a rock star."

"Well, I really like you, Casey," he replied. "And it's not because you're an accountant."

I swooned. "You're awesome. Thanks for coming here for me today, Jake... it was such a great surprise, and it means a lot to me."

Jake stared at me in his sexy way, hair falling into his eyes and his head tilted to one side. "I think I have a crush on you, Casey Caldwell."

"Really?" I whispered shyly.

"Really." He bent down and kissed my neck. "I spent the entire barbecue watching the clock so I could leave and come see you."

"I'm so happy you did." I nuzzled into him.

"Dude?" We heard Kyle from inside the car.

"I know," he bristled at his brother, and then toned it down for me. "I really have to go now."

"When does your flight leave?"

"An hour and fifteen minutes."

"Oh no, Jake," I laughed. "Go."

I wrapped him in a hug and whispered in his ear, "I'm going to miss you, Jake McKallister." Then I kissed his full lips.

Jake stared at me like I was some prize to be won, and said, "I'm going to miss you more, Casey Caldwell."

He made me feel special in a way I'd never felt before.

"Call me once you get to Germany, okay?"

"I will."

We kissed again, and then he opened the car door and got in. As they drove away, Jake waved at me. My heart skipped a beat. I turned back to the crowd gathered outside the restaurant. I was ready for them.

24

JAKE: THE STAR TREATMENT

We hit traffic on the way to the airport despite it being a Sunday. By the time we pulled up in front of the arrival terminal, I had exactly forty-eight minutes before my flight took off.

"Are you sure you don't want me to come in there with you? I can park real quick... or hell, I can just leave the car parked here for a few minutes," Kyle said.

"And get it towed away? No, I told you, I'll be fine. Don't worry. I'm going to check in and then immediately go through security," I reassured my brother.

"Okay. Call me as soon as you're on the plane, so I don't worry."

Normally, little brothers didn't worry about their adult siblings making it through an airport by themselves, but there was nothing normal about my situation. Being famous came with certain challenges – getting through crowded public areas being one of them. I jumped out of the car and grabbed my guitar, backpack, and duffle bag out of the back seat.

I leaned into the open window and said, "Thanks for the ride. I'll text you when I'm there. Oh, and good luck on the show."

Kyle smiled. "Don't know what I got myself into."

"You're going to rock it," I replied. "See ya, Kyle."

"Yeah, see ya. Oh, and one more thing... she's awesome."

I nodded at Kyle before turning around and walking into the airport. Keeping my head down, I headed straight for the first class passenger line and was relieved to see there was only one person in it. I got in line just as the man in front of me was called up. I took out my phone and pulled up my flight information. As soon as I heard the whispering, I knew I had been spotted. There was a difference between crowds in public places like this and crowds who were gathered to see me at a concert or in front of my hotel. Those who specifically came to see me were usually big fans, and they assembled in one place. They fed off each other's energy, and the results were loud and crazy, but at least those crowds were controlled, and I could choose how much interaction I wanted to have. But being spotted in a public place was unpredictable. If I was lucky, people would just whisper, stare, and take pictures. If I was unlucky, I would find myself in the middle of an unruly mob. I wasn't sure how this particular day was going to go, and I could feel the tension of uncertainty building up inside me. I carefully avoided eye contact until I was called up to the counter.

"Next first class passenger please," the ticket agent called. I walked up to the counter and smiled at the middle-aged woman. She looked stunned when she saw me, but recovered quickly and plastered a professional smile on her face. "Welcome to United Airlines. Where will you be flying today?"

"LA then on to Frankfurt, Germany," I replied.

"Can I have your passport, please," she asked. As I was handing it over, her fingers accidentally brushed past mine.

"Oh... I'm... sorry," she stumbled on her words. Her face turned a crimson shade.

"No problem," I offered.

"Okay, well let me... .um... " She was looking at me trying to string her sentence together. Finally, she just gave up, waved her hand, smiled and started typing into her computer. "Oh, yes, now I remember... do you have any luggage to check?"

"No. I was going to just carry on my duffle bag and guitar."

She stared at me again for a longer than comfortable moment, then resumed typing. Okay, now this was getting a little awkward.

Finally, she looked up and said, "Okay, so we have you in seat 2A to Los Angeles and then 3C on the second-floor first class lounge from LAX to Frankfurt on Lufthansa. Just have them scan your phone for boarding. You're going to have to proceed directly to your gate as soon as you go through security."

"Will I have enough time to get through it?"

She looked over to the security line. "Yes, you should be fine. I'll call the gate and let them know you're making your way through security. If you'd like, I can get you special assistance."

"Yeah, that would be great," I said. "Just someone to take me to the gate."

"Of course," she agreed and got on the phone immediately. She spoke to someone for maybe twenty seconds, then hung up and started typing again. I waited.

Finally, she looked up smiling. "So you're traveling to Germany with just a duffle bag?"

"And a guitar," I smiled.

"Oh right, and a guitar," she repeated. "Wow, you travel light."

"I'm on tour in Europe. All my stuff is there. Just took the weekend off."

"You left Europe to vacation in Arizona? Interesting choice."

"My brother's wedding, actually."

"Oh, okay, that makes more sense," she replied, biting her lower lip.

"So am I all set then?" I asked, needing to move this along so I wouldn't miss my flight.

"Yes...yes...of course...sorry, I got distracted," she said, sounding flustered. I looked at my passport still in her hand. Time was ticking.

"Um..."

"Oh, geez," she exclaimed, then handed it back to me. "Didn't realize I still had that. Well, have a wonderful flight."

"Thanks," I said, then turned away from the counter. Standing behind me was a man in a United Airlines uniform.

"Mr. McKallister? Please follow me."

The man led me toward the security. Someone called my name, and I was stupid enough to look up. Cameras snapped in my face. More people called my name. I smiled and waved, then looked away. I could see a crowd forming, and I tensed up. The assistant moved behind me to try to slow the tide of people. The lady checking tickets at the opening of the security line saw us coming and immediately waved us to a special line. The United rep unlatched one of those temporary barriers and told me to step through. I did and he came in after me and shut it.

"This way," he said and led me the back way through the security line until I came up to the TSA officers checking IDs. I felt bad bypassing the line of people waiting to get through security, but I was in a hurry and being chased, so it was in everyone's best interest to get me through quickly. The rep spoke to the TSA agent, who in turn, looked up at me, unimpressed. He nodded gruffly, and the rep came back to me. "He'll take you next."

"Thanks, I appreciate that."

The TSA officer finished with the entire family he'd been checking. The first person in line stepped forward, but the officer put his hand up to stop her. He then turned and motioned me forward.

"I was next in line," the older woman complained.

I looked at her apologetically and said, "Sorry."

She gave me a dirty look.

"Madam, please step back. You'll be called in a moment."

"Oh, sure, fine. I've only been waiting for twenty minutes, but please, take him first."

Feeling like a total shithead, I stepped forward. I didn't blame her for being annoyed. I would have been too. Usually, I declined special treatment in the name of humanity; however, I had little choice but to accept this one. As the officer was checking my passport, I heard someone behind me whisper, "Don't you know who that is?"

"Should I?" she said with clear annoyance.

"That's Jake McKallister."

"Who?" she asked.

"The rock star."

I left for the security screening after that and didn't hear her reply. I didn't care. I was just relieved that the man hadn't said *the kidnapped kid* instead of *the rock star*.

By the time I finally got my guitar back, after it had gone through a thorough inspection, I was very happy to see an airline employee in a golf cart waiting for me. At this point, my flight was scheduled to take off in only fifteen minutes.

Lucky for me that I had that cart because my gate was clear around the other side of the terminal. When we pulled up to the gate, everyone else had already boarded, and the crew was waiting for me. Because I'd wanted to see Casey again, I was holding up an entire plane. That was a dick move. I quickly scanned my phone and walked down the ramp to the plane. As I entered the cabin, the flight attendant for first class came straight over to me and helped me store my guitar. It was a small plane, with only two rows of first class. When I looked up to find my seat, one hundred sets of surprised eyes stared back at me, and the whispering started. I slid into my seat, pulled out my phone, and texted *on plane*.

"Oh, sorry," the flight attendant apologized. "You have to turn that off. We'll be pushing back in a few minutes."

"Sorry," I said, sliding it to plane mode and putting it back in my pocket.

∼

The flight to LA took just under an hour. As we waited for the doors to open, a couple of passengers behind me asked for my autograph. I signed several tickets, half a dozen iPhone cases, and an assortment of other items. I posed for pictures with a few passengers who were close enough to get them. The people were very friendly, and I didn't mind, since I had nothing else to do. Plus, I was in a good mood thinking about Casey. I couldn't wait to talk to her again.

I had a nearly three-hour wait for my connecting flight in LA. The minute I stepped out of the plane, an airport representative was there to greet me. I was whisked into a cart and driven to a private lounge. That was one of the perks of stardom. The unwritten rule was, if you had to ask for special assistance, you weren't famous enough to get it. Most places I went, people were waiting to whisk me away to a private location. I never complained. It made my life easier, and also the lives of the other passengers, who were routinely inconvenienced by delays caused from surging crowds and overzealous paparazzi. Still, for a kid from a middle-class background, the first class lifestyle annoyed me at times. There was pompousness to the whole thing. If I could just sit and wait for my flight undisturbed in the waiting area like everyone else, I would. But that had become nearly impossible for me over the last two years. So I accepted the rides and the special services offered to me.

I was taken to a first class lounge and given the 'VIP-est' of the VIP rooms. Whoever got this room tended to be the most famous person in the airport at that moment in time. As long as Angelina Jolie didn't walk in, I was golden. The minute I closed the door to the rest of the world, I felt myself relax. After spending so much time around crowds and my family and wedding guests, it felt good to be alone with my thoughts. Despite my job, being around large groups of people made me anxious.

I spent my time in isolation writing. I needed to get out a song that had been playing in my head for the last few hours. Every word, every lyric, was about love and possibility. Casey's image danced in my head. God, I had it bad.

Just before it was time to begin the boarding process, someone arrived to shuttle me to the gate. This time, I arrived a few minutes before boarding. The minute I stepped off the cart, I was spotted. Sometimes people stayed back and gawked, but today I was almost immediately approached. A group of tourists asked for my picture and autograph. I tried to politely accommodate as best as I could, but the crowd grew pretty large. The airline employee who had accompanied me tried to deflect the crowds, but she was quickly overwhelmed.

One attractive young woman sidled up next to me for a picture and whispered seductively in my ear, "I want to join the mile high club with you." I raised my eyebrows and gave her a sideways look. It wasn't the first time I'd been offered such a thing, but it was the first time I had no interest in even entertaining the thought. Casey was the only girl who held any interest for me anymore. I took a second look at the woman and couldn't help but smile when I thought of Keith's assessment of my groupie-sluts. My brothers thought I sought out these types of women; but in reality, they approached me. The truth was, I had never put any effort into wooing a woman – until Casey came along.

Over the intercom, I could hear a call that first class on my flight was boarding. With the help of the rep, I tried to disengage from the crowd, but they weren't letting me pass. Soon, the airline employee was behind the crowd and no help at all.

"Sorry, I have to board now," I stated, as I tried to push my way toward the gate. No luck. People kept pushing pens into my hand, kept asking for selfies. I put my hands up and said, "Sorry, I have to get on my flight." Still, I was not allowed to pass.

Finally, a gate agent came up to the crowd of people and said, "We are boarding. Please let our guest by, or the flight will be delayed."

I started to make my way forward when someone grabbed my guitar from behind. "I've been waiting," he replied angrily. I stopped and turned. A man in his thirties was trying to pull me back. *Jesus Christ!* This was getting out of hand. I felt my heart rate start to rise.

"Let go," I demanded forcefully.

He didn't release me. I pushed him to let me go, but he yanked harder on my guitar, knocking me off balance. I stumbled backward. Then a young guy who was wearing a US marine's baseball cap pushed through the people and grabbed the man, pulling him off me.

"Back off!" the marine shouted. "Everyone. Back off!" As if by some miracle, the crowds parted, and I had a clear path to the gate. I turned to the guy who'd helped me and thanked him. He just waved it off, still gripping the offending guy's wrist. I walked straight to the flight attendant and handed her my phone. She scanned it and handed it back.

"I'm so sorry," the woman apologized. She looked horrified.

I nodded. I was still shaken by the encounter, but I didn't want to show it. I walked down the ramp, trying to put some distance between the mob and myself. My heart was beating wildly. *That was frickin' ridiculous.* I got onto the plane and was immediately led upstairs. Today of all days, I was incredibly happy to be flying on a 747 with a second floor first class, so I wouldn't have to deal with all the people coming on.

Once the flight had taken off, I finally allowed myself to relax. What had happened in the terminal was excessive and crazy, but it was becoming more common than I liked to admit. I'd always prided myself on my independence and not needing bodyguards.

But I was in a different place now than I'd been when I first started my career. Back then, I was more of an oddity – still in my teens, the kidnapped kid who'd released an unexpected hit song called "Dare." But there was no respect back then, only pity. I was viewed as a one-hit wonder and not a serious musician, and if I was recognized, people usually kept their distance, probably because they were not entirely secure in my sanity.

As that one hit song turned into many, though, the fact that I'd been kidnapped became less and less important, although it was always there, like the elephant in the room. Instead of being mocked as a one-hit wonder, all of the sudden I was hailed as a child prodigy by the powers that be in the music world. With more success came an increase in the crowds. The fear and pity people once reserved for me turned more toward admiration for my musical abilities. My admirers felt freer to approach me. But I'd always been able to move around freely without assistance.

That had all changed with the release of my last album a little over a year ago. It spawned four number ones on the Billboard charts and was the top-selling album of the year. In addition, a song I wrote and sang for a movie soundtrack also became a huge hit. Suddenly, I was catapulted into mega-stardom and found myself for the first time a full-fledged celebrity. Overnight, it seemed, I was a household name, and not just for getting myself kidnapped. To be known for something positive and of my own choosing was liberating. I was no longer just someone's victim. People started to look at me differently. I was a rock star, riding the wave of success. Pretty soon, getting around became more difficult. Fans started approaching me in large numbers, and they were getting progressively younger and louder. Women and girls were throwing themselves at me. I slowly started coming out of my shell, and my confidence soared. Through it all, I'd tried to stay grounded, although I'd be the first to admit to being a spoiled asshole from time to time.

My thoughts returned to Casey. I wondered how she would

deal with all this. I certainly wouldn't willingly put myself into this madness if I wasn't getting a direct benefit from my fame. But what benefit would Casey get? Nothing. It hadn't been the same situation when I was with Krista. She was already famous, and used to the cameras and the crowds. Was it fair to subject Casey to all this? Probably not – but it was beyond my control. Casey would have to make that decision for herself because, after last night, I was all in. Casey was now running the show.

25

CASEY: LONG DISTANCE ROMANCE

I got up early the next morning, giddy with excitement. Just the idea of getting to talk to Jake again gave me shivers. He'd promised to call or Facetime me, and I was holding out hope that he wasn't full of shit. I showered and did my hair and dressed in a cute outfit. I wanted to be prepared for any scenario. At 11:00 am, my phone rang with a Facetime request from Jake. I screamed out my excitement before answering it.

"Hi," I said. "You made it!"

"I did." Jake was smiling.

"What time is it there?"

"8:00 pm. Germany is nine hours ahead."

"How was your flight?"

"I almost got mauled in the terminal at LAX, but otherwise, it was good."

"What the hell? What happened?"

"Just some unruly passengers who wouldn't let me board."

"What do you mean? Were they actually restraining you?" I asked with genuine concern.

"Sort of. This psycho grabbed my guitar and yanked me back.

I lost my balance and almost fell over. I had to be rescued by a marine."

"No way! Oh, my god. That is scary. Are you all right?"

"Yeah, of course."

"You're so nonchalant about it," I said, and then mimicked his tone: "I almost got hit by a bus today... no big deal."

"I hate to tell you this, but getting mobbed is just a normal day for me. I would be scared if I weren't being chased through an airport."

I shook my head. "Your life is crazy, Jake."

"I know," he acknowledged.

"Don't you ever get tired of it? Being stared at and chased?"

"Yeah, sometimes, but I get to do what I love every day. It's a tradeoff that I'm willing to make."

"Yeah, that's true. I feel the same way about accounting."

Jake laughed. "I'm sure you do." His phone bounced a second.

"Where are you?"

"I'm in my tour bus heading to the next venue."

"How long will that take?"

"I have no idea. The concert is tomorrow night. The rest of the guys are already there."

"So you got picked up at the airport in your tour bus?" I asked in surprise.

"Yep."

"That's funny. Why didn't you fly to the city you're playing in?"

"Because then I would have to take another flight on one of those tiny planes. I decided it was safer, and more comfortable, on my bus."

"So you like traveling in the bus?'

"Yeah, it's pretty sick. I have everything I need in here, so I don't usually get bored."

"I've never seen inside a tour bus before."

"You want a tour?"

"Heck, yeah."

Jake started walking me through the bus. We went past some bunk beds into the bedroom. I even made him take me in the bathroom. I was in awe of the opulence. He walked me back through the bus until we were once again in the sitting area.

"Wow, fancy."

"You should see the one I have in the States."

"Better than this?" I asked in surprise, because this was the most luxurious bus I'd ever laid eyes on.

"This is a rental. The one I have in the States I own, so I decked it out."

"Oh, wow, that is something I would like to see. Does it have a bed where we could make out?"

"Why, yes it does," Jake said, giving me his sexy smile. "Now I really can't wait to show you."

Neither could I.

Jake walked back to where he'd been sitting when he called me.

"So how many guys are usually on your bus?"

"Just me."

"I thought tour buses were always loaded with a bunch of sweaty guys."

"Yeah, all the sweaty guys are required to have their own bus... away from me."

"Oh really? Is it in their contract?"

"It's in my contract," Jake said, with a haughty tone to his voice. "My tour, my rules."

We talked for two hours that first day. There was no awkwardness or hesitation. We just talked and laughed as we got to know each other better. Each day, Jake would call me and each day I learned more about him as a person. One thing became perfectly clear to me: Jake was everything I'd ever wanted in a guy. I had fallen so far that there was no getting back up. And I grew closer to him every day. I needed to see him – talk to him –

just to get through the day. Luckily, Jake seemed to feel the same way. When he wasn't performing or doing press, he was traveling from place to place on his tour bus, and during those long drives, we had hours to talk. I was up at all times of the night and was exhausted for my waitressing shifts, but it was worth it. Getting to know Jake was the most exciting and rewarding experience of my life.

He was a rare find, that was for sure. Not only was he beautiful and funny and talented, but also he had this unique way of looking at life that I found incredibly intriguing. To say that Jake was wise beyond his years would be an understatement. It was more like he'd already lived a full life and was halfway through the second. If the masses only knew the depth of the man he was, they would be in awe. It gave me such an incredible sense of responsibility and pride to know that one of the planet's most misunderstood human beings had opened up his life to me as if it was the most natural thing in the world. I had fallen completely and helplessly in love with him. It was a terrifying thought that Jake had the power to destroy me. Incredibly, though, I sincerely believed that my heart was safe in his capable hands.

26

JAKE: LASSEN

After talking to Casey, I was on a high. I bounded around the bus trying to find things to do. I tried watching TV but couldn't concentrate because I kept drifting back to our conversations. I tried writing a song but was too distracted by all the feelings swirling around in my brain. I tried playing the keyboard but was having trouble just piecing a melody together. One thing was for sure: if I didn't sort through my feelings about Casey, my next album was going to be a big pile of crap.

Needing some distraction, I headed to the front of the bus.

"Hey, kid," Lassen said.

"Hey, you want some company?" I asked.

"Sure."

I plopped down in the passenger seat. Lassen looked over at me and furrowed his brow.

"What?" I said, although I knew exactly why he was giving me that look.

"Seatbelt."

I rolled my eyes. "I don't wear a seatbelt anywhere else on the bus."

"I don't care. Up here you wear your seatbelt. How many times do we have to argue about this, kid?"

I sighed and strapped in. Lassen, formally known as Bob Lassen, was my driver, and the only person I allowed to call me *kid*. He was a gruff man in his mid-fifties. Standing 6'1 and weighing around 300 pounds, Lassen was an imposing figure. He rarely smiled and was not big on social interactions. He had a tendency to be short-tempered and judgmental. Needless to say, Lassen didn't have a lot of friends. In fact, I wasn't sure if maybe I was his only friend. During his off months, he never mentioned hanging out with anyone, and while on tour he didn't socialize with the other drivers or crew.

Lassen spent most of his time on the bus. When we were parked, he drew the curtains over the windows and shut the partition to enclose his own space, which included a bed and a TV. I think he did it as much for his own privacy as for mine. People always asked me why I kept someone as anti-social as Lassen on the payroll, but they didn't know the man like I did. They didn't know that Lassen was there for me when I really needed someone. They didn't know he was one of the few people in the world I fully trusted, and they certainly didn't know Lassen wouldn't hesitate to lay down his life for me. Lassen was more than just an employee; hell, he was more than just a friend. Bob Lassen was like a second father.

Lassen had started as a long haul truck driver while still just a teen. He married his high school sweetheart and had three children. As he crisscrossed the country in his big rig, Lassen set up shop with another woman in another household, and had two children with her. Essentially, he had two wives on opposite coasts that knew nothing of each other. He managed to keep up the lie for nearly ten years. When it all blew up in his face, Lassen started drinking heavily and went through a mental breakdown. He lost everything: his homes, his wives, his children, his job. It took him almost five years of alcoholism, depression, and homelessness before he pulled his life back together. Lassen eventually found peace, got sober, and started working for an Asian vacation company, driving busloads of foreigners to American tourist attractions.

After a few years of that, he got a job driving tour buses with my record label and was assigned to me on my very first tour. Back then it was just me, the band hired to play with me, a crew/manager/guardian, and Lassen. All the guys were at least fifteen years older than me and most were openly hostile. Obviously, they didn't like working for a sixteen-year-old kid who, they incorrectly assumed, was a one-hit wonder. They had no respect for me and wasted no opportunity to let me know. It was really a horrible year. I was still struggling with the effects of the crime I'd only barely survived; I was missing my home, my dog, and my family; and the people I was living in close quarters with every single day treated me like shit. To make matters worse, they were all into hard partying, slutty women, and doing drugs. My only escape was up front with Lassen, the only other sober person on the bus.

I'm not sure if it was just a pity thing or what, but Lassen took me under his wing and kept me safe. We talked about a lot of things on those long and lonely nights rolling down the wide-open roads. Things he'd never shared with anyone. Things I had never shared with anyone. The wounded, lost, sixteen-year-old musician and the ex-alcoholic, anti-social, polygamist bus driver. We couldn't have been more different – or more alike.

As my star began to rise and I was able to hand pick who I wanted on my team, Lassen was always at the top of my list. A couple years ago, he quit driving for my label and now exclusively drove for me. It was nice to have someone I trusted with me when I traveled, but just as nice to have that person make himself scarce when I wasn't in the mood for company. Lassen understood that balance without me ever having to say a word.

"How was the wedding?" He asked.

"It was good," I answered in my typical non-committal way. I caught myself and added, "Actually, it was really fun."

"You have a chance to talk to Mitch?"

"A little. He was pretty busy getting married and all, but yeah."

"I hope he appreciated the effort you put in to get there."

"He did," I replied, thinking back to our confrontation. I didn't want to tell Lassen about it because he would get pissed. His devotion to me was absolute. Whether I was at fault or not, Lassen was always on my side.

"How did the song go with Quinn? Did he do a good job?"

"Yeah. He was a little timid singing, but I was proud of him. My mom was ridiculous, taking all these pictures of us together on stage like some momager from hell."

Lassen turned up his lip. It was his version of a smile. "You think he's good enough to break out?"

"I don't know. He's really talented, but he's shy."

"So were you," Lassen commented. "And look what happened."

I grinned, then shifted in my seat. Pain shot through my knee. I must have flinched because Lassen looked over.

"How is it?" he asked, with concern in his voice.

I shrugged. "It's fine."

"No, it's not."

"Then why did you ask?" I challenged.

Lassen shook his head but didn't answer. He knew better than to argue with me about my knee. We sat quietly for a couple of minutes, and I watched the road pass under the tires. I liked driving at this time of night when there weren't many cars out – it was like the roads were lonely and welcoming our passage. I watched a sign go by with these weird lines and what appeared to be a stick figure getting run over. I wondered what the hell it meant. Yet, at the same time, I didn't give a shit. I pondered, as I always did, how Lassen knew where to go in all the foreign countries he drove through. I used to ask him, but he would just shrug and not respond, so I stopped asking.

"I met a girl," I blurted out.

Lassen didn't say anything. I didn't know if he was waiting for me to elaborate or if maybe he didn't hear me. But when I looked over, he nodded. Lassen was a man of few words.

So, for some reason, I just kept going. "She's a college student. She studies accounting. She's really funny, and I think I really like her."

Still nothing? Come on Lassen, you're killing me here.

"And I don't really know what to do."

Lassen nodded.

Jesus. Sometimes he was like talking to a frickin' wall.

"I mean, I want to see where this goes, but I'm not sure if I have it in me, you know?"

"Have what in you?" Lassen finally responded.

I didn't answer because I didn't really know what to say.

Lassen sighed. "I've known you a long time, kid." Long pause. "And you trust my judgment, right?"

My stomach tightened. I wasn't sure I wanted to hear what was coming, but I nodded anyway.

"You have it in you, kid. You've always had it in you."

27

CASEY: FIRST CLASS OFFER

That first couple of weeks after meeting Jake I kind of just floated through my life in Arizona. I had trouble concentrating on anything that didn't have to do with a certain rock star. After an article appeared in the local paper about Jake's visit to Outback Steakhouse, my connection to him spread fast. I became somewhat of a celebrity at work. My co-workers were continuously asking me questions about Jake and the status of our relationship. I was honest when I told them I didn't know. Jake and I had never discussed what we were. Certainly, we were more than friends, but we weren't exclusively together, either. Even my boss, Tony, seemed overly interested in my relationship. He'd been extremely impressed with Jake during his visit to the restaurant, and asked me almost daily when 'my boyfriend' would be visiting again.

Jake's visit had given a boost to Outback Steakhouse, and we were busier than ever. Tony had framed the picture of himself and Jake on the wall for all to see. I was starting to see the side of celebrity that Jake had talked about. It really was a strange phenomenon. Everyone had a story, real or made up, about their connection to Jake. It was sort of funny but also a little disturbing. I understood better why Jake hid who he really was only for those he trusted. There were a lot of people out there willing to take advantage of another for their own gain.

Case in point was the reporter who arrived at the restaurant asking for 'the girl Jake had come to see.' My co-workers pointed her in my direction. I was promptly offered a large sum of money to give an exclusive interview about Jake McKallister. Of course, I would never dream of betraying Jake's trust like that, but I feared the unscrupulous reporter would make up a story and use my name as her source. So terrified was I of this that the minute she left I called Jake and told him what had happened. And shockingly enough, he didn't seem at all surprised. Instead, he apologized for not warning me that this could happen. I was shocked that such an occurrence was common in his world. Jake coached me on how to handle a situation like that if it were to happen again.

We had been talking for two and a half weeks when Jake presented an offer that I couldn't refuse.

"So I was wondering, do you have a passport?"

"Yes, why?"

"You do?" Jake seemed surprised.

"Yes. I'm not a country bumpkin, Jake. I've traveled a little bit."

"I didn't mean it like that," he said sheepishly.

"I know, I'm kidding. So why do you want to know if I have a passport?"

"'Cause I was thinking maybe you'd want to use it."

"Keep talking."

"Well...I have three shows in London this weekend, and I was wondering if you want to come."

"Really?" I asked, lighting up with happiness. He wanted me to visit him!

"Yeah. I could buy you a ticket in one of those fancy first class sleeper seats that you're so jealous of."

"You want me to fly to London?"

"Yeah, why not?"

"Why not?" I laughed. I thought about it for a minute, and realized that I might never get an offer so appealing for the rest of my life. "Yeah, why not?"

"Wait, does that mean you'll come?"

"Heck, yeah, I'll come."

"Great. I'll book your ticket right away so you can't change your mind."

"I don't want to change my mind. But, Jake, just book me a regular seat. I don't want you to spend that kind of money on me."

"Casey, it isn't that much money."

"Yes, it is. I'm perfectly fine flying coach. Promise me, Jake, or I won't go."

"Okay, fine. Should I book you a seat near the bathrooms too so you can be even more of a martyr?"

I laughed. "I'm not Mother Teresa. Just get me a window seat at least a few rows up from the porta-potty."

"Oh, my god, you're so demanding."

28

JAKE: NO TAKE BACKS

I didn't have much time to prepare for her arrival. I'd been thinking about inviting her to visit me, but the London idea had come to me on Monday and I was going to be in town on Thursday. I assumed the chances of her having an active passport or that she would actually say yes were pretty slim, but I had to ask anyway. When she agreed to come with no hesitation, I was psyched – but soon the nerves set in. What if we didn't have the same chemistry in person that we'd had the first time? What if things were awkward between us? Then it would be a long-ass weekend.

29

CASEY: LONDON CALLING

F our days after getting the invitation of a lifetime, I stepped off the airplane in London. It was, by far, the best flight of my life. Jake totally went back on his promise to get me a seat in coach and surprised me instead with that damn luxury sleeper seat in first class. It was hard to be mad at him when I was pampered like a princess for eleven hours. By the end of my flight, I finally understood what all the fuss was about. Flying first class was incredible, and I could definitely get used to such treatment.

A driver was waiting for me with a sign in baggage claim. He loaded my luggage and drove me to a hotel called The Langham. It was a grand hotel in a picturesque area of London. As we pulled up, I noticed a large gathering of people held back by fencing on the sidewalk in front of the hotel.

"What's this?" I asked the driver.

"Fans. Jake McKallister's arriving at the Langham soon."

"Oh… " It was weird now to think of Jake as a celebrity, even though I clearly remembered my reaction to him the first time I saw him. There was this thrill that couldn't be explained. "Do a lot of celebrities stay here?"

"Quite a good number, yes, madam."

"Is it always like this when famous people arrive?"

"No, no... it just depends on who it is. The better looking the boy is, the more screaming girls show up," he said, as if it were common knowledge.

I nodded. How could I argue with that logic? Jake was the best-looking boy I'd ever seen. I paid the driver a tip with the pounds that had been delivered to me by overnight Federal Express. As I walked toward the entrance, I looked over at all the young girls and women, hoping beyond hope to catch a glimpse of the guy I was about to spend the weekend with. It freaked me out a little bit. I'd never had to share a boyfriend with millions of adoring fans.

I checked into my room, a suite overlooking Portland Place and Regent's Park. It was the size of the hotel I'd stayed at for the wedding, but it was clear that this place was much more opulent. Everything gleamed in maple wood, and there was a beautiful freestanding tub in the middle of a marble bathroom. I wasn't sure if Jake would be sharing this room with me or not. In planning the trip, we'd never actually discussed living arrangements, and now I was left wondering.

Because Jake wasn't expected to be in London until the late afternoon, I decided to take a nice nap and a luxurious bath before he arrived. When he finally knocked on the door around 5:00 pm I was on pins and needles. I opened the door and flung myself into his arms.

"Oh, shit," Jake replied, a bit stunned. "Nice to see you, too."

I wrapped my arms around his neck and kissed him heatedly. Once I finally pulled away, Jake said, "Okay... I was worried it might be awkward, but I guess not."

"Thank you. Thank you. Thank you," I exclaimed, giving his lips quick pecks between the thank-yous.

"For what?"

"For bringing me here. For not forgetting me. For being so hot," I gushed.

"I missed you, Casey."

Turned out Jake had his own room, and when he went across the hall to shower, I got dressed up to go out. Jake said he had a surprise planned for me. When he came back, he was wearing a light blue button-up shirt with black jeans and a slim-fitting quilted black jacket that hung open. He seriously looked like he'd stepped off a fashion runway.

"Damn, you're looking fine," I complimented him.

"So are you. I like that outfit."

"This old thing?" I joked. "It's something I threw together at the last minute." In reality, I'd gone shopping before making the trip to London. It had taken me hours to pick out three outfits. This one showed a little Victoria Secret enhanced cleavage, which was what I assumed Jake liked about it.

We walked down the hallway and got in the elevators. "When I came to the hotel earlier, you had a fan club out front."

Jake shook his head, grinning. "Oh, yeah... that. I'm kind of a big deal, Casey."

"Yeah... I'm starting to figure that out," I agreed. "So did your fans go crazy when you pulled in?"

"I came in a back entrance."

"What? Oh, no way. That isn't fair," I complained, punching him in the arm. "Poor girls... waiting out there all day and then you slip in the back entrance."

"Sorry." Jake said as he rubbed his arm. "I had no idea it would bother you so much."

"Do you ever say hi to them?"

"Yeah, of course I do." Jake flashed me a sexy smile. "But I was eager to see you."

"Oh, well, in that case," I flirted. "You're forgiven."

"Would it make you happy if I went out and said hi to them?"

"Actually, that would make me rather happy, yes," I said with a serious British accent.

Jake fixed me with an uncertain stare before shrugging and saying, "Okay, you asked for it."

We stepped out of the elevator, and the hotel manager rushed up to Jake to ask if there was anything he could do to make his stay more pleasant.

"No, everything's perfect, thank you. Could you order me a taxi, though?"

"I'll have one of our drivers pull round. Would you like for me to arrange a discreet pick-up?"

"No, the front is fine. Thanks."

"Sir, there's a crowd gathered outside."

"I know. I plan on greeting them," Jake said.

"Very well, but if you'll be so kind as to give me a moment to gather my security team, things will go much more smoothly for all of us."

Well, it took more than a moment. Jake's tour manager was in the lobby when Jake made the request to greet his fans, so the manager insisted Jake's private security team needed to be out there as well, in order to help control the crowds. So then we had to wait for all those guys to come down from their rooms.

"I shouldn't have said anything," I whispered to Jake. "I feel bad. Now your guys are being inconvenienced because of me."

"Don't feel bad, Casey. It's their job."

"I know, but... "

"Casey," Jake interrupted me. "I pay these guys to drop everything and come running when they're needed. It's what they signed up for. This happens all the time, so stop feeling bad."

"Okay." I smiled. "I'm done."

"Finally." Jake grinned.

Just then we got the all clear. Jake took hold of my hand and led me outside. A roar came from the crowd, followed by shrill screams of "JAKE!" The crowds started pushing on the barriers. It was nuts. The security warned the crowd to stop pushing as Jake headed straight for them.

"Are you ready for this?" he whispered in my ear. I nodded a bit apprehensively this time. This was intimidating. How did he do this every day?

Jake walked up to the throngs of screaming girls and even some guys. He signed their autographs, took pictures with them, and chatted effortlessly. Again I found it interesting that there was no sign of the detached Jake from the rehearsal dinner. He seemed so comfortable around his fans and treated them like they mattered. And they loved it. They loved him. It didn't take much for a celebrity to make others happy. Jake continued to sign autographs and talk to the crowd even after our car arrived. Then abruptly he turned, waved at the crowd, and walked away. Grabbing my hand, he led me to the car and we ducked into the back seat. You could hear the disappointed fans calling out to him as we drove away. I looked over at Jake.

"Trust me, it's best this way," Jake explained. "I hate disappointing people, especially my fans, but I can't stand there all night signing autographs either, you know? And I've learned that if I give them any warning that I'm leaving, they start begging and pushing and crying. Then I feel bad. So I make it quick and decisive, like pulling off a Band-Aid... striking before they even know what's happening."

~

That evening, Jake took me on a private dinner cruise down the Thames River. It was a magical experience. We saw all the lights. Then it was on to the London Eye, where we were given our own private carriage with a large window. We actually didn't get to see too much of the sights, though, since we were making out most of the time. When the ride was over, we didn't want the date to end, so we decided to take a walk. Because it was dark, Jake was more easily able to blend in with a crowd. As we were strolling through the streets, the wind picked up and clouds filled the dark skies. As the first raindrops hit our heads, Jake pointed out a pub and we slipped in. It was crowded inside, with music blaring. We weaved in and out of people until we arrived at the bar. Jake was wearing his jacket with the hood pulled up. No one noticed him.

He leaned over and shouted in my ear, "Gotta buy you your first draft beer."

I nodded. There had to be at least twenty people trying to buy drinks at the bar. Initially, we were completely ignored. Then Jake pulled down his hood, exposing his famous face, and, suddenly, several bartenders were eager to serve us. Jake ordered us two pints of bitter, and we found our way to a little table in the corner of the bar.

"This place is crazy."

"The Brits take their beer seriously."

"Jesus, I guess. That was intimidating. I like how you used your fame to get served," I mocked him in a playful way.

"I know. That was impressive, right? Sometimes it comes in handy. Cheers."

I took a sip and tried not to gag. It was so bitter! I must have made a face because Jake laughed at me. I gave him a dirty look and took a big gulp, then opened my mouth to show him I swallowed it. Jake shook his head in amusement. Maybe it was the atmosphere or the excitement of the pub or my smoking hot date, but about halfway through my pint, I was actually somewhat enjoying my beer.

That is, until the pub owner came over and introduced himself, then set two more pints on our table and told us it was on the house. *Crap! More beer?* Jake shook the man's hand and chatted easily with him for a few minutes before asking about catching a cab. The man offered to call one for us, so Jake arranged with him to have one pick us up in twenty minutes.

Having become slightly tipsy after finishing off my first pint and starting on my second, I got a little 'handsy' with Jake under the table.

"Check, please," he whispered, grinning.

"I'm ready when you are."

"It's considered rude if we don't finish."

"Oh, god. I can't drink another one of these. You have to help me then," I demanded, a bit belligerently.

Jake grinned. "Jesus, I thought I was a lightweight, but you're already an angry drunk, and you've only had a pint."

"It's not that. I just want to get you back to my room so we can have a repeat of our last night together," I whispered.

"You mean on our first date?"

"Uh-huh."

"So wait… does that make this our second date?" Jake teased.

"It does."

"I remember on the first date hearing you say that you didn't have any rules on a second date."

"You heard right," I said, with a clear suggestion in my voice.

Jake picked up my drink and started chugging it. I laughed.

We finished off our drinks and got up to go. Cameras flashed as we walked by, but no one stopped us. While we were in the pub, the storm had settled over London, and rain was hammering down on us as we ducked into our cab. Ten minutes later, we pulled up to the entrance of our hotel. I looked over at the fence that had once held back hundreds of fans and was shocked to find two lone figures standing under a single umbrella in the drenching rain. One looked like a younger girl. I pointed them out to Jake.

"Are you kidding?" he said. "What are they doing in the rain?"

"Waiting for you, I think."

The cab came to a stop, Jake paid, and we got out.

"Jake? Jake?" cried a girl. Jake waved at her as we ran in the pounding rain from the car to the hotel entrance. Once under the awning, Jake said something to the doorman, then put his hand on my back and guided me into the warmth of the lobby.

I started toward the elevator when Jake said, "Hold up a second, Casey." I stopped and looked at Jake in confusion. He nodded toward the entrance. We waited maybe a minute before the doorman escorted in the two people who had been waiting in the rain. They were drenched from head to toe, but the looks on their faces were ones of pure joy and excitement. It was a young teenage girl and probably her mother.

"I hope you weren't out there waiting on me?" Jake asked, with genuine concern in his voice.

"We were," the woman said, shivering. "Not my idea – hers." She pointed to the girl. "My daughter Lauren is just such a huge fan. It's her dream to see you in person, but we weren't able to get tickets to your concert, so I promised to bring her here instead."

Jake turned to the girl and reached his hand out. She took it and looked like she might faint. "Well, then, it's nice to meet you, Lauren."

She made a weird sound and swooned.

"We were here earlier when you came out of the hotel and signed autographs, but we were all the way in the back of the mob. This is the first time we've ever done something like this, so we didn't know we needed to get here eight hours in advance. Anyway, we never managed to get close enough to get your picture. My daughter was just devastated, so I told her we'd wait until midnight, and if you didn't return by then, we were going home. There were lots of fans who stayed, but once the rain started up, people kept leaving until it was just the two of us left," the mom said.

Lauren gazed at Jake in awe. She appeared to be fourteen or fifteen years old. Looking up shyly over her thick glasses, Lauren was an awkward girl.

"I don't know if I'm worth all that trouble," Jake started to say, but Lauren interrupted.

"Oh, you're worth it," she replied timidly. "I can't believe I'm standing here with you right now."

Jake smiled. "Do you have something you want me to sign, Lauren?" Lauren got out a picture inside a plastic bag from under her jacket and handed it to him along with a black sharpie. She was standing there shaking, but it was impossible to tell if it was because of excitement or if she was freezing. Jake wrote something on the picture and then posed with Lauren for a photo.

"You're so talented... and so nice. I'm never going to forget this," Lauren said, with such sincerity that I thought she might cry.

Jake smiled, looking kind of embarrassed. He glanced at me, and I grinned. He then addressed Lauren. "So, your mom said you couldn't get tickets to my show."

"No," Lauren stated, looking forlorn. "Mum tried, but they sold out too fast, and the second-hand tickets were too expensive. But that's okay. This is even better, getting to meet you in person."

"Well, I'd really hate for you to miss out. Maybe you'd like to come as my guest, instead?"

Lauren stood there a moment like she couldn't believe her ears. She was speechless. Then a huge smile broke out over her face. "Really?" she shrieked, unable to control her excitement. "Yes. Yes! I would love to be your guest."

"Great. Then I'll see you backstage, and we can talk more... when you're dry, okay?"

"I... I can't believe this. Yes... Yes! Thank you."

"How about three tickets? So you can bring your mom and a friend?"

Lauren's eyes filled with tears. "You're so nice."

Jake got out his phone and asked the mom, "What day is best for you?"

"We'll make any day work. Whatever's best for you."

"What's your name?"

"Angela Millbrae."

Jake typed her name into his phone and then wrote a few more lines of texts before sending it off. "So, I just put all three dates on here. You can go any of these days... or all of them, if you want. When you get to the arena go to the will call window, tell them your name, and show your ID. They'll give you three VIP passes. If there's any problem at all, ask them to page Sean Wilson, okay?"

"You mean I could go to all three concerts... as your guest?" Lauren asked in amazement. She was looking close to vomiting.

"If you want, sure."

Lauren exclaimed excitedly, "Thank you. Thank you. Thank you. Thank you! You're the best. Thank you."

Jake nodded, smiling. We parted ways then. Jake took my hand, and as we were walking to the elevators, I glanced back to see Lauren happily hugging her mom and Angela beaming with excitement for her child.

As soon as the elevator door shut, I wrapped my arms around Jake's neck and kissed his lips. "Just when I think I can't possibly like you any more than I do, you go and do something sweet like that."

Jake shrugged. "It's not a big deal. I get a certain number of tickets to every show."

"That's not the point. You made that girl so happy."

"I have a soft spot for kids, especially ones who seem vulnerable, like Lauren. Small gestures mean a lot to them."

"So if Lauren had been some pretty and privileged rich kid, would you have given her the tickets?"

"No."

I smiled. "You're a softie, Jake McKallister."

He nodded.

"I like it."

"Yeah?" Jake asked, then kissed me. The elevator door opened on our floor. Jake took my hand and led me to his room. Without a word, he opened the door and steered us in. I ogled him like a piece of meat before flinging myself into his arms. We started kissing roughly. I grabbed at his shirt and pulled it over his head. I stared at his bare chest and took in his tattoos and scars. Damn, he was so sexy. For a brief moment, I felt a bit like Lauren... faint and lucky.

"You're yummy, Jake," I purred, and kissed him. He attacked my neck. I groaned, pushing up against him. I was definitely going to have a hickey in the morning. Jake hastily pulled my shirt over my head as he continued to attack my neck with kisses. His hand snaked around my back and his fingers deftly unfastened my bra. Yeah, he'd done this kind of thing before. Jake's tongue trailed down my neck until it arrived at my left nipple, and he swirled it over the sensitive skin. The next few minutes were spent in that vicinity. Jake's foreplay was so erotic that I was groaning involuntarily. Without warning, he lifted me up and I straddled him as he pushed me up against the wall. We were kissing so intensely that it was almost painful. Jake's fingers dropped down and he began to manipulate me through my pants. My hips were thrusting into him. It was just pure and wild lust. I could not get enough of him. It felt like we were devouring each other. Jake put me down for a minute, and his tongue trailed down my stomach as he unbuttoned my pants and pulled them off me. He then took hold of each of my hands and dropped to the floor on his knees. With my arms pinned to the wall, Jake's tongue was everywhere, swirling along my thighs and over my vagina. I was squirming all over the place, my body convulsing in ecstasy. I screamed and jerked in pleasure. Luckily, I was too horny to feel embarrassed. All the built-up tension and excitement of the past few weeks had brought me to this point – pinned up against a wall having the most sexually amazing experience of my life.

As for Jake, he was totally turned on by my little display of lustful ecstasy. He groaned as he sank his tongue inside me. I gasped. He probed me inside, slowly at first and then progressively faster and more aggressively as my hips moved to his rhythms. That damn tongue was everywhere, licking and flicking and sucking and fucking. I'd never in my life felt anything even remotely like what Jake was doing to me. I shamelessly pushed deeper into him. My legs were shaking so badly that had Jake not been pinning me against the wall, I would not be upright.

At some point, Jake's finger slid inside me, effortlessly finding my g-spot as his tongue attacked my clit. The dual symphony totally destroyed me. I lost it in glorious fashion, bucking wildly before sliding down the wall and landing brusquely on my ass, panting as Jake coaxed the last of the orgasm from me.

When it had passed, I was totally spent. My head was spinning and I couldn't think straight. Jake stood up, lifted my limp body off the floor, and carried me to the bed. I'm not sure if he tripped or if I was too heavy or what, but he unceremoniously dropped me on the bed, falling over the top of me in the process.

"Smooth," I said. We both bust out laughing.

"You like that?" Jake grinned as he adjusted his body until he was lying on top of me. "That move always slays the ladies."

"I'm sure," I giggled, then wrapped my legs around him. His bulge was pushing against me. I groaned as I grabbed his ass through the tough fabric.

"Please, Jake. Take them off," I moaned. Jake rolled off me and pulled down his jeans.

He kept his boxers on as he crawled back on top of me, and our bodies just molded right back together. My hands were groping his ass, my hips thrusting into him. Jake moaned. Slowly, I slid my hands under the fabric of his boxers, and instead of soft flesh, I felt little ridges of raised skin. More scars. He tensed a moment, and I could feel his uneasiness. I wanted to turn his attention back to the task at hand.

"I want you," I whispered in his ear as I pulled his boxers off. My hands were on his ass again. The tension in his body eased and soon he was back to his lustful self, licking and fondling my breasts as I gripped his rigid cock in my hand and manipulated it. Jake bucked against my strokes, then groaned and pulled away. My body went cold.

I put my arms out to pull him back down, but Jake was reaching for a condom. I saw his bare back for the first time. Scars there, too. Jesus Christ. The reality of his life shocked me. What must it have taken for him to survive? But before I could give it another thought, Jake sank back down on me and thrust in. I gasped in surprise at the aggressiveness of his need and wrapped my legs around him, accommodating his impressive girth. Jake drove into me roughly several more times, then calmed down and his strokes became slower and more intense. Everything inside of me quivered in need. He would pull out and thrust in. Slow, fast, hard... my head was spiraling from the ride. But Jake didn't forget me even when his own lust had yet to be tapped. His fingers found my clit and he manipulated me as he tended to his own need. We thrust together for several minutes. He was reading my body for signs, waiting for me to catch up to him. Was this guy for real?

I was babbling incoherently as I approached another orgasm. Jake was panting into my ear. His groping was sending me over the edge. As an earth-shattering orgasm rocked me, Jake let loose at the same moment, and together we rode out the most amazing fuck of my life. It was unlike anything I'd ever experienced. He was just on a different level from any other guy I'd ever slept with – not that I'd had a multitude of partners. Truly, I hadn't known that sex could be like this. Jake was awakening things inside me I didn't know were there.

After collapsing on top of me, he was like a dead weight. I had to push against him. "Jake, you're crushing me."

"Oh, sorry," he said, still panting, as he slid off me and rolled onto his back. We both just lay there, breathless.

Finally, I found my words. "Wow."

Jake was silent.

"I mean, wow-wow, right?" I rolled to my side to look at him.

Jake turned his head and a smile spread across his face.

"You're like… good at this," I said, and then joked, "Way to go, stud."

"Yeah, well, I jacked off earlier so I'd be more impressive."

"Shut up." I gaped "You didn't."

Jake smirked.

Yeah, he probably had.

"Well, no matter how you got there, it was amazing… thank you."

Jake turned to his side. "You're thanking me… for fucking you?"

"Uh-huh." I smiled and kissed him.

"Well, then, I'm not really sure how to respond to that… you're welcome, I guess. It was my pleasure."

We woke up the next day to angry banging on the door.

"Oh shit!" Jake swore as he shot up. "What time is it?"

More banging. "Jake! Open up!" Jake got up, wrapped himself in a towel that was hanging over a chair, and stumbled into the other room to open the door.

"What the hell are you doing?" I heard the angry voice question.

"I overslept. No big deal."

"You overslept?" he mimicked angrily. "No big deal? You do realize that you have press in one hour, right?"

"You work for me, Sean, so lay off the attitude," Jake snapped back. I smiled. Jake didn't take shit, and that impressed me. If that were me getting yelled at, I would have been apologizing profusely. Everything was silent for a few seconds.

"Shit, sorry, Jake. I was just freaking out a bit. When you didn't show up at the venue for the sound check and you wouldn't answer your phone, I got worried. It's not like you. I had to drive all the way back here."

"I'm sorry about that. I made a mistake. I'll jump in the shower now. Let them know I might be a bit late."

"Okay," I heard Sean reply.

"And Sean?"

"Yeah?"

"If you ever talk to me like that again, you won't have a job. You hear me?"

"Yeah, I do. I'm sorry."

Jake shut the door and I heard him walking back to me. He had a sheepish smile on his face. "Why is it that every time we sleep together people get pissed?"

"I don't know, but it's annoying," I said, rolling my eyes. "I mean, why can't people just be happy that we're getting laid?"

"I know." Jake agreed, then bent down over me to give me a kiss. "I was really hoping for a quickie this morning, but sadly, that isn't going to happen. So get your ass out of my bed and get ready. You have fifteen minutes."

CASEY: CONCERT CHERRY

Jake and I arrived at the O2 Arena in London about forty-five minutes late for his press tour. I watched him get interviewed a dozen times about his music and tour. He even helped with a giveaway – the grand prize being two VIP tickets to the night's concert. I found it interesting that no one asked him about the kidnapping, probably the single biggest story Jake could tell. It must have been a condition to his appearing on their shows that they not ask him personal questions.

Once Jake finished with the interviews, we went to another room where a buffet was set up. Jake and I had slept through breakfast and lunch, so we were both starving. We went back for seconds before going to the dressing room. Jake led me to a couch, and we both dropped down into the comfy cushions. Jake sat glassy-eyed on the couch.

"You look tired," I commented.

"I'm exhausted. Someone kept me up all night."

"Hey, you weren't complaining last night," I reminded him.

"Who said I was complaining? I was simply stating a fact."

"Well, unfortunately, I have plans to keep you up all night tonight, too."

"Promise?"

"Promise." I lifted my little finger like I was pinky swearing, and Jake hooked his finger in mine.

"Aren't you tired, too?" Jake asked.

"Yeah, but I don't have to perform a concert for 20,000 screaming fans."

"I'll wake up by then...hopefully."

"Hopefully? That doesn't sound promising. Let's take a nap. Sleeping is my favorite."

"Oh, well in that case... " Jake smiled and readjusted his body on the couch. He held his arms out and I sank into him. We fit together so perfectly. I cuddled in his arms, and within minutes we were both asleep.

We were awakened, for the second time in a day, by an older woman. She was much nicer than the manager had been, gently nudging Jake awake.

"Sorry, sweetheart. I hate to disturb you, but you have to get dressed."

"Okay," Jake replied a bit groggily. "Can you give me a minute?"

"Of course, hon. I'll be just outside. Come get me when you're ready," she responded sweetly. She walked out and shut the door behind her.

"Who's that?" I whispered in my sleepy haze.

"Marcy. She works for me."

"What's her job?"

"Her job title is Mom."

"Mom?" I laughed.

"Yeah. She just kind of does everything a mom would do. She keeps the household running smoothly. She takes care of anything that has to do with the band and preparing us to go on stage. And then after the show, she takes care of all that, too. She's older, her kids are grown, and she likes traveling with her husband, so it works out perfectly."

"Damn, that sounds like an awesome job."

"She likes it." He shrugged. "Personally, I wouldn't want to be picking up all our sweaty clothes and washing them, but Marcy doesn't seem to mind."

"I'd work for you."

"Oh, really? What would your job be?"

"I'd be your manager, for sure."

"My manager?" He grinned.

"Yeah, so I could boss you around."

"Oh, of course."

I snuggled into Jake's body feeling happier than I'd ever remembered being.

"Did we actually sleep?" he asked.

"I think so." I yawned.

Jake reached over and grabbed his phone to check the time. "Oh, shit. We slept for almost an hour."

"Really? I must have fallen asleep immediately."

Jake tapped my ass. "Time to get up."

"I know. It's just so cozy here." I pouted, but nevertheless, I untangled myself from his arms and pushed off him to stand up. Jake gasped in pain, grabbing his knee.

"Oh, my god," I cried. "Are you okay? What did I do?"

"Nothing. It's okay. I have a bad knee. You just kind of clipped it on the wrong spot," he said, playing it off like nothing was wrong.

"I'm so sorry. I had no idea. You should have said something, so I would have been more careful," I replied. I felt horrible about hurting him.

"It's fine, Casey. I didn't mean to react like that."

"Yeah, would you please try to keep your pain levels down when I'm with you?" I joked. "Geez. You're so selfish."

Jake winced. Pain was clearly still swimming through his eyes as he rose from the cushions, but he wrapped me in a hug.

"I could nap with you all day," he said, changing the subject.

I wanted to ask him more about his injury, but I could tell he didn't want to talk about it, so I let it go. I looked up at him, and his famous face struck me for a moment. I felt a rush of excitement course through me. I leaned into him and gave him a long, adoring kiss.

"What was that for?" he asked.

"Do I need a reason?"

Jake smiled, then walked over to let Marcy back in. It was our last moment of peace because the minute the door opened, it was a dizzying parade of people coming in and out of the dressing room. Jake seemed completely calm and collected. He was obviously used to all the activity. About a half hour before show time, a line of British celebrities came in to meet Jake. Some I knew and some I didn't. Some brought their children. Jake was friendly and engaging, and I was impressed with his ease. He introduced me to everyone by just saying, "This is Casey." Of course, the celebrities were nice to me, but they were only interested in Jake. Once he'd greeted all of them, the doors were shut and final preparations were made. Sean, the tour manager, appeared in the doorway. He'd been coming every five minutes for the last half hour.

"You're on in five," he said this time.

Jake just nodded and turned to me. "Are you ready?"

"Me? Are *you* ready?" I laughed.

"I do this every day, Casey."

Jake took my hand and strode confidently down a long corridor. There were people moving all around us. Some ignored Jake, like his crew who were used to being around him, but those who worked for the venue stopped and stared and whispered when Jake walked by. As we came to the end of the hallway, a door was opened and Jake was directed through it. The minute we stepped through, a burst of excitement erupted from a line of people held back by barriers. Behind them, I could hear the roar of the crowd in the arena. I spotted Lauren and Angela, and the two people who had won tickets earlier in the day, as well as about thirty more people. This was obviously the VIP section.

"Do you know any of these people?" I asked.

"No. These are mostly giveaways or family of someone who owns the arena or has lots of money to buy their way in," Jake whispered. "And now I have to schmooze with them." He grinned at me and squeezed my hand before letting it go and walking over to the line of VIP ticket holders. He went down the line signing autographs and taking pictures with the lucky fans. Jake paid special attention to Lauren and her mom. Lauren hadn't brought a friend; I hoped that didn't mean she didn't have one to bring. I felt sad for the sweet girl. But there was only happiness on her face now. Jake thanked her and her mom for coming – as if they would really want to be anywhere else on this earth at that very moment.

"On in two," came a shout. The lights went off in the arena, and the crowd roared. Jake signed autographs for a couple more people, then waved at the VIP holders as he walked toward the stage. He grabbed my hand as he passed by. I smiled up at him, proud to be with him. We stood at the edge of the stage. The noise was deafening. A sold-out crowd of thousands, all waiting for Jake... and he seemed completely calm. Jake chugged a bottle of water, then jumped in place a few times.

"Thirty seconds," Sean called out to Jake.

"Oh, my god. This is crazy. I can't believe you're going out there. I would be completely terrified. Are you even nervous?" I asked in awe.

A smile spread across his face. "You know, it's just another day at the office."

I shook my head. The spotlights went on and crisscrossed the stage. The roar of the crowd got even louder. Music started playing. The screams were riotous.

"Okay, gotta go to work." Jake grabbing my face and kissed me playfully before being handed a microphone and singing the first notes of a song. The crowd went berserk. Jake walked a little way out on the stage, but he was still shrouded in darkness. He sang a couple more lines to the song before the lights suddenly went on and all hell broke loose. The roar was ear-splitting. Jake confidently strolled out onto the center of the stage to the overwhelming approval of the crowd. He started to belt out a song I had heard many times. *Good god.* I felt light-headed. How the hell had I ended up here... with him? I was practically trembling with amazement. I'd never felt more privileged or more ecstatic.

I watched with fascinated elation as Jake sang his first few songs. He was so comfortable on stage, and had an energy and excitement to him that was incredibly endearing. I was amazed at how he talked to the audience – like they were his friends. I could see why he was a star. His fans loved him. From the side of the stage, it was hard to see. I wanted to go more toward the front so I could watch his performance better. I looked back toward the VIP section. Everyone was gone. I saw a side exit and figured the crowd went out there. I walked over to a guard.

"Excuse me," I said. "Does that exit lead to the front of the stage? I was hoping to get a better view."

"There's no better view than the one you just had," the guard said smiling. "But yes, if you go through that door, there's a small viewing area in the front. It's the next best thing."

"Do you mind?" I asked.

"You're the girlfriend. You can go wherever you want."

I smiled at that. *Yeah, I think I just might be the girlfriend.*

I found my way out to the front of the stage and watched the rest of the concert from there. It really was an incredible experience. I now totally understood the draw and why people paid the money they did to see artists perform live. It was such a rush. The music; the lights; the hot singer. I was mesmerized. I walked over to

Lauren and Angela, and they welcomed me. They were curious about my relationship with Jake and oohed and ahhed when I told them how we'd met and that this was the first time we had seen each other since. I stayed next to them the entire show, and we had riotous fun singing together along to the hits. By the end of the concert, I found mother and daughter so endearing that it felt like I had two new best friends.

I wasn't sure if Jake was aware that I'd left the backstage area until toward the middle of the concert when he was performing on the long stage that went between the crowds. He was reaching down touching people's hands. I extended my arm with the same excitement everyone around me had and jumped up and down screaming. I actually didn't even think Jake knew I was there until, just before touching my hand, he made eye contact, grinned, and then jerked his away like we were playing slaps. I laughed out loud as Jake took off to perform on the other side of the stage.

The music came to an end in a flurry of lights and fire and sound. I mistakenly assumed the show was over, and asked Lauren and Angela if they were going to head back to the VIP area. They informed me they were going to wait for the encore. I'd completely forgotten about that and felt like an idiot. I tried to play off my musical ignorance with an "Oh, yeah," but mother and daughter still laughed at me. I stuck my tongue out at them playfully. I really was having the best time. Jake came back out after that and sang three more songs before it was over. I was drenched in sweat and ecstatic over what I'd just been part of. I was just so incredibly impressed with Jake. His talent was undeniable.

The fortunate crowd I was with made their way back inside to the VIP area. The friendly guard I'd spoken to earlier was no longer there. He'd been replaced by a new guy.

"Um... I'm... uh... I'm Jake's girlfriend," I said awkwardly. It felt like I was lying or bragging when I said those words. Jake and

I had never discussed if I was his girlfriend or not, but it seemed to be an accurate assessment of our relationship. Jake wouldn't have invited me here if he wasn't at least somewhat interested in me. But for a guy who could have anyone he wanted, maybe I was reaching for things when I identified myself as his girlfriend.

The suspicious guard looked my sweaty, disheveled self up and down. I could not have been real impressive-looking at this point, so I totally got why he wouldn't believe me. "Where's your artist pass?"

"I don't have one. I came with Jake."

"Uh-huh, but I can't let you through... not without an artist pass. You actually shouldn't be back here at all without, at the very least, a VIP badge," the guard said gruffly. "I'm going to have to have you escorted out."

"She's Jake's girlfriend." Lauren stepped in for me.

"Well, then he should have given her a proper pass," the guard said sternly.

"He's expecting me back there," I tried.

"Look, maybe you're his girlfriend, maybe you aren't. It doesn't matter. If you are his girlfriend, then you'll appreciate that my job tonight is to protect your boyfriend. And that means that no one goes back to see Jake McKallister without the appropriate authorization."

What he said made sense, but that didn't solve my problem.

"Can you call Jake?" Lauren asked me.

"Good idea," I said, and took out my phone. I dialed Jake's number, but there was no answer. I hung up.

"He didn't answer?" Lauren asked. I shook my head. The guard was on his phone now. I was starting to get a bit worried. Was he calling for backup to have me thrown out?

"What about Sean Wilson?" Angela suggested. "You can ask to have him paged. That's Jake's manager, right?"

"Yeah," I said, thinking that after what happened this morning,

Sean would probably rather see me thrown out of the arena than let me back with Jake again. "I should do that."

Just then my phone rang. I looked down and it was Jake. Thank god. "Hello?"

"Where are you?" Jake asked.

"In the VIP section. The guard won't let me through. Apparently, you were supposed to get me an artist pass or something... and now they want to throw me out of the joint."

"Hold on. I'm coming to save you," Jake said, with an amused voice, and hung up. I stood there a couple of minutes before the door opened and Jake walked through.

The VIP crowd saw him too and cheers went up. Jake waved at them as he walked up to the guard, who looked instantly worried.

"She's with me," he said.

"Oh, sure... of course. I'm sorry about that. She didn't have a pass. For your protection, I'm strictly forbidden from allowing anyone through without one. I hope you understand," the guard stumbled, clearly trying to explain himself.

"No, I get it. You're doing your job. It was my bad," Jake said and patted the guard on the shoulder. A look of relief crossed the guard's face, and he let me through immediately. "She's always wandering off. I can't leave her alone for a second," Jake said, smiling mischievously at me.

"Oh, shut up," I replied, then turned to Lauren and Angela and hugged them both. "Thanks for helping me."

"Of course," Angela said, turning toward Jake. "This girl is a real sweetheart."

"Yeah, she's okay," he said off-handedly.

I gasped like I was offended, then started laughing. Lauren and her mom joined in.

"And thank you again for the opportunity to come backstage. It's just been such a special night," Angela said.

"I'm glad you had fun. Are you coming again tomorrow?" Jake asked.

"If you don't mind," Angela said.

"No, not at all. I need someone to keep watch over Casey here." Jake waved in my direction.

"I think someone better get his girlfriend a pass for tomorrow," she countered.

"Thank you," I said throwing my hands up in the air before addressing Jake. "See this is all your fault."

"Yeah, yeah." He agreed, nodding his head. "You ready?"

"Yep," I said, turning to Lauren and Angela. "See you tomorrow."

Jake grabbed my hand and led me back to the dressing room.

"I'm going to have to keep better track of you," Jake said sternly. "What were you doing on the other side, anyway?"

"It was my first concert, remember? I wanted to really experience it."

"And you couldn't do that from the side of the stage?"

"Well, I couldn't see your pretty face," I teased. Jake crossed his eyes and tried to make himself look ugly. He failed miserably. "Oh, and by the way your, hair... that man bun thingy. Was that for my benefit?"

"Maybe," Jake replied coyly. "Actually, I was about to take a shower when you interrupted me with your whole 'damsel in distress' bit."

"Again – your fault, not mine."

"How was I to know you were going to wander off and get lost?"

I was going to argue with him some more, but he was just too cute, so I kissed him instead. "Get on with it, then."

"With what?"

"Your shower. I want to get you back to the room so I can do something special for my hero."

"Okay, yeah... I like the way you're thinking."

CASEY: NO REGRETS

I woke Sunday morning snuggled next to Jake. This fairytale weekend was going to come to a close soon, and I wanted to squeeze in every last second with him.

"I don't want to leave you," I said, tilting my head and giving him a kiss. "I'm going to miss you so much."

"Don't, then."

I propped myself up on one elbow and looked at Jake. "Don't what?"

"Don't go. Stay with me."

I stared at him a second, then shook my head in shock and said, "Really?"

"Yeah, why not?"

God, how I wanted to say yes! But I had responsibilities back home that I couldn't just walk away from. "I wish I could – I really do – but I have to get back."

"Why?"

"I have to work, Jake. The money I make during the summer pays my rent and helps with my college all year long."

"Okay, so what do you make working all summer?"

"You mean how much money do I make?"

"Yeah, for the entire summer."

"I don't know. If I'm lucky, I get about six."

"Grand?" Jake asked in surprise.

"No, dollars. Of course, grand," I answered, sarcastically.

"Wow."

"Wow, what?"

"I'm just...uh...out of touch with how much people make."

"What? Is that like nothing for you?"

Jake had the decency to look embarrassed and shrugged.

I considered his reaction to my shitty pay. "Why? How much do you make?"

"I don't know. A lot," Jake answered, casually. "I have an idea. What if I give you six thousand dollars to cover the summer, and then you can stay with me?"

"You're going to pay me to stay with you?"

"Well, when you put it that way, it makes me sound like a creeper."

"I'm kidding," I said, laughing. "That is such a sweet offer, Jake. It really is, but I can't take that kind of money from you."

"Why not?"

"I don't know. It's wrong. Besides, I wouldn't be able to pay you back."

"It's not a loan. I don't do loans."

I looked at him. Was he seriously offering to pay all my expenses?

"I want to say yes so bad, Jake, but I just can't. I'll get fired, and I need that job once school starts."

"If they fire you, I'll personally go to the manager and beg for your job back. Tony and I are like this," Jake said and intertwined his fingers together. "I can be pretty convincing when I want to be."

"I'm getting that."

"You can't blame me for wanting to spend the summer with my girlfriend."

"Am I?" I asked, my heart skipping a beat. It was the first time he'd called me that. "Your girlfriend?"

"Seriously? Do you require a formal request?"

I shrugged, letting him know in no uncertain terms that yes, I did require it.

"Okay, then. Casey Caldwell... will you be my girlfriend?"

I paused and hesitated, making him wait. "Well... I don't know... " I then squealed and wrapped my arms around him. I gave him a long, lingering kiss before saying, "I would love to be your girlfriend. Nothing would make me happier."

"Damn, you were making me sweat there for a minute."

"Yeah, right." I rolled my eyes.

"So what do you say? Are you going to stay with me or what?"

"I would love to, Jake but, seriously, I can't."

"Why not? What's more important than us being together?"

That gave me pause.

"Just say yes – like you did when I asked you to come to London. "

"That was for three days. Do you have any idea what my parents would do to me if I stayed here with you all summer?"

"It's nothing they won't get over... eventually," Jake said. "If I'd listened to everything my parents wanted me to do, I wouldn't be here today."

"Yeah, but I'm not brave like you."

"Look, Casey. I like you... a lot. This – what you and I have going here – it's good. You can't deny it."

"I don't deny it. It's incredible."

"So then we owe it to ourselves to see where this goes. If we separate and live our own lives for the next three months – right now, at the very beginning of our relationship – can we really get it back to where it is now?"

"I... I don't know." Now I was worried. I didn't want to lose him. If I left, would he move on?

"All I'm saying is, there's an easy solution for us to be together.

I have the money. We pay your rent for the summer and put the rest aside for college. I'll beg your employer to give you your job back, and your parents will eventually forgive you. If you don't want to stay with me, that's one thing... but if you do, there's no logical reason why you can't." Jake was clearly pleased with his argument, and I couldn't help but smile back. What the hell was I thinking? The guy I was falling in love with was asking me to stay with him for the summer... to go on tour with him... any girl's dream scenario. How could I say no to that?

"You'll beg for me?" I asked coyly.

"Of everything I just laid out in my speech, *that* is the only thing you got out of it?" Jake laughed.

I nodded innocently.

He sighed. "Yes, Casey. I will beg for you."

"Then how can I refuse?"

"You'll stay, then?" Jake's face lit up. He looked so happy.

"I'll stay," I said and hugged him.

"Damn, you didn't make that easy."

"Nothing in life worth fighting for is easy."

Jake smiled, then leaned over and kissed me. "No, you're right about that."

We kissed for a few minutes before I pulled away and said, "I do have one condition."

"You have conditions now?" Jake asked, looking slightly worried.

"I only have clothes for three days. You're going to have to take me shopping, *Pretty Woman* style."

Jake grinned. "Deal."

I had to make the call to my parents. I was worried what their reaction would be. What I was doing – taking this chance with the guy I liked – it was totally out of character. I waited until I thought my parents would be awake before making the call. Thankfully, my mom answered.

"Hello?"

"Mom, it's me."

"Oh, thank god! I've been trying to call you."

"Yeah, sorry, I've had it on airplane mode so I don't get charged for calls. Is everything okay?"

"Yes, of course. I was just so curious, and I'm so happy to hear your voice. Your name didn't come up on my phone."

"Oh, that's because I'm actually calling from Jake's phone. He has an international plan, so it doesn't cost me anything to call from it."

"You're calling from Jake McKallister's cell phone?"

"Mom, you don't have to use his full name," I laughed, even though I myself routinely used it.

"I know, it's just weird for me to hear you say it so casually, like he isn't some huge celebrity," my mom said in awe.

"Well, he's not just a celebrity anymore. He's my boyfriend."

"Your boyfriend?"

"Yep. I made him formally ask me, and then I accepted," I announced proudly.

"That's my girl."

I laughed.

"Wow, I just can't believe it," she said, with incredulity in her voice.

"Honestly… neither can I. It's all so unreal. I keep asking myself how I got so lucky to snag a guy like him. I have to look around to see if I'm being punked or something. I seriously have no idea what he sees in me, but I'm not complaining."

"What do you mean 'what he sees in you'? You're a beautiful, funny, intelligent woman."

"Aw, thanks, Mom."

"But you guys are moving really fast."

"Not really… I mean, I've already known him for about a

month."

"Yes, but you've only spent five days together. Is that really enough time to know you want to date a person?"

"If Jake asked me today, I'd marry him tomorrow," I said, only half-joking. "He's that amazing. You just have no idea."

"But you can't possibly know that much about him."

"That's the thing, Mom. In other relationships I've had, we went on dates and slowly got to know each other; but with Jake, because we couldn't do anything else but talk, everything was accelerated. I literally spent hours upon hours just talking to him. I know way more about him at this stage of our relationship than I've ever known about any of my other boyfriends."

"Have you talked about the kidnapping?"

"Mom, no, of course not."

"He's never said anything?"

"No, why would he?"

"I'm just saying – there's a whole huge chunk of his life that he hasn't shared with you. And that isn't small stuff. Trauma like that stays with you and has a tendency to surface later in a relationship."

"And if it does, we'll deal with it. But honestly, Mom, everything Jake has been through in life made him the man he is today, and he's special. He has this extraordinary strength and wisdom that I've never seen in a guy his age. You'll understand when you meet him. I'm telling you, Mom. Jake is the catch of a lifetime."

"You're gushing," she said, laughing. "You sound head over heels for him."

"I am. I can't help it."

"Well, he sounds amazing."

"Oh, he is. I can't wait for you to meet him. You'll love him."

"I'm sure I will. I can only imagine how exciting it all is for you. But here's what I'm worried about: you're falling so hard, so fast. Are you sure he feels the same way? Otherwise, your heart is going to be broken."

"I know, that scares me, too. But I don't want fear to keep me from taking a chance at love. Jake is worth the risk to my heart."

"And does he feel the same way about you?"

"I honestly think he does. Jake isn't shy about expressing to me how he feels. He's told me he's falling for me. Jake acts like he's the lucky one to be dating me, and not the other way around. He just makes me feel so special."

"I hope I get a chance to meet him someday soon."

"You will."

"So, then, you guys are talking about moving this relationship forward once he comes home from tour?"

"We really haven't talked about it. I think it's just assumed."

"How could you make that work, with him in LA and you in Arizona?"

"I don't know, but I think we'll figure it out. This feels like a mature, grown-up relationship. We have great communication."

"So I take it that the two of you have been... uh... romantic?"

"Mom? Geez."

"Just tell me that you were smart and safe."

"Mom? Of course."

"Okay, sorry. I had to ask."

"No, really, you didn't," I scoffed.

"Oh, don't be such a prude," she said dismissively, "So what time is your flight again? When do you leave London?"

"Um... actually, that's why I called. I'm not flying home today."

"What? Casey, you only got those three days off."

"I know. I called my manager today and told him I wouldn't be back this summer."

"This *summer*? You quit?"

"Jake asked me to stay with him. I'll get to tour with him and see Europe. It's the chance of a lifetime, with I guy I really like. I know this is totally out of character for me, but I owe it to myself to see where this goes."

"Oh, Casey."

"Mom, please understand... I love you and respect your opinion, but I'm staying in Europe with Jake for the summer, and nothing you say will change my mind."

"And how are you going to pay for this European trip?"

"I'm not; Jake is."

Mom sighed, and then said, "This relationship... maybe it's going somewhere, I don't know, but what I do know is that your future is your education. You need that summer money to help us pay for your school. Your dad and I can't pick up the slack. You know after his surgery he hasn't been able to work."

"I know, and I promise you, my education won't suffer. I'll be back in mid-August to prepare for the upcoming school year, and I'll graduate next spring as planned, I guarantee you that. As for the money, Jake's taken care of it. He transferred $6000 into my bank account this morning. That will pay the rent for the next two months and keep me solvent until I can start school again."

"He loaned you $6000?"

"Not loaned – gave."

"He just gave you $6000?"

"Yes, Mom. He's a multi-millionaire. $6000 is like pocket change for him."

"Casey... please... this is... think about what you're doing. You're too smart to throw everything away for a guy. I see the appeal. I do. He's handsome and charming. He's famous and he's a rock star. I get all that. But, honey, he's a fling."

"That's the thing. I don't think he is. I think... I think he's the one."

My mom didn't reply to that statement. After a few moments of silence, I said, "I'm sorry if you don't agree with my decision, but I'm not changing my mind. Maybe I'll get hurt, but I'm willing to take that risk. I feel... I feel like if I don't take a chance on this relationship, I'll regret it for the rest of my life. When I'm fifty and looking back on the summer of my twenty-third year, what would I rather that memory be of? Traveling through

Europe with my incredible boyfriend, or working shifts at Outback Steakhouse? I love you and Dad. I want you to be happy and support me, but ultimately it's my decision, and I've made it."

There was silence on the line. "Mom?"

"I'm here."

"Are you okay?"

"Yes. Just a little shocked."

"Don't be mad."

"I'm not mad... it's just... It's hard to support this when we haven't even met Jake. He's a musician, Case; they don't have the best reputations. What if he gets tired of you and just abandons you somewhere in Europe? How would you get home?"

"Jake is sincere, and he would never leave me stranded. Can't you please trust my judgment? You always said I had a good sense for people. Why does Jake have to be any different?"

Mom seemed to be considering what I said. Finally, she sighed and said, "You're right. You have good judgment, and if you believe in him, then we just have to trust that you're making the right decision. I just hope he understands how much you mean to us."

"He does."

"I need to be able to get in touch with you at all times."

"Jake's going to put an international calling plan on my phone. That way, if you call me from the home phone, there'll be no charge to you."

"Is he there now?"

"Jake? Yeah, he's in the other room."

"I want to talk to him."

"What? Mom, no."

"Yes, Casey. Put him on the phone."

"Oh god," I said, under my breath, and opened the door. I walked into the other room and faced Jake. "My mom wants to talk to you."

Jake's face dropped. He looked horrified. I almost laughed. He mouthed, 'What do you want me to say?' I shrugged as I put the phone on speaker.

"Hello?" Jake said into the receiver.

"Hi, Jake, this is Linda, Casey's mom.

"Hi."

"I asked to speak with you because I need you to make me a promise."

"Okay."

"No matter what, you'll keep my daughter safe."

"I promise I will. We'll be staying in nice hotels in safe areas, so you don't need to worry. You have my word that nothing bad will happen to her."

"Good, because she means the world to us."

"I know she does. And she'll be safe with me."

"Okay. And if anything happens and you're no longer together, you have to promise me that Casey will have the ability to get to an airport and fly home to us."

"Don't worry about that. Casey has an open-ended airline ticket in her name. She can go home whenever she wants."

"Oh… That's good."

"Listen, Linda. I just want you to know that I wouldn't ask Casey to stay with me and upend her life in Arizona if I didn't really care for her. I know how this probably looks to you, because of who I am, but I want you to know that my intentions are honest."

"Okay…well that makes me feel better."

"And when I get off tour, I'll come and meet you."

"I look forward to that. And Jake, I'm counting on you to take care of my daughter."

"I know and I will. I promise."

"Okay. Thank you. Goodbye, Jake."

"Bye. Here's Casey again."

He handed the phone back to me with a thumbs-up.

32

JAKE: HEADED IN THE RIGHT DIRECTION

I couldn't believe how happy I was when Casey agreed to stay. The last couple of days had been beyond my expectations. Not only did we get along great, but the sex was incredible. For the first time in my post-Ray life, I felt excited about my future – like I was headed in the right direction with a woman who made my heart beat faster and made me feel like I was a pretty frickin' awesome guy. And the more time I spent with Casey, the more confident I felt about our relationship.

Yes, the nagging voice in the back of my mind was still there, but I was holding it back as best I could. What had my therapist said back when I was a kid? It was a choice. How I decided to live my life was up to me. If I wanted to be miserable, then I would be. And for some reason, that was the path I'd chosen for myself; I couldn't even remember why. But I didn't want that any longer. I wanted to be happy. It was a choice.

Before my Sunday concert, I took Casey to Harrods so she could buy some clothes. Although I offered to buy her anything she wanted, Casey was careful with her choices. This was a girl who was used to living on a budget, who didn't feel comfortable spending too much money, and I respected her wishes. After the store, we headed to the arena. This last concert was a matinee performance and then we would be back on the road for the UK portion of the tour.

33

CASEY: THE TOUR BUS

Jake's final London concert was a blast. Because Angela and Lauren had come faithfully to every show, Jake surprised them with artist passes for the final performance. They were able to hang out in the green room and watch the last concert from the side of the stage. To say they loved it would be an understatement. They gushed over both Jake and me – but mostly Jake. They told him over and over how wonderful he was. I certainly didn't disagree. When it came time to say goodbye to Angela and Lauren and head on to the next city, I was surprised that I was actually sad to see them go. They were always going to be a part of this incredible weekend.

But, for me, the fun wasn't ending. I got to spend the whole summer touring with my rock star boyfriend! I was still wrapping my head around it all. Jake wanted me to stay. He wanted me to be his girlfriend. I felt so happy... and lucky. So when I boarded Jake's tour bus for the first time at the arena after the show, I was giddy with excitement. No matter where our relationship took us, I felt certain that this would be the adventure of a lifetime.

The bus was seriously amazing. Walking inside it was like

walking into another world, one where rich people lived. The interior was dark wood with black leather furniture, granite counters, and hardwood floors. Recessed lighting illuminated the interior. Every convenience of home was aboard this bus. I walked around in awe. This place was incredible. Jake's room had a queen size bed, exercise equipment, and a bathroom, and shower. He had a keyboard and recording equipment and various musical instruments. It was so 'rock star' cool.

"Wow, Jake. I'm impressed."

Jake smiled. "Your bag should be in the bedroom."

"Yeah, I saw it."

Just then an older, sour-looking man came up behind Jake: Lassen. Jake had warned me about him and said he might not be very personable to me. He explained that Lassen was very protective and that I shouldn't take it personally if he wasn't overly friendly.

"Casey, this is Lassen, my driver."

"Hi." I smiled widely and went in to shake his hand.

He took it and said gruffly, "Good to meet ya."

"You, too."

"I'll stay out of your way as much as possible."

"And I'll do the same," I promised.

"I can work with that," Lassen replied.

We took off for the next city that night, a quick two-hour trip to Birmingham. The buses would stay the night in the arena parking lot. I asked Jake why he stayed in a hotel some nights and in the bus others. He explained that it depended on how much time would be spent in the city and how long the bus ride was between the cities. Usually, if it was two nights or more, they got a hotel room.

"But…"

"I know what you're going to say," Jake stopped me. "We're going to be in Birmingham for two nights."

I was impressed. That was exactly what I was going to say.

"Since we just had three nights in a hotel and will have two nights in a hotel at the next stop, we decided this one would be a bus leg. A few years ago, pretty much every leg was a bus leg, but now that I have multiple concerts in different cities, we're getting spoiled."

"Right, because traveling in luxury buses is such a drag," I sighed.

"This one isn't. But imagine one with twelve other guys. I guarantee you, it isn't luxury," Jake said, wrinkling his nose. "Most of the time the toilet is clogged. There's a permanent sweaty sock smell in the air, and the couches – I'm not kidding – they're sticky."

"Eww... God. Gross."

Jake shrugged. "I'm just saying."

"Guys are disgusting... present company excluded."

Jake nodded. "Hey, I'm starving. You want me to make you a sandwich?"

"We just ate," I informed him. There was always a big spread in the green room after the concert.

"I know, but I'm hungry again. I burn like a thousand calories on stage. Those lights are so damn hot."

"I'll make you a sandwich," I offered.

"You know how to cook?"

"You don't cook a sandwich, dork."

"I know that." He rolled his eyes. "I meant in general."

"I can cook the essentials. And I make a mean salad. Otherwise, I'm useless in the kitchen. Why? Can you cook?"

"I can make pretty much anything out of a box or a bag," Jake said proudly.

"Nice. So multi-talented."

"Uh-huh, right."

Jake and I made his sandwich together, but he got more on it than he bargained for, since I kept adding stuff from the refrigerator just to annoy him. We kind of got into a little bit of a food fight when I 'accidentally' flicked a piece of turkey onto his arm. That turkey was then thrown back and forth a number of times before Jake caught it and shoved it in his mouth. Hey, at least he wasn't a germ-a-phobe.

As Jake ate, we sat at the little table and talked. We had such an easy rapport. Jake was never boring; I felt like I couldn't learn enough about him. That was so intriguing to me. Before I knew it, Lassen was pulling into the arena.

"Damn, that was fast," I marveled.

"Yeah, this was a quick one. The trips aren't all so short. Wait until we have to drive from Glasgow to Dublin. We have to drive all the trucks and buses onto ferries."

"We're going to Scotland and Ireland?" I asked incredulously.

"Yeah," he responded offhandedly, apparently not nearly as impressed as I was. "I have the itinerary if you want to see it."

"For sure. I'm jealous. You get to see so many historic places."

"Honestly?" Jake shrugged. "I don't usually see much more than the inside of the arenas in the cities I visit."

"No way? Jake! Why not?"

"Because this is my job. I'm not on vacation."

I shook my head. "Well, I hate to tell you this, buddy, but when we get to Paris, I'm going to the Eiffel Tower – with or without you."

"Well, I hate to tell you this, Casey, but I've already played in Paris."

"No, you haven't."

He nodded.

"Well, shit." I frowned. "I need to see that damn itinerary."

"I'll figure out a way to get you to Paris," Jake promised.

"I was just kidding. Anywhere we go will be exciting for me. This is all just one giant adventure."

Jake smiled. "So… "

"So what?" I grinned back.

"You want me to give you a tour of the bedroom?"

"You already gave me a tour."

"I meant a tour of the bed."

"Oh, in that case… "

We retired to the bedroom and were making out when I straddled Jake's naked body and stared down at him adoringly. Scars crisscrossed his chest, but instead of being unsightly, they gave Jake a tough, powerful aura. I ran my finger over one. Jake tensed, looking embarrassed, then put his hand on mine, stopping me.

"Don't," he said.

"Jake," I protested.

"Casey… just" – The look in his eyes gave me pause; he was giving me a warning that I was crossing the line – "don't."

I stared at him a second and considered telling him he shouldn't be ashamed of his scars, but thought better of it. Jake seemed to want to avoid the topic altogether. My little lapse in judgment had totally ruined Jake's erection. He was all tensed up, so I reached back and grabbed his dick. It didn't take long for it to get back to where it had been before I touched his scar. I lowered myself onto him and slowly rode him. As I did, I lay down on him and started kissing his neck.

"I think you're perfect," I whispered in his ear.

Jake didn't respond. He didn't look at me. He just aggressively flipped me over and had his way with me.

34

JAKE: WORLDS COLLIDE

Dammit, I felt like a fucking idiot. Casey hadn't meant anything when she touched my scar. I'd snapped at her and acted like a freak. I wished I could take it all back and pretend that I was unaffected by something as innocent as her touch. But it was out there now, like the giant elephant in the room. It made me sick to watch the best thing that had ever happened to me collide with the worst thing that had ever happened to me – Casey's purity vs. Ray's depravity. Those two worlds didn't belong together. But, whether I liked it or not, they would have to co-exist. I had to figure out a way to be okay with it.

I knew Casey was. I truly believed she was there for me and that she didn't care about my scars. But somehow her acceptance of me and the fact that she thought I was perfect made me feel even more flawed. What kind of a man was I if my girlfriend had to reassure me that I was 'pretty' every time we had sex?

35

CASEY: WRITTEN ALL OVER HIS SKIN

I woke up around seven in the morning. Jake was still sleeping. I lay there awhile, thinking about what had happened last night. His reaction had taken me by surprise. Whatever had happened to him, Jake was obviously not okay talking about it.

I looked at my sleeping boyfriend. Although I knew he wouldn't appreciate it, I traced his body with my eyes anyway. His scars entranced me. There were a few that were deep and jagged, and the skin around them folded into one inverted pocket. These scars were encased in tattoo designs, as if he were trying to minimize their shocking existence. It was obvious something violent and terrible had happened to cause scars like that. Had he been stabbed? Other scars were long and shallow, as if the tip of a knife had been dragged across his skin. Still others were sharp and deep, like something had struck him. And then there were other smaller and singular scars, like the faded ones on his cheek, in one eyebrow, and along his jawline. Jake's wrists, ankles, legs, and butt were also marked up, but those scars were faded. I wondered if he'd had laser surgery or even skin grafts to reduce the scarring. I knew a little about that sort of stuff because a friend of mine had been in a serious car accident as a child and had undergone a series of treatments to diminish her scars.

My eyes focused on his knee. It was a mess. Deep jagged scars crisscrossed the area. Those looked more like surgical scars, but I couldn't be sure. I could see now that his knee was swollen. No wonder he'd yelped in pain when I'd accidentally touched it. When I finished categorizing all of Jake's visible scars, I tried to wrap my brain around what must have happened to him all those years ago to cause such trauma to his body. I also couldn't help but wonder what that would do to a person's psyche. How could someone go through something as horrible as what Jake clearly had, and not come out of it without internal scarring? Was Jake hiding that part from me? Was my mom right? Was the trauma of what he'd suffered going to come back to haunt us some day?

After waiting nearly a half hour for him to wake up, I finally had to get up and use the bathroom. Once I was done, I glanced over – he was still out. I wanted him to sleep, so I pulled on a sweatshirt, just in case Lassen was around, and tiptoed into the living room area of the bus. Lassen's partition was closed. I relaxed. I made some Keurig coffee and picked up the itinerary. It was the size of a book. Curious, I opened it up and read through the list of all the cities we would be visiting, getting more excited by the second. Then I flipped the page and there was an overview of the first city on the list. It told a little about the history of the city, listing notable restaurants and interesting places. I continued flipping through the book until I came to Birmingham. I read through the summary of the city and was immediately interested in Aston Hall. Jake had told me he didn't have anything to do until 1:00 pm that day, so I decided I was going to take him sightseeing.

I returned to the bedroom and climbed onto the bed where my snoozing guy lay. Careful to avoid his knee, I kissed him all over, like a dog licking his master.

"Wake up. Wake up," I sang out. "Everybody wake up."

"Oh, god," Jake groaned. "You have terrible pitch."

I nudged him again. "Get up. We're going sightseeing."

Jake rubbed his eyes. "We are?"

As it turned out, taking Jake on an outing wasn't as easy as hopping in a car. Advanced preparation was a must. When I told him where I wanted to go, Jake called his tour manager and told him to make it happen. I could only imagine the look of annoyance on Sean's face when he heard that. I told Jake that it wasn't a big deal, and we didn't have to go, but he insisted that he too wanted to see Aston Hall.

Two hours later, the museum director was leading us on a private tour through Ashton Hall. The Hall had been built in the early 1600s and had been a private home until it was turned into a public park and museum in the 1800s. The director carefully avoided the other tourists as she guided us through the mansion, even taking us to rooms that were off limits to the general public. I wondered if Jake always got this kind of special treatment. Not that I was complaining; I was directly benefitting from his celebrity status. No driving. No waiting. No being herded around like cattle. Hell, yeah!

After touring the mansion, Jake and I strolled through the lush gardens alone. It was a chilly day, so he was wearing a baseball cap with a hoodie pulled up over it, and no one gave him a second look. We walked the gravel paths and marveled at all the colors. Together, we tried to determine what flowers we were looking at. Jake was no help at all. I teased him relentlessly, and he seemed to love it. He was so relaxed and acted like he had nothing better to do than hang out with me all day, even though the reality was that in seven hours he would be performing in front of thousands of screaming fans.

Much to Sean's relief, we made it back on time. Jake had a number of things he needed to do, so I retreated back to the bus. Lassen was in the living room when I came in, and he immediately rose to leave.

"You don't have to leave on my account," I said.

"I always give Jake his privacy when he's on the bus."

"Jake's not here."

"I was on my way out anyway," he said, and quickly exited.

I had to admit I was glad he left. I still didn't know the man and felt a bit uncomfortable around him. Jake trusted him, but that didn't mean I automatically did. I had to get used to having another person in the bus with us. I mean, geez – Jake and I were having sex only a few feet from where Lassen slept. It was a little weird, if you asked me.

After the concert, we hung out in the green room for a while, and Jake introduced me to the roadies. Nearly every one of them was long-haired, tattooed, or both. Pretty much every other word out of their mouths was the f-word, and they knew how to pound down the liquor. They were kind of like a rolling band of rock n' roll carneys. Most, maybe even all of them, were older than Jake. Some even looked to be in their fifties and sixties. They all had rough exteriors, but most of them were really nice guys. And they loved me. Who knew that my particular brand of crude humor would play so well to the roadie crowd?

Jake hung back and let me take the lead. He seemed to be enjoying himself, but he definitely didn't act the same way with these guys as he did with his brothers. I also noticed that the roadies seemed a little reserved with him – like when one guy made an offensive joke toward me, he stopped himself mid-laugh and looked over nervously at Jake. I wasn't sure what their relationship was like with him, but it was clear that Jake was in charge, and they looked to him for direction. When Jake laughed at the joke, everyone else seemed to almost exhale in relief.

I also was introduced to the band members and the two backup singers, Carmen and Sasha. They were older, in their thirties or forties, maybe. They seemed very interested in me, asking all kinds of questions about my life. I got the impression they were sizing me up, determining if I was worthy of dating

Jake. I wasn't sure if I was passing their test, but after a while, they stopped grilling me.

Carmen and Sasha weren't the only women I met. A couple of the band members had girlfriends traveling with them, and one of the guitarists had his wife and kids with him, although I didn't get to meet her because she was putting the kids to bed. I tried to befriend the two girlfriends, but they weren't very friendly. They kept giving me these looks. Then, at one point, I heard one of them whisper, "She's not even that pretty."

That would become a recurring comment that I would learn to accept from Jake's fans. They were extremely critical of the way I looked. It was like the minute they saw my hand in Jake's, it was war. The sideway glances, the nasty comments, and even the physical jostling really hurt my feelings those first few weeks. But Jake was always there, protecting and defending me. More importantly, he was there to steadfastly justify my significance in his life to any detractors. He tried to ease the sting by telling me that the fans were jealous of me because I was beautiful. But I knew the truth: they were jealous of me because I had him. Over time, I cared less and less what they thought of me. After all, I was the one who got to roll around on the bed with their fantasy every night.

That first night in Birmingham was a blast. We spent so long in the green room talking and telling dirty jokes that the arena staff finally had to ask us to clear out so the janitors could clean up.

After Birmingham, Jake's traveling crew of nearly sixty people boarded one of eight buses and twelve semi-trailers and continued on through the UK. The trucks and buses would roll into town, and it would take about six hours to assemble the stage and props. Local crew was on hand to help with the setup, and everything ran like clockwork. I'd never considered what it took to put on a tour the size of Jake's. It really was a massive production. I was amazed at the sheer number of staff needed.

There were stagehands and sound engineers and lighting guys; there were security personnel and truck drivers and musicians. And Jake, at twenty-three-years-old, was their boss. Although he had Sean to run the day-to-day logistics, Jake still had a hand in almost everything. I watched him handle stressful situations with a maturity that belied his years.

While we were in the UK, Jake played concerts in Manchester and Sheffield in England, and then on to Glasgow and Dublin. In every city, Jake and I would go sightseeing. Although at times sneaking him out unseen was challenging, we both came to love our little outings. Some days Jake wouldn't be recognized at all, and other days he'd get mobbed. After one particularly gnarly fan encounter in Ireland, Sean insisted we have security with us, and Jake reluctantly agreed. I felt safer knowing there were people there to back us up if we got into an unmanageable situation. As strong and fearless as Jake was, even he could not handle an unruly mob on his own.

That first month I was with Jake was a whirlwind of activity. After the UK stops, we drove through the Channel Tunnel into Europe. Jake performed three to five concerts a week and was in a new city or country every three days on average. I saw and experienced things I'd only read about or seen on TV. Ancient cities, soaring cathedrals, million dollar yachts, and movie stars. It was really a dream come true, and to witness these things with Jake by my side made me feel so fortunate to be living this incredible life.

Jake, for all his world travels, had really never ventured out to see the cities he was touring in. With me by his side, he seemed eager to experience everything these spectacular cities had to offer. There were times that we would sightsee all day and then Jake would have a concert that night. We'd come back to our hotel or into the bus after the shows and be exhausted but exhilarated. Inspired by our experiences, Jake would stay up late into the night writing. Our special moments were becoming songs. I loved watching him work. He was such a creative person. The way he blended words together and crafted the sounds mesmerized me. He was truly an artist.

Although things could not have been going better in our relationship, there was always that nagging worry that he was holding back on me. I had to wonder if it was my own imagination talking. If his horrible past hadn't been written all over his skin, would I still think he was being guarded? Probably not.

The truth was, Jake had been more open and affectionate with me than any other guy I'd ever met. Did it really matter than that he never spoke of the unimaginable trauma that had shaped his young life? Was he not entitled to that one privacy? I sighed. At this point, it didn't matter what he was hiding from me because I was completely and hopelessly in love with him. Every time he walked in a room, my heart swelled with love. He took my breath away every single day. And in the bedroom, I'd become a person I didn't recognize. I should have been embarrassed by my lack of inhibition, but Jake never made me feel self-conscious. The way he looked at me, the way he treated me, always made me feel so desired.

As far as I could tell, Jake was falling for me too, but he hadn't expressed it in exactly those words. And there was no way I was going to tell him how I felt until I knew for sure where his head was. Again, that uncertainty crept into my mind. I wished I could just sit him down and ask him all the burning questions I had. But Jake had a way of avoiding questions he didn't like. Case in point: his knee. It was clearly getting worse with each performance. The swelling was noticeably visible now, and Jake winced in pain when he didn't think I was looking. I'd asked him several times what was wrong with his knee, but Jake always found a way to distract me – namely by being so damn sexy and flirty that I would forget my head if it wasn't attached.

One night while we were traveling on the bus, I was lying

with my head in his lap when I asked, "So, how exactly did you become a rock star?"

"I have no idea."

"I mean, like, how did you get into the music business?"

"Oh... When I was sixteen I entered a talent competition. I was spotted by a music scout and offered a record contract."

"Well, that was easy."

Jake flashed me a sly grin.

"What?"

"It would have been easy if I hadn't lied about my age and who I was."

I stared at him in surprise and then sat up. "Okay... you have my undivided attention now. I want to hear this story."

"Your head was in my lap. I'm pretty sure I already had your full attention," he said, trying to distract me with his sexiness. *Nope. Not this time, buddy.*

"Just tell me, Jake," I demanded.

"It's a long, boring story. You don't want to hear it, trust me."

This was what I was talking about – little moments like this when I would ask a seemingly innocent question and it was met with resistance. "Actually, I do. And who cares if it's long? We have an eight-hour drive."

Jake sighed. It was obvious he didn't want to talk about it. After a pause, he finally said, "Okay, so remember when I was that weird homeschooler?"

"Yes... but I was kidding about that," I giggled.

"No, you weren't." Jake grinned. "Anyway, I was obsessively practicing for hours and hours every day. I was playing the piano and the guitar, I was writing songs and singing. My mom kept telling me I had a nice voice and that my songs were good enough to sell... but, you know, she's my mom. She's supposed to say shit like that. I wasn't sure if she was just trying to boost my confidence or if I was actually somewhat good. The only way to find that out was to compare myself to others. So without telling my parents, I sent in a tape and was selected to perform in a talent competition in LA."

"Why didn't you tell your parents?"

"Because I didn't want anyone that I knew to be in the audience, just in case I really sucked and totally embarrassed myself."

"Makes sense."

"Yeah, but there was a problem with that logic," Jake continued.

"What was the problem?"

"I was sixteen and couldn't sign up for the competition without parental consent. So I went and got myself a fake ID, making myself eighteen. That way I was a legal adult."

"Even though you weren't."

"Right, but that isn't the point. I also changed my name on the fake driver's license to Jake Ryan."

"Your middle name?"

"Yeah."

"Jake Ryan is a way cooler rock star name than Jake McKallister," I teased. "Just saying."

"I know. That would have been sick, right? I wish I could have kept it."

"Why didn't you?"

"Well, I'm trying to tell you. Stop interrupting." Jake sighed. "I warned you it was a long boring story."

"Sorry. Go on."

"Anyway, I performed in the competition, and as it turns out, there was a music scout in the audience. He came up to me after the show and asked me to come to the studio to sing that same song for his boss. A few days later I went to the studio, performed it, and was offered a contract. But I signed it as eighteen-year-old Jake Ryan."

"Isn't that a federal offense?"

"I don't know. Probably." Jake shrugged. "But I was underage so maybe it didn't count."

"And your parents didn't know?"

"No. They had no idea."

"Wait –how were you getting to LA by yourself?"

"I drove. I was sixteen. I had a driver's license. The studio was only a forty-five-minute drive from my house."

"Oh, okay."

"So anyway… Jesus Christ, you interrupt a lot," Jake teased.

"I know. I'll try to shut up."

"Thank you. So *anyway*, apparently the music label does a routine background check on all their artists. They took my fingerprints. I didn't think I was in the system, but it turned out I was, so about three weeks later, while I was in the studio laying my first tracks, the results came through. Not only did they find out I was not eighteen, but they also figured out who I really was."

My eyes grew large with surprise. Okay, this story was getting good. "What happened? Were they mad?"

"Furious! The producer and the studio lawyer drove me back to my house. They informed my parents what I'd done and told them to be prepared for a lawsuit."

"How did your parents react?"

"Obviously, they weren't real happy with me." Jake shrugged.

"I bet. So what happened? Did you get sued?"

Jake gave me a look like I was interrupting again, but then he grinned.

"Sorry. You know I can't keep my mouth shut," I laughed.

"I know. You just can't help yourself."

"Seriously. I can't," I agreed.

"Okay, so, when we didn't hear from the studio for about two weeks, we thought maybe they forgot about suing me. But then we were called into the record company and met with the head honcho – the CEO of the record company. He said he'd listened to a couple of my tracks and was impressed. He then pulls out a new contract all ready for my parents to sign."

"Well, that was good, right?"

"No, because the asshole didn't care if I could sing. Offering me that contract had nothing to do with my talent or lack thereof. He was just smart enough to realize that he could make money off who I was. Basically, his intention was to exploit my past in order to sell albums. I saw right through him and flat out fucking refused to take his offer. Then a couple weeks later, we got a big envelope in the mail. All that was written on the cover letter was 'Choose.' One set of papers was a declaration of intention to sue, and the other was the record contract."

"No way," I said, shaking my head in disbelief. "You were blackmailed, Jake."

"Oh, trust me, we knew that. But my options were limited. I either signed with them as Jake McKallister, or I went to court as Jake McKallister. Either way, I was going to be paraded through the media again. In the end, I chose what I thought was the lesser of two evils," Jake said. I waited for him to elaborate, but he didn't.

"What you thought?"

"Yeah, those people made my life miserable."

"So... I mean, you were basically forced into this life."

Jake nodded. I couldn't read his expression, but he seemed subdued.

"You're probably the biggest rock star in the world, and you never even wanted to be one?"

Jake stared at me and then shrugged. "No, I wanted to be one. That was, like, my dream when I was little. I just didn't want it the way it was being offered to me. I'd finally faded out of the public eye, so the last thing I wanted was to be stared at again like some circus freak."

I nodded. "But you had no choice?"

"No. I mean, I did it to myself by lying and then signing that contract in the first place. But I was just a dumb kid. They took advantage of that."

"That's really terrible, Jake. I'm sorry that happened to you."

Jake glowered at me for a second and then said, with some edge in his voice, "I didn't tell you that so you'd feel sorry for me, Casey."

"And I wasn't feeling sorry for you, Jake," I responded with the same edge. "I was pissed that some asshole CEO blackmailed you into doing something you didn't want to do. There's a difference."

Jake stared at me for a long, uncomfortable moment, and then his shoulders drooped and he said, "I just really don't like pity."

"And I've never pitied you," I said, trying to control my annoyance. "It pisses me off that you'd even think that. You see how I look at you, so don't insult me."

Jake raised his eyebrows, surprised at my burst of anger.

"Asshole," I couldn't help but add.

A smile spread slowly across Jake's face.

"I swear to God, Jake, if you laugh at me, I'll hitchhike home."

"To America?" he grinned.

I gave him a dirty look, but I could feel the anger melt away. Jake's smile just slayed me.

"I'm sorry, Casey. I was an asshole. You were right. You're always right."

"And it would be wise for you to remember that."

He smiled again. I smiled back.

"You're a jerk sometimes."

"I know."

He grabbed me and pulled me into his arms and attacked my neck in kisses. "Forgive me," he said, kissing me for real this time.

When our hot kiss ended, I asked, "Was I mad at you?"

Jake nuzzled my neck.

"So did you win?"

"Win what?" Jake asked, confused.

"The talent competition. Did you win?"

"Oh," Jake said, shaking his head. "No. I came in third."

"Third?" I scoffed, giggling. "God, what a loser! I mean you weren't even second best."

Jake laughed along with me. The tension was completely gone.

"Are you still with that studio?"

"No. As soon as my contract expired, I got myself a nice, new contract with their biggest competitor." Jake smiled.

"Nice. What happened after you signed with the first studio?"

"I recorded my album, and when it was released three months later, the studio basically promoted me as 'Look at the poor kidnapped boy. Isn't that cute? He's trying to sing.' It kills me to say this, but that guy was right. The publicity stunt worked. People were curious. Interest was high. My songs started playing on the radio, and then they started selling. I probably wouldn't be where I am today if they hadn't used the kidnapping as a marketing tool. But I still think it was a shitty thing to do."

"I agree. And you told me that you went on tour by yourself."

"Yeah, I did. When my album started selling, the studio hastily threw a tour together. My parents couldn't figure out a way to travel with me without losing the house, so the studio convinced them to let me go with Steve, my assigned guardian. He was supposed to be like a makeshift parent – you know, oversee my homework and make sure I ate and slept and got to the shows on time. But Steve was basically the opposite of that. His only concern was getting me to each performance. He didn't give a shit about my homework or if I ate or slept. I heard him, on several occasions, brag about getting paid to be my babysitter, but in reality he was just getting paid to party. The studio also hired a group of guys to be my band, and they were all way older than me and hated playing backup for a kid they considered to be just a novelty act. To make matters worse, I was traveling the country on a tour bus with a bunch of guys who regularly drank, did hard drugs, and routinely brought skanky hookers back into our cramped living quarters. I would be, like, lying in my bunk trying to tune it all out but, I mean, it was like a frickin' brothel in the bus. And Steve was as bad as the rest of them. It was a really bad situation for anyone, much less a sixteen-year-old."

"Why didn't you tell anyone? Your parents?"

"I wasn't close with my family."

"You weren't? Why?"

"It was complicated back then... and, I don't know, I guess I just kind of felt like I deserved the misery."

I grabbed his hand and shook my head. I wanted to show him sympathy, but I didn't want him to confuse it with pity. "I wish I'd been there for you."

"I'm glad you weren't there. You wouldn't have liked me much back then."

"Yes, I would have."

"No, Casey, you wouldn't have. I promise you. I was so fucked up."

"So how did you get from there to here?"

Jake stared at me for a second, then looked away. He avoided my question by saying, "It wasn't all terrible on that first tour, though. At least I had Lassen."

"Lassen drove for you back then?" I asked in surprise.

"Yeah. He and I were the only two sober ones on the bus. I spent most of my time up front with him. He became my guardian and watched over me and protected me. Without him, I don't know if I would have made it, honestly."

"Huh. Wow," I said, shaking my head. I had a whole new respect for Bob Lassen.

36

JAKE: LOSING CONTROL

For one month Casey and I had been traveling through Europe together, and it was hands down the best time of my life. I was in love with a beautiful woman. Casey was everything I could ever have asked for. But just as I knew it would, reality finally caught up to me. My life was quickly spiraling out of control. I was trying hard to hold it all together, but the pain at times was unreal, like jagged knives stabbing into my knee. And as my knee swelled to twice its size, so did my anger and hate. I was powerless to stop the demons surging through my body and soul. Ray was everywhere. His evilness invaded me. I was descending back into Hell.

I was losing her. Day by day I could feel her slipping through my fingers. Soon she would be gone, and I would have no one but myself to blame. If I couldn't make it work with Casey, I would never be able to make it work with anyone. The realization that I was doomed to a life of loneliness hurt more than I ever thought it would. Now that I'd had a taste of what love was, I knew how much I would miss it.

Two times in the last week I'd experienced flashbacks during sex. The first one came after her hand ran down my back in a way that made my body revolt in panicked horror. Suddenly, it was not Casey in bed with me. I gasped in shock and pulled away violently. She apologized profusely, assuming she'd accidentally brushed up against my knee. I didn't correct her. How could I explain to her that, for a brief moment, she'd become my rapist?

After that, I tried to avoid intimacy with her. But Casey didn't understand what was happening to me. My excuses would only hold for so long. The night before, when she'd initiated sex in the most erotic strip tease ever, I couldn't control myself. I loved her. My body wanted to be with her. I gave in to her need... to my need. I kept telling myself it was going to be okay, but I was too much in my head. Too worried about another visit from the demon. And Ray did not disappoint. *You like that, don't you, boy?*

This time I jumped up from the bed angrily. *I fucking hate it!* I wanted to scream at him. I was shaking with uncontrolled fury. *I hate it! I fucking hate you!* My fists were clenched, and my face was contorted with vengeful rage.

Upon seeing Casey's horrified face, I battled my way out of the flashback. Shame filled my soul. I was not worthy of her. Tears filled her eyes. Casey finally understood that more was happening than just my knee.

"What was that?" she questioned, looking dismayed.

I didn't answer her as I pulled my pants back on.

"Jake. Please. What's happening? Just talk to me."

I shook my head, too furious with myself to even come up with a plausible explanation.

"Did you... did you just have a flashback?" she asked.

Her question floored me. How? How did she know?

"What do you know about flashbacks?" I spat out.

"Just what I learned in psychology class."

I looked at her. Psychology class? "Casey, you have no frickin' clue what you're dealing with."

"So tell me."

I laughed, bitterly.

"Jake, I feel you pulling away. I want to... "

"What? You want to help me? Is that what you want?"

"I...yes. Is that so bad?"

"It's not bad. It's just not going to happen."

"Why not? When the flashbacks come, tell me what to do."

"I can't predict them, Casey."

"But there's something that triggers it."

I looked at her and shook my head.

"You know what triggers it, Jake. I can tell you do, but you won't tell me," Casey said, her voice cracking. Tears were now rolling down her face. "Why now? You weren't having them before."

"I've had them before. I just haven't had them with you."

"So what has changed? Is it the pain? I can see how much pain you're in, Jake. It's getting worse."

I sighed and dropped my shoulders. "This is who I am, Casey. That guy you met? That was me pretending to be the guy I wanted to be. I'm a fucked up piece of shit. I have nothing to offer you. This is it!"

Casey didn't say anything for a long time. She got dressed. I stood there. Finally, she uttered, "How convenient."

"What?"

"I said...how convenient," she repeated, but now there was an edge to her voice.

"What's that supposed to mean?"

"You tell me you don't like being pitied, but when it's convenient for you, look at you playing the pity card."

I didn't respond. She wasn't wrong.

"Don't try to get me to feel sorry for you, Jake McKallister. I won't. I know who you are, and to suggest that I don't is just insulting. This isn't who you are. This is you in pain. This is you afraid. You're giving up on us because it's easier for you to call it quits than to face the things that torture you. I won't give up on you as easily as you're giving up on me!" Casey cried, and then stomped out of the room.

37

CASEY: THE PAIN OF KNOWING

We didn't talk the rest of the night and into the next day. I was terrified. Jake was definitely pulling away from me. The past week, in addition to the pain he was clearly in, he'd also seemed sad and despondent. I wanted to help him, but he was so defensive. And I wasn't the only one noticing the change in Jake's demeanor. He was short-tempered with his crew, with Sean getting the brunt of his anger. Jake seemed focused solely on getting through his concerts, which clearly were becoming more difficult for him.

Sean and Lassen and I had tried to get him to see a doctor, but he refused, saying he knew what was wrong and there was nothing that could be done about it. Anytime I brought up his injured knee, Jake rebuffed me. I realized that whatever had happened to his knee was somehow related to the kidnapping, but so far, that area of conversation was off limits to me. Last night's confrontation was proof of that. Something I did triggered a flashback. The look on his face when he jumped out of bed took my breath away. It was pure, agonizing fear. He was clearly reliving something terrible that had happened to him. My heart ached for him in a way I couldn't explain. I loved him so much, his pain was my pain. I wanted desperately to help him, but I also understood that his pain might run too deep to ever be assuaged. Just thinking about it made me cry.

That day we kept to ourselves. Jake had things to do to prepare for his concert that night, and I stayed on the bus and read a book on my iPad. An hour before the concert, I went into the arena and walked into his dressing room. Jake was slumped miserably in his chair. He looked visibly ill.

"Are you okay?" I asked, alarmed.

Jake didn't answer.

"Jake?!"

"I'm fine," he mumbled.

I walked over to him and felt his forehead with the back of my hand.

"You aren't fine. You're burning up," I said in concern.

Jake stood up and limped over to his bag.

"You can't perform tonight, Jake. You're sick."

"I'm not sick. It's my knee. The swelling is causing the fever," he said as he dumped a few ibuprofen pills in his hand and swallowed them down. "It's not a big deal. I can perform."

"If you have a fever due to the swelling, Jake, that means you have an infection. You need antibiotics."

"Oh, I wasn't aware you were a doctor," he replied in a condescending tone.

Anger gripped me. I glared at him. "Asshole."

Jake shook his head like I was being annoying.

"Oh... I'm sorry. Am I being an annoying bitch? Forgive me for being worried about you. But, you know what? If you want to pass out on stage, be my guest. I'm going back to the bus," I said, as I opened the door.

"Casey..."

"No. You can talk to me when you can treat me with respect," I spat, as I stomped out of the room.

I breezed past a surprised Sean, saying loudly enough for him to hear me, "He has a fever. He's burning up and can barely walk. Someone needs to do something. He won't listen to me."

"Wait, Casey... where are you going?"

"Back to the bus. I'm not going to watch him pass out on stage," I said as I stomped off.

I went back to the bus and was changing into my sweats when I got a text from Sean.

"He won't listen to me either. I'll keep an eye on him during the show."

"He's burning up."

"I know. I can tell."

"He needs to drink a lot to stay hydrated," I texted back.

"Okay, I'll make sure he does."

"Thanks, Sean."

"He doesn't mean it, Casey. It's the pain talking."

"I know."

"Considering what he's survived, it's amazing he isn't angry and withdrawn all the time."

"Yeah, I know."

"But Jake really likes you, Casey. I've never seen him happier. Don't give up on him."

It touched me that Sean cared. We had become unlikely friends in the past couple of weeks, and both of us were worried about Jake's decline. At first, I assumed Sean was only worried because it was his job to worry, but now I understood that he genuinely cared about Jake's well being.

"I'm not going to give up on him. I promise."

"Good. And I'll talk to him... convince him to see a doctor."

"Okay, thanks."

Later that night, after the concert, Jake stumbled in. Somehow he'd managed to stay upright for the show, but he was looking worse than before. His skin had taken on a flushed color and sweat was rolling down his face and neck.

"You don't look good."

"I don't feel good. I need to sleep."

"Did you take a shower?" I asked.

"Yeah."

"You're just dripping sweat."

"Sorry. Do you want me to sleep in a bunk?"

"Of course not." I scooted over and he collapsed on the bed next to me. He was out in seconds. Concerned, I watched him for a while before falling back to sleep. I woke up to Jake screaming out in pain. I shot up in the bed. His body was radiating intense heat. I felt Jake's forehead – he was on fire. The bus was moving. I checked the clock. It was four in the morning. His screaming stopped suddenly.

"Jake?"

No response.

"Jake, wake up."

He groaned.

"Jake?" I shook him. His eyes rolled in his head. Something was wrong.

I jumped out of bed and ran to the front of the bus. Lassen was at the wheel.

"You need to get to a hospital – now," I shouted.

"What's happening?" he replied in alarm.

"He was screaming in pain, and then he just passed out. I can't wake him up," I said, a sob escaped my throat.

"Jesus…Is he breathing?"

"Yes, but he's burning up, Lassen. I mean, you can feel the heat coming off him."

"Okay. I'll call Sean and get directions to the closest hospital. Get some ice packs from the freezer and put them on his wrists to cool him down."

"Okay," I said, with tears running down my cheeks.

"It's okay, Casey. I'll get him to a hospital."

I ran back to check Jake before going to the refrigerator and pulling out all the ice packs we had. I placed two on his wrists, one on his forehead, and one on his knee. Jake roused but started screaming in pain again. He threw the ice pack off his knee.

"It hurts. It hurts," he muttered, incoherent. His eyes were rolling in his head. "I didn't mean to... I'm sorry. Don't... noooo... just kill me. No more. Just kill me. Please. Don't hurt me anymore."

It took me a moment to realize Jake wasn't talking to me. He was having another flashback. He was talking to Ray, the guy who'd kidnapped him. Tears were rolling down my cheeks as I listened to Jake plead with his kidnapper to end his suffering. How bad must it have been for him if he was begging to die?

"It's me, Jake. It's Casey. Tell me what I can do to help you," I cried.

Jake stopped talking. His eyes found me and he tried to focus, but the fever was pulling him back.

"I'm here, Jake. I've got you," I said as I grabbed his hand. "Look at me."

"Casey?" he whispered.

"Yes. Keep looking at me," I urged. I didn't want him to have to go back to that terrible place in his mind. I started talking to him about all the things we had done and all the places we had gone. Jake listened. He even tried to smile when I reminded him of funny things. I kept Jake's attention away from his pain... away from his torment.

Thirty minutes later, Lassen pulled the bus up to the entrance of the emergency room at a hospital somewhere in Germany. He ran out of the bus and a few minutes later came back followed by a doctor and two nurses. By this point, Jake was barely conscious. He groaned in pain but was otherwise lethargic.

The three health care professionals circled around the bed. The nurses seemed momentarily stunned by their famous patient, but the doctor was unfazed. He checked Jake's eyes and felt his pulse. He said something to one of the nurses in German and she quickly exited the bus.

"Jake, my name is Doctor Stoltz. Can you hear me?" the doctor asked in near perfect English.

Jake didn't answer.

"Jake, open your eyes."

Jake's eyes fluttered open but closed just as fleetingly.

"Has he taken anything?" Dr. Stoltz asked me.

"Um... he's been taking a lot of ibuprofen and Tylenol," I replied.

"He means drugs," Lassen said, looking pissed by the question.

"No. Jake doesn't do drugs."

The doctor looked at Lassen. "I need to know if he's taken anything so I can help him." Then he looked at me. "Miss?"

"No," I said. "At least I don't think so. Jake isn't a drug user."

"How long has he been like this?" the doctor asked.

"Well, like this... about an hour, but he's been in extreme pain for about a week."

"Where is his pain?"

"Left knee," Jake answered for himself through gritted teeth.

Dr. Stoltz moved down to Jake's knee and lifted the sheet.

"Don't touch it!" Jake screamed out suddenly. "I need an orthopedic surgeon."

"I'm just going to take a look," the doctor said, as he went for the Velcro wrap.

"No," Jake jerked up. "I swear to God... Don't fucking touch it!"

I was absolutely shocked. Jake never spoke to people like that... ever. "Jake, he's trying to help you," I tried.

"Only..." He clenched in pain. "Only a surgeon... "

"Okay. Don't worry, I won't touch it," the doctor said. Just then two men came in carrying an ambulance stretcher. "Jake, we're going to transfer you to the cot."

"I can do it," Jake responded. He sat up, but immediately got lightheaded.

"Just lie back. It'll be easier," the doctor said, as he laid Jake back down. To my surprise, Jake didn't protest. The two men quickly transferred him onto the stretcher, was strapped him in, and carried him off the bus. They immediately wheeled Jake away, so I went to the waiting room.

Lassen sat down next to me. Within thirty minutes, the waiting room filled up with roadies and band members. All the buses and trucks in the tour had been notified that Jake was in the hospital, and all had turned around and come back. The streets outside the hospital were lined with semis and tour buses all baring the Elevate World Tour logo. It must have been quite a sight for the hospital staff as they started trickling in for their a.m. shifts.

I could hear Sean on the phone, debating whether Jake could perform his next concert, which was scheduled to start in sixteen hours. I could only hear one side of the story, but it was obvious Sean was being pressured into making a decision.

"Look, I'm not doing anything until I talk to Jake. If I cancel it and he's okay to perform tonight, it'll be my head. What? No, I'm not saying that. I seriously don't know if he will physically be able to get up on the stage. Just wait for him to be seen by a doctor, that's all I'm asking."

I looked at Lassen.

"They should cancel it," I said. "You saw him. He can't even stand up."

"I know, but maybe he just needs some antibiotics. I don't know. But I will say, it's not that easy to cancel a concert. Sean is right to wait," Lassen replied.

At least an hour after arriving at the hospital, a pretty dark-haired nurse walked over to me.

"Are you Casey?"

"Yes." I stood up.

"Come with me, please," she said, and waved me toward the door.

"Is he all right?" I asked.

"I'm not allowed to give out patient information. You can ask him."

I couldn't help but notice her flawless face and perfect curves as she pointed me to an open door, and I made a silent prayer she wasn't Jake's nurse. As I came in, I saw him lying on a hospital bed with one arm over his face and an IV in the other. Jake looked less flushed now, but I could tell he was still in extreme pain. He heard me come in and lowered his arm, then reached it out and took my hand. I sat down next to his bed. We didn't talk for a moment, but I understood that it was Jake's way of saying sorry. I picked up his hand, turned it over and kissed the back of it. Jake smiled weakly.

"You look a little better," I said.

"Yeah, they mixed a little morphine in with my IV cocktail."

"Gotta love morphine." I paused. "Have you seen the doctor?"

"Yes, but I don't want an ER doc touching it. I'm waiting for an orthopedic surgeon."

"Yeah, I know. You made that pretty clear."

"Why? What did I say?"

"Well, you pretty much threatened the ER doc with death if he touched your knee."

"No, I didn't," Jake groaned.

"Oh, yes, you did."

"Shit, that's not good."

"Don't worry. I'm sure he's heard worse. You're hardly the first aggressive guy to come into his ER in pain."

"What else did I say?"

I thought about his ramblings about Ray and the kidnapping, but I knew to keep that information to myself. "Mostly you were just mumbling incoherently. Blah, blah, blah. I don't know. I wasn't really listening," I said, sidestepping the question.

"Look, Casey. I know I've been a miserable jerk. For what it's worth, I'm sorry."

"It's worth a lot. You're forgiven." I smiled.

Jake shook his head like he didn't believe me.

"Give yourself a break," I whispered. "You've been in a lot of pain. I'm not mad. I promise."

Jake squeezed my hand and then suddenly tensed. He grimaced as pain rolled through him again.

"I thought they gave you morphine."

"They did, but not enough to knock me out. I want to be awake and coherent when the orthopedic surgeon gets here."

"Well, where is he? It has been almost two hours?"

"I think." Jake gritted his teeth. "I think he's coming from Belgium or something."

I laughed. "Was that a joke, Jake McKallister?"

He nodded.

"I like 'Morphine Jake' better than 'Tylenol Jake.'"

Jake attempted to laugh, but it came out more like a gasping groan.

A few more minutes passed before a tall man in green scrubs walked into the room.

"My name is Doctor Weiss," he said with a thick accent. He shook Jake's hand.

"Jake," he said, then glanced toward me. "My girlfriend Casey."

"Nice to meet you both. Dr. Stoltz tells me you have effusion in your knee."

Jake nodded.

"Let me take a look," the doctor said, as he began to pull apart the Velcro. On first contact, Jake gasped. The doctor paused. "I'll be careful."

Jake nodded and looked away, biting his lip as the pain increased. The doctor got the wrap off and mumbled something I didn't understand. Jake's knee was twice the normal size, and red and purple.

"How long has it been this swollen?"

"About a week and a half."

"Okay, sorry, but I have to palpate the knee. I'll be as gentle as possible," the doctor said, lightly pushing on several different areas in Jake's knee. Jake cringed, gasped, and groaned throughout the exam. The doctor stood back up and picked up his chart.

He looked over it before asking, "Is your blood pressure normally high?"

"No," Jake replied.

"On a scale from one to ten, what is your pain level?"

Through gritted teeth, Jake managed to say, "It ranges from eight to ten."

"How long has it been at this level?"

"A couple of days."

"You told Dr. Stoltz that you had an earlier injury to this knee."

"Yes."

"What kind of injury?"

"My knee was crushed."

"In an accident?"

"Not exactly."

"What kind of injury then?"

Jake glanced at me, then hesitated a second before saying, "It was smashed by a sledgehammer."

My mouth dropped open in shock.

"A sledgehammer?" The doctor repeated, not sure if he'd heard right.

"Yes," Jake said, avoiding my astonished expression.

"I'm not sure if I'm understanding the word correctly. Are you saying it was smashed with a metal hammer?"

"Yes, you're understanding it right."

"Deliberately?" the doctor asked, still too surprised to accept Jake's answer.

Jake looked away and said, "I was kidnapped when I was a kid. I got this injury then."

Doctor Weiss stared at him, clearly shocked by Jake's admission, before clearing his throat and saying, "Okay. I see. Um... uh... do you have your original kneecap?"

"No," Jake said, wincing in pain.

"How many surgeries have you had?"

"Uh...two knee replacement surgeries."

"How often does it swell like this?"

"Um...I've only had it this bad one other time."

"And you had a replacement after that last swelling?"

"Yes."

The doctor nodded. "I need to check your mobility." He raised Jake's leg by the ankle and bent the knee several times. Jake was gripping the sides of the bed with white knuckles. Sweat was dripping down his face.

"Sorry. Almost done," the doctor said. He pulled Jake's leg up and slightly to the side. Jake jerked forward, in a state of agony. The doctor gently put his leg back down.

"Okay, well, obviously there is a tremendous amount of fluid in the knee, and that is probably what's causing the majority of your pain. That will, of course, need to be effused. But the dark coloring and the high fever suggests a secondary infection."

Jake nodded. "Do whatever you need to do. I just need to be on my feet and ready to perform by tonight."

"I don't... that isn't advisable," the doctor said. "You will need to rest that knee for a few days after I drain it, or the fluid will come right back. And raising your heart rate when you have an infection can be dangerous."

"I get what you're saying and, trust me, if I had the luxury of time, I would jump at the chance to take a few days rest, but I'm in the middle of a tour. Tickets have been sold. Stadiums have been booked. I can't just postpone. It would be a logistical nightmare. I'm just asking for a temporary solution... something to get me back on my feet so I can perform. I won't consent to anything more. So please... just drain the fluid, give me a lidocaine and a steroid shot and some antibiotics, and I'll be on my way."

Dr. Weiss seemed to be considering what Jake said. He was obviously trying to decide what to do. He looked at Jake, down at the chart, and then back at Jake before finally clearing his throat and saying, "This is a unique situation."

Jake nodded.

"I understand your dilemma and will honor your request, but please understand... the choice you're making isn't medically advised."

"Yes, I understand."

"All right, then. I want to move you to a more sterile environment. I'll have the nurse bring you in when the room is ready."

"Okay, thank you."

Dr. Weiss walked out of the room.

"Are you sure about this?" I asked. "I really think you need a few days' rest."

"I don't really have a choice, Casey."

"Yes, you do. Postponing your tour isn't the end of the world. No one would fault you."

"You don't understand this business like I do. Music execs don't look kindly on that sort of thing. And it's not just the tour, it's the publicity. I'll be crucified. The rumor mill will be working overtime. Before you know it, they've have me in rehab recovering from a drug overdose or some other made up bullshit."

I looked at Jake in stunned surprise.

"I'm not making this shit up, Casey. That is what will happen. I guarantee you," Jake replied.

Two nurses came in: the pretty one from earlier, my silent prayer clearly not answered, and an older, sour-looking one who didn't speak English. She grunted her commands in German to the younger nurse. As the very attractive younger nurse went about her tasks, she smiled and chatted in fluent English with

Jake. I could tell he was not feeling up to talking, but he politely responded to her anyway. I sat there next to him like I was invisible. The nurse never once acknowledged me. I was annoyed. Was she really flirting with him when he looked about ready to pass out? I guess that was definitely a perk of being famous: you could look and feel like shit but still be hot.

And my poor Jake was sick as a dog. He barely had the energy to lift his head, yet still, the nurse seemed a little too interested. I think Jake sensed my irritation and mentioned weakly to her that I was his girlfriend. The nurse actually gave me a thorough once over. It occurred to me that I was without makeup, in sweats, and my hair had been hastily pulled back into a messy bun. I imagine I deserved the contemptuous look I received. I could almost hear her describe me to her friends, telling them that Jake could do so much better.

In a few minutes, the nurses were wheeling Jake out the door.

"Hold on for a second," Jake said. The nurse stopped pushing the bed. He looked at me and reached out his hand. I walked up to him and grabbed it.

"Can you get my phone and call my parents? I don't want them to hear on the news that I'm in the hospital. You can call the home contact."

"What do you want me to tell them?"

"Just tell them I had swelling and needed to get the knee drained. Tell them I'll call when it's over."

"Okay."

"Don't worry. I'll be fine," Jake whispered in my ear, then pulled me to him and kissed me.

"I know," I whispered back. "I'll be here waiting."

Dr. Weiss walked up to us and grinned. "All right. How do you say it? Let's get the show on the road."

Jake nodded as he dropped my hand. I watched him get wheeled away. I went back to the waiting room. I told all the band and crew what was happening and that Jake was still planning on performing that night. They nodded like they never doubted it for a minute, but I saw Sean actually sigh in relief.

I went out to the bus to get Jake's phone and nervously dialed his home. Aside from the brief exchange at the wedding, I'd never spoken to Jake's parents. I hoped Jake's dad answered; he seemed less intimidating than the mom. No such luck. Jake's mom, Michelle, picked up my call. It was obvious by her groggy voice that I'd woken her up.

"Hello? Jake? What time is it?"

"Mrs. McKallister? I'm sorry to wake you."

"Who is this?" She seemed instantly awake and immediately concerned.

"I'm Casey Caldwell, Jake's girlfriend. He asked me to call you."

"Is he all right?"

I could hear the panic in her voice.

"Jake's okay, but he's in the hospital."

Michelle gasped.

"His knee swelled up, and he was in terrible pain. He got really sick and feverish, and then this morning he passed out."

"He was unconscious?"

"No, not really. It was more like he was unresponsive. Lassen drove him to the hospital. He's with the doctor now having the fluid drained. They're going to give him antibiotics and then release him."

"They're releasing him today?"

"Well, they wanted to keep him for a few days, but Jake refused. He has a concert tonight."

"Good Lord. Is he even going to be able to perform?"

"I don't know. Jake thinks so, and there's no talking him out of it. And I tried."

"He's so damn stubborn."

"Yes, he is," I agreed. "Anyway, Jake didn't want you to hear on the news that he was in the hospital and get worried. He told me to tell you that he'll call as soon as he gets back on the bus."

"Casey... is that your name?"

"Yes."

"Thank you for letting us know. Can you keep his phone on you so we can call for updates?"

"Yes, of course. If you like I can call as soon as he's done with the procedure."

"Yes, please do that. When did it begin?"

"They're just getting started now. The doctor thought it might take about an hour. I'll call as soon as I know anything."

"Thank you, Casey."

I hung up and my tension eased. That wasn't so bad. Michelle and I had something very important in common: we both loved Jake with all our hearts. She only wanted the best for him. I would just have to prove to her that I was best for him. I spent a few minutes making myself look a bit more presentable by changing into a Henley long sleeved shirt and jeans, brushing my hair into a ponytail, and putting on a little eye makeup. Lassen walked in.

"I was just heading back," I explained, feeling guilty that I was taking the time to make myself look better when Jake was in torturous pain.

"He'll be in there a while, I think," Lassen replied.

I nodded as tears filled my eyes.

"He'll be all right. Jake's a tough kid. He's been through way worse than this."

"You'd know."

Lassen looked at me in surprise.

"Jake told me he talks to you."

"Oh."

"How much do you know about what happened to Jake during the kidnapping?"

Lassen hesitated.

"I know you can't tell me what he went through. I just want to know how much you know."

"I know some things."

"Do you know what happened to his knee?"

Lassen nodded.

"So you knew it had been crushed by a sledgehammer?"

Lassen nodded again.

Neither of us spoke for a moment.

"What kind of a monster does that to a kid?" I wondered. Tears threatened to pour out.

Lassen shook his head.

"What kind of monster does that?" I questioned, angrily. Then I started bawling. "I mean, how am I... how can I help him heal when he's been through something I can't even comprehend?"

I cried and cried. All the stress of the past few days poured down my cheeks. Lassen stood there awkwardly, looking highly uncomfortable.

I pulled myself together for his sake.

When I finally stopped crying, Lassen said, "You can't heal him. Just love him. That's all he wants."

"I do love him."

"I know." He shifted back and forth a few times before clearing his throat and saying, "Sean wants me to get some sleep so I can safely drive later."

"Yeah, of course."

Lassen walked away, looking relieved to be getting away from me.

After fixing my makeup again, I went back to the waiting room and sat with Jake's guitarist Eric and his wife, Kayla, the couple traveling together in a motorhome with their three kids. Kayla and I had become friends, and Jake and I had spent some time together with them and their kids. Kayla had the baby monitor up to her ear. All three kids were sleeping inside the locked motorhome steps outside the emergency room.

As we waited for Jake's procedure to be completed, the hospital began to fill up with staff and patients. It was nine in the morning, and the typical hurried activities of a busy hospital were swirling around us. The waiting room was bursting at the seams with not only all of our people but the patients who were coming in on a steady basis. All the drivers had been ordered to sleep, and some of the crew had followed suit. Some had also headed over to the cafeteria, but at least half were still waiting in the room with me for word on Jake's condition.

It was well over an hour before I was summoned again. Dr. Weiss was waiting for me at the door.

"Jake asked that I fill you in on his condition."

"Is he all right?" I asked in concern.

"Yes. I was able to drain almost all the fluid. He's feeling much relief."

"Oh, good." I smiled with relief.

"I gave him a dose of morphine to settle him down. He's sleeping now. I've recommended to Jake that he stay the night; however, he's adamant that he wants to leave. So, at the very least, Jake will need to stay until the next dose of antibiotics can be given to him intravenously."

"Okay. Does Jake know this?"

"Yes. I told him. He wasn't thrilled, but he agreed. I'll be back to check on him in a bit."

After the doctor left, I quietly crept into Jake's room to find him still sleeping. His face was flushed and he still looked feverish, but he also looked peaceful. The mask of pain that had clouded his senses, even in sleep, was mercifully gone. Jake's knee, although bruised, resembled normal size again. I bent down and gave him a kiss. Jake didn't even stir.

Since he was sleeping, I stepped out to call his parents.

Michelle answered on the first ring. "Hello? Casey?"

"Yes. I just talked to the doctor. He was able to drain most of the fluid, and Jake was feeling better. He's knocked out on morphine right now. They'll release him in about two hours."

"Okay. Good. Have you seen him since the procedure?"

"Yes."

"How does he look?" I could hear the strain in her voice.

"A lot better than before. He isn't as flushed and feverish. The doctor said he would be fine."

"That's good," her voice cracked.

"Are you okay?" I asked.

"Yes. I just... I worry."

"I know. So do I."

"How is his... um... his mood?"

I hesitated. She obviously had been through this with him before. I didn't want to worry her, but I didn't want to lie either.

"He's been struggling this past week."

There was silence on the other line.

"But before that, he had been really happy. I think now that the swelling is down, he'll feel a lot better."

"Hopefully, yes," she said.

I could hear the anxiety in her voice.

"Have we met before, Casey?" Her voice softened.

"Yes. At the wedding, actually."

"You're the girl from the wedding?" she asked in surprise.

"I am."

"Jake invited you to go on tour with him?"

"Not right away. We talked on the phone for a couple of weeks, and then he invited me to visit him in London. Once I was here, he asked me to stay."

"Really? So how long have you been with him then?"

"A little over a month. I have to go back in three weeks because I start my senior year at the end of August."

"You're a college student?"

"Yes. I'm studying accounting."

"Do you live in Arizona?"

"I do."

"Jake never tells me anything. I didn't even know he had a girlfriend," Michelle said, sounding disappointed.

I didn't know what to say, so I stayed silent.

"Anyway, once Jake is awake, will you have him call me?"

"Of course. And, Mrs. McKallister... Don't worry. Jake is surrounded by people who love him. When the band and crew found out he was in the hospital, they turned around and came back. Everyone is in the waiting room. No one wants to leave until they know he's okay."

There was a moment of silence before Michelle said, "Thank you, Casey. That makes me feel a lot better actually. You seem like a lovely young woman."

"Thank you," I replied, surprised.

We said our goodbyes and then hung up. I walked to the waiting room to inform the others that Jake was doing well, but that he would need to wait a couple more hours before being released. There was a sense of relief in the air. The concern was genuine.

I returned to Jake's bedside and sat with him for nearly two hours until the pretty nurse came in and connected a new IV bag. She glanced at me and I was insecure enough that I secretly hoped she noticed I wasn't as homely as she'd once thought. The nurse turned her attention back to Jake. She seemed to be assessing more than just his health. I was used to women ogling my boyfriend, so I didn't know why it bothered me so much. Jake was always so good about deflecting his admirers, but in his vulnerable state, there was no protection. Without Jake defending my honor and validating my presence in his life, I was nothing more than a gold-digging groupie.

As the nurse checked Jake's blood pressure and other vitals, the tightening of the blood pressure cuff roused Jake from his morphine-induced slumber.

"Hello again," the nurse cooed.

"Hey," Jake answered back, groggily.

"I just attached the IV, so once it's empty the doctor will come in and discharge you."

"Okay, thanks." Jake turned his head and saw me. "Hey, babe."

"Hey, yourself." I smiled, then took his hand and squeezed it. "You look better. Are you still in pain?"

"I'm not feeling anything right now."

"I bet."

"You think they'll let me take an IV filled with morphine for the bus?"

"Oh, yeah, I'm sure." I played along.

The nurse left the room. Maybe she realized three was a crowd.

"I called your parents during and after the procedure to let them know how you were doing."

"Was my mom freaking out?"

"She was sufficiently concerned, but I eased her fears."

"Thanks."

"I think she's a little pissed at you, though."

"Why?"

"Because apparently you never mentioned to her that you had a girlfriend."

Jake suddenly looked guilty, like he'd been caught in a lie. "I know. I'm sorry. I just didn't want all the questions. I'll tell her all about you, I promise. I mean, after the week we've had, you're still my girlfriend, right?"

"You aren't getting rid of me that easy."

"I don't want to get rid of you." Jake frowned. "I really am sorry."

"I know."

Jake stared at me a long moment. "So are the guys at the venue yet?"

I laughed.

"What?" He grinned, as if we were sharing some joke.

"They're in the waiting room."

"No, they're not." Jake stopped smiling. "Why didn't they keep driving?"

"Well, because about five hours ago we didn't think there was going to *be* a venue. I mean, even you have to admit that it's a little hard to put on a Jake McKallister concert without Jake McKallister."

Jake was not happy. "Dammit. I thought I just had to worry about getting myself there. Now I have to worry about everyone else."

"You don't have to worry about anything. Sean is handling it."

"Can you get him for me?" Jake said, still frowning.

"No."

"No?"

"Not if you're going to get mad at him. Sean has been on the phone non-stop since you were brought here. He's been trying to hold off the label. They were pushing to postpone. Sean saved the tour. He's the only reason you can still perform tonight. So you will play nice," I admonished.

Jake looked at me like he wanted to argue, but instead, he sighed and said, "You're right. I'll be nice."

I smiled and patted his shoulder. "Good choice. And just so you know, the guys weren't told to come back. They just did. They wanted to be here for you."

Jake mumbled something, then asked, "Has the media picked up on this?"

I hesitated, then nodded. "There are buses and semis lining the street for two blocks. With the tour logo on the sides, it was a little hard to miss."

"Are there reporters?"

"Yes."

"Great," Jake replied in frustration. "What are they reporting?"

"Just that you were brought to the hospital."

Dr. Weiss strolled in. "How are you doing, Jake? You look better."

"Yeah, I feel a lot better."

The doctor picked up the chart and looked over it. "Blood pressure is normal. Fever is down. I think you're turning the corner."

"Does that mean I can get out of here?"

"You have about thirty more minutes. I'll start the discharge orders."

"Okay, great. Thanks."

After the doctor left, Jake turned to me and asked, "Can you go to the bus and get me some jeans and a long-sleeve shirt? Some underwear and socks too, and my tan leather shoes? Also some toiletries. I want to take a quick shower before braving the cameras."

"Yeah, sure."

"And please send Sean in. I promise to be nice."

38

JAKE: PULL IT TOGETHER

After Sean left, I lay back on the bed. Although I was feeling way better now that my knee had been drained, the past week had shaken me. The flashbacks; lashing out at people who didn't deserve it; pushing Casey away – it had to stop. She'd forgiven me for my dick behavior this time, but she wasn't going to put up with it forever. I had to figure out a way to get my shit together. I couldn't let what happened last week happen again, even if it meant having my knee amputated. That had been an option for me since the kidnapping, but my parents had decided against it, hoping I would regain normal use of it over time. Obviously, that hadn't happened. Basically, I lived from one cortisone shot to the next. The pain was always there – but sometimes, when it swelled up like it had, it became unbearable. And the shitty part was, it was never going to get any better. Every tour was the same: the swelling increased after each show until I was in excruciating pain.

The nurse came into the room. "Are you doing all right?" she asked, in a slight German accent. Her hand rested on my arm.

"Yeah, better."

"That's good. You know, I'm a big fan of your music and just you in general. You seem like a very down to earth guy."

I looked up at her. How in the hell could she tell that? I'd been writhing in pain for the majority of the time she'd been around me.

"Oh, yeah, well, thanks." I smiled, although I was really not in the mood for a conversation. "How much longer now?"

She checked the IV bag. "Just a few more drops. Are you so eager to leave?"

Seriously? Who would want to remain tethered to an IV in a hospital? "I have a concert tonight that I need to get to, so yeah... kind of eager."

"Well, I know you're leaving, but if you're ever in Germany again, you can give me a call." She pressed a note in my hand, presumably with her number on it.

I looked down at the paper, shocked she would have the balls to do this while she was working. Plus, she'd clearly seen Casey. "I have a girlfriend," I stated matter of factly.

"I know, but let's be honest. What are the chances you'll still be with her next time you're traveling through Germany?"

"Hopefully, the chances are high," I replied.

"You like her a lot, then?"

I didn't respond. My relationship was none of her business.

"Seems like a waste, if you ask me."

Well, I didn't ask you, I wanted to say, but I held my tongue. I wasn't going to give a complete stranger the satisfaction of getting into a discussion about my girlfriend and me.

"You're too young to be tied down right now. Why limit yourself? Have a little fun."

"Yeah. Been there, done that."

The nurse gave me a look of pity.

"Anyway, just put my number in your phone under German Gia. I'll make it worth your while."

Just then, Casey walked in holding a pile of my clothes, looking disheveled and a bit sweaty, but the minute she appeared in the room it brightened. As if sensing tension, Casey glanced at German Gia and then at me. I smiled. She smiled back.

"Perfect timing," the nurse said to Casey. "I was just about to remove his IV."

"Oh good," Casey replied, her face bright and happy. God, how I loved her. Casey had an inner beauty that radiated and ignited everything it touched. How could any woman ever compete with her?

German Gia grabbed hold of my arm and, with her nail, traced a line to the IV. I looked up at her in surprise, and she smiled. I glanced over at Casey, hoping she hadn't seen it, but one look at her face told me she had. Once Gia was busy pulling the needle out of my arm, I raised my eyebrows and gave Casey the look, the one that said both, *What the fuck?* and *I'm totally not into her, I swear to God.* Casey smiled and rolled her eyes. I loved that about her. She didn't blame me every time something like this happened. It was like we were partners in this bizarre world I lived in, where nurses actually hit on their patients.

As soon as I was free, I swung my legs over the side of the bed and attempted to stand up. I immediately got dizzy. Gia grabbed me by my arm and sat me back down.

"You might be a little light-headed from the morphine," she said. She was back to being my nurse, thank god. "Take a couple deep breaths."

I did and it helped. I stood up again, and this time, I felt stronger. I took a few steps to the bathroom. "I'm going to take a quick shower."

"Has the doctor cleared that?" Gia asked.

"I didn't ask, but I'm going to take one anyway," I said.

Gia raised her eyebrows, then smiled. "Well, okay then. A decisive man. I'll give you your privacy."

Casey brought me my stuff from the bus. "Do you want me to stay in here, just in case?"

"Just in case what? I fall flat on my face?"

"No, just in case the nurse comes back."

39

CASEY: PREPARED TO FIGHT

Jake was discharged, and the only thing he had left was to brave the media. All the staff and crew got back in their buses and semis. The line of vehicles stretched for blocks. It was a sight to see, but the tour staff wanted to show a united front. Everyone would retreat together. Lassen pulled Jake's bus to the entrance of the ER.

Jake was standing with Sean and Eric inside the room, making final preparations.

"Jake, do you want me there, or should I go to the bus?" I asked.

"What do you want?"

"I would prefer to not be on camera. I haven't showered or anything today."

"I think you look beautiful."

"That's sweet." I smiled. "It's a lie, but still sweet."

"Go. I'll meet you there in a couple of minutes."

I walked out of the room, through the ER, and headed toward the bus. At least a dozen reporters and camera crews were waiting, held back by hospital security. As I knocked on the bus door, several reporters called out questions to me. Lassen opened the door and I slipped in.

"Is he on his way?" Lassen asked.

"Yes. He should be here any minute. He wants out of here as much as we do."

"Oh, I can only imagine," Lassen agreed.

"Thanks for everything this morning," I said, obviously referring to my crying fit.

He shrugged.

"It's just frustrating sometimes. I want to help, but I don't know how."

"I know how you feel. I'd do anything for Jake. I love that kid," Lassen said, clearing his voice. I could tell he wasn't used to sharing his feelings, and he was now done.

"Me too," I nodded, smiling. I was really starting to love Lassen. "Did you get any sleep?"

"I did, actually. Sean made all the drivers go and sleep for a few hours. We only have a six-hour drive. Sean hired extra staff for tonight to help with set up."

We heard a commotion outside.

"Sounds like show time," Lassen said, and he opened the bus door.

Jake walked out of the hospital looking healthy and strong. I knew he wasn't, but the reporters didn't need to know that.

One female reporter called out, "How are you feeling, Jake?"

Jake smiled and waved but didn't respond. A barrage of questions followed.

"Jake, what brought you to the hospital?"

"It's being reported that you passed out."

"Do you have HIV?"

"Did you have a drug overdose?"

"Are you entering rehab?"

Through all the intrusive questions, Jake's neutral facial expression stayed the same. He focused on getting to the bus.

"Are you canceling the show in Cologne tonight?"

Jake ducked inside the bus.

Sean then turned to the reporters. "Jake was brought to the hospital with a fever. He hadn't been feeling well for a few days. He was treated with antibiotics, then released. The tour dates haven't changed. Jake's feeling better and looking forward to playing in Cologne tonight. Thank you."

Sean climbed in, and Lassen shut the door and got in the driver's seat. We pulled out of the ER and joined the line of buses and trucks as we made our way to the next concert.

Sean and Eric had come on the bus with us. The men had a lot of scheduling issues to hash over. After reminding Jake to call his mom, I happily retreated to the bedroom and changed the sheets, as Jake's sweat was all over the old ones. After making the bed, I collapsed under the fresh linens and fell fast asleep. When I woke up hours later, Jake was snoozing by my side. We were still driving. I got up and went to the living room area. The other guys were gone. We must have stopped somewhere while I was sleeping. I went to check on Lassen.

"Hey, how are you doing?" I asked him.

"Good."

"Are you getting tired?"

"Nope, doing good. Don't you worry."

"I'm not worried. You're a decent driver," I joked.

He curled his lip up.

"Are we stopping soon?"

"In about an hour. How's Jake?"

"Sleeping. He looks a lot better and isn't feverish anymore."

"Good."

"How about some company?"

"I wouldn't mind some," Lassen mumbled.

I settled in the chair next to him and we chatted until he pulled the bus into the arena parking lot. After we were parked, Lassen and I went to the kitchen and got some food. We continued talking. Lassen was a really interesting guy. At fifty-eight, he had really lived the life, driving for some of the biggest musicians in the business. With the stories he had, Lassen could write a best-selling book. But he was loyal to his former employers and would never divulge the names of the people we were talking about.

A while later Jake walked in, looking all scruffy but wearing a lopsided smile on his face. "Are you having a party without me?"

"Yep. A grilled cheese sandwich and glass of milk party. Very trendy."

"I can see that. You mind if I join?"

"I don't know. What do you think, Lassen, do we have room for sickie here?"

Lassen laughed. He shoved the last of his sandwich in his mouth and stood up. "Party's over for me. I need to sleep. Have a good concert tonight. Don't pass out in the middle of a song." Lassen patted Jake on the shoulder and winked at me.

Jake's mouth dropped open in shock when he saw Lassen's wink. "What the hell is going on here?" he questioned. "I feel like I'm in an alternate universe right now. Since when are you charming?"

"Since you brought home a girl worth charming," Lassen said as he walked away.

"Thanks for keeping me company," I called out.

He waved but didn't look back.

Jake watched Lassen disappear behind the partition. "You two are getting friendly. Do I need to worry?"

"You don't have to worry about anyone. Although I can't say the same about me."

Jake's eyebrows scrunched in confusion, as if he were trying to remember what he'd done wrong.

"Your nurse?" I said, crossing my arms in front of me.

"Oh geez, I know. How unprofessional was that?"

"I was afraid to leave you alone with her when you were out cold."

"You didn't, I hope."

"I have to admit, she totally intimidated me."

"Why?"

"I don't know. She kind of looked at me like I was a bug she wanted to squash. When you aren't around to defend our relationship, I guess I just feel like a money hungry tramp."

"Casey," Jake admonished. "All that matters is what you and I know."

"True, but it can still be intimidating at times. Especially when you throw a hot nurse into the mix."

Jake shook his head. "You don't get it, Casey. You're all I see."

I reached out and touched his face. No guy had ever made me feel as special as Jake did... or as insecure. There was so much to say, but it would have to wait.

"What time is the concert?" I asked, changing the subject.

"Eight."

"You realize you're on in an hour and a half?"

"Yes. That's why I woke up."

"I'm just surprised people haven't started pounding down the door."

"That should be happening in about five minutes."

"Are you feeling better?" I asked, putting my hand to his forehead.

"Yeah, I'm a little out of it, but the pain is nearly gone."

"You had me scared, Jake," I admitted.

"I know. Sorry."

Just then came a knock on the door. We both looked at each other.

"Right on cue."

I nodded. "Are you sure you can do this tonight?"

Jake shrugged. "I guess we're about to find out."

He got up and went to the door and let Marcy in.

"Hey, sweetheart. How are you?" she asked.

"I'm hanging in there."

"Don't take this the wrong way, but you look like shit."

Jake laughed. "I know."

"I have your clothes here," she said, patting a bag. "Do you want to shower here or in the arena?"

"The arena."

"Are you ready to head over then?"

"Yep. Are you coming?" Jake asked me.

"Yeah, I'm just going to shower and change."

"Okay, I'll see you there," Jake said, then bent down and kissed me.

Jake performed that night, and you'd never have known he'd spent the better part of the day in the hospital. I think he felt the need to prove to the naysayers that everything was fine. He was definitely a pro.

After the concert, we came back to the bus, and it was on to the next city. As Lassen drove, Jake and I hung out in the kitchen. We chatted like we had before he got sick. It was so fun and easy. I felt so happy. Our connection was back and as strong as ever.

Jake surprised me by bringing up the injury to his knee.

"Are you... uh... okay with what I told the doctor today? You looked a little freaked out."

I paused before answering him. "No, I'm not okay. I just can't believe he would do that to you."

Jake didn't say anything.

"It's just... you've never talked about the kidnapping to me, ever. And then, out of nowhere, you drop an atomic bomb on me."

"I know." Jake nodded. "Sorry. I should have prepared you. It's just hard for me. I just don't... um... can't... talk about it."

I paused when he said *can't*. My heart ached for him.

"I just don't get how you can be the guy I know, but have this whole horrible past just lurking in the background. How do you separate the two?"

Jake shrugged. "I don't know. I used to not be able to separate them at all, and I was so miserable but, over time, I had to, or I wouldn't have survived."

"So when you're with me, are you hiding your past, or is it not really a factor?"

"I think a little of both. It's been ten years, so the passage of time has made things easier, I guess. And overall I'm a happy guy. I love my life. I have a great job, a great girl. But sometimes the past won't let me be happy."

"Is that something that will affect our future?"

Jake sighed. "I can't answer that. I don't know. I'm sorry."

"You don't have to be sorry, Jake. I just want to know what I'm up against because I'm prepared to fight for you... even when you try to push me away."

Jake looked away. "I want to be a better man for you, Casey. I really do."

"I already think you're a better man, Jake. I don't want you to change. I just want you to be at peace with who you are."

Jake's eyes softened. "Thank you, Casey."

"For what?"

"For accepting what can't be changed."

I touched his hand and gazed into his eyes. "You look tired."

"I'm exhausted, even though I've been sleeping almost all day."

"Well, I'm thinking it might have something to do with the fact that you've spent the past week in excruciating pain, then spent the wee hours of the morning in the hospital followed by a high energy, two-hour concert."

Jake grinned. "Yeah, maybe that's it."

We retreated to the bedroom. When we lay down, Jake opened his arms and I snuggled into him. He hadn't wanted to cuddle with me for at least a week. It felt so good, like I had him back. Jake didn't say anything, but kissed my forehead a few times. I just enjoyed the closeness.

Then out of the darkness, and out of the silence, came the three words I'd wondered if I would ever hear from Jake: "I love you."

My heart felt ready to explode. I sought out his eyes. He was looking at me with such tenderness.

"I love you too, Jake. I've loved you since the day we met."

Jake smiled. His eyes were heavy, and he didn't say anything else before sleep took him. I lay awake playing those three words over and over in my head. He loved me. No matter what else happened, Jake loved me.

40

JAKE: WHERE HATE LIVES

I woke up the next morning feeling better than I had in weeks. The throbbing was gone in my knee, and the dark cloud that had been hanging over me had dissipated. Last night I'd told her I loved her. It was something I'd been feeling for a long time, but for some reason, couldn't convince myself to admit. But after everything that had happened last week, she needed to know. I loved her. She loved me. The rest should have been easy. But as with everything else in my life, nothing ever came easily.

The goddamn flashbacks plagued me with doubt and worry. My ability to be intimate with Casey was in question, and it was something I couldn't just ignore. If we were going to move past the problem, I had to admit to Casey the truth behind the flashbacks and tell her what triggered them. But in order to do that, I had to admit things to Casey that I wasn't sure I could.

"You okay?" Casey asked. Her face was scrunched up with worry. I'd had no idea she was awake and watching me.

"I'm... yeah," I stumbled on my words.

"Do you regret what you said to me last night?"

"No. I love you, Casey. There's no reason to regret that."

She smiled up at me. "I love you, too. I have wanted to tell you for so long, but I didn't want to scare you off. Sometimes you seem so skittish."

I sighed. "I know. All this is new to me. For a long time, I didn't think I had the capacity to love another person like this. You kind of blew into my life like a hurricane and turned everything upside down."

"Wow, you make me sound so charming," she teased.

"In a good way, Casey. I needed my life to be shaken up. I was too stuck in my ways. Too lost in my head. You woke me up. You showed me that I could love."

"Why would you think you couldn't love?"

Honest or not? Do I tell her how I really feel? I love her and she deserves to know.

"Because... " I hesitated. "I have so much hate inside me that I didn't think there was enough room for love."

Casey sat up. She grabbed my hand and said, "You hide it well."

I nodded.

We sat in silence for a minute.

Then Casey lifted my hand and kissed it. "Well, then I guess we'll just have to fill up that space with so much love there's no more room for the hate."

"I don't know if it's possible, Casey. The things he did... I don't think I can let it go."

"No one benefits from your hate," Casey whispered. "He's dead."

"I know. I killed him."

Casey nodded but didn't seem shocked or even concerned.

"That doesn't scare you?" I asked in disbelief.

"No."

"Well, it scares the shit out of me. I know exactly what I'm capable of."

Casey shrugged. "Anyone is capable of killing if they're pushed far enough."

How could she be so nonchalant about my admission? I killed someone... albeit a sick, twisted serial killer, but still. "I don't believe that it doesn't scare you just a little. There are a lot of people out there who think I'm a cold-blooded killer."

"But you know you aren't. I know you aren't."

"How do you know?"

"Because Jake, you're a good person with a kind heart. It isn't your fault that you were put into a position where you had to fight for your life. If you hadn't done what you did that day, there would be no you. And if there were no you, there would be no us. And if there were no us, well, that would just be a damn shame."

41

CASEY: DECISION MADE

We arrived at our next location and checked into a hotel. Jake had a much-needed day to rest before his show the following night. We decided to order in and just relax. Jake had slept more than usual after his hospital stay. After our talk earlier in the day, Jake seemed a little sad. I wished I could make him believe that I loved him unconditionally and that what happened in his past did not need to affect our future.

Since arriving at the hotel, Jake had been on the phone. I didn't know who he was talking to, but he'd asked for privacy and I gave it to him. When he finally came out of the bedroom, he seemed more upbeat.

"Everything okay?" I asked.

"Yeah. I was talking to a surgeon in the States."

I looked at him in surprise.

"We were discussing my options for my knee. He's one of the best orthopedic surgeons in the country, who specializes in knee replacements. He's agreed to fly to Los Angeles and operate on me. They have these new state of the art knees now. He thinks it would really improve my mobility and maybe even help with the pain."

"That's great. When would this happen?"

"In October or November. We'll set a date once I get back," Jake said, and then hesitated.

"What is it?" I asked in concern.

"Um... here's the thing. If he gets in there and decides a new knee won't really benefit my situation, then another doctor would be prepared to amputate."

"Wait... what?" I replied in shock. "You're having your leg amputated?"

"Well, hopefully it won't come to that – but, yeah, it's a possibility that I need to be prepared for."

I shook my head. "I just... I don't understand. This is so sudden."

"It's not sudden. Because of the nature of my injury, amputation has always been a risk. My parents refused it when they were presented with that option after the kidnapping. They hoped I'd regain normal use of my knee over time. But that hasn't happened. Casey, I'm tired of fighting this knee. I fucking hate it. I hate that every time it hurts, I have to remember how it got this way."

"How *did* it get that way? What could possibly have happened that would cause that asshole to shatter your kneecap with a sledgehammer?" I asked.

Jake sat there for a few seconds. Obviously, he was deciding if he was going to share such personal information with me. Then, to my surprise, he murmured, "I tried to escape. That was my punishment."

I blinked back my shock, then shook my head and whispered, "Jake."

We sat there silently for a moment.

"I can't even imagine the pain. It must have been unbelievable."

Jake didn't respond. He looked upset, so I didn't push it. I was feeling sick to my stomach just thinking about what Jake was not saying.

"Where would they amputate?" I asked, solemnly.

"Above the knee. I won't have a natural bend anymore, so my mobility will be limited. This might be my last tour for a while."

Tears immediately filled my eyes. "You love touring. You're an amazing performer."

Jake shrugged. "I've been performing for seven years straight. I need a break anyway. And it's not like I'd be sidelined forever. They've made a lot of advancements with prosthetics; I'll be on my feet again. It just might take some time."

I was trying to take it all in. "I can't help but worry that you're doing this for me, because of what we talked about earlier."

"No," he said, taking my hand. "I'm doing this for me."

"Well, if you want to do something nice for yourself, get a massage or something. Don't have your leg cut off," I replied, with a miserable smile.

Jake shook his head. "It's not like I'm choosing this. Trust me, this surgery is going to suck either way, but it has to be done at some point. The recovery for knee replacement is gnarly. It takes months and is really painful. If I'm not going to see a huge improvement, I just don't see a point of putting myself through it, you know. The amputation, yeah, it'll be rough, but eventually the pain will fade."

"But you won't be able to live this life anymore." I gestured around us.

"I don't care. I don't need it."

I stared at him skeptically.

Jake sighed. "My knee holds me back, Casey. It tethers me to the past in a way that isn't healthy. I mean, you saw what happened last week. I'm doing this to improve my quality of life – to improve *our* quality of life. I can't do that until I get this taken care of."

I nodded, squeezing his hand. "You're the bravest man I've ever known."

Jake didn't say anything.

"And you're pretty damn hot, too."

Jake grinned. I think he was relieved that I changed the subject. "Speaking of hot, are you purposely wearing those shorts to get a rise out of me?"

"If you're rising, it's your own damn fault." I smiled.

"Your ass cheeks are practically hanging out!" Jake exclaimed. "I'm only human."

"Then come and get it," I offered.

42

JAKE: FLASHBACKS

I picked Casey up and dropped her unceremoniously on the bed. I was on her straight away and we were kissing feverishly. As we urgently stripped off our clothes, a moment of anxiety gripped me. It was going to happen again, and then she was going to see what a freak I was. *Stop! Dammit!* Why couldn't I just stop thinking and just enjoy being with her? Why did I always have to worry about Ray joining us?

As if sensing my apprehension, Casey whispered, "Talk to me, Jake."

"It's nothing."

"Is there anything I can do differently?"

"No," I said, letting frustration creep through me. I sat back up. "It's not you, Casey. It's... "

"What?" Casey asked, looking at me with such love that all my defenses fell.

"It's him," I sighed.

Casey sat back up too. "Ray?"

I didn't answer. Silence filled the gaps.

"Do you mean Ray?" Casey tried again.

I nodded and took a deep breath.

Casey ran her fingers through my hair, and then laid her forehead against mine.

Just tell her, I screamed in my head. Just get it over with, then let Casey decide if I was still worth her love. I pulled away from her.

"He... you know... I'm sure you do... you have to," I rambled.

"He sexually assaulted you," she finished the sentence for me.

I nodded. A feeling of relief washed over me. It was out there now. The dirty truth. No more hiding. No more lying. "I was a kid. I tried to fight him off, but... I was a kid."

Tears filled Casey's eyes. "I know. I'm so sorry, babe," she said, and took my hand. "And that's not pity talking. It actually hurts my heart that someone hurt yours."

We sat there quietly for a while. For the life of me, I couldn't come up with one damn thing to say.

"What happens during the flashbacks, Jake?"

There was no point in lying anymore. "I just... sometimes... like if you touch me in a way... or say something that reminds me of something... you know... it just... it triggers something... and then it's not just us anymore... do you know what I mean?"

"Yeah. I think so. Can you pinpoint specific things?"

"No, because sometimes it doesn't bother me and sometimes it does."

"So how can we work through them?"

"I don't know if we can, to be honest. That's what makes it so fucked up."

We sat there quietly for a minute before Casey asked, "Don't take this the wrong way, but have you ever had therapy?"

"I've described to you how overprotective my mom is... so, yeah, of course, I have."

"But not recently, I take it?"

"I never really saw a reason. I was dealing okay with everything until I met you. God, that sounded bad. I didn't mean it in a negative way. It's just... I figured out ways around the flashbacks by never getting too close to anyone. If I had sex once with someone and had a flashback, they were never going to know. I could make some excuse that I wasn't feeling it. But, to be honest, when it was impersonal sex I rarely got them anyway, so I wasn't worrying."

"So you worry more with me?"

"Yeah. I want to make you happy. Before we have sex, I start worrying about having the flashbacks, and then I worry about what I'm going to say to you and I worry that you're going to think I'm a freak."

"Jesus, Jake, it's amazing you can even get a hard-on with all that anxiety."

Her brash assessment of my angst surprised me and I couldn't help but grin.

"Look, babe, I'm not trying to make light of this. I know you're suffering. I can see it. But now that you've been honest with me and I know what's going on, and you aren't in horrific pain... you don't need to worry anymore. If a flashback comes on, no biggie, we'll deal with it."

"You say that now, but what if they don't stop? What if they get worse?"

"So we don't have sex for a while... or ever... as long as we have intimacy and love and communication, that's all that matters."

"Oh, great." I shook my head in frustration. "That's not enough for me, Case. If I can't be a real man for you, then you need to find someone who will."

"You don't get it. I don't want anyone else. I only want you... forever. I know we can work through this and be where we were before. Why are you fighting this?"

I didn't reply to her. I just stared off into space.

"Look at me," she whispered.

I lifted my eyes to meet hers.

"Stop second guessing yourself and start believing in us."

"I do believe in us."

"If you did, you wouldn't be questioning my loyalty to you."

"It's not you, Casey. It's me."

"No. When you say that I need to find a 'real man', you're putting this all on me. That's not fair. There are two of us in this relationship. Both of us need to work to keep it strong. I feel like you aren't giving me any credit – like my love for you doesn't matter."

"I didn't mean it that way."

"We don't choose who we love, Jake. It just happens. It can't be explained and it can't be broken as long as we both protect it. I'm prepared to keep what we have safe. Are you?"

I thought about what she said. Casey was right; I wasn't giving her the credit she deserved. She'd never wavered in her devotion to me. If anyone could get me through this, it was Casey. I stared her in the eye before responding, "I am."

A dazzling smile formed on Casey's face. She put her arms around my neck and kissed me. "It's you and me forever, buddy... and don't you forget it!"

"I won't."

"In fact, I'm going to be like Krista and never let you break up with me."

I laughed and pulled her to me. "I don't want to," I said, as I attacked her neck in kisses. "I have an idea."

"What?"

"Can we try again?"

"I thought you'd never ask."

And this time around, Ray was nowhere to be found. The worry that had plagued me the past two weeks was gone. Maybe it was her unwavering belief in us, or maybe it was that we were stronger together than apart. It was like we had agreed to partner up and defeat Ray where he played. Afterward, when we were lying in each other's arms, I felt so hopeful. Casey was right. What we had was special, and I was prepared to fight for us.

43

CASEY: MEET THE PARENTS

W e lay on the bed talking for so long that we totally forgot to order our dinner, so finally Jake called room service at 10:00 pm. Twenty minutes later there was a knock on the door, and Jake disappeared into the bathroom so there wouldn't be any awkwardness with the waiter. I let him in and watched him set everything up. I noticed him glance around the room several times. Obviously, he knew who was staying there.

When he was finished setting up, the waiter asked, "Is there anything else I can get you, madam?"

"No, thank you. It smells amazing." I gave him a tip and the waiter left, but not before taking one more disappointed look around.

Jake came out of the bathroom wet and totally naked. I couldn't help but marvel at him. He was so beautiful. I remembered how self-conscious he was about his scars when we first met, and now he was totally comfortable parading around nude. I smiled adoringly at my boyfriend.

He looked up and smiled. "What?"

"I was just admiring the view."

"It took that dude forever to set up. I got bored and decided to take a shower." He grinned.

I melted.

Jake slipped on his boxers and a T-shirt and sat down opposite me at the table. We dug in.

"So, we really haven't talked about what we're going to do this year, with us living in different states and all," Jake said.

"I know. I've been avoiding the topic because it makes me sad. I wish I'd met you earlier so I could have put in a transfer to a school in LA."

"You'd do that? Move to LA?"

"Seriously? I would move wherever you are."

"I actually don't think it's too late to transfer," he said.

"It is for a public school. You have to apply in the winter. I have a friend who did that, so I know. But I'm not sure about private schools. I couldn't afford those anyway."

Jake gave me a look. Money was no obstacle for him. "But what if a private school would accept a late transfer? I mean, would you really want to leave Arizona... leave your family?"

"Yes, Jake. You're my family now. I want to be with you."

Jake put down his fork. He flashed me a sheepish grin.

"What?" I asked.

"I've actually had someone look into that. There are a few private schools in LA that have accounting programs, and one of them is only about ten miles from my place. They'll all accept late transfers."

I stared at Jake in shock. "Really? You actually researched it?"

"Well, I had my agent back home look into it. In order to do a late transfer, you have to have the Dean sign off on it. And if he won't, I'll persuade him."

I smiled. "I... I don't know what to say. Would you want me to move there?"

"Yeah, I would. Once I have my surgery, I won't be able to travel for a while, and with you in school, it might be hard to see each other very often. I mean, we can make it work, so don't feel like you have to move–"

I jumped from my seat and flung myself into his arms. "Are you kidding me? Of course I want to move. I just want to be with you. I'm so happy right now. It's like a weight has been lifted off me."

"Well, okay then. After dinner, let's pick out your new school."

We spent the rest of the night going over my options and making plans. I decided I wanted to go to the university closest to Jake's place. We both agreed that I should have my own apartment near campus, not only to make it easier school-wise but also to appease my parents, who were sure to be skeptical about my move. Of course Jake wanted to pay for everything, and I wasn't really in the position to refuse.

Mid-August came before I knew it. The summer of my life was coming to an end, but thanks to my incredible boyfriend, our impending separation didn't seem so daunting. I had so much to do before moving to LA. I broke the news to my parents and friends the day after I was admitted into my new school. My parents were not happy, but I was 100% sure of my decision and didn't give them an opportunity to protest. My friends were sad to see me leave but thrilled by the reason for the move. Taylor found a replacement roommate, but made me swear that she could come and visit whenever she wanted. She also requested to sleep with Jake, but I vetoed her on that point.

Before I knew it, I was back on a plane for the States. Leaving Jake was one of the hardest things I'd ever done. I was so in love, and the idea of being apart from him even for a day hurt my heart. I even contemplated just brushing off my education and staying in Europe with Jake, but I'd made a commitment to myself that I would get my degree, and that was what I was going to do.

The move to Los Angeles was easier than I'd imagined. Jake had my new apartment furnished, so really all I needed to bring were my clothes and a few other essentials. He also set up a bank account in my name with enough money in it to keep me going for a long time. We had talked about it and agreed that I wouldn't get a job right away. I wanted to be there for him after the surgery, and if I were tied to a job in addition to my studies, free time would be difficult. Not having to focus on anything but completing my education appealed to me more than I cared to admit. I'd always been an independent, working girl, but it felt good to be taken care of for a change.

I started my senior year with Jake still away on tour. I missed him fiercely but stayed in constant contact with him. Our relationship went back to those first days after we met at the wedding – the hours spent on the phone while he traveled from city to city – but now I didn't just have to imagine what he was experiencing, I could see it in my mind because I'd lived it. It really had been the trip of a lifetime.

I poured myself into my studies and found my professors at my new school to be much more accessible and willing to help than those at my old. I was excited to be learning so much. I met a few friends in my accounting classes the very first week of school, which made me very happy since I'd actually been worried about having to eat by myself in the cafeteria like a loser. The thing with college is you meet one person, then it seems you have a huge group of friends. I even started hanging out with them in the evenings and on the weekends and went with them to school events. But I didn't tell anyone about Jake. It seemed like bragging to dangle my rock star boyfriend in front of these people.

Jake came home the last week in September. I was so excited that I arrived an hour early to LAX and ended up waiting another hour and a half for him to go through passport control, claim his bags, and then get searched while going through customs. But none of that mattered when I saw him walk through the doors and head up the ramp. Excitement coursed through me. He was wearing jeans, a T-shirt, and a baseball cap. He was flanked on either side by security and another attendant had his bags on a cart.

It took a matter of seconds for him to be recognized. I heard one girl call out, "That's Jake McKallister!", which caused a flurry of activity. Jake acknowledged the crowd as he scanned the faces. I knew he was looking for me. I stood toward the end of the ramp holding a sign. When he saw me, a big smile spread across his face, and then his eyes traveled upwards to my sign, which read 'Cake'. He nodded, amused. And then I was in his arms. He picked me up and kissed me, and the crowd around us oohed and ahhed. Cameras flashed around us.

Jake put me down and whispered in my ear, "I missed you so much."

"Me too."

"I like your sign," he said, looking pleased.

"I thought you would. It's short and sweet."

"Just like you."

"Hey, I'll have you know I'm 5'6. That's taller than the average woman."

"Geez, sensitive," Jake teased. "Did you bring your car?"

"No. I ubered here, since you said you had a car that was picking you up."

"I do. I was just making sure. We better get out of here before we end up on a magazine cover."

Jake came home on a Monday, and by Friday we were on a plane flying to Arizona to meet my family. Jake was so nervous as we walked up the driveway.

"Relax, they're going to love you, Jake," I said.

"Yeah, I doubt that Casey," Jake replied. "I'm any father's worst nightmare."

"I told you, my dad tries to act tough. You just have to get through the crusty exterior into the soft goodness inside."

"One, that's nasty," Jake cringed. "And two, something tells me I won't be warming his heart."

I squeezed his hand and whispered, "You worry too much. Relax. Just be yourself – only nicer and cuter and more successful."

Jake gave me a sideways look and rolled his eyes.

I laughed. "You're taking this way too seriously. I mean really, how can you get better than you already are? You're the whole package, baby," I said and slapped his ass.

Jake spun around and playfully grabbed my hand. "Hey, keep the hands waist up when your father is within a twenty-five-mile radius."

"You don't think he knows my hands have been waist down?"

"Okay, you're really starting to freak me out now. You better not make any kind of sexual references around him. I'm not kidding. I'm nervous enough already."

"I won't." I grinned.

"Seriously, Casey. Promise me?"

I sighed. "God, you're no fun. Fine. I promise."

I opened the door and called out, "Hello? Mom? Dad?" I then grabbed his ass and squeezed.

Jake looked at me intensely.

I whispered, "That was just to get me through the weekend. I'm done now."

Before Jake could react, we heard my mother's squeal from across the house.

"You're early," she panted, as she rounded the corner with an apron on. I looked at her in surprise. My mother never wore an apron. She usually didn't care if she sat down to dinner with a little food slopped on her shirt. *Someone's trying to impress.* My mom came straight to me with a big, excited smile on her face and gave me a quick hug. Then she turned her full, and giddy, attention on Jake.

"Jake, it's so nice to meet you," Mom said, as she reached out her hand.

Jake smiled and shook it. "It's really nice to meet you, too. What would you like me to call you – Mrs. Caldwell, or…?"

"Oh, please, call me Linda."

"Linda, thanks for having me over this weekend," Jake said.

"The pleasure is ours. You're a busy guy – we just really appreciate you taking the time to come and meet us. I'm sure Casey's told you we're a pretty relaxed bunch, so please make yourself at home. I hope you like lasagna. Casey said you like Italian food," Mom rambled.

"I love lasagna."

"Oh, good," Mom said, as she patted Jake's arm. Then to me, she said, "Why don't you put your bags in your rooms? And then meet me in the kitchen."

"Okay." I grabbed Jake's hand. We dropped his bag off in the guest room and then I led him to my childhood bedroom. I stopped him before we got there.

"Before you enter, I just want to explain myself."

"Uh-oh… what?"

"Remember that I was a teenager when I decorated this room, and that I haven't lived at home for several years."

"Yeah, yeah… step aside." Jake grinned. I tried to block him from entering. We wrestled before he playfully pushed me out of the way. He opened the door, looked around, then started laughing. Even though I no longer lived at home, my room remained largely unchanged from the boy-crazy teenager that decorated it. Hot pink décor and millions of pictures and posters, some of half naked celebrity guys – none of Jake, thank god – decorated the walls.

"Wow." Jake eyes sparkled as he looked around in awe. "You really liked pink."

"And naked guys too, apparently."

"Yeah. You perv," Jake chuckled. "I just... I don't really know what to say."

"I know," I frowned. "It's awful."

"I love it."

"You do?" I asked, blushing from embarrassment.

"Yeah. This is like out of a movie or something."

"I know," I laughed.

"I can tell that you were a happy kid."

I heard maybe just the faintest bit of melancholy in his voice.

"I was a happy kid," I said and watched Jake for a reaction. "Does that... um... make you feel bad... because yours was, obviously, not as happy?"

Jake looked at me for a second, then shook his head. "Contrary to popular belief, Casey, I had the most kick-ass childhood ever. It was thirteen and up that sucked."

"Well, it doesn't suck now, does it?" I asked, as I wrapped my arms around his waist and kissed him.

"No, twenty-three and up has been pretty good so far." He grinned.

"Uh-huh," I mumbled, getting grabby with him. "Too bad you have that twenty-five-mile radius rule, because I think you and I could have lots of fun under my hot pink sheets."

Jake wrestled free of me. "You promised me, Casey."

"You're such a goody-two-shoes. You're a disgrace to rock stars everywhere."

"Really? Okay, then, how about when you meet my mom I run my hand up your shirt and grope your boob? I'm sure that will make just as good a first impression."

I winced. "Oh yeah. I see your point. I'll be a good girl."

"Thank you."

We walked back to the kitchen. "Where's Dad?"

"He just went to the store for me. Your brothers should be here any minute. Have a seat," Mom said, staring at Jake with a

star-struck smile on her face. Jake and I sat on the barstools.
Mom was still staring.

"If you take a picture, it'll last longer," I teased her.

"Oh, sorry," she said. "It's just ... you're more handsome in person."

"Oh...thanks."

"Mom, let's not be creepy," I rolled my eyes. "We're trying to make a good impression, remember?"

"That's not creepy, Casey. It's simply an observation."

"Yeah, Casey. Let your mom observe," Jake teased.

Mom laughed out loud. "Ha! You're funny as well as handsome. I can see why Casey likes you."

"Still creepy, Mom."

As Mom finished making a salad, we chatted easily. We'd only been there for ten minutes, and Jake already seemed totally comfortable and relaxed around my mom. But then, we both knew she wasn't going to be the problem.

My dad walked into the kitchen about five minutes later. He stopped in his tracks when he saw us.

"You're early," he said, with very little emotion.

"Why does everyone keep saying that? We aren't that early," I replied. "Dad, this is Jake." Jake got up out of his chair and went to shake my dad's hand.

Dad reached out for his. "How do you do?" he said formally.

"Good. It's nice to meet you," Jake responded, with the slightest falter in his voice. Jake was always so confident and in control; it was funny to see him nervous.

My dad looked Jake up and down, lingering on a tattoo on Jake's arm, then dropped his hand and gave me a hug. "Look at you," he said and held me back at arm's length. "Since when do you wear dresses? Are you going all Hollywood on me?"

"Dad," I said smiling. "I'm not twelve anymore."

"Don't remind me." He smiled. "You do look beautiful, honey. I've missed you."

"Ahh... thanks. I missed you too, Dad."

Dad looked at Jake again and said, "Well, welcome to our home, Jake. We've been waiting a long time to meet you."

"Yeah, I'm sorry about that. I would have come sooner, but I've been out of the country for awhile."

"Yes, I know. My daughter was with you," Dad said abruptly.

"And she had a wonderful time. Thank you for taking such good care of her, Jake," Mom jumped in, covertly slapping Dad on the arm.

"Of course. I wouldn't let anything happen to Casey," Jake said, glancing apprehensively at my dad.

Just then, the door opened and my brother Miles and his wife, Darcy, walked in with their two kids, Sydney and Riley. The kids ran in to hug my parents, and then I got my turn to kiss and hug my little niece and nephew.

Miles walked straight to Jake and said, "Hi, I'm Miles."

"Jake. Nice to meet you."

"And I'm Darcy."

"Nice to meet you, too."

"And these are our kids. This is Sydney and this is Riley."

"Hi, Sydney. Hi, Riley. I'm Jake."

Sydney smiled shyly and ducked her head on her mom's leg. Riley was busy hitting Miles in the leg with a plastic sword. Neither one of them answered back.

"Sorry, they're a little shy when they first meet someone new," Darcy explained apologetically.

"No worries."

We made some small talk in the kitchen as my mom finished up dinner. Sydney was no longer hiding behind Darcy. She'd taken an interest in Jake and was eyeing him when she asked, "Are you Auntie's boyfriend?"

"I am," Jake answered.

"You have long hair," Sydney said, wrinkling her nose to show her distaste.

"Sydney!" Darcy gasped, looking horrified.

Jake raised his eyebrows as he reached for his hair. "Do I?"

Sydney laughed. Her facial expression changed from judgmental to delight.

"I'm so sorry, Jake. She just says things sometimes without thinking," Darcy said, flustered.

"Trust me, it takes a lot more than that to offend me."

"Well, that's good, then, because this family doesn't hold back," Darcy replied.

"I'm getting that vibe."

Riley now wandered over. "Do you like thords?" he asked, with his signature lisp.

"Yep. They're my favorite plastic weapons," Jake responded casually. I loved how natural Jake was with kids. He never talked down to them.

"Mine too," Riley said, as he swung his through the air and pretended to stab Jake.

"Riley, no stabbing the guests," Miles said, and pointed the sword the other direction.

"Oh, my god, we really aren't that bad of parents... I promise," Darcy said, shaking her head and looking embarrassed.

"I'm actually around kids pretty often, so I know how they operate," Jake replied.

"The guitarist in his band has three kids who were on tour with them," I added. "Jake has been known to babysit on occasion."

"Really? You babysit?" Miles asked. "Darcy, did you hear that? He babysits."

"I don't babysit." Jake disagreed. "My friend brings his older two over for piano lessons, and then he conveniently disappears. There's a big difference."

Everyone laughed.

"How old are the kids?" Darcy asked, looking less stressed.

"Nine, six, and two."

"I'm seven," Sydney replied.

"No way?" Jake joked. "Me too."

"No, you're not," they screamed in unison, giggling.

"Okay, you got me. I'm twenty-three."

"You're old," Riley commented.

Jake made a face.

"He's not old," Sydney giggled. "Papa's old."

"Hey, you leave me out of this!" Dad bellowed from across the room, but there was a smile on his face.

"I'm five," Riley interrupted.

"Five? Are you in kindergarten?" Jake asked.

"Yes."

"I'm in second grade," Sydney said proudly. Sydney was now just inches from Jake, looking up at him in awe.

"Wow, so you can read now."

"Yes. I can read since kindergarten," Sydney said importantly.

"I can read, too," Riley interrupted again.

"No, you can't," Sydney said.

"Yes, I can," Riley whined.

"Sydney, Riley knows how to read kindergarten words," Darcy said, coming to his rescue.

"Yes, but *I* can read whole sentences." Sydney insisted, importantly.

"Big deal, so can I," Jake boasted.

Sydney thought that was hysterical. She laughed and laughed.

"What's your favorite subject in school?" Jake asked her.

"My favorite subject is math," Sydney proclaimed.

"My favorite subject is math, too," Riley repeated.

"No, it's not," Sydney said in an irritated voice. "You're just copying me."

"You know what my favorite subject in school was?" Jake asked, in an attempt to distract them from their argument.

"No!" Riley said with excitement.

"What?" Sydney asked with interest, momentarily forgetting about her dispute with Riley.

"Recess."

Both Sydney and Riley laughed. So did their parents.

"That's not a subject," Sydney said, grabbing onto Jake's arm.

"Yes, it is, and I was good at it," Jake replied.

"I'm good at recess, too," Riley said, jumping up and down.

"Me too," Sydney agreed.

And that was all it took for Jake to win over my niece and nephew. From that moment on, they followed him around everywhere, chattering endlessly. Miles and Darcy kept apologizing, but Jake just shrugged it off like it was no big deal.

My other brother, Luke, arrived in his typically loud manner. "I'm here!" he sang out. He was always fashionably late. Luke pulled me up into a big bear hug, then eyed Jake and said jokingly, "You look just like Jake McKallister. Has anyone ever told you that?"

"Yeah, a few people actually."

Luke let me go and shook Jake's hand. "Nice to meet ya, man. I'm Luke."

"Nice to meet you, too. I'm Jake."

"Damn, it's weird to see you here. I still haven't been able to wrap my head around the fact that my baby sister is dating a rock star." Luke rumpled my hair. I slapped his hand away. "Of course, it'll seem more real when I'm standing backstage at one of your concerts picking up on your groupies."

"Luke!" my mom admonished.

"I was just kidding, Mom, geez," Luke said.

"Could you please just let Jake get acquainted with us first before you go scaring him off?"

"That's impossible. I have four brothers."

"Oh, well, in that case," Luke said mischievously, "I wasn't kidding."

"I'll try to make that dream come true for you." Jake grinned.

"Yah!" Luke exclaimed, pumping his arm in the air.

"Yeah, all right, Luke. Good luck with that," Mom shot back.

"What, you don't think I got game, Mom?"

"No, of course I do, honey. Mommy thinks you have lots of game."

We all laughed at that. Luke huffed like he was mad, but he wasn't. Jake looked on with amusement.

We stood around chatting with my brothers for a few minutes until Mom called out, "Dinner is served."

We walked over to the table. Jake was about to sit when Mom said, "Oh, not that one, Jake. It's wobbly. Luke, you sit there instead."

"Oh, of course," Luke said, rolling his eyes and making a scene about having to sit in the broken chair.

"Well, I don't want our guest falling to the floor... you I don't care."

"Yeah, I mean Jake is used to luxury... but me? I wouldn't know what I'm missing. Right?"

"Right," Mom said. "Exactly."

I turned to Luke and said, "Jake's got an 1100-square-foot townhouse from the 70's. It's definitely not luxurious."

"What the... ? Why in the hell do you not live in a mansion?" Luke asked incredulously.

"Luke, language," Miles admonished, as he glanced at his two kids.

"Sorry. Why the heck do you not live in a mansion?"

Jake shrugged. "I don't need one. I'm on tour most of the time."

"Well, that just sucks," Luke whined. "You've totally ruined my impression of rock stars. Thanks, Jake!" For effect, Luke threw his arms up in the air dramatically.

"Sorry to disappoint you. If it makes you feel any better, I have a sick tour bus."

"Yeah, it makes me feel a little better," Luke sighed.

Jake laughed. I could tell he was really starting to hit it off with Luke.

We all found our seats and began eating. My brothers started teasing me about living in California, so I teased them about being idiots. Jake just listened with an amused look on his face.

"Where are you originally from, Jake?" Mom asked conversationally.

"California."

Everyone looked around at each other in surprise, then erupted in laughter.

"Dude, you could have said something while we were ripping your state to shreds," Luke said.

"I thought it was funny."

"Are you from the LA area?"

"I grew up about fifty miles north of LA."

"By the ocean?"

"Yeah."

"Okay, so this is going to be one of those stereotypical Southern California questions. Are you a surfer?" Miles asked.

"I was. I haven't surfed in a long time. When I was a kid, my dad and brother and I surfed every morning before school. I had the bleach-blond surfer hair and everything."

"Ahhh… cute," I said, absently stroking his hair. "I can't picture you blond."

"How come you don't surf anymore?" Dad asked.

"Um… I have a bad knee."

Dad nodded.

"Well, here's another stereotypical Southern California question. Have you ever been attacked by a shark?" Luke asked.

Everyone laughed again.

Jake got a strange look on his face and said, "Well… actually… "

"You didn't," I countered. I couldn't tell if he was kidding or not.

Still, Jake had a weird look.

"Okay, but not like a great white or anything?" I asked uncertainly.

Jake shrugged.

"Seriously?" Miles asked in shock.

"No, I was just kidding. But if I'd been attacked by a shark of *any* kind, I feel like it should have counted. Geez, Casey."

That got a big laugh.

"Seriously, man, I couldn't surf just for fear of getting attacked by a shark," Luke commented.

"No, Luke, you couldn't surf because you wouldn't be able to get your fat ass up on the board," Miles insulted.

Luke reached over and punched him.

"How old were you when you first started surfing?" Mom asked.

"Like six or seven, so I didn't really know sharks were something to fear until I was a little older. One time, two dolphins swam up and started circling me. My dad told me to put my feet up on the board and sit still. It wasn't until we were back on shore that he told me dolphins will sometimes protect humans when sharks are near. I was a little freaked out by that."

"I can imagine," Mom commented.

"Did you stop surfing after that?" Darcy asked.

"No. But whenever I saw dolphins I pulled my feet up onto the board. My dad used to say that there's no reason to invite a shark to have a snack."

"Dude, if you were surfing at six years old, there would be no reason to put your feet on the board. The shark could have just come out of the water and swallowed you whole."

"No doubt," Jake agreed.

"Your mom was fine with you surfing at six years old?" Darcy asked, looking over at Riley.

"No. But Kyle and I were such brats back then that I think she was just happy to have us out of the house."

"What do your parents do for a living?" Dad asked.

"My dad is a postman, and my mom is a music teacher."

"Really?" Mom questioned in surprise. "I didn't realize you came from a middle-class background."

"Yeah... What type of family did you think I came from?" Jake asked curiously.

"I don't know... like an entertainment family," Mom said, looking a little embarrassed.

"What, Mom, like the Partridge family?" Luke teased.

Everyone laughed.

"No. I don't know. Maybe," Mom replied, flustered.

"No, I'm the only professional musician in my family."

"What do your siblings do for a living?" Dad questioned. He seemed interested in Jake, and that was a good thing. If my dad didn't like someone, he usually got quiet and detached from the conversation.

"The two youngest, Gracie and Quinn, are in middle and high school. Then I have another younger brother, Kyle, and he works for me. My older sister Emma is a nurse. Then Keith owns a surf and skate shop in my hometown. My oldest brother Mitch – he's actually my half-brother, my dad's son –he lives here in Arizona and is an appraisal officer, or something like that."

"And you're the only singer? How did that happen?" Miles asked.

"I'm the only professional one, but most of my siblings can carry a tune."

"Well, that's more than you're going to get in this family," Miles joked. "Have you heard my little sister sing?"

"I have actually," Jake said, cringing. "I wasn't impressed."

"Hey!" I pretended to be offended.

"Wait, hold on a minute," Luke interrupted. "If my calculations are correct, you're a middle child, too."

"Yep, smack dab in the middle," he said. "Three older, three younger."

"Oh, that sucks. I'm sorry, man," Luke consoled, then looked at my mom accusingly, "I bet they make you sit in the wobbly chair when important company comes over, too."

Jake nodded with a frown.

"Oh, boo-hoo," I said.

"Hey MCS is a real thing," Luke said seriously.

"MCS?" Darcy asked.

"Middle Child Syndrome," Luke finished.

Jake laughed.

"Sorry to break up your little pity party, but there is no such thing as MCS," I shot back.

Luke gasped as if he were offended. "Back me up here, Jake."

"Sorry, you're on your own. There's no winning an argument with Casey."

Everyone agreed.

"I hear ya, brother," Luke said, still laughing.

The conversation drifted off Jake for a while. We chatted about the kids and about Dad going back to work. Jake seemed to visibly relax with my family, as if he no longer found the prospect of interacting with them intimidating. But of course, it didn't take long for the discussion to center around Jake again. He was, after all, way more interesting than anything else my family had to talk about.

"Why do you have tattoos?" Sydney asked, after studying Jake for most of the dinner.

"'Cause I like them," Jake answered, matter of factly. "And they're sick."

"He's a rock star, Syd. He has to look the part," Luke added, as if he knew Jake's motivations.

"What's a rock star?" Sydney asked.

"Someone who sings and performs on stage for lots of people," I said.

"Like Justin Bieber?" Sydney asked, with a little-added interest.

Luke looked between the two of them in amusement.

"Um…" Jake's eyes widen. "Sort of, yeah."

"Do you know Justin Bieber?"

"I've met him."

"You have?" Sydney's eyes were huge. "Are you famous, too?"

Jake looked kind of embarrassed.

"Yes, he is," Darcy answered for him.

"Are you on TV?" She stared right at Jake, wanting the answer to come from him.

"Sometimes, yeah," Jake answered.

"What's your name?"

"Jake McKallister."

Sydney looked Jake up and down, and then said, "Well, I've never heard of you."

Everyone laughed at her precociousness.

"Ooh… shot down by the second grader!" Luke said holding his arms up for effect. I could see a bromance in the making.

"That's probably a good thing," Jake said to Sydney.

"How do they put the color on?" My niece continued with the inquisition.

"What?"

"Sydney, why don't you give Jake a break with the questions?" Miles said.

Sydney ignored her father. "The tattoos. How do they put in the colors?"

"Oh… with tiny little needles," Jake replied.

Sydney gasped, putting her hands to her mouth. "Yuck. Did it hurt?"

"No, not really," Jake replied.

"How many do you have?"

"A lot."

"Can I see them?"

Jake laughed. "No, I don't think so."

"Why not?" Sydney demanded.

"Because I would have to take my shirt off at the dinner table. I'm pretty sure that would be considered bad manners," Jake explained.

"After dinner then," she responded.

Everyone laughed, including Jake, who then looked around the table and said, "A little help here?"

"Sydney," Darcy began, trying to suppress her mirth. "It's not appropriate to ask someone to take their shirt off."

"At least not until you buy them a drink," Luke whispered to Jake.

"All right," Mom said, attempting to rein in the conversation. "Let's move on. I don't think I told you guys the story about Aunt Stacy getting caught in a hurricane when she was on vacation."

Mom proceeded to tell the lively story, and the focus went off Jake for a short while. Sydney finally seemed to lose interest, and she left the table to color.

"So, Jake, have you always wanted to be a professional musician?"

"Um... yeah, when I was a kid I did. My mom's a music teacher, and she started training all of us how to play the piano when we turned three. I really took to it and picked stuff up much faster than my siblings. Mom was shocked when she discovered I could hear something once or twice and then recreate it without written notes."

"Really?" Dad asked, seemingly impressed.

"So hold on," Luke cut in. "I can play you a song right now, one you've never heard before, and you could play it back to me?"

"I might have to hear it a couple of times, but yeah."

"Damn," Luke said, sitting back and looking awestruck.

"How rare is it to be able to do that?" Mom asked.

"I don't know, really. When I was younger I just thought of it as a cool parlor trick that I could impress my friends with. But now that I work as a musician, I can definitely see the benefits. I pick up new instruments easily, and I can hear the melody in my head while I'm writing a song."

"Huh, that's interesting. So your mom picked up on this and cultivated your talent?"

"It would seem that way, yeah." Jake smiled. "I thought of it more like punishment when I was young, though. All the other kids got to be outside playing, and I was stuck inside on the piano."

"Ahh, poor guy," Mom sympathized. "I bet you thank her now."

"I do, actually," Jake agreed.

"You were really young when you got started in the music business, weren't you?" Darcy asked.

"Yeah. Sixteen."

"Dude, you're like a musical prodigy," Luke complimented.

"I don't know about that," Jake replied, humbly. In fact, he was often referred to as a prodigy, and from everything I'd seen of him and his extraordinary talent, I completely agreed with that assessment.

Dad cleared his throat and said, "How many months out of the year are you away on tour?"

"It varies."

"But you're away quite a bit, isn't that right? I can imagine it would be tough to live a normal life."

"Who wants a normal life?" Luke asked. "I live a normal life and, I gotta say, it kind of sucks."

I wasn't sure where my dad was going with his line of questioning, but I assumed he was assessing how long I would be away if our relationship lasted.

"Traveling is part of the job for sure. Most musicians make their money touring nowadays. There's not a lot of reimbursement to be had from traditional record sales, now that everything has gone digital."

"So, in order to be successful, you pretty much have to live your life on the road?"

"I have for the past seven years, yeah, but that was because I was establishing myself. Now that I have a pretty loyal fan base, I can cut back some."

"And have you?"

"Um… I plan to. I always say I'm going to take a break, but then I come off tour and release an album, and I'm right back out there."

"Is it addicting?"

"Honestly, yeah. I really like performing, but this time, I'm definitely taking a break from touring for awhile."

"What's different this time?" Dad asked curiously.

Jake grinned and looked at me. "Well, a few things."

My family picked up on his reference and laughed.

"Not only do I want to stay in town while Casey finishes her senior year, but I'm also going to have knee surgery next month, so I physically won't be able to perform."

"Oh wow, I'm sorry to hear that. What happened to your knee?"

"Just an old injury," Jake said, without elaborating.

Thankfully, my family didn't push for further details. We passed around the food and chatted easily with each other. Jake was enjoying all the family gossip, even though he had no idea who we were talking about.

"So I gotta ask," Luke said, bringing the conversation squarely back to Jake. "Being famous and all, you gotta meet lots of women. How'd my baby sister here catch your eye?"

"Her sense of humor. She was so funny. She just kind of blew me away the minute we met. It didn't hurt that she was beautiful, either."

"Oh, stop," I said, all the while motioning for him to continue.

"We just had instant chemistry, right?" Jake asked me.

"It was for me," I agreed. "I mean, what's not to like?"

"So you must have some insane stories to tell about fans and groupies," Luke said.

"I have lots, but most I can't say in front of kids."

"Oh, okay, now I'm interested. You gotta give me something."

"Let's just say I've been asked to sign pretty much every body part there is," Jake replied.

"Even the meat and potatoes?"

"Yes, even the meat and potatoes." Jake nodded.

"Ooooh, gross," the guys groaned in unison. "Seriously... why would they even want those things signed? I mean, what could possibly be the purpose of that?"

"Um, so they can have my signature tattooed on."

"Noooo," the guys screamed.

"Yes," Jake cringed.

"HOLY... SH... "

"Luke," Mom shushed him.

"Sorry, SHOOT. So do you sign them?"

"No, of course not. Do you really think I want my signature forever inked onto that?" Jake pretended to shudder.

"Tell me another crazies story."

"Um... Oh, this one time, I was at the grocery store, and there is this guy who keeps staring at me. He's like peering around the aisles."

"Creepy."

"Yeah. So finally this guy comes up to me and we make eye contact. He then puts his hands up, you know, like he's trying to talk down a suicide jumper and he starts approaching me slowly." Jake demonstrated to my family with his hands. "And he's saying things like, 'It's okay... take it easy... just relax.' He's talking to me like he's trying to tame a wild animal. So weird. Then he says to me, 'Easy... it's okay... I don't want to talk to you, I just want to take a picture with you.'"

"No, he didn't?" Darcy gasped.

"I swear."

"What did you do?"

"I walked away."

"Geez, what a weirdo," Dad said.

"You know, the older I get the more I realize how many weird people are in the world," Mom said. "I mean, how do people get so... odd?"

"That's easy," Luke said, looking smug. "Weird people breed weird kids. I mean, think about it. Who is a weirdo going to marry? Well, another weirdo, of course. And then those two weirdoes pop out mini weirdoes. It's the circle of life, people... crazy style."

We all laughed.

After dinner, we retreated to the living room. As Jake walked in, he stopped in front of the piano.

"I didn't know you had a Steinway," he said to me.

"A what?"

"The piano... it's a Steinway."

"It belonged to my grandmother, and it was passed down to me by my mother."

"Only because it's such a huge waste of space, and she didn't want it in her living room," Dad grumbled.

"Like it would fit in her living room. She lives in a mobile home, Dave."

"Yeah, yeah. I think she purposely moved into one so she wouldn't have to take the damn piano."

Jake glanced back and forth between my parents with an amused look on his face.

"Anyway, it hasn't worked for as long as we've had it."

"It doesn't work?" Jake asked in disbelief.

"I mean, some of the keys are broken. I looked into getting it fixed, but it was too expensive. Someday, maybe," mom said.

"The only way we're fixing that thing is if we win the damn lotto. And even then, we'll have to have bought every single other thing we ever wanted first," Dad griped.

Jake looked back and forth between my parents, grinning at their verbal sparring.

Mom gave Dad a warning look, and he shut up.

"I can get it into working condition for you," Jake offered.

"Seriously? You know how?"

"Yeah. I fix all my own instruments. Do you have a music store in town?"

"Bensen's is on Main Street."

"Sweet. I can stop in there for some supplies tomorrow."

"Really, Jake, that isn't necessary. We didn't ask you here so you could work."

"It's no chore at all. I have all weekend. I love fixing things. You'd actually be making me happy."

Mom smiled and patted Jake on the shoulder. "I would love it, then. Thank you, Jake."

"Well, Dad," Luke cut in. "Looks like you just won the Lotto."

〜

We all settled down on the couches in the living room.

"So, Casey, have you made friends at your new school?" Darcy asked.

"I have. I met this group of girls that I really like."

"What do they think about you dating Jake?"

Jake looked at me inquisitively. "Yeah, Casey, what do they think?"

I could tell I had a guilty look on my face when I said, "I haven't told them."

"You haven't told them?" Mom asked. "Why not?"

"When we first met, I didn't say anything because I hardly knew them, and then once we became friends it seemed weird to just blurt it out. I didn't want them to think I was bragging."

"So now you're just lying?" Mom nodded. "That's so much better."

"I'm not lying. I'm just omitting the truth."

"So are you never going to tell them?"

"No, I am. I'm just waiting for the right moment."

"Like when they see a picture of the two of you together in *People* magazine?" Mom asked.

"Right. Just before that."

"Dude, does it bother you that she's keeping you a secret?" Luke asked.

"I just got back from tour. I didn't even know I was her dirty little secret until a few days ago."

"That's not at all what you are," I said, hugging him. "I just don't want to share you yet."

"Uh huh, right. Oh, speaking of sharing, Linda... I think you might have something that I really need to see," Jake said.

"What?" I asked, looking at him in surprise.

"A certain binder."

Understanding dawned on me.

"Oh, no, you don't," I squealed, as I attempted to cover his mouth with my hand.

"What?" Mom asked, looking between the two of us questioningly.

"Casey's banana binder," Jake answered.

"She told you about that?" Mom asked, laughing.

"She did, and since then it's been my dream to get a look at it."

"I have no idea where it is. Casey might have destroyed it. But I promise you, Jake, if I find it, you'll be the first to know."

"I'd appreciate that."

After that, we talked for over two hours about all kinds of topics, from my dad's back surgery to how his recovery was going. We talked about the kids' school and Luke's job. Conversation flowed freely. At eight, Miles and Darcy announced it was the kids' bedtime and they'd be leaving soon. They changed the kids into pajamas and got them all ready for bed in hopes that they would fall asleep in the car on the short drive home. Darcy sat down to read them a story, but the kids insisted that Jake read it to them instead. Always a good sport, Jake settled onto the couch with my niece and nephew on either side of him and read them a story.

While Jake was occupying the kids, I got up to use the bathroom and was cornered by Darcy.

"Wow, Casey," Darcy whispered to me. "Jake's an awesome guy."

I smiled and nodded.

"He doesn't act like some huge celebrity. He's just really down to earth... and good with kids. Sydney and Riley love him."

"I know. I love watching him with kids. He'll make such a good daddy someday," I gushed.

"Okay, hold up, girl," Mom said, coming up beside us. "Let's just get you through college first."

"Obviously," I said, rolling my eyes.

"That being said," Mom continued, "do not, under any circumstances, let that one go."

"Trust me, you'd have to pry my cold, dead hands off him before I let go."

"I don't think he wants to go anywhere, Linda. Just the way he looks at her... Jake is definitely in love with you, Casey."

Jake must have heard his name. He looked up from his book and gave me a quizzical glance. I smiled warmly at him. He returned the sentiment, then went back to the story.

"I love him," Mom whispered. "He's wonderful. Even Dad thinks he's a genuine guy. He told me he was impressed with Jake."

"He did?" I sighed with relief. "Jake was so nervous about meeting him. He told me he was any dad's worst nightmare."

"Well, that's probably true on paper, but Jake is no nightmare. You were right to stay in Europe with him. He's something special."

I gave my mom a happy hug.

Later, we followed Darcy and Miles and the kids out to the car. As we were saying goodnight Sydney said, "Can you come to my game tomorrow, Jake?"

"What game?"

"My soccer game."

"What? I'm not invited?" I said, looking sad. The kids laughed.

"You can come, too," Sydney giggled.

"Wow, that is so nice of you," I teased.

"That sounds fun," Jake said, looking at me. "What are we doing tomorrow?"

"No big plans."

"Do you usually go to her games?" Jake asked my parents.

"Yes, but we were going to hang out with you and Casey instead tomorrow."

"You don't have to go," Miles said, then whispered to Jake, "You don't have to feel obligated. You can just tell her you're busy if you don't want to go."

"Actually, that sounds like fun," Jake replied. "If it works with you guys."

"Of course," Darcy said excitedly. "We would love to have you come."

"Yay!" Sydney and Riley squealed.

"Are you going to score a goal for me?" Jake asked.

"Probably not," Sydney replied.

"Probably not?" Jake laughed. "Way to have confidence, girl! You were supposed to say, heck yeah!"

"Heck yeah!" Sydney screamed.

44

CASEY: LIFE'S LITTLE INSECURITIES

Jake, my parents, and I got to the soccer fields about ten minutes before Sydney's game was to begin. Sydney saw us coming and left her team to run up to us. We all gave her a hug and she grabbed Jake's hand and led him to her side of the field. No one had noticed Jake until he crossed over the grass in front of all the players and their parents. Then there was an audible sound of surprise followed by whispering, staring, and pointing. We set up our chairs next to Miles and Darcy as Sydney went back to her practice. The entire crowd was now staring at Jake and snapping photos of him with their cell phones. He ignored them and chatted easily with my brother.

Mom whispered in my ear, "Is this going to be all right? Maybe bringing him here wasn't a good idea. What if he gets mobbed?"

"We didn't bring him, Mom. Jake wanted to come. He makes his own decisions. He'll be fine. He's used to dealing with crowds, don't worry."

The game started a few minutes later, and Jake was thoroughly enjoying watching Sydney play. He and my dad were chatting throughout the match about how the game was played and what the different positions were. My dad had grown up thinking only baseball, basketball, and football were real sports, and Jake had never seen a soccer match in his life, so they were bonding over their common ignorance of the game.

When halftime rolled around, parents of Sydney's teammates came over to Miles and Darcy and said hello to Jake. A few asked him to take pictures with their daughters. Jake graciously obliged, which opened the door for others who started wandering up to him asking to take pictures, too. It was interesting to watch Sydney's reaction to the attention Jake was getting. She was quickly realizing Jake was famous – on the same level as her idol Justin Bieber. She seemed in awe of Jake but also possessive. When people asked for his picture, Sydney would try to steal him away. As soon as the game started back up, Jake asked those still waiting to take a picture with him to hold off until after the game, so he didn't miss anything.

As it turns out, Sydney's team lost, and she did not score a goal. But with all the praise we lavished upon her, she still felt like a winner. The first thing she did when she got off the field was grab Jake's hand, and she refused to let go until we were in the car headed back to my parents' house.

After a lunch of sub sandwiches, Jake and I decided to go to the music store to buy the supplies Jake needed for the piano. Problem was, Sydney wasn't giving Jake much breathing room, and she insisted on coming, too. And since Sydney wanted to come, so did Riley. Jake made the mistake of saying they could come if it was okay with their mom; and once the invitation was out, there was no turning back.

After bribery didn't work on Sydney, Darcy agreed to let them go. It wasn't that she didn't trust us taking them; it was more that she didn't want to inconvenience Jake. Darcy insisted we take her minivan since the kids' car seats were already in there, but Jake refused to drive it, swearing it would ruin his rocker cred if he was seen at the wheel.

The music store was a challenge. Riley was all over the place, and I was the one running after him. Sydney stuck like glue to Jake. He chatted a few minutes with the ecstatic staff at the music store, got the supplies he needed, and took a few pictures. Then it was off to Target, where Jake promised to buy the kids one toy each. Before going into the store, Jake put on a baseball hat and a hoodie. It didn't help much. People noticed him right away but thankfully left him alone, for the most part. Jake plopped the kids in a cart and rode on the front like it was a skateboard. The kids screamed in delight as the cart sailed down the aisles.

Once in the toy area, Jake lifted the kids out of the cart. Riley found a sword and was done right away, but Sydney had to go up and down every row three times before making her final decision. People had started gathering at the ends of the aisles, peering down at Jake. He ignored them, as always. His focus was solely on our little quartet.

Once the kids were happy with their choices, Jake put them back in the cart and started riding it again. He looked over at me with a big grin on his face. I shook my head in amusement. Jake was like a big kid himself, and the little kids loved it.

We were headed toward the front of the store to pay when I heard someone call my name. "Casey?"

I looked up and saw Alicia Sanders, a girl I'd gone to school with. We had sort of been friends in elementary school, but lost touch in middle school and hardly ever exchanged words after that. She walked up and hugged me. Jake put the brakes on the cart.

"Hi, Alicia," I said.

"It's so good to see you," she said to me, without actually looking at me. Her focus was solely on Jake.

She stuck her hand out to him and said, "Hi, I'm Alicia, a friend of Casey's."

Oh, I didn't realize you still were.

"Oh, hey, nice to meet you," Jake replied in a pleasant manner. I guess he assumed she really was my friend.

"Wow, this is so crazy. I'm a huge fan. I just love your music. I think 'Catch My Light' is the best song ever written," Alicia gushed.

"Oh, thanks."

"Do you have a new album coming out soon?"

"The beginning of next year."

"Ooh... I can't wait," she cooed.

I stood there in the aisle watching my 'friend' make friends with my boyfriend. Alicia could not take her eyes off Jake. *Hello, I'm over here.* Clearly, she was more interested in him than me.

"So, what have you been up to?" I asked, lamely.

She reluctantly turned her attention to me. "Oh, you know, working, hanging out."

I nodded. "Where do you work?"

"I'm a brow specialist at Ulta."

"Oh, yeah?"

"Uh huh, and damn would I love getting my hands on your brows."

Jake raised his own brows in surprise and then grinned. My fingers went to my eyebrows as I smoothed them down. They weren't that bad, were they?

"So, Casey, I heard that you were dating Jake, but I thought it was just a rumor... until now."

"You heard? How?" I asked, in surprise.

"Everybody's been talking about it. Twitter, Insta."

"Seriously?" I questioned. I didn't know our relationship was trending. I glanced over at Jake to check his reaction, but he wasn't paying attention. He had his hands full with Riley, who was actively trying to climb out of the cart now that it was no longer a race car. Alicia looked over, too.

"Oh, my god, Casey! Those aren't yours, are they?" Alicia

asked with clear judgment in her voice as she fixed her eyes on Sydney and Riley.

Jake jerked his head up upon hearing her question. His lip turned slightly upward in amusement as his eyes darted back and forth between Alicia and me, as if convinced he was about to witness a girl fight.

"No. They're my niece and nephew. We're taking them out to buy them a toy," I said, feeling the need to explain. Now I was really annoyed. Clearly, I wasn't old enough to have a kid Sydney's age, unless I'd had her at fifteen.

"Oh, geez... I was gonna say, ho, you get around," Alicia smoothly insulted.

Jake burst out laughing, and Alicia beamed. I was slowly simmering. Plastering a fake smile on my face, I gave Jake a warning death stare and he stopped laughing.

"Let's go!" Sydney said as she tugged on Jake's arm.

Yes. Thank you, Sydney.

"Yeah, we better go," I said to Alicia. "It really was nice to see you again."

"You know, I have a great idea. I'm having a little gathering tonight. Why don't you and Jake come over? Melissa Espy and Ashley Gonzales and Haley Reyes will be there... Oh, and I can invite Tommy too if you want. We're really good friends now."

"Tommy Schultz?" I asked in disbelief. My ex-boyfriend?

"Yeah, he moved back here after college. He works at Chase Bank."

"Why would I want him there?" I responded with the slightest bit of edge in my voice.

"Oh, I don't know. I thought you might want to reminisce or something."

I scoffed out loud. Reminisce with my old boyfriend in front of my new one? Yeah, great idea. "No, that's okay."

Jake looked back and forth between Alicia and me, no doubt curious about our exchange.

"Tommy is Casey's old boyfriend," Alicia offered up smugly.

Are you frickin' serious? That was a bitch move. What if I hadn't told Jake about him? What if Jake were a jealous guy? Which clearly he wasn't, judging by the grin on his face and the clear amusement in his eyes.

"Oh, really?" He turned to me. "You sure you don't want to catch up with him, Case?"

"I don't have a burning need, no." I smiled back, but I was only pretending. Inside, I was pissed.

"Bad blood, huh?" she said, then added, "He dumped you right?"

Oh, my god... Alicia was coming close to becoming the first woman I punched in the vagina. Jake seemed to finally figure out that Alicia was *not* my friend, and that she was actively dissing me. He put his arm around my waist protectively and pulled me close.

"Lucky for me," Jake replied, staring down at me admiringly. At that moment, I really didn't deserve his devotion.

I glanced up at him before turning to Alicia and saying, "Anyway, we can't come tonight, but thanks for the invite."

Alicia completely ignored me. "Maybe Jake can come then."

"We're actually having dinner with my brother and his wife tonight, so, yeah, it won't work," Jake replied.

"What about tomorrow? We can do a barbecue." Alicia kept trying. "I really would like to catch up with Casey."

Yeah, sure you would.

"We're flying back to LA tomorrow," Jake answered.

"You live there, Casey? In LA?"

"Yes. I go to school there now."

"Oh, wow, so are you guys, like, living together?" she asked, looking impressed.

Jake and I exchanged glances. Although I spent most nights at his place, it wasn't something I intended to share with Alicia. "I have my own apartment close to school."

"Well, maybe someday." She practically batted her eyelashes at Jake.

I'd had enough. "Okay, well, it was good seeing you, Alicia."

"You too. Look me up on Insta or Twitter, okay? My user-name is @Aliciabrowsbaby. It's easy to remember."

"Sure," I answered, making a mental note to do everything in my power to forget that very catchy username.

"And Jake, it was so nice to meet you." Alicia took his hand again. "I actually follow you. You should follow me back."

"I don't really follow people," Jake replied, dropping her hand.

"I know... because you're a celeb. I get it. But since we know each other now, you wouldn't have to worry about me Twitter stalking you or anything."

Jake grinned knowingly. Alicia had stalker written all over her.

"Hey, would you mind if I, uh, maybe got a picture with you?"

"Um... " Jake said, glancing around. The last thing he wanted was to have a bunch of Target customers asking for pictures. "Yeah, sure, but real quick, so more people don't start asking."

"Yeah, yeah. Sure. Casey, can you take it?"

Why the hell not? I thought grumpily. I took her phone and quickly snapped a couple of pics, then handed the phone back to her.

Jake immediately started pushing the cart. I waved goodbye to Alicia, and we made a quick exit. Onlookers followed us to the front. As we waited in line, several people requested to take pictures with Jake, but most just snapped photos without asking.

When we got to the front of the line, the kids put their toys up on the conveyer belt. The cashier, an older woman in her fifties, greeted us warmly and asked how we were doing and if we'd found everything we were looking for.

Before Jake or I could respond, Sydney blurted out, "He's famous."

The cashier burst out laughing.

"Sydney!" I gasped in embarrassment. My niece looked at me like she didn't understand the problem.

"I know." The cashier nodded.

Looking amused, Jake said, "I paid her to say that."

When we arrived home, Jake was eager to tell the others about Sydney's declaration at Target. It got a big laugh. I didn't know why, but I was still annoyed by the whole encounter with Alicia. Jake usually defended me to women who were hitting on him, but he hadn't done that today. I felt like he'd encouraged the attention. While he went about fixing the piano, I went outside and had ice tea with my mom and sister-in-law.

"Is everything okay?" Mom asked.

"Yeah, why?"

"You just seem... quiet."

I looked at my mom. She knew me well. I sighed. "Just annoyed."

"Why?"

"When we were at Target, Alicia Sanders came up to say hi. Remember her?"

"Sure."

"Anyway, I haven't talked to her since middle school, and she comes up and acts like we're best friends and then proceeds to try and set me up with Tommy Schultz, steal my boyfriend, and hate on my eyebrows."

"Good lord! In that order? I can see why you're annoyed. That's a lot to happen on a trip to Target," Mom joked.

"What did she say about your eyebrows?" Darcy asked.

"She said she would love to get her hands on them. You know, implying they look like shit."

"I think you have nice eyebrows."

"Well, you have to say that because you're my mom."

"No, actually that isn't in the Mom Handbook."

"Uugghh," I groaned and covered my eyebrows with my hands.

"Okay, so I get the whole trying to steal your boyfriend, but I'm confused about the Tommy Schultz part," Mom said.

"Yeah, so she invited us to her house tonight, and then asked if I wanted her to bring Tommy over so we could reminisce about old times... in front of Jake!"

"Oh, that's not cool."

"I know. That's what I thought. And she was totally flirting with Jake the entire time. Like, I'm just standing there, invisible."

"No offense, Case, but doesn't your boyfriend 'get hit on everywhere he goes?"

"Yeah, but not by a girl who introduced herself to him as my friend."

"Yeah, that is pretty low," Darcy agreed.

"What did Jake do when she was flirting with him?" Mom asked.

"Nothing. I swear, sometimes he's so oblivious. I don't think he even realized until the end that she was hitting on him."

"God, I love him. He's so damn cute." Mom's eyes danced with amusement.

"Don't defend him." I pouted, even as my mood lightened a bit.

"Sorry if I don't feel too sorry for you. You knew what you were getting into when you met him. He can't help the attention he gets, and as long as he isn't acting on it and he's coming home to you every day, does it really matter?"

"I'm usually okay with it. But today rubbed me the wrong way. I don't know, I guess I'm just cranky. I'm PMS-ing."

"I could tell," Mom laughed. "Don't take it out on Jake... at least not until he's finished my piano."

As it turns out, it took longer than an hour for Jake to finish with the piano. He was still working on it when Mitch and

Kate arrived at the house. Mom had invited them over for dinner. She insisted Jake stop so that he could visit with his brother, but that didn't happen. Instead, Mitch sat on the piano bench and talked to Jake while he finished, and Kate and I caught up on everything that had been happening in both our lives. What were the chances when we were waitressing together, years ago, that we would one day both end up with McKallister boys?

Luke came over just as Jake was finishing with the repairs. Jake started playing an instrumental song on the piano, and Mom came running in to listen. When he was done, I looked over and saw tears in her eyes.

"Are you okay?" I asked.

She smiled. "I just... my grandma would have been so proud to hear Jake play her piano so beautifully."

"I had no idea it could make those sounds," Dad said.

"Yeah, it's a funny thing, these pianos," Jake teased. "They make noise."

After Jake taught Sydney and Riley a few notes on the piano, we retreated to the backyard for a barbecue. Gathered around the fire pit, we talked late into the night. By the time Mitch and Kate and the rest of my family left, my parents were exhausted and went straight to bed. Jake and I stayed up to watch "Saturday Night Live." When it was over, Jake turned off the TV and yawned.

"So, have you followed @Aliciabrowbabe yet?" I asked.

"You're saying it wrong. It's @Aliciabrowsbaby." Jake corrected as he put the emphases on the word 'browsbaby.'

"Wow, I'm impressed. You were really paying attention," I said, with just a hint of accusation.

"What's that supposed to mean?" he questioned.

"I didn't really appreciate that you laughed when she made that dig about my eyebrows."

"You're pissed about that?" Jake replied.

"I'm pissed that you seemed a little too eager to flirt with her," I spat out.

Jake looked at me in surprise. "Are you for real right now?"

"Uh... yeah, I am, actually."

"I thought she was your friend. I was just being nice."

"Yeah, well, try being friendly without making me feel like shit next time."

"Jesus, you're being a bitch right now."

"Whatever."

He sighed in frustration. "Okay, first, I was not flirting with her. She was flirting with me. And second, the brow comment was funny, and if you weren't on the rag you'd have laughed, too."

Oops. Wrong thing to say, buddy. I could feel the heat rising. I got up and stomped off to my room.

Jake appeared at my door a few minutes later with that cute lopsided smile on his face. I fought to stay pissed. He'd been rude and insensitive. *But look at him... No. Stay strong.*

"I'm pissed at you."

"Yeah, I figured that out all by myself."

"Good for you." I nodded but refused to look at him.

"Okay, Casey, here's my apology. I'm sorry for suggesting that your bad mood might somehow be related to that time of the month. It was wrong of me. Please don't kill me," he said, cowering helplessly.

I couldn't help but laugh. "You're just digging your hole deeper and deeper."

"I know. Truce?" He reached out his hand.

"Truce." I shook it. Jake pulled me into a hug. We didn't talk for a minute or two. Finally, I said, "I'm sorry. I got jealous. It was stupid."

"You don't have anything to be jealous of. You know you're my girl. Those others, they're just interested because I'm famous. It has nothing to do with me."

I scoffed. "You always say that, but it has everything to do with you. You're gorgeous, Jake. Women would hit on you regardless of your job."

Jake didn't respond.

"Seriously? Have you looked in a mirror lately?"

He shook his head.

"Oh, come on," I scoffed.

Jake focused on me. His expression changed. Then he said in a serious tone of voice, "I don't look at myself in the mirror."

"Why not?" I asked, perplexed.

Jake paused, then shrugged and said, "I'm kidding. I'm going to bed. Good night, babe. I love you."

He gave me a kiss and then walked out of my room.

"I love you, too," I called out after him.

What was that all about? Another one of Jake's many mysteries. I changed and got ready for bed. I crawled under the sheets and lay awake wondering what he meant. Why wouldn't he look in a mirror? Unable to sleep, I threw the covers off and walked down the hall to the guest room. I quietly opened the door. Jake was sleeping, or at least pretending to sleep. I crawled into bed with him and wrapped my arms around him. Jake's body settled into mine. We didn't speak, but I could tell he was awake.

"Why don't you look in a mirror?" I whispered.

Jake lay there a while without speaking, and I wasn't sure if he heard me.

"Are you awake?"

"Yeah."

"Why don't you look in a mirror?" I asked again.

Jake sighed. Instantly, I understood it had something to do with the kidnapping.

"Why don't you look in a mirror?" I asked for the third and last time.

"The day I escaped," he started, but then stopped abruptly. I waited. "That day... uh... I got injured pretty bad. I couldn't walk, so I crawled or dragged myself around until I could find a phone and call for help. I found one on a dresser in a bedroom. There was a mirror attached to the back of the dresser. As I pulled myself up, I caught sight in the mirror of this… this thing… this bone-thin bruised and bloodied creature with dead eyes and wild, blood-streaked hair. I gasped and looked behind me, sure I was about to be attacked by this beast. There was nothing there."

Silence filled the air. No more words came from Jake.

After a minute of quiet, I finally finished the story for him. "You were the creature."

I could feel him nod. "For years afterward, if I looked in the mirror, I saw him and I hated it. He was just a fucked up reminder of what I'd become. So I stopped looking."

I hugged him a little tighter but didn't say anything. A calm settled around us before I whispered, "You're looking at him the wrong way."

"What are you talking about?"

"The creature. You see him as negative. But, Jake, he was so brave and so determined to live. He persevered against great odds." My voice broke with emotion. "He doesn't deserve your scorn. If you look in the mirror and see that boy again, you should thank him."

Jake didn't respond to me. In fact, we didn't speak again. Jake seemed to fall asleep immediately. I lay awake, listening to his rhythmic breathing. My love for him was beyond all reason. Most days, Jake was the man I'd met the first night, so funny and talented and intriguing. And then there was the man with secrets – a man so tortured by his past that he blamed the boy he once was. There was so much sadness buried deep inside him. Moments like tonight, where he bared the tiniest bit of his soul to me, were so few and far between. I wanted to help him see himself the way I saw him, but I knew pushing him would only serve to draw him deeper inside his head. Since meeting Jake, I'd researched a lot about how to approach survivors of abuse. The key was to wait for a moment when Jake himself offered up a piece of his past. And with gentle nudging, possibly pull out a little more than he had originally planned on giving. Although I wanted so much more from him, I knew I needed to be patient. He was worth the wait.

I woke up to sunlight streaming through the windows. Jake was not beside me. I bolted up, worried and feeling like a jerk. I had been so concerned about stupid stuff like eyebrows and flirting, while Jake was forced to deal with real issues. I wondered if he looked at me like some stupid little girl with laughable problems. The minute I stepped out of the guest room, I heard his voice in the kitchen. I wandered in. Jake was standing over the stove with a spatula in his hand. My mom was beside him, and Dad was sipping coffee at the table.

"Hi, honey," Mom said cheerfully. "I'm teaching Jake how to make omelets."

"Good lord." I smiled.

I walked over and kissed my dad on the cheek, then went to Jake. He gave me a quick side hug and went back to his task at hand.

"Scoot the spatula under it here. Just halfway. Good. Now flip that part on top of… oops." Mom laughed as all of the filling came out of the omelet. "You have to flip it faster."

"You could have told me that before I flipped it." Jake complained as he tried to scoop the filling back into the omelet.

"How long have you been awake?" I asked him.

"About an hour."

"Why didn't you wake me up?"

Jake shrugged. "I was letting you sleep because you were a little salty yesterday."

Mom snickered, and Dad grinned from behind the newspaper.

"You're both traitors," I teased. "One weekend and you already like him more than me."

They didn't refute my claim. I loved that they loved him. I gave my mom a happy kiss.

"I love you, Mom. Thanks for taking care of my guy."

"Are you kidding? I'm enjoying every minute," she said, putting her arm around Jake.

He was concentrating intensely as he scooped his omelet out of the pan and onto a plate. "My first omelet," he pronounced proudly.

It looked like scrambled eggs.

Jake posted a picture of his culinary creation on Twitter, and we both laughed when @Aliciabrowsbaby retweeted it.

After our late breakfast, Jake and I packed up our stuff. Our flight was scheduled for 2:00 pm. Miles and Darcy and the kids came over to say good-bye, as did Luke. It had been a great visit. My family had welcomed Jake with open arms. Sydney started crying before we got in the car, clinging to Jake. Apparently, he was charming even to seven-year-old girls. Jake promised he would visit again soon. And he meant it, telling me that spending time with my family was like spending time with a bunch of Caseys.

45

CASEY: THE MCKALLISTER FAMILY

Once back in LA, Jake called home to his family, and we made plans to visit Saturday. I was a nervous wreck the whole week of school. I'd met most of his family already, yet still I was filled with anxiety. I didn't know what to expect. One thing was certain: I was very thankful I hadn't gotten frisky with Jake around my dad, or the payback would have been a bitch.

We left around three on Saturday. Jake drove us along the coast, and told me little stories about what he did on this or that beach and pointed out the spots where he'd surfed. It was heartening to see him in an environment that obviously made him happy. An hour later, we pulled up to an enormous electric fence surrounded by stone and flowering vines. I gaped in shock at the enormous plantation-style ranch house that sat back on the property. I turned to Jake.

"Where are we?"

"My parents' house. Where did you think we were?"

"Um... I thought you said your parents were middle class."

"They are. I bought them this house," Jake said, as he placed his thumb on a security scanner and the fence opened.

"Oh, well, shit."

"I wanted to do something nice for them."

He drove through the gate and pulled up in front of the house.

"Well, this is definitely nice," I said, as I stepped out of the Jeep. Jake took my hand and led me up the front porch. A teenage girl threw open the door and flung her arms around Jake's waist.

"Gracie," Jake hugged his baby sister. She beamed. After a minute of mindless chatter from her end of the conversation, he introduced us. Grace exchanged a quick *Hi* with me before grabbing Jake's arm and pulling him through the front door. Their dad was standing just inside, wearing a Hawaiian shirt, shorts, flip-flops, and a big smile on his face.

"Casey, this is my dad, Scott."

"It's nice to meet you," I said as I held my hand out, but Scott didn't take it. He came in for the hug instead. *Okay, then.*

"Casey, it's so good to meet you," he said, patting my back. "Come in. Come in. Michelle will be here in a minute. She just went up to change clothes."

"No, I'm here," she said from behind him as she walked in. She came directly to me and gave me a hug. "Casey, it's so nice to see you again. I really look forward to talking to you."

"You, too."

Wow, they were way friendlier than I'd expected.

"Jake, you have to come and see," Grace said excitedly. "Debra had babies."

"No way," Jake replied. "Where are they?"

"In the music room."

"Why in the music room?"

"Oh, trust me, it wasn't supposed to happen that way," Michelle cut into the conversation. "I had a box all set up in the family room, but Quinn left the door to the music room open, and Debra snuck in and ended up having her babies in there."

"Who is Debra?" I asked, confused.

"Our cat."

"Who names their cat Debra?"

"We give all our animals the most unoriginal human names we can think of," Grace explained. "We have another cat named Carl. And a dog named Mark."

"Seriously?" I laughed.

"Don't ask," Jake said, rolling his eyes. "It was my dad's brilliant idea."

"That's hysterical."

We followed Grace into the music room and as Jake dropped to the floor to pet the tiny white kittens, I peered around the room in shock. Every wall was covered in framed honors. Every shelf held trophies and awards. And every accolade in the room had Jake's name on it.

Jake glanced up and saw me looking around. "My mom insisted."

"Only because they were all over the floor of his townhouse. He hadn't bothered to do anything with them. He had Grammys lying on the floor. Can you believe that? Someone had to do something."

"Oh, yeah, right, mom... you didn't put these up to save them, you just put them up to brag," Jake teased.

"Can you blame me? Look at these awards." She raised her hands to the room. "I'm proud of my boy."

"I don't blame you at all," I said. "I would do the same thing. This is impressive."

"Not as impressive as this," Jake said, as he held up the most adorable little kitten next to his face. "Can we keep it, Casey? Can we, please?"

"You can have them all," Michelle offered.

"Do they have names yet?" Jake asked his dad.

"As a matter of fact, they do," Scott answered proudly.

"Oh no," I giggled. "I can't wait to hear."

"Okay, so we've got Dennis, Karen, Cynthia, Ronald... and this little guy here is Chuck."

We all laughed.

"I have nothing to do with this," Michelle said, shaking her head.

"The names may change depending on whether they're male or female."

"You don't know that yet?" Jake asked.

"Son, it's a little hard to see wieners at this stage of the game."

"God, Dad, you've got to get a hobby or something."

We left the kittens behind, and Michelle led us out into the backyard. A gorgeous covered patio with beautiful outdoor furniture circling a large fire pit was the centerpiece. It was so fancy that with just the push of a button, the entire patio could be enclosed in glass. Just beyond the outdoor room was a giant beach-entry pool with a swim up bar, two slides and four waterfalls, grotto caves, and two hot tubs. Beyond the pool was a guesthouse and a full-size basketball court. *Wow. Nice gift, Jake.*

Mark, a shepherd mix, came running up to Jake and started jumping all over him.

"Hey, buddy, where were you?" Jake asked, kissing his dog's face.

"With me," Kyle said as he walked in. He came right up to me and gave me a hug. "How are you doing, Casey?"

"I'm good. What about you?"

"Yep. Good. Hey, thanks for taking care of Jake while I was away."

"No problem. How was the show?"

"What show?"

I looked at him, confused.

"He can't talk about it until after it airs," Scott explained. "If he does, they can take his first born child – it's in the contract."

"Oh, geez, okay," I laughed. "Forget I asked."

"I'm going to go get the drinks and snacks," Michelle said to me. "I'll be right back."

"Can I help?"

Michelle paused like she was surprised by my offer. "I would love that. Thank you."

I got up and followed her into the kitchen.

"Jake looks good," Michelle expressed. "He seems happy."

"Yeah, he does. I think he's relieved the tour is over. It was taking a toll on him physically."

Michelle nodded. "It always does. I think he'll need another knee replacement at some point."

I didn't say anything. Jake planned to tell his parents about the surgery today.

"So, Casey, were you a fan of Jake's before you met him?"

"No, not really. I mean, I thought he was a good singer, but I'd never been to a concert of his or anything. To be honest, when I met him at the wedding, I didn't expect him to even talk to me."

"Really? Why?"

"He's way too cool for me," I stated. "I'd be the last girl you'd expect to date a rock star."

"Why is that?" Michelle asked, her eyes taking me in with interest.

"I'm just not that exciting."

"I don't know. Jake obviously thinks you are. Did you know you're the first girl he's ever brought home to meet us?"

"He told me."

"I'm not sure if it was because he was embarrassed by us or because he knew the relationship wasn't going to last, so why bother?"

"Definitely the latter. How can you possibly be embarrassed by a family who names their kitten Chuck?"

Michelle smiled. "I suppose so. You seem to have a good sense of humor, Casey."

"That's how I snagged your son."

"Oh, really?" Michelle put down her pitcher of iced tea. "Do tell."

After I explained our whole 'meet cute' story, Michelle actually laughed. "I can only imagine how that prank went over with Jake."

"He was sufficiently horrified."

"Oh, I bet he was." Michelle's eyes flickered with amusement, much like her son's. "Huh. I have to say, Casey, you aren't at all what I was expecting."

"That's what my parents said about your son," I replied.

Michelle seemed surprised. "I didn't know Jake had met your parents."

"We went there last weekend."

"They liked him?"

"They loved him."

Michelle lifted her eyebrows. "Wow."

"That surprises you?"

"I...yes. I guess it does. I mean, he must have felt very comfortable with your parents, if they were able to see him for who he really is."

"Oh, yeah. Two days was all it took for them to like him more than me," I joked. "Sunday morning I woke up to find Jake and my mom making omelets together."

Michelle didn't comment, but I could tell she was pleased.

Jake walked into the kitchen. "Everything okay in here?"

"Of course," Michelle replied. "I was just getting to know Casey. Were you checking up on me, Jake? Making sure I wasn't scaring her off?"

"Hey, I wasn't implying anything," Jake said holding up his hands.

"You give me no credit." She shook her head. "We'll be out in a minute. You can take the pitchers."

Jake's eyes fixed on mine, and he gave me a look like he was asking if I was okay. I nodded happily. He seemed to relax, then grabbed the drinks and left.

"You told me on the phone you were a college student. What are you studying?" Michelle asked.

"Accounting."

"When will you graduate?"

"This is my last year."

"Good for you. And then what do you plan on doing?"

"Well," I hesitated. "I guess it depends on Jake. We're just kind of figuring everything out. Ideally I'd like to do freelance work so I could travel with him. It would be tough to make things work with him on the road and me in an office."

"You'd be willing to do that for Jake?"

"I'd do anything for him," I replied honestly. "I promise you, Michelle, I have no ulterior motives. I just really love your son."

Michelle stared at me for a moment, eyes misted over, and then she quickly looked away. She cleared her throat and said, "Are you ready?"

I nodded. I wasn't sure if I'd just blown it. Michelle was harder to read than her son.

We carried the snacks outside to the patio. Michelle explained why some of her kids wouldn't be joining us: Keith was out of town; Emma was working; Quinn had already made plans before Jake called. So it was just Grace, Kyle, and Jake. Grace was taking full advantage of her time with Jake. She was nestled up next to him on the couch. He'd bought her some stuff on his travels, and it was obvious from her expression that she loved her gifts. I took the seat beside Jake's dad, and I was glad I did. Scott was a riot. He was so easy going.

Jake's parents told me all kinds of funny stories about him and Kyle growing up. I laughed so hard when Scott said that he and Michelle had 'indoor kids' and 'outdoor kids.' Jake and Kyle were clearly their outdoor kids. In the summer, when they were really little, Scott would throw the two boys outside in the backyard, like dogs – his words, not mine. Scott said he even had to go around the yard and board up any holes in the fence to keep them from slipping through. The boys would happily stay out there all day, skateboarding on the ramps Scott built for them, and then at night they were allowed inside to eat, shower, and sleep.

Scott talked about taking the boys surfing every morning when they got a little older and how the three of them would have to sneak out before Michelle woke up because she didn't approve of them going out before school. It was funny. People just assumed Jake had had a horrible upbringing because of what happened to him but, like he told me before, he'd had a 'kick-ass' childhood. It explained a lot about Jake as a person. That fun-loving, flirty, easy-going side of him was a product of how his parents raised him; and the reserved, sad, self-doubting side of him was a product of Ray's cruelty. Both people lived inside Jake, each fighting for control. I decided right then and there that I would make it my mission in life to make sure Ray would not win. I would fill Jake's life up with so much love and happiness that there would be no place for that monster to hide. Jake might have killed Ray, but I was going to destroy him.

The visit with Jake's family went well. Scott seemed to love me. The jury was still out on Michelle. She was friendly and interested, but not overly so. I didn't force a relationship. I was just myself and hoped she would come to appreciate that.

46

CASEY: DIRTY LITTLE SECRET'S OUT

Jake spent the next few weeks in the studio laying tracks for his upcoming album. He had a deadline of sorts – he wanted to have a finished album before the surgery, and time was running out. I barely saw him. He worked long into the night. I mostly stayed at my apartment during that time, not only because he was so busy but also because I had midterms.

The week after coming back from my parents' place, I was having lunch in the cafeteria with a few friends when a guy I knew from class named Brandon came up, out of the blue, and loudly asked, "Are you Jake McKallister's girlfriend?"

My friends laughed like it was a silly question. Surely I would have shared something that note-worthy with them had it been true. But I was so stunned by the question that I just sat there in silence. All of the sudden their laughter faded, and they stared at me in astonishment. Students from the several tables closest to us turned around in interest too, having heard the question and being surprised by my lack of reply as well. Brandon stood there, waiting for my response.

"Well, are you?" he demanded.

"Where did you hear that?" I asked, glancing over at my confused tablemates.

"A friend of a friend works in the admissions office. He told me he'd heard Jake McKallister's girlfriend had transferred here and that she was an accounting major. He was wondering if I knew who she was. Anyway, you're the only transfer student I know... plus the only one hot enough to date a rock star," Brandon declared.

My friends' mouths had dropped open in response. Now it seemed the entire cafeteria was staring at me. I didn't really know what to say. Brandon took my silence as an admission.

"Damn, you *are* his girlfriend! I knew it!"

"Shhh," I said in irritation.

"Wait," my friend Dani said. "Hold on. You're Jake McKallister's girlfriend?" Her last word dripped with disbelief.

I looked around at all the shocked faces and replied, "Yes."

"The same Jake McKallister who's a rock star?"

I grinned. Was there any other? "Yes."

There was a collective gasp from the cafeteria, followed by stunned stares thrown in my direction.

"Wait. You're dating Jake McKallister?" Julianne asked in shock, still not quite believing my admission.

I nodded.

"You're flipping dating Jake McKallister?" Julianne's voice was higher-pitched this time.

"Yes, Julianne. I don't think the people in the next building heard you."

"You're with Jake McKallister?" she said quietly this time.

"How many times are you going to ask me that?"

"As many times as it takes to believe you."

I shrugged.

"Why didn't you say anything?" Dani asked.

"I told you I had a boyfriend named Jake," I answered feebly.

"Yeah, but that isn't the same thing as saying you have a boyfriend named Jake McKallister. Totally different story, sister."

"I know... I wasn't trying to deceive anyone. I wanted to say something, but it just never seemed like the right time. I'm sorry."

"What else have you not told us?" Hope asked, not seeming as amused as Dani.

"As far as big, shocking revelations? That's it."

"I mean that's just... I can't even believe it," Julianne said, shaking her head. "He's like my favorite artist of all time. I've even told you that, and... and you were *dating* him and you never said anything!"

"I know. I'm sorry. I didn't say anything in the beginning because I didn't really know you guys. Then once we became friends, it just seemed awkward to bring it up, like, 'Oh and, by the way, I'm dating Jake McKallister.' It seemed like I would be bragging."

"Well, Jesus Christ, Casey, you have reason to brag," Dani teased. "But I get it. There really is no good way to reveal to your girlfriends you're dating a hot rock star. No matter what, we're going to hate you."

I groaned. "Oh, great."

Dani hugged me. "I'm just kidding. You're awesome, Casey. In fact, it makes me like Jake even more, knowing he chose a girl like you. He has good taste."

"Well, I don't know about that, but thanks."

"How did you meet him? At a concert?" Hope asked.

"No. I met him at a wedding for my friend and his brother. We were paired together. I was a bridesmaid; he was a groomsman."

"And you just hit it off?"

"Yep. Instantly. And we've been together ever since."

"And you transferred to be closer to him?"

"Yes."

"Do you two live together?" Dani asked.

"No. I have my own apartment. You've been there, remember?"

"Yeah, but I never saw a picture of Jake in there. Not once."

"What, were you expecting a signed poster or something?"

"Something like that, yeah."

"Where does Jake live?" Julianne asked.

"He has a place in Santa Monica."

"So after you leave class, you go and hang out with Jake McKallister?" Julianne asked. She still seemed to be having trouble grasping all this.

"Yep. That's usually how a relationship works."

Julianne shook her head. "Sorry... I'm still totally shocked."

"I can tell. You have this weird look on your face."

"So, I mean... are we going to get to meet him?"

"Eventually, yeah. But you're going to have to get in line. I barely get to see him anymore."

"Really? Why?"

"Jake's super busy right now. He just got back from tour and is recording his new album. He rarely leaves the studio nowadays."

"Oh, that's too bad," Dani whined. "Nope, sorry. I can't conjure up any sympathy for you."

I laughed.

"You met during the summer when he was on tour, then?"

"Yes. After the wedding, he flew back to Europe. Then not long after that, he invited me to come for a visit and I stayed. Poor guy couldn't get rid of me."

"You even went on tour with him?" Julianne pouted.

"I did. Best summer ever. We traveled on a tour bus in this long caravan, with all the other band members and crew. It was like a big, dysfunctional rock n' roll family," I reminisced.

"I really, really kind of hate you right now," Julianne said, probably only half joking. "You're living my dream."

"Sorry," I said. "I can't even believe it happened sometimes."

"Don't take this the wrong way, but is he, like... normal?" A guy with glasses and long sideburns asked from the next table over. I didn't know him, but now I hated him. I gave him a dirty look. "I mean, come on. He spent a lot of time with a serial killer."

"Don't be a douche, Rawlings," the guy sitting with him said.

"I'm just saying," the asshole said smugly.

"If by normal, you mean that he knows how to conduct himself in public and treat other people with respect, then yes... he's perfectly normal. Maybe he needs to give you some lessons."

Everyone chortled at my burn.

The asshole shook his head, looking annoyed.

"Do you have a picture of the two of you together?" Hope asked.

"Yeah," I said and pulled out my phone. I picked out a picture and said, "This one was taken after one of his concerts."

After everyone at my table had seen the picture, and a few people from other tables who had come over to take a look, my phone ended up in Dani's hands. Just as she was about to pass it back, it buzzed.

Dani looked down at the screen and squealed. "Oh, my god, he just texted us, Casey!"

"Us?" I laughed. "Give me my phone back."

"He wrote, *kickin' us out at 4:00. Want me to come by and get you?*"

"Dani, I can't believe you read it."

"It just popped up. I didn't mean to. Can I text him back? Please... please."

"No."

"You're so selfish," Dani protested. "You get him all the time. I'm just asking for one little text."

"Fine. One text," I consented, rolling my eyes.

"Yah!" Dani cheered, as she bent over the phone and started texting something. She giggled as she sent the text.

"What did you write?" Julianne asked.

"I put, 'Well, hi there handsome.'"

"No, you didn't." I gasped.

"Casey?" Jake texted back almost immediately.

Dani read it out loud.

"He knew right away it wasn't you."

"Because I would never say that to him and he knows it," I laughed.

"No, I'm Dani, Casey's friend. I jacked her phone so I could say hi."

A couple seconds passed before Jake texted back, "Oh, she finally told you about me, huh?"

"She did and we are sufficiently impressed."

"*That means a lot*," Dani read aloud.

"He's joking," I added.

"I got that, Casey."

"So I hear you're working on a new album. You got any songs on there about Casey?"

Jake didn't respond for about a minute.

"Where did he go?" Dani complained to me.

"I don't know." I shrugged.

"Are you still there?" Dani asked.

No response.

"I told you he's been busy," I tried to explain.

"Yeah sorry," Jake finally texted back. "Still here."

"I thought you ditched me."

"No. I'm in the middle of recording a song. And yes there might be one or two about Casey."

"Can't wait to hear them. Sorry to interrupt while you're recording."

"No worries."

"Okay just one more question. What's the name of the song you're recording?"

"Random Attack."

"I'll remember that. I'll give Casey back her phone now. Thanks for being a good sport Jake. Hope we get to meet you soon."

"Yeah. For sure."

~

After Brandon dropped the bomb, word spread across the campus like wildfire. Within a twelve-hour period, it seemed, everyone knew who my boyfriend was. There was a lot of staring and whispering going on. Luckily, my friends didn't seem any different. They still treated me the same way, but I did get some good-hearted teasing. Because I showed up alone to everything, it became the running joke among my friends that I was delusional and that I really wasn't dating Jake at all. According to my friends, Jake was just my phantom boyfriend. It was pretty funny, but not entirely without merit. Even I was not seeing as much of Jake as I would have liked.

47

CASEY: THE MILLION DOLLAR CONFESSION

The weeks leading up to Jake's surgery were hectic. Not only was he putting in the long hours in the studio, he was also recording an original song for a soundtrack. In addition, he had a couple of videos to film and a handful of press appearances. I didn't understand why he was trying to cram everything in all at once, and became visibly annoyed with him on more than one occasion. In fact, his workload actually caused us to have some of our first real fights. After each argument, Jake would promise me that he was almost done, and when everything had been completed, he would devote all his time to me.

But that didn't happen. The album ran longer than expected, and by the time it was complete, Jake had only five days to spare. And he didn't spend them relaxing... or with me. He holed himself up in his townhouse and became quiet and withdrawn. I assumed his behavior was related to the impending surgery, but he wouldn't talk to me about it at all. I tried to be supportive and encouraging, I really did, but my patience was wearing thin.

Three days before his scheduled surgery, I came home from school to find Jake sleeping in the middle of the day, something totally out of character for him.

I nudged him awake and asked if he was okay.

"Yeah," he said groggily.

"Are you sick?" I asked in concern. If he was, would they cancel the surgery?

"No," Jake said harshly. "I just want to sleep, okay?"

I was taken back by his brash attitude, so I turned and walked out of the bedroom. Irritated, I opened my book and tried to focus on studying. A few minutes passed before Jake came out of the bedroom. I ignored him. He went into the fridge and made himself a sandwich. The tension in the air was strong. He sat down in the chair opposite me and ate his sandwich in silence. He seemed out of it. He wasn't looking me in the eye. Instantly, I got a bad feeling.

"What's your problem?" I grumbled.

Jake looked up at me, then shook his head and went back to eating.

I pretended to lose myself in my studies, but I couldn't concentrate. I was getting madder by the second. Finally, I slammed my book closed and stood up. "You know what, Jake... I'm not going to play this game with you. If you feel like filling me in on why you're being such a frickin' dick, I'll be at my apartment." I grabbed my backpack and headed for the door.

"Casey, stop."

"You know, I don't think I will," I spat out, and opened the front door.

"Casey, please, stop." Jake sounded a bit worried now.

"Why? I came here so we could spend time together before your surgery, and you're acting like such a jerk."

Jake just stared at me.

"What, Jake? You got nothing for me?"

"Give me a break. I've had a rough day."

I turned to him and said, irritably, "Are you going to talk to me about your rough day, or am I going to have to guess?"

Jake put down his sandwich and shook his head. Finally, he said the words that made my body tremble in fear.

"I... I don't think... " Jake sighed. "The surgery. I have a bad feeling."

It felt like I'd been slapped. "What do you mean? What kind of bad feeling?"

"I don't know. It's just a feeling. Like I'm not going to survive."

I stared back at him in shock.

"That's why I've been acting weird all week. I'm scared I'm about to lose everything."

I shook my head. "No... that's... no."

Neither one of us spoke for at least a minute. Finally, I whispered, "It's normal to be apprehensive before surgery, Jake."

"I know. I've had fourteen surgeries over my lifetime, Casey. I know what to expect."

"Jesus, Jake, if you have a bad feeling about the surgery, call it off. It isn't too late," I said, trying to control the fear in my voice.

"I can't do that."

"Yes, Jake. Yes, you can. Pick up the phone and tell them it's off."

Jake shook his head.

"You're telling me you think you're going to *die*, but you refuse to call off the surgery? I'm not sure I understand your motivation here."

"Well, when am I going to do it, Casey?"

"I... I don't know... But not now, not when you feel like this." Tears pooled in my eyes.

"I can't just ignore the pain and hope it goes away. It won't. I know. I've tried. My knee is a fucking mess, and putting the surgery off won't make it any easier for me later on."

I stared at Jake for a while before whispering, "I don't know what to say."

"There's nothing you can say, Case. It's just a shitty situation, and there's nothing I can do but take the risk."

Tears rolled down my cheeks. "You're basically telling me you think you're going to die, Jake. How am I supposed to respond to that?"

"I'm sorry. I shouldn't have said anything but... I... I don't want to be alone tonight."

"You won't be," I said as I hugged him. "You just have to talk to me. I hate when you shut me out."

"I know. I'm sorry. I get lost in my head sometimes."

I led him to the couch and we sat down. He wrapped me in his arms as we sat in silence. So much was going through my mind. Jake had suffered immeasurably in his life, and now he believed the surgery to repair some of that suffering could actually kill him. Life was so unfair sometimes. I leaned my head against his shoulder, overcome with worry.

"You're going to be okay, Jake." I finally said.

"You think?"

"I know."

"Why?"

"Because you survived a serial killer. No way is surgery going to be the thing that takes you down."

"It was a fluke that I survived, Casey. There was no skill or bravery involved."

"Hold on, I'm not finished. You're also going to survive because you're going to have babies with me someday."

"I am?" Jake asked, smiling. "I'd like that."

"And they will be the cutest little nerdy, rocker babies you ever saw. They're going to be beautiful and funny and smart and talented."

"Hold on... I thought you said they were going to be mine," Jake joked.

"Right, but you forget, they'll be half mine, too," I said, playing along.

"Oh, right." Jake smiled.

"And the third reason why I know you're going to survive is because if you don't, I will kick your ass."

"That might be a little hard to do, if I'm dead and all," Jake pointed out.

"Oh, I'd find a way. There is nothing more dangerous than a woman scorned."

We sat quietly for a few minutes holding hands, then Jake bent down and kissed me.

"I love you," he said, and then added, "so much. I hope you know that."

"I do. Of course, I do. And I love you, too."

"No matter what happens, don't ever forget that."

"Nothing's going to happen, Jake. You're going to go into that surgery and come out with a new knee. Then you're going to wake up and see my dorky face smiling back at you. That is all that is going to happen... Because, dammit, the universe owes you that much."

"Damn right it does." He smiled. "You know what else it owes me?"

"No, what?"

"Last minute surgery sex."

"Jesus Christ, Jake, if all that was a show to get me to open my legs for you, all you needed to do was give me that sexy little head tilt of yours and you'd have had me."

Jake spread his hands. "What can I say, I'm dramatic."

He reached down and cupped my ass, pulling me down. He climbed on top of me and started nibbling on my neck as I giggled.

"On the couch?" I questioned. "What are we, sixteen?"

"Would you prefer a wall?" Jake asked, referencing our first encounter.

"Oh god, don't remind me. I was such a slut."

"No, you were the hottest chick *ever*."

"*Was?*" I teased.

"Well, I mean, you still are; but that night, sliding down that wall..." Jake shook his head at the memory. "It was so damn hot."

"I have a deal for you."

"Okay," Jake said, looking hopeful for another wall encounter.

"Yeah, no, buddy, not what I was offering. You can't even get on your knees at this point. The deal is: you recover from your surgery, and then you'll fly me back to that hotel, get us that exact room, and we'll have a repeat."

Jake smiled. "I'm down for that. Does that mean I'm not getting any tonight?"

"I didn't say that," I said, then stood up and offered my hand to him. "But I'm not doing you on the couch."

The evening before the surgery, I lay in Jake's arms on the bed, my finger tracing lazy lines on his chest. I kept circling one of the deep scars surrounded by a tattoo.

"It's a stab wound," Jake offered up, completely out of the blue.

Stunned by his admission, I figured I would try my luck for the second time and ran my fingers lower and pointed at another deep gash encased under ink.

"Stab wound."

I touched a third, similar scar.

"Another stab wound," he confirmed.

I ran my finger over a long, thin scar running the length of his arm.

"Knife."

"And the two deep ones on your back... are those stab wounds, too?"

Jake nodded.

"So five in all?" I asked.

"Yeah."

Jesus. What the hell? Although I'd assumed as much just by looking at his scars, the confirmation of such horrible violence shocked me. Neither of us said anything for a minute.

Finally, I asked the question I'd wondered since first hearing his story all those years ago on the news. "How... I just... I can't figure out how you did it. How did you escape... especially after getting stabbed five times?"

Jake looked away. He didn't answer me. Maybe he couldn't.

"Sorry, you don't have to tell me."

It was quiet for a long time, and I figured we were done talking. Then Jake surprised me.

"I've been offered millions of dollars to answer that question."

"I'm sure. Have you ever told anyone?"

Jake hesitated, and then said, "Lassen."

"Lassen?" I asked in surprise. Wow. They were closer than I ever suspected. "He knows a lot. You'd never guess."

Jake nodded. "Lassen knows how to keep his mouth shut."

"So do I."

Jake stroked my hair. "I know."

I looked at his face. He was stressed. I didn't want to upset him the night before his surgery. I rose up and kissed his cheek. "Never mind. Let's talk about something else."

"Okay," Jake agreed, seemingly relieved.

We lay there silently as I tried to come up with another topic to discuss.

Finally, he sighed and opened up. "He thought I was dead."

"What... what does that mean?" I asked.

"Ray... He thought I was dead."

"After he stabbed you?"

"No, before he stabbed me, he" – Jake hesitated – "he strangled me."

I didn't know what to say, so I remained quiet.

"Maybe when he'd checked my heartbeat or pulse or whatever, maybe I'd actually stopped breathing, I don't know, but I woke up on a piece of plastic on the floor of the basement, still very much alive."

"What happened? Why did he strangle you?"

"I… that's a story for another day. The point is, he strangled me and he thought I was dead and he laid me on a piece of plastic that he planned to wrap my body in when he buried me. When I woke up, he was outside digging my grave."

"Jesus," I mumbled. My heart was racing. Was this really happening? Was Jake really telling me this?

"When I was… uh… there… he always kept restraints on me, but this time when I woke up, they were off."

"Because he thought you were dead."

"Right. I understood pretty quickly what was happening. I tried to come up with some kind of a plan."

"To escape?"

Jake hesitated. "No. Not to escape. To die."

I gaped at him in shock. "Why would you want to die?"

"I didn't *want* to die, Casey. All I ever wanted every minute of every day was to live, but the kind of living Ray was offering wasn't living – it was just slow dying."

I nodded. I couldn't believe he was telling me all this.

"The thing is, I'd given up long before Ray strangled me. When he took out my knee about a week before the escape… that's when my hope died."

I stroked his arm, speechless.

"Anyway, I was trying to come up with a plan to be dead before he got back down into the basement and found me alive. Ray had used a knife on me plenty of times, as you can see," Jake said as he pointed to his body. "So I got it and sat back down on my plastic and prepared to cut my wrists."

"I… I don't understand. If you had the knife, why didn't you use it on Ray?"

"Because I'd already tried that, Casey. That's why I'm having surgery tomorrow."

"Oh," I answered, numbed by the horror of what I was hearing.

"And, honestly, I really didn't think he could be killed. He was like a real life monster. No matter how hard I tried, I just could never get the upper hand with him. I knew if I tried to stab him, he'd just wrestle the knife out of my hand and start stabbing me. I could never win with him... ever. So I decided I only had three choices. Number one was to let him find me alive and be forced to continue living the hell I was in. Number two was to stab him and get stabbed back and hope to God he killed me. And number three was I could take my own life."

Jake inhaled roughly, then turned his head and grimaced as if the memory physically hurt him. "Number three was the safest bet and involved the least amount of pain and suffering."

"I just... God... I don't know what to say."

"I started cutting," Jake pointed to the faded marks on his wrists, "but killing myself when I didn't want to die proved more difficult than I thought. I was struggling to make that final cut to sever my artery. And while I was gathering my courage, the worst thing that could possibly have happened, happened."

"What?" I asked, all wide-eyed and horrified.

"He opened the basement door. I didn't know what to do. I panicked. I just lay back down on the plastic, hid my bloody wrist with the knife behind my back, and played dead. Ray came down the stairs, and I listened as he was doing things around the basement."

"He never came over to check on you?"

"No. And thank god he didn't, because it would have been obvious I was still alive. I had sweat and tears on my face, smeared blood up my arms, and my heart was pounding so loud I could feel it vibrating in my throat. I was paralyzed with fear."

"What did you plan to do?"

Jake shrugged. "I had no plan. I had no idea what was going to happen. At that point, things were just going to have to play themselves out."

"Were you prepared to use the knife to defend yourself?"

"I don't know if I was thinking of anything at that point. It was just indescribable terror. It was kind of like that car ride after Ray kidnapped me. I knew something bad was going to happen, but I didn't know what. Like I was in a horror movie and had come to the finale. I was just scared out of my mind. I'm surprised I managed to keep myself from crying out because I was just emotionally destroyed at that point. My body was shaking. I think that's what finally caught Ray's eye. I could hear him walk over to me. He nudged me with his shoe and said, "Are you still alive?" He then got down on one knee and put his finger against my neck to feel for my pulse."

I gulped back my horror.

"That moment... it's something that still haunts me today... it was like everything was happening in slow motion. I knew Ray was about to discover the truth, and I couldn't let that happen. I pulled the knife out from behind my back and thrust it into the side of his neck. Ray's eyes widened and he jerked back screaming. I could tell he was shocked. I mean, he'd thought, up till that point, that I was dead, so he definitely was not expecting me to suddenly come back to life... and with a knife in my hand.

"As for me, the moment I thrust the knife into him, I knew I'd started a war I couldn't win. There was no turning back. I pulled the knife out of his neck and aimed for his chest. This time, Ray reacted more quickly. He grabbed for the knife, but the blade sliced through his hands and plunged directly into his chest. Ray screamed and grabbed my hand, which was still gripping the knife, and we wrestled for it while it was still lodged in his chest. He punched me in the face, and I lost control of the knife. Ray actually yanked it out of his own chest. God. The look on his face... I was going to pay for what I did."

Jake stopped talking for a moment and took in a long, deep

breath. "Anyway, I tried to scramble away then, knowing that I was about to get stabbed, but Ray grabbed my ankle and yanked me back. He then thrust the knife into my back. Before I had a chance to even react, he stabbed me again. Using my trapped ankle, he flipped me over onto my back. I was still squirming fiercely. He stabbed me in my side. I could see the blood pouring off the blade as he raised it up again. I think he was aiming for my heart, but I made a last second attempt to fight him off and Ray got my stomach instead. The blade went straight through my body and hit the concrete under me. It made this horrible wet clanking sound. I'll never forget it. Then Ray jerked the knife up, back through my body. I just collapsed back to the floor. I was done. I remember looking him in the eyes as he raised the knife again. I knew it was over, and this feeling of relief flooded through me... if only for a split second because at that moment Ray gasped, grabbed his chest and screamed."

"What happened?" I asked, my eyes wide with shock.

"I had no idea at the time. I thought he was reacting to the pain from the stab wound, but I later learned that the blade had pierced his heart and he was actually having a heart attack. I kind of watched the whole thing play out, still trapped under him. Ray screamed a strangled cry and grabbed for his chest. Then the knife dropped from his hand, landing next to us. Ray was too preoccupied with the heart attack to realize his mistake until I reached for the knife. He saw me and grabbed for it too, but I got to it first. We both struggled for control over it, but at that point, I was actually the stronger of the two of us, and I came up swinging. I stabbed Ray two or three more times until he toppled to the side, falling off me. He rolled onto the ground, screaming in pain. There was blood everywhere. I was slipping on it. He kept trying to grab for the knife, so I kept stabbing him. It seemed like forever before he stopped moving." Jake looked away. Silence filled the air.

After a minute, I finally found my voice. "Why have you never told anyone this story, Jake? I mean, you let the media rip you to shreds on a daily basis. You let them call you a killer. If they knew this story... my god."

I stared at him. When he didn't respond, I moved on. "How did you get away?"

"At first, I didn't. I just assumed I was dying. I'd been stabbed four times and I couldn't breathe, because one of the stab wounds had punctured my lung and partially collapsed it. I had a brief thought to try to escape, but I couldn't get my body to cooperate. At that point, I just had nothing left. I collapsed and rolled back onto my piece of plastic and wrapped myself into it. I never expected to leave the basement. I just lay there and waited for death."

"How long did you lie there?"

"I don't know really. I think I might have been going in and out of consciousness. I just lay there and waited and waited. And when death didn't take me right away, fear took over. I started thinking about my mom and how much I wanted to hear her voice again. That's when I decided to try to get out of the basement. I thought that if I could get myself up the stairs, I could call my mom and she would give me the peace I needed to pass on."

Tears that I'd been holding onto began rolling down my cheeks.

"Anyway, I got out and called my mom and got rescued in the process. And... that... is my escape story."

I stared at him in awe. "I... I don't know what to say, Jake."

"Don't say anything."

"I won't. I promise."

"No. I mean, I told you about the escape, and now it's done. I don't want to ever talk about it again. Okay?"

Shocked, I could do nothing but nod in agreement.

48

JAKE: IMPENDING DOOM

The feeling of impending doom consumed me for weeks leading up to the surgery. I tried to force myself to be positive, but nothing eased my fears. If I was going to die on that operating table I needed to make plans – lots of plans – not only to protect the people I loved, but also to safeguard my legacy.

Getting my sixth studio album finished was incredibly important to me. I felt it was some of my best work and a great way to say goodbye, if it came to that. I also visited my safe deposit box at my bank and retrieved an unreleased album that I'd recorded years before. It was once a concept album called *36 Days*, and it was special because it told the story, in musical terms, of the entire kidnapping from start to finish. But upon completion, the finished product was too raw and revealing. It would have been like opening up my life for the world. In the end, I couldn't release it, so instead, I hid it away in a safety deposit box and recorded new tracks and released a different album. I'd never been back to the box until yesterday. If something happened to me, *36 Days* would tell the story I had never been brave enough to tell while I was alive.

I had my attorney draw up a new will and left strict instruc-

tions on when the album could be released – five years to the day
of my death – and who would benefit from the profits. I also
made sure to include Casey and her family in my will. If something happened to me, I wanted to know she would always be
taken care of.

But all of that paled in comparison to the most drastic step I
took to keep my legacy alive. I sent for the owner of one of
LA's largest sperm banks. He left our meeting with a vial of my
jizz. Casey would never have to find out; unless, of course, I
died. Then she would be totally shocked that I'd thought far
enough ahead to consider her future. I knew Casey loved me. I
knew that our love was deep enough that it would take her a
long time to move on... just as it would for me if, God forbid,
something was to happen to her. I also knew she wanted my
babies. I looked at it like an insurance policy: if I died during
surgery, at least there was a chance for a part of me to live on.
And I knew without the slightest doubt that Casey would be an
excellent mother to my child. And, of course, if I did have children, the will stipulated that all my wealth would transfer to
them.

I felt ready. Everything had been completed, and there was
nothing left to do but get the surgery over with and pray to God I
survived. Once upon a time, I wouldn't have cared. My life meant
nothing to me then; but now, when I had the world at my feet
and an amazing woman to love me, I wanted to live. I had so
much more to accomplish and to experience.

I'm not sure why I told her about the escape last night. I
hadn't intended to. It was a moment of weakness or a moment of
courage, I'm not sure which. I don't know why I'd held onto the
truth so tightly. Casey was right – if the media knew the real
story behind the escape, I'd be treated differently, maybe with
more respect. But that was the thing: I preferred the contempt. I
preferred that people thought of me as some deranged killer
instead of the scared, weak, helpless kid I was. There had been

nothing brave or heroic in my escape. At one horrible moment in time, luck had swung in my favor.

I woke up with a jolt early on the day of the surgery. Oh, god... I forgot. In all my doomsday preparations, I completely overlooked some of the most important people in my life – my fans. After everything they had done for me over the years, how could I go out without giving them something? Careful not to disturb Casey, I eased my weary body out of bed and grabbed my computer.

A few hours later I was back in bed, but this time with a hospital gown on. My family was there, circled around me like I was already lying dead in a coffin and they were at my viewing. Everyone was upbeat and positive, assuring me that the surgery would go fine. Only Casey knew of my fears. She stood in the background looking terrified. I wished I'd never told her. How stupid could I have been?

A doctor came in to inform me they were ready to sedate me. I asked him for a minute. Then I turned to my family and smiled.

"No worries. I'll be fine," I lied to them. We said our goodbyes, as one by one my family members exited the room until it was just Casey and my mom and dad.

"I'll be here when you wake up, Jake," Dad said, patting my shoulder.

"Okay. I love you, Dad."

"I love you too, son."

He walked out of the room, worry etched upon his face. I saw a tear roll down his cheek. My dad had always been the more emotional one.

I turned to Casey and held my hand out for her. She grabbed it and I pulled her down and kissed her. Casey rested her forehead on mine. She was overcome with emotion.

"Remember what we talked about?" she whispered.

I nodded.

"I'll kick your ass."

"I know." I smiled.

Then she whispered in my ear, so my mom wouldn't hear, "Come back to me, Jake. Promise."

"I promise," I whispered back, hoping and praying I could keep my promise.

"I love you," she said. I could hear the anguish in her voice.

"I love you, too."

Casey kissed me one more time then slipped out the door. I saw tears in her eyes too. Damn. I had to make it. It would crush my family if I didn't.

My mom walked up to me after Casey left and grabbed my hand.

"Are you okay? You seem... "

She didn't finish her sentence. She didn't have to. I knew what she meant. My mom and I had been through a lot together. She could read my emotions very well.

"I'm okay. Just a little scared, I think."

"You're going to be okay. That girl is counting on you."

"I know. I'm going to fight, Mom. I always do."

Tears threatened to flood my mom's eyes, but she valiantly held them off. "Yes, you do. You have fought so many battles, Jake, but you always come out the winner. And you will again today."

"Yeah," I responded, but there was hesitation in my voice.

"You have to believe. I feel like you're doubting yourself. Don't ever do that. You're too strong and too brave to let doubt creep into your mind. This is just another battle to win."

"I'm tired of always fighting, Mom. I'm tired of all this shit. I just want... " I sighed, gulping back my emotion. "I just want peace."

"I know you do, sweetheart," she said, stroking my hair. "And it will come."

"When?"

Mom didn't have an answer for me. We were silent for a moment.

"Sometimes, we just have to be happy with what we have. And you have so much: a family who loves you, an amazing career, and a wonderful girl who adores you."

I smiled at just the thought of Casey. "I know. I shouldn't complain."

My mom shook her head. "It's okay to feel the way you do. Just never forget what's most important. You'll get through this and be stronger for it."

I nodded.

"Mom?"

"Yes?"

"I want you to promise me something."

"Okay."

"I want you to take care of Casey. Make her feel like a part of our family. She's scared. She hasn't been through this with me like you have. Let her lean on you if she needs to."

Mom nodded. "I will. I promise."

"I love her."

"I know," she said, still holding back the tears.

"Thanks... for everything. You've always been the best mom. You never gave up on me, even when I gave up on myself. I love you so much." My voice broke.

"I love you, too," she replied, her voice cracking. "You're going to be fine."

It sounded more like she was trying to convince herself of that more than that she truly believed it.

"I know," I lied.

Mom smiled, then let go of my arm. "I'll see you soon."

I nodded as she walked out of the room.

49

CASEY: THE VIGIL

The surgery was scheduled to take upwards of five hours. I was a nervous wreck. What Jake had shared with me the other day played over and over in my mind. An hour into the surgery, I heard Quinn call over Keith and Kyle. They all hovered over Quinn's phone. Moments later, they looked up with shocked expressions on their faces.

"What is it?" Michelle asked them. Kyle took Quinn's phone and walked it over to Michelle. I saw her read whatever it was, and then she too looked up in surprise. "When did he post this?"

"Just before the surgery," Kyle answered.

Now I was curious. I stood up and walked over. "What's up?"

"Jake...um," Kyle started.

"Is he okay?" I cut him off, fear circulating through my bones.

"It's not about his surgery. Did you know he was going to post this?" Michelle asked, holding up Quinn's phone.

"Post what?" I replied.

"Jake issued a public statement."

I shook my head. "About what?" I asked.

Michelle handed me Quinn's phone.

To my fans,

Today I'll be having surgery. This will be my 15th operation in the past ten years and my third knee replacement. There is a chance that, during the surgery, it may become necessary to amputate my left leg just above the knee. Because I've never publicly spoken about my past, the possible outcome of this particular surgery will undoubtedly come as a shock to my devoted fans. Please know this isn't a decision I've taken lightly.

For the past ten years, I've struggled with a variety of health issues as a result of injuries sustained from a crime committed against me as a young teen. Over the course of the month-long ordeal, I was subjected to a wide range of cruelties, and my life was repeatedly threatened. It was a world I did not understand, one that I struggled to survive in. Extreme desperation pushed me to make difficult decisions. I attempted, and failed, to escape on multiple occasions. The price I paid for those botched attempts was always swift and brutal. One such punishment, the repeated bludgeoning of my kneecap with a blunt object, resulted in the injury I'll be having surgery for today. I've fought long and hard to save my leg, but sometimes even the best efforts fail. My hope is that today will be a whole new beginning.

And in the spirit of new beginnings, I'm calling out the media for the years of attacks on my character and for unfairly scrutinizing me for the actions I took all those years ago to save my own life. On the day in question, I was a critically wounded thirteen-year-old kid fighting to stay alive in the hands of a knife-wielding serial killer. To all who condemn – it's easy to judge from a position of safety. I have not, nor will I ever, apologize for defending myself. I'm only alive today because he's dead.

And finally, to my seriously incredible and faithful fans:

thank you. Through it all, you've stood by me, supporting me unconditionally. Your acceptance and love have given me the strength to push forward in times of weakness. I'm only where I am today because of your loyalty and compassion. For that, I'll forever be indebted.

Jake

"Wow," I breathed out. "I'm shocked."

"Me too," Michelle replied, as she sat down next to me, looking defeated. "He's always been so private. I can't believe he would open himself up in that way."

I nodded, knowing what Michelle didn't – that it was Jake's way of saying goodbye to his fans. No way would I tell his mother that. It upset me that Jake felt the way he did. He could not possibly know how this would end.

"Has he ever spoken to you about the kidnapping?" Michelle asked quietly.

"He's told me some things."

"Like what?"

"Um…about his knee and how he escaped."

Michelle nodded. "He obviously trusts you."

"Well, it's hard for him to talk about. I don't push him."

"That's smart. I've never been successful trying to pull information out of him. That's been hard for me – not knowing. He came home so broken. You wouldn't even have recognized him as the man he is today. But when he was that shattered boy I wanted to know everything, because I felt like it was the only way to protect and help him – but the more I pushed, the more he pulled away."

"Did you ever get the story out of him?"

"No. I got bits and pieces. I mean, I know some of what happened to him because of his injuries; but to this day, I have no idea what Jake went through."

"Jake told me the only people who know things about his kidnapping are you and Scott, Kyle, and Lassen."

"Lassen? Really?" Michelle said, clearly surprised. "I didn't know they were that close."

"They are. I think Jake has confided a lot in Lassen."

"Huh, that's interesting. Jake always manages to surprise me."

I laughed. "Yeah, he's never boring or predictable, that's for sure."

"No." Michelle said ruefully. "He definitely isn't. He's always been that way, though... since he was little. I used to call him my free spirit."

I nodded, smiling.

Then suddenly, Michelle's face turned sad. "That man – he tried to take Jake's spirit. He did everything he could to break him. And he almost won, but Jake, even when he had nothing left in him, he fought. He always fights, Casey. Jake always wins."

I sat with the McKallister family as we awaited word. I had a long conversation with Emma, whom I'd never spoken to before. She came across as reserved, but like her famous brother, once she felt comfortable, she opened up. We talked for a long time, mostly just mindless chatter, but it was what we both needed to take our minds off Jake lying on a table nearby, unconscious and cut open. Maybe his leg had already been amputated. The image took my breath away. The hours ticked by slowly.

Finally, the doctors came out to deliver the good news: the operation had been a huge success. Not only had Jake's leg been spared, but the doctor was successful in removing previously unseen bone fragments, which he believed were a major cause of Jake's recurring pain. A new, state of the art knee replacement had been surgically inserted. Jake had done remarkably well during the surgery, and the doctors were incredibly pleased.

Jake woke up in recovery and was moved to the ICU. When I came in, he was groggy but awake.

"You made it." I beamed.

"Yep. Only 'cause I was scared of you," he responded in a hoarse voice.

The relief that swept through my body was immense. An entire day passed, and Jake was awake and alert. Things looked great. Doctors were pleased. We were all so relieved.

But then twenty-two hours after the operation, tragedy struck. Kyle and his dad and I were in the room when it happened. Jake was talking like everything was fine, and then he stopped abruptly and said with fear etched across his face, "Something's wrong." He then convulsed in pain and started gasping for air.

Kyle ran from the room screaming for help. A doctor I'd seen before but who wasn't one of Jake's regular ones came rushing in. Behind him were two nurses pushing a cart.

"We've got to protect his airway before it closes. Hold his arms," the doctor said to Scott and Kyle. I watched in horror as the doctor shoved a tube down Jake's throat as his father and brother held down his thrashing body. Once he was intubated, the doctor, who had been calling out orders during the entire shocking ordeal, pushed Jake's bed out of the room and ran with him down the hall. Scott, Kyle, and I followed after until the doctor finally pushed Jake through some double doors. We were blocked from entering by a nurse in surgical clothes.

"That's my son," Scott demanded.

"He's being taken to surgery. You can't go in. I'm sorry."

"THAT'S MY SON!" Scott screamed. I could clearly see the panic on his face.

"Sir, you need to keep your voice down. Go to the waiting room, and I'll have someone come out and talk to you as soon as possible."

Scott looked ready to explode.

"Dad," Kyle said, grabbing Scott's arm. Scott ripped it away. "Dad, come on."

"Your mom. You need to get your mom, Kyle." Scott looked frantic now.

"I will. Come sit down. Your blood pressure, Dad. Come and sit down. I'll get Mom. Okay?"

Scott looked at the doors and then at Kyle and then at the doors again. Then he started crying. I stood there helplessly.

"Casey, I need your help," Kyle said to me.

I nodded. He grabbed Scott from one side and I steadied him from the other. He was almost limp in our arms as we led him to the waiting room. When we got there, it was filled with people. I looked at Kyle for direction.

"Let's take him back to Jake's room," Kyle grunted with effort. We continued on down the hall with Jake's distraught dad.

"I don't understand," he was mumbling. "He was fine a minute ago. I don't understand."

Kyle looked at me with dread in his eyes. I looked back in dismay. We got to Jake's room and sat Scott down onto a chair. A nurse appeared in the doorway.

"What happened?" Kyle asked her.

"It's possible he threw a clot," she replied.

"Will he need surgery?"

"Yes."

"God," Kyle said, dropping his head. He swayed a little to the right, and I grabbed his arm. Kyle stood there quietly a second, then shook his head and looked up at the nurse. "My dad – he has high blood pressure, and he isn't doing well. Can someone check him?"

"I will. Let me get a cuff," the nurse said, and hurried out.

"I'm going to go outside the door and call my mom. I don't want my dad to hear, okay?" Kyle whispered. "Can you keep an eye on him?"

"Yes, of course. Are you okay, Kyle?" I asked.

"Yeah. I… I'm just…." Tears filled his eyes. "I'm okay."

I let go of his arm and he walked out to call his mom. The nurse came in to check Scott's blood pressure, which turned out to be high, but not dangerously so.

"I want you to rest here. Don't get up. I'll check you again in twenty minutes to make sure the numbers are coming down," the nurse said, and then left.

I stepped over to Scott and rubbed his arm.

"Why?" he questioned. "I just don't understand. Why can't he ever just catch a break? Hasn't he been through enough?"

I didn't know how to respond, so I stayed silent and let Scott vent. Kyle stood in the doorway. He looked worn.

"Did you talk to your mom?"

"She's on her way."

"She just wanted to take a shower. She was counting on me to keep him safe."

"It's not your fault, Dad. It's better you were there and not her. She wouldn't have been able to hold him down."

"They just shoved the tube down his throat… Jake was gagging."

"They had to secure his airway," I said. "There was no other choice."

We all waited in the room until Michelle came in with Emma. She looked at Scott in concern.

"Is he all right?" she asked Kyle.

"Yeah, I had a nurse check him out. His blood pressure was a bit high, but she checked again a few minutes ago and it was down."

"Don't worry about me. I'm not the problem," he mumbled. "They've got Jake back in surgery."

"I know. I spoke to a doctor. He's going to try to find out what's happening and give us an update."

"Okay. Yeah. I should have thought of that," Scott said, sounding a little disoriented.

"They also have a private waiting room they're going to open for us. Emma, can you get dad a candy bar from the vending machine? Kyle, I need you to call Keith."

Michelle took over. Thank god. We just wandered around following her orders. She stayed calm and collected the entire time, and the rest of the family followed her lead. She was definitely the glue that kept them all together. I looked at Michelle in a whole new light. I now understood how Jake had made it through those early years. Michelle would never have allowed him to give up. She was my new hero.

It wasn't until hours later that we learned what had happened to Jake. Despite all the precautions the doctors had taken with Jake, as well as the anticoagulant medication he was on, he still developed a pulmonary embolism – a clot from the knee that traveled up his body and entered his heart, causing his heart to arrest and blocking the flow of oxygen to his lungs. Jake was rushed into surgery to remove the clot and afterward was placed in a medically induced coma and attached to a life support machine. It was unknown whether Jake had suffered any brain damage from the lack of oxygen. We would have to wait until he was removed from the coma and the machines to see what damage had been done.

Within hours of the pulmonary embolism, rumors began circulating that Jake was brain dead and that he was about to be taken off life support. Media descended on the hospital, and the streets outside filled up with thousands of crying fans. Police were brought in to control the crowds. After his public statement, Jake's incredible story of survival filled the airways once again, but this time, his courage and perseverance were revered, not questioned, and his struggles touched the hearts of millions.

Things spiraled so completely out of control as Jake lay sedated and on the ventilator that the hospital administration begged his parents to agree to a news conference. At first, they were adamant about protecting Jake's privacy, but when the worried crowd outside began to unintentionally block ambulances and disrupt the normal functioning of the hospital, Jake's parents consented to allow Jake's doctor to give a press conference.

They did a good job easing the fears of the crowds, but Jake's condition was anything but stable. Three days after being placed in the coma, Jake was weaned from the drugs. We all gathered as Jake was removed from the machines. We were warned that if his heart did not start beating on his own, that he might need defibrillation, and that if he didn't breathe on his own, he might need more time on the ventilators.

A few tense minutes followed when it looked like Jake's heart might not start beating on its own. The doctors prepared the paddles. Then, suddenly, the lines on the monitor started moving. Jake heart was beating, and he was breathing on his own. The relief was overwhelming. All that was left now was for Jake to wake up.

He didn't. Doctors performed a variety of tests on him. An EEG was given to measure his brain activity, and it appeared that he had normal function – yet still he didn't wake up, making doctors fear his brain was damaged more than they had originally suspected. It appeared he had slipped into a coma. Nothing they tried, or we tried, could wake him up. This was not what Jake had predicted: hovering between life and death. That was no way for a man like Jake to live.

50

JAKE: PURGATORY

I was awake, but everything was dark. I tried to open my eyes, but they remained shut. I felt nothing. No pain. I didn't know where I was. I faded in and out for what seemed like forever until I started hearing voices – Casey, my mom, my dad, Kyle – they were all calling to me. I could hear their stress and fear. I struggled to wake up. Why couldn't I wake up? Was I dead?

I could feel Casey touch my face. I could taste her tears on my lips. What was happening? "Wake up," she kept telling me. "You promised. Wake up." I was trying, I really was, but I was stuck. Not alive. Not dead.

51

CASEY: KYLE'S TRUTH

Four days after he'd been removed from the ventilators, I sat in the private waiting room with Kyle waiting for word on another test that was being performed on Jake. Kyle and I had become close since this all began. There was an unspoken understanding between us. Both our lives revolved around Jake. Neither of us really knew what to do without him. I saw Kyle's head dip and he buried his eyes in his hands. He'd barely slept in days. I got up and walked over to him.

"Can I get you anything?" I asked.

He shook his head and didn't look up.

"He's going to wake up," I said.

Kyle nodded, then glanced at me. His eyes were red.

"It's his fault," Kyle whispered.

"Whose fault?" I asked, upset that he would blame Jake for this.

"Ray. If it weren't for him, Jake wouldn't be in a fucking coma," he emoted angrily.

"Oh," I said, not knowing how to respond. We sat silently for another minute.

"I was there. Did you know that?"

"Where?"

"With Jake when it happened."

I sat down. "I... I guess I knew that. I mean, I remember hearing in the news years ago something about his brother witnessing the kidnapping."

"Ray came up to us with a gun in his hand. He had a mask on. He forced us to lie down on our stomachs. He threatened to kill us if we didn't do what he demanded. If I did something wrong, he'd kill Jake. If Jake did something wrong, he'd kill me. I can't tell you how terrifying it was. It messed me up, Casey. I still have nightmares about that day. And I only spent five minutes with him."

I rested my hand on his arm. "I'm sorry."

"I mean, can you even imagine what it must have been like for Jake? I used to obsess about it... try to imagine that it was me who had been taken and not Jake. The things he had to do to survive... I wouldn't have lasted a day in there."

"You don't know that."

"Oh, I know that. I'm a follower, Casey. I've never desired to lead. I always had Jake for that. He was always the coolest kid and the bravest kid, and the most talented kid. I was none of that, and you'd think I'd resent him for it, but I didn't. I was just happy to bask in his greatness. Hell, I'm still doing that."

"Who can blame you? He's pretty great." I smiled.

Kyle glanced at me. He smiled weakly. "You aren't kidding. Jake fought a serial killer for thirty-six days and lived. I mean, what kind of mental toughness does it take to do something like that?" He shook his head in awe. "No. I wouldn't have lasted a day."

"You never know how strong you are until you're put to the test."

"Yeah, I guess," Kyle agreed, looking worn. "Sometimes... " He stopped himself.

"What?"

"Sometimes I wonder if this is just all 'Final Destination' stuff. What if Jake cheated death all those years ago? What if everything since that day has been leading up to this?"

"I don't believe in superstitions," I said firmly. "Jake survived because he was stronger than Ray. It was his fate to survive, not the other way around. He will wake up, Kyle."

"When? I just want him to be okay," Kyle said, his voice breaking. "I just want him to give me that look."

"What look?"

"The annoyed one. It's how I get him to acknowledge me. I just irritate the hell out of him until he's forced to pay attention," Kyle explained.

I laughed. Then a thought occurred to me. "That's not a bad idea, actually."

"What?"

"Annoying him. Maybe it will wake him up." I brightened.

"Are you serious?" Kyle asked, looking at me skeptically.

"Is it going to hurt?"

"I guess not."

"Let's go, then. Let's annoy the shit out of him until he screams at us to stop."

Kyle and I went into Jake's room and sent Emma and Scott away, telling them to get some food. We then proceeded to do all the things that normally irritated the hell out of Jake. Kyle told stupid jokes and gave him wet willys and poked him; I sang right in his ear. At one point, while Kyle was playing typewriter on Jake's chest, Michelle walked in.

"What are you doing?" she asked, looking horrified.

"Annoying him," Kyle responded with a grin.

"You're doing what?"

"We're doing things to annoy him," I backed Kyle up. "He hates all these things. We figure at some point, he's going to wake up and punch Kyle in the face."

Michelle looked on in shock. "That is the stupidest thing I've ever heard."

Kyle and I peered at her, uncertain if we should continue.

"Well, go on," she said, a smile breaking out across her face. "Don't let me stop you."

So we spent the rest of the day being the most annoying people on the planet. Michelle even got in on the action herself, questioning Jake about sex and tickling his toes. Jake didn't wake up, but it was a stress reliever for all of us.

As the days passed with no change in Jake's condition, sadness consumed me. I'd never been much for prayer, but I prayed now. Grief overwhelmed me. My mom showed up at the hospital at some point. I hadn't even known she was coming. I spent my days at his bedside talking to him, pleading with him, threatening him. All he had to do was wake up; but he didn't. He just didn't. *Wake up, Jake!*

EPILOGUE

I looked out over the crowd where my family was gathered. The cap on my head kept slipping down, and the oversized gown dwarfed me. I'd waited a long time for this day to come, and everybody I loved was in the stands supporting me. Well, almost everyone. My thoughts turned to Jake. I wished he could be here with me on a day like this. I shook my head. No, I would not let his absence bring me down today.

I plastered a smile on my face, and when my name was called, I proudly walked across the stage to accept my diploma. Afterward, I made my way through the crowds until I found the people I was looking for, and I was smothered in hugs and congratulations. Not only was my family there to support me, but so was Jake's. What with all we had gone through together, they'd become as close to me as my blood family.

Michelle came up and enveloped me in a warm hug. "Congratulation, sweetie," she said, and kissed my cheek. "I'm so proud of you. Honors and everything."

"Thanks, Michelle." I exhaled loudly.

"Hey, none of that," she instructed. "This is your day. Don't let anything ruin it."

"I won't. I just wish he were here with us," I replied.

"I know." She nodded. "He should be here, but there's nothing we can do about it, so just enjoy this moment."

"I am." I smiled. God, how I loved that woman.

Kyle came up and wrapped me in a gigantic bear hug. He had a big smile on his face as he lifted me off the ground and shook me.

"Stop it, you dork." I laughed and smacked him.

"Yeah – get your hands off my girl!"

I looked out over the crowd for the source of that voice I knew so well. My eyes focused on a man with glasses and a full, shaggy beard. I didn't even recognize him at first, but then he smiled that adorable lopsided grin of his, and I ran over to him and flung myself into his arms.

"Casey!" my mom admonished. "His knee. Careful."

I ignored her. Jake's knee was fine. She just liked to baby him because she adored him so much.

"Have you been here the whole time?" I asked.

"Uh-huh, but I had to sit with Lassen in the nosebleed seats. Man, those things suck. I have a whole new appreciation for my fans."

"Who did this for you?" I pulled on his beard.

"A makeup artist I hired. She did such an amazing job I didn't even recognize myself."

"Well, if you looked like this, why didn't you sit with everyone else?"

"Because… imagine Duck Dynasty sitting down in the middle of our families. It would have been totally obvious that it was me in disguise. But with my man Lassen here, no one would suspect a thing."

"Hey, are you calling me a redneck?" Lassen huffed, but there was an amused look on his face.

"I'm just saying you and I are way more compatible now that I look like I just walked out of the backwoods," Jake teased.

"Did the university know you were coming in disguise?"

"Nope," Jake said, and put a finger to his lips. "They're probably still wondering why I didn't show up in the designated viewing room."

I smiled up at my wonderfully hairy boyfriend. Even looking like a mountain man, he was still the most beautiful man I'd ever known.

Jake kept his promise: he came back to me. It happened suddenly. Gracie was the only one with him at the time. She'd been talking about the kittens and had taken her phone out to show him a picture, when all of a sudden, after spending two weeks in a coma, Jake just opened his eyes.

What followed was not some miraculous recovery. It took time. Although Jake could remember everything and seemed to have normal cognitive abilities, his motor skills needed work. Because he'd been lying unresponsive for so long, his body was slow to respond, and his knee needed the movement it had been lacking while he was in the coma. A team of physical therapists worked with him around the clock. Jake took his first tentative steps on his new knee three days after waking up. Within a week, he was walking short distances. He was released from the hospital after that and went home to his parents' house. His physical therapy continued uninterrupted. Jake wanted to recover more than anyone – it frustrated him to not be able to do things that he was used to being able to do.

Within a month of waking from the coma, Jake was playing his songs on the piano again. There had been some worry that his vocal cords could have been damaged during the intubation, but when Jake started singing again, it was clear they had recovered nicely. Things were slowly improving for Jake. Every day, he made progress. After six months of recovery, Jake was nearly back to his old self. In fact, he might even have been better than his old self because the pain that had been dogging him for years was finally under control. He still had some issues, but it was nothing like it was before.

Probably the single biggest challenge Jake was dealing with now was how to handle his fans and the press. After his well-received public statement and his near-death experience, Jake had become somewhat of a hero. His fame had soared to new heights, and he was more popular than ever before. If people hadn't known who he was before, they knew now. His kidnapping, and the fate of the other victims of Raymond Davis, became front-page news again. But this time, Jake was not cast as the villain; instead, he was portrayed as who he genuinely had been – a courageous kid who'd saved himself from a vicious killer. The world now followed his every move. Jake was not exactly thrilled by his accelerated fame – in fact, he was decidedly embarrassed by all the coverage – but he was quickly coming to terms with his new normal.

It was for that reason that Jake was asked to stay away from the graduation proceedings. My school's administration worried that his presence would be too overwhelming and that the security necessary to keep people away would be too costly. They also argued that his being at the graduation might take away from the experience of the other families and graduates. Jake was instead encouraged to go to a viewing room and watch the proceedings on a TV screen. Although I wanted him there with me in the stands, I understood the university's position. This wasn't just about me; there were other graduates who deserved their day as well.

"Do you know who that is?" Darcy asked Sydney and Riley, as she pointed to Jake.

Both looked up at him, and then Sydney's eyes brightened and she burst out, "JAKE!"

"Shhh!" All the adults in our group shushed in unison. Sydney flung herself on Jake. I was forced to give up my guy to an eight-year-old. He spent a minute chatting easily with my niece as I gazed at him in awe. He was the best thing that had ever happened to me. I never took him for granted anymore. I loved him so much.

Jake caught me staring and smiled. He whispered something to Sydney, and she giggled and walked away. Jake came up to me and kissed my lips through his hairy beard.

"I forgot to tell you," he stated. "Congratulations, babe. I'm proud of you."

~

We moved our party to a private location after the graduation ceremony was complete and all the pictures had been taken. My mom and Michelle had worked together to put the party on for me. They'd become friends at the hospital while Jake was in the coma, and had kept in touch ever since. It turned out to be a pretty big bash with my family and Jake's, and my friends from Arizona, and some of Jake's band and crew that I'd become friends with.

After dining on catered steak, chicken, and ribs from a local barbecue joint, the party broke up around 12:00 am. It was just Jake and I and our moms and a couple of others who stayed to clean up. Jake pulled me aside and handed me an envelope.

"What's this?" I asked.

"Open it." He grinned.

"It's so heavy!" I exclaimed excitedly. Inside the envelope were plane tickets... like twenty of them. "What is this?"

"The party isn't over yet," he said. Both Jake's family and my family came back in the room. They were toting suitcases.

"What the?" I looked out over all my excited loved ones.

"We're flying to Tahiti."

"All of us?"

Jake nodded, smiling.

"When?"

"In about six hours."

EPILOGUE

"**O**h, my god!" she exclaimed, shocked. She jumped up and kissed me. This was the reaction I was hoping for. I was a little worried Casey wouldn't appreciate having no time to prepare, but this was the only way to surprise her and have all the family together in order to make the trip.

If I had to be honest, the vacation was not only a celebration for Casey and all the hard work she'd put into getting her degree, it was also a thank you to our families for all the support and love they had given us the last few months. It hadn't been an easy road for either of us since I woke up from the coma.

Those weeks in the hospital were a blur to me now. I was transported to my parents' house after being released, and my mom doted on me hand and foot. Usually I wouldn't have been able to stand such treatment, but I was too weak to protest.

Casey struggled to complete the semester while spending most of her time in the hospital or at my parents' house with me. She made the two-hour round trip drive nearly every night and stayed the weekends until the winter break mercifully arrived and gave her four weeks off. I was worried about the stress on her, but the more I worried about her, the more stressed she became.

Two physical therapists alternated treatments for nearly eight hours a day every day. It was truly exhausting, but regaining my strength was all I wanted. I hated being dependent on others. One week into Casey's break, I insisted on moving back to my place over my mom's strong objections. As grateful as I was to her for all she'd done, I was reaching my breaking point. I was used to being independent and making my own choices. But at home being cared for by my mom, it was like I was back to being the child and I couldn't take it anymore.

Besides, Casey and I needed alone time. Our relationship had really taken a backseat to my rehabilitation, and recently she'd been more of a nurse than a girlfriend. I wanted to be me again. I wanted us to get back to where we were before the shit that crapped down upon our lives happened. And aside from a quick romp in the bathroom at my parents' house, we hadn't had sex in a really long time.

Moving home was the push I needed to get my life back together. Interest in me had skyrocketed after I nearly died. An outpouring of support had flowed in from all over the world, and once I got home I started back with my music. For a while there in the hospital, I worried that I might never regain the fine motor skills necessary to continue as a musician. It took a lot of hard work to get back into the rhythm of things, but I finally felt confident in my abilities again.

As soon as I was doing well enough, I started back on social media. I wanted to keep my fans updated on my progress. The response was overwhelming and humbling. My new album came out in the beginning of January and debuted at number one, and it had been sitting at the top of the charts ever since.

Casey was at my side through all the craziness. Both of us were ready for her to be done and graduated. She decided to put off getting a job right away in order to travel with me for a while.

I had a lot of commitments set for the summer, and she wanted to be with me. I secretly hoped she wouldn't work at all, but it was not my place to say. I'd let that decision be up to her.

The chartered private jet whisked the whole McKallister/Caldwell group to a resort in Tahiti, where we all had adjoining over-the-water huts. We spent several days lying in the sun, playing in the water, and doing various water sports. On our fifth day, we all took a boat to a private island for a day of sunbathing and barbecue. It was May 30th, one year to the day since Mitch and Kate's wedding… and one year since Casey and I had met. A lot had happened in the past year, but it was all worth it to get us to this point in our lives.

I looked over at Mitch. His arm was around his wife, who was now four months pregnant. Life just moved forward at lightning speed, and if you didn't get on the ride while you could, you were going to be left behind. That wasn't going to be me anymore. I wasn't wasting any more time. My past was no longer in control – my future was.

Casey came up behind me and wrapped her arms around my waist. "Are you okay?" she asked.

"Yeah, I'm good. You wanna take a walk down the beach with me?"

"Sure." She smiled.

I took her hand and we wandered along the water line, not really talking, just enjoying each other's company.

"Ahh… look," Casey said. "Someone must be getting married here later."

She pointed to an arch that was covered in flowers and surrounded by a little white fence.

"Oh, yeah," I commented. "Let's go take a look."

We walked up the sand until we came to the fence. I stepped over it.

"Jake. You can't do that."

"Why? I'm just looking."

"There's a security guard over there," she whispered, as she gestured toward him with her eyes.

"If he says anything, we'll leave. Come on," I said, holding my hand out.

Casey wouldn't take it. "Jake, no." She glanced over to the security guard.

"Live a little. What's he going to do?"

Casey hesitated, uncertain what to do.

I sighed. "If he comes over, I'll give him a fifty."

My hand was still out waiting for hers. Finally, she grabbed it and stepped over the fence. I guided her to the arch and we walked under the flowers.

"Oh, wow, Jake, this is so pretty," Casey said in admiration. Then she got a better look at the flowers. "Wait, these are gardenias and stephanotis and peonies... these are all my favorite flowers. That is crazy. What are the chances?" She smiled as she took in the sight with wonder in her eyes.

After a few seconds, she turned to me and said, "Isn't that crazy?"

"Not so crazy," I responded.

She searched my eyes, confused.

I knelt down on one knee.

"What are you... oh, my god, Jake... " Casey gasped, covering her mouth with her hand. Tears immediately sprang up in her eyes.

"This is all for you, Casey," I said, as I opened my hand to reveal a tiny box with a sparkling two-carat cushion-cut yellow gold diamond engagement ring inside.

Casey looked at the ring, then at me, then back at the ring. She seemed genuinely shocked.

"Will you marry me, Casey Caldwell?" I asked as I slipped the ring on her finger.

Casey was beaming from ear to ear as tears rolled down her

cheeks. She dropped to her knees and wrapped her arms around my neck. "Yes. Yes. Of course, yes. I love you."

We sat in the sand and kissed under the arch of Casey's favorite flowers. After a couple of minutes, we heard cheering back at the BBQ.

"Did they all know what you were planning?" Casey asked, grinning.

"No. Only Kyle, and he was sworn to secrecy."

"Well, they figured it out."

"A lot quicker than you did. I thought I was going to have to knock you out and drag you under the arch for a minute there."

"I know. I didn't want to ruin some girl's dream day. But that 'some girl' turned out to be me," Casey gushed, her eyes glowing with happiness and love.

I nodded, smiling. Casey wasn't 'some girl' to me. She was my world, and my future. We were no longer just Jake and Casey.

Today we officially became 'Cake.'

The End

❦

Can't wait to read more? Find out what happened the day Jake went missing and why it has haunted Kyle to this day... **One-click** The Theory of Second Best **now!**

He wants to step out of the shadows but sins from the past keep him shackled to his brother's side.

Kyle

You probably don't know me. I'm Kyle, younger brother to one of the world's most famous rock stars.

I've carved out a comfortable existence touring with my famous brother and living in the lap of luxury with no real commitments or plans of my own. When the opportunity comes to compete on a reality show, I jump at the chance. I mean what else do I have to do?

But life hasn't always been this easy for me. I was once a messed up kid. Can you blame me?

I was there the day Jake disappeared. I saw it all. And now I keep the secret...

Kenzie

I lead the world's most boring life. No really, I do. In fact, I'm fairly certain the only reason I made it on the reality survival show *Marooned* in the first place is because I've never ventured further than three hundred miles in any direction from my hometown in all my life. You know, the whole 'fish out of water' contestant? Yep, that's me.

And now, I'm here on an island occupied by a cast of quirky characters so much more interesting than myself. Take Kyle, for example, the very cute and very entertaining Southern California beach boy with shaggy hair, a generous smile, and an uncanny ability to forgive.

Not even four hours had passed and I already had a starry-eyed crush. Ah man. This one-sided attraction had all the makings of disaster... one that would play out in front of an audience of millions.

One-click The Theory of Second Best **now!**

* * *

Sign up for my newsletter to find out when I have new books.

You can also join my Facebook group, <u>The Banana Binder</u>, for exclusive giveaways and sneak peaks of future books.

I appreciate your sharing my books and telling your friends about them. Reviews help readers find my books! Please consider leaving a review for Cake A Love Story_on your favorite book site.

Turn page to meet Kyle's love interest Kenzie>

ALSO BY J. BENGTSSON

Made in United States
Orlando, FL
28 April 2023